# THE ARTS OF SPIES AND BUTTERFLIES

# THE ARTS OF SPIES AND BUTTERFLIES

## AN ADAM WALKER NOVEL

### VALERIE NIEMERG

*For David.*
*If you can learn to sing, I can learn to write.*
*Save me a seat near the basses.*

**From the Institute Catalog**

Level I — Average Extraordinary Talent

Level II — Extreme Prodigy in One Skill

Level III — Prodigy in a Study and/or Skill and Related Fields

Level IV — Prodigy in Multiple Areas of Intellectual Pursuit

Level V — Unlimited Learning Capacity in Skill and Intellect

Level VI — A. Walker

# PRELUDE

*"I guess I should start by saying, I'm sorry. I know if you're watching this, if you've found your way to this recording, well, I'm sorry."*

# RACHEL

1977

RACHEL BERTRAND STRODE THROUGH THE CHURCH, HER BLACK heels clicking on the stone floor. Though still barely thirty years old, Rachel had long-ago retired from field work when this moment came. Inactive. Out in the cold.

This is not her story. This is her epilogue.

Once upon a time, when she took blind cold orders from distant voices, Rachel would have chosen this church for its high arched ceilings that could swiftly dissolve conversations, masking them in its echoing corners. She would have draped an ivory lace over her head and knelt down reverently about halfway up the aisle, always on the left side. She'd rub some beads in her fingers that tinkled together softly while she waited for her contact to sidle up beside her. Their shared words would mingle with the whispered petitions around them and disappear into the arches above, information passed, orders given, destinies decided.

Today though, it felt like sitting inside a photograph, a piece of her history, preserved by some thoughtful entity who now watched to see what she would do next. As if anything mattered anymore. The eyes of the stone-cold statues fell upon her with curious questions. The scent of stale incense and wood polish filled the space with the trickle of the fountain at the back and the occasional murmurs of the scattered old women.

Of course, she was absurd. No one was coming. There was no target, no focus. No Rachel, really. She shivered, hoping even ancient walls could not hold the echoes of one's former self.

Beneath an aging Scottish tapestry, a small curtain opened, and a man stepped out from a confessional. Rachel rose, then ducked into the vacated closet, pulling the curtain shut behind her. She sat in the darkness and listened to the mutterings of the penitent on the other side of the stall. What would it be like to have such ridiculous sins?

When her screen slid open, a man's voice offered a speedy blessing and an enduring silence.

"Am I supposed to say something now?" she said.

"Have you never been to Confession?"

"No."

"Well, I can't grant you the Sacrament if you're not Catholic. I'm happy to help you start the process."

"That's not why I came in here."

"Then why?" asked the priest.

"I don't know. I only came into the church because I remembered this place. I used to come here, but it was always just a forgery. I wanted to know what it feels like."

"To be forgiven?"

"I doubt there's a category of forgiveness for me," she said. "I used to find killing people an easy thing to do." She clearly heard the old man stop breathing on the other side of the screen. "Don't worry," she said, mildly amused. "I don't do that anymore."

The priest straightened his vestments. "Well, that's a start. But..." He paused for a moment, as though searching for just the right words, the shortest phrase, the quickest sermon he could give. "Forgiveness waits," he said at last.

"What?"

"It's not like missing your flight. Forgiveness waits for you."

"Well, I wouldn't even know where to start," she said. "Whose forgiveness do I need first? The people I've killed, or those I've betrayed? Which side is right?"

"Just one. Listen, you came into this church today. Usually, that happens because something is compelling you to be here: a change in health, a new romance, a child."

At first, she did not respond, as though trying to rinse away the old man's words from the air around her. A solitary slit of light streamed past the sad, frayed edges of the velvet-curtained door. Unbidden, Rachel's thoughts slipped through it to a room full of wiggling children and the smell of chalk. At a tiny desk in the center, a little girl sat, her hands folded neatly together, her black curls held on her head by an ineffectual barrette of a pink, rhinestone butterfly.

"Whoever it is, they need you to live your life," said the priest, his voice slowly stretching outward so that his words resounded from the end of a long, imagined, echoing corridor. "Stop dragging it around."

Rachel felt dizzy and gripped the sides of the little wooden closet.

"Tell me why you came in here," he added. "Be done with it already."

"I told you. There are many things." She faltered. Why had she come in here? The tiny space smelled musty and confined. Her plane was leaving soon. An impulse seized her, to jump up, whisk past that curtain, skirt back down the aisle.

*Coward.*

"There is this one thing," she said. "It follows me. The rest, I think I understand, like it made sense somehow. But this thing… I've been rewriting it in my head for years, just to get through the day. Playing the same scene over and over. I can't make it go away."

"You can't make it go away?"

"No."

"Now that," said the priest with a smile she could not see, "is a beautiful confession."

An hour passed before Rachel stepped out of the confessional, dizzy and curious. As if shouting in protest, Glasgow's weather expressed its finest spit and spew, hammering water onto the crowded rush-hour sidewalks outside the church. It felt personally directed, like Heaven's outrage at what she had just spent an hour doing, and now Almighty invisible powers reached down from the sky with outraged watery tentacles. How dare she.

That was funny. Watery tentacles. And that Heaven, if there was such a place, would choose this for its wrath. There had been many other hours Rachel had ill spent, covered in blood and cool thoughtless acts of obedience. And they had mostly been followed by bright and sunny afternoons sipping sleek Scotch on patios in Valencia. Heaven, if there was such a place, must not control the weather.

So, she stepped down into the rain. Drenched commuters scampered through the puddles, around her, returning to their cold little flats. Out of habit, she scanned the perimeter, found four dark spots but no suspicious shadows, a car double parked across the busy street. She hadn't had a tail in years.

*They need you to live your life. Stop dragging it around.*

In a far corner of her vision, a shadow approached like a dark wave through the evening mist. It stepped with a familiar urgency, encroaching and raising something above its head. Seconds melted into minutes, and even the drops falling around her slowed as her inner alarms blared awake. Instantly and automatically, she raised an arm to block the blow, grabbed the instrument with both hands, and used the attacker's own weight to propel them backwards against the stone steps. She swiped the weapon away and flung it backwards as the assailant cried out.

"Please stop. Just take it!" An innocent woman cringed before her.

Rachel beheld the umbrella in her hands.

"I'm so sorry," she said, stepping back. "I thought you were…"

Other pedestrians stopped to gape, intervene, help the woman up. A man in a raincoat stood between them, his arms raised.

"I'm sorry," Rachel repeated, and she stepped back again, dropping the umbrella to the wet pavement. "I didn't know, I mean, I wasn't thinking." When she stepped back a third time, her heel missed the edge of the sidewalk and she slipped, sprawling into the lane, just as a taxi sped past to make a rush-hour traffic light.

In the fleeting second between impact and darkness, Rachel felt the cool rain drops on her lips and saw the different colors of shoes splashing in the gray puddles. She smelled the sweet smoke of a nearby cigarette, heard the fleeting grumble of a city bus. Life had been going on all this time, like so many colors on a wondrous tapestry, waves of harmonies passing in a symphony, or in the sun-bent fluttering of a pink, rhinestone butterfly.

# 1ST MOVEMENT: TALENT

*"Kelli, you remember the question? And the answer? You must never tell anyone, you understand?"*

*"Oui, Maman. Personne. Je comprends."*

# ONE

## February 1977

BUTTERFLIES AND FIREFLIES AND LOCUST SONGS AND GOLDFISH ponds, and once upon a night, in Amiens, France, there lay a little girl, weaving her tiny fingers in and out of an old afghan while listening to the walls. They did not speak, or sing or whine, the walls, but creaked wickedly at unexpected intervals. What made that sinister sound? Were witches hiding there? Cursed women with jagged fingernails and serpentine tongues who could seep through tiny cracks or small unpainted spots? Or perhaps they used invisible doors, hidden within the closets or down between the curly legs of the nightstand?

Now of course, Kelli's *maman* had told her many times that witches were not real. But this testimony did not convince Kelli. It seemed that every story she had ever heard centered on the machinations of a sinister malformed woman who impelled the heroes into their destined despair. And besides that, Kelli was a very clever child. She understood that Maman often told her things, just so she would not be frightened.

For example, whenever Kelli asked about her Papa, Maman

would only say that he was lost in the war. Not that he died, or he was killed, but that he was lost. So, Kelli always imagined her father still wandering endlessly somewhere, through a forest where the fighting had long ago stopped. Perhaps he had discovered a house of candy and a witch who turned him into a cookie. Maybe that's what happened to all the people who died.

Kelli carefully studied her darkened surroundings. Only a thin wash of streetlight penetrated the lace curtains of Madame Girard's guest room. The old lady's dressers, which stood so tall and fancy in the daylight with their white doilies, bronze handles, and porcelain knickknacks, had again, magically morphed into blackened, sinister forms in the darkness.

*Pop! Crack!*

Kelli stiffened beneath her covers, her ears tingling to attention. She pulled Petite Pearl close, rubbing the doll's smooth nylon skin against her cheek. Pearl and her stitched-on blue gingham dress submitted willingly to the asphyxiating clench of five-year-old terror. *Just one more night, Pearl.*

Tomorrow, Maman would return from her trip, and Kelli could go home to the cozy suburban house that didn't smell like old perfume and where Maman always left a little light on at night. Then Maman would go back to work in the building with the mirrored windows that reflected the Cathédrale. Maman had left for this trip on Friday, promising something special would come for Kelli on Sunday, the night before she returned. *Something wonderful.* Kelli had spent most of Friday and Saturday conjuring visions of purple princess toads, or magical keys that could open any window into a bright flower garden.

But her elderly babysitter, Madame Girard, seemed to announce "Bedtime!" at an earlier hour each evening, and despite the cleverest of protestations, this evening was no exception. Kelli had been speedily teeth-brushed, face-wiped, and night-gowned up with the efficiency of a *Capitaine de l'armée.*

"But Maman promised. Something wonderful tonight. Remember?"

"Wonderful will have to wait until tomorrow," Madame Girard had replied. "Your *maman* will be home then and will probably give it to you herself."

"But Maman said Sunday. That's today."

"Not for long. Now go to sleep."

Kelli clutched Petite Pearl and pulled the lace curtain aside. She peered out onto the cold, blue lane, scanning every dark corner for any lurking, wiry figures with pointy, blackened teeth. In the cone of light under the streetlamp, something fell, wafting like a tiny fairy cradle, down, down, down to the lifeless pavement. Kelli gasped and sat up. Another tuft appeared, lilting downwards, and then another, until an entire silent chorus of feathers danced together through the blue light.

Naturally, she held her breath in a stunned anticipation. So far, it had been a very disappointing winter for a five-year-old. No snowballs, no sledding, no frost-bitten noses or wild, whitened adventures. Just cold and damp, even through Noël. It wasn't right. But now, as though all complaints had been filed and registered with the proper authorities, the horrible weather inadequacies of the past months had been recognized and addressed with this perfect symphony of soft lovely flakes dancing in mystic silence just beyond the windowpane of Madame Girard's guest room.

*Pearl! Maman has made it snow!*

Without any regard for shadows or creaks in the walls, Kelli jumped off the bed and dashed across the floor.

"*Qui est là? Kelli?* Is that you?" Madame Girard cried from her darkened suite.

Kelli tore down the stairs and undid the bolt. When she pulled open the front door, a bluster of flakes wafted into Madame Girard's foyer.

"Kelli? Kelli! *Qu'est-ce rue tu as?*" Madame Girard, loosely wrapped in a shawl, reached the landing at the top of the stairs just as Kelli leaped outside. "Kelli, come back, foolish girl!"

Feet bare and nightgown flapping, Kelli held out her arms and let the crystals tickle her nose with cool, wet kisses. She spun, moving to an orchestral accompaniment, Pearl swinging delightedly at her side. *Brisé, brisé, chassé, assemblé, arabesque,* round and round, fingers reaching falling flakes, coming together, Heaven and Earth in an amicable duet, a soft moving dance, while hungry witches scampered off, their impotent brooms waddling between their legs.

———

Ironically, on the same dark and cold February night in 1977, across many miles and over a mighty iron border, another, very different sort of dance took place. A black, formless shadow slid unnoticed through the vigilant Moscow streets with an out-of-place elegance, a graceful ease between the structures and mounds of blackened snow. *Brisé, brisé, chassé, assemblé, arabesque,* round and round, but not quite so. He did not really dance of course, but moved with such an ease, a confident elegance, that, had anyone seen his efforts, they might have called it such.

A few short bocks from Dzerzhinsky Square, the figure approached a building whose many dark windows towered high above, releasing only scattered splinters of captive light. A sign hanging from the gates in the front lot read in Russian, "1st Moscow Watch Factory," but its cold and empty lots were carefully lit. An astute observer might notice the tiny heads that surveilled the property from far above.

With a few soft clinks, the figure in black scaled the fence and landed inside the compound, where he scurried away like a rodent, quickly melding into shadow. A guard emerged from a booth to investigate and lifted a radio to his lips, but whatever soldier stood posted on the roof across the street saw only darkness.

The shadow, whose name was Adam, crept along the base of the building. He withdrew a rope and hook from inside his coat and swung it out through the night air until it latched onto the bars of a window. Adam scaled the wall, repeating this maneuver, until he reached the top.

Three men patrolled on the roof. He could hear their voices, their chilled breathing, and the crunch of their boots on the graveled floor. Two shared a cigarette on the southwest corner, their AK-47 assault rifles dangling loosely from their shoulders.

"You think they could kill us out here in this cold?"

"They know it. Don't sit down. Couple years back, somebody did die up here. Froze up like a piece of meat, right on that ledge. I'm serious. They used to only have two up here. One on each end."

"Vodka tales."

"No, this is true. They had to break off his fingers to get the weapon out of his hand. Don't sit down."

A pair of silenced taps sped through the brittle air from Adam's pistol and the guards fell like puppets, their bodies quickly stiffening and their words dissolving into the cold Moscow air.

*Everyone should hope to be so lucky in death.*

Adam crossed the roof in a series of acrobatic bounds. He met the third guard as he rounded the corner of the elevator maintenance room, his foot striking the man in the face and breaking the soldier's neck.

Landing in a crouch, Adam's ears perked. Something was not right. Across the street, the rooftop watchman let his rifle drop on its strap and raised a radio to his lips. Still down on one knee, Adam took aim and sent a bullet over the street, searing through the soldier's neck. A second hit his skull. Soldier and radio fell with a distant, muffled thud.

The clock had begun. Somewhere in the floors beneath him,

an American diplomat was enduring the worst of Soviet hospitality. Adam had at most ten minutes to find the man and execute their mutual escape, or they would both die. He swiped a radio from the soldier with the broken neck, scaled the elevator mechanical room, and removed the grate, disappearing into the building with an alarmingly silent grace.

———

Almost three weeks after Kelli's late-night ballet in the snow, Robert Durand peered through the conference room window at his legal offices in Amiens, France, looking for her. "Marianne, I thought you said the Bertrand girl was in here."

His receptionist looked up, her fingers suspended over her typewriter. "She is."

"Well, she's not there now. Did she go to the restroom?"

"Keep looking." Marianne returned to her typing.

Durand studied the curiously empty room. A cup of orange juice and a small assortment of pastries sat untouched on the table. A few chairs had been moved away to a back corner, where they stood facing outward. But no five-year-old girl.

"See the chairs in the back?" Marianne said without looking up.

"She's behind them?"

"Maybe."

Durand sighed. "Get the babysitter." Gingerly, he opened the door. "Kelli? Are you back there?" He stepped toward the cluster of chairs. "Kelli, it's Mr. Durand. Can you come out so I can speak to you?"

The silence did not surprise him. Since learning of her mother's untimely death, his five-year-old client had not spoken a word to anyone. Whether she was unable to process what had happened, or just traumatized, he couldn't guess. He lowered himself stiffly to the floor and searched between the chair legs.

Gingerly, he pulled a chair away. Kelli sat curled into a ball, hugging her knees, her wide eyes staring into emptiness in his general direction as she rocked slightly back and forth, silent as mist.

The babysitter Girard stepped in the room. "Oh no. I was afraid of this."

"What is she doing?"

"First time, I found her in the bathtub. Next time, under a desk."

"Has she always behaved like this?" Durand asked.

"No, no. She was a very lively, happy child before..." Madame Girard stood wringing a handkerchief in her bony hands. She seemed to have more difficulty breathing every time she came to the office. Durand couldn't blame her for not taking the girl on. She was too old to accept such a responsibility. For weeks, he had scoured France for any family but found not even an alcoholic uncle to claim the child. He couldn't keep the girl with the old woman any longer. She would have to be taken to a state facility.

"Kelli?" Durand called. "Can you come out here for a minute? I need to talk to you."

At last, his tiny client unwrapped herself and crawled out, allowing the lawyer to guide her to the table. Durand held a small gray envelope in his hand, surely the oddest part of this whole ordeal. The mother's will had indicated a security box at a Paris branch of the Banque De France be opened in the event of her death. He had hoped to find some surviving relative to open the box, but instead, death certificate and will in hand, he himself had traveled to Paris, again hoping to retrieve some clue to Kelli's kin. What was in the box? No money, no jewels. Just this small rubber envelope that would only be useful if it contained a list of names and phone numbers.

"Kelli." The lawyer spoke softly, because the girl always jumped when someone interrupted her stare. "I have been looking for someone who could take care of you. Some family. Can you help me? Do you know anything about your father or his family? A last name? A picture? Did you ever meet anyone, a grandmother or a cousin perhaps? Anyone at all?"

She lifted her knees up to her chest, burying her nose.

He placed the envelope in front of her. "Your mother left this for you."

Durand ripped the package open, and a charm bracelet tumbled out onto the table with a jingle. It was a pretty piece with thick coils tightly interwoven, a work of craftsmanship, probably real gold. The odd collection of charms included a tiny ballerina, a pistol, a lock, a chess pawn, an airplane, a karate fighter, a sailboat, a character from some eastern language, a plain flat circle, a large dagger, the symbol for *pi*, and one dimpled, gold nugget.

"Kelli, does this mean anything to you? Do you have any idea why your mother would go to so much trouble to keep it safe?"

The lawyer sat back and readjusted the clasp of the useless trinket for her to wear, far too bulky and enormous for her tiny wrist. It disturbed him, how easily she gave him her arm, thoughtlessly obeying every instruction, like a lifeless ragdoll with everyone else telling her what to do.

———

Inside the Moscow compound, Adam leaned over the dark elevator shaft, studying its contours with a flashlight. Gloves on, he mounted the framework and descended between cables and walls in a seamless series of moves, landing with silent grace atop the car.

He located the control box and started the car up in maintenance mode, riding on top to just below the sixth floor. He activated the outer door latch and pried the doors apart. A thin line of light streamed across his masked face. Too many feet, too much activity.

He pushed the door closed and raised the elevator to halfway past the next floor. Again, he disengaged the outer door latch and peeked through. This hallway was dark and empty. Adam disengaged the maintenance controls and slipped down on to the cool tiled floor.

White walls and doors wound like a maze on the seventh floor, each marked only with a number and a small viewing window. He might have spared a fleeting thought that inside each tiny room a prisoner of the state festered in visions of a dismal future: best case to die alone in this small white tomb, lose their senses, or be shipped off to labor, soon to dissolve into faceless history.

*Only the Fokus mattered.* His directive. The object of his mission.

Rounding a corner, Adam doubled back, planting himself against the wall. A nearby cell opened, breaking the silence. Two soldiers emerged, lugging something wrapped in a white sheet. They dropped their cargo and wiped their brows.

"Makes you wonder what they're feeding them, huh? Weighing that much?"

"This one came in heavy."

"How do you know that?"

"They're all traitors. Liars, living double lives. Eating double rations. And we get stuck lugging their fat lazy carcasses. Let's go. We've still got the fourth floor." The men departed, leaving their load behind on the cold tile floor.

Adam crept up to the discarded bundle, squatted, and moved the sheet aside. A thin, lifeless man in his fifties stared blankly out, his body cold and blueish. Adam covered him back up and continued towards the stairs, passing many more white doors and sheeted bundles on his way. He entered the stairwell and leaned over the railing. From an outer pocket he pulled a tiny object shaped like two small milk bottles soldered together around an electric panel. He held his breath, engaged the device, and dropped it between the railings, watching it tumble into the darkness of the stairwell below. It landed with a distant clink.

He entered the sixth floor and inhaled again. Warmth of bodies filled the hallways, breaths, heartbeats, soft conversations. Feet plodded around, making tremors on the tiled floors.

Six or seven people in the hallway, not counting the ones behind doors. Stealth would not be possible.

Footsteps approached from his right. He grabbed a man in a white lab coat and pinned him against the wall with a hand over the man's mouth and nose. He jabbed a pistol deep into the man's gut. Adam whispered a name in the man's reddening ear and watched his eyes wander guiltily down the hallway to his left.

Adam quickly rendered the man in the lab coat unconscious, then crept away. He backed against a wall, listening to the voices of Russian men in the hallway just beyond the corner. He visualized the long white hallway, so similar to the one on the floor above. The unique colors of each soldier's voice laughed together. One smoked a cigarette. Another pair stood on watch closer, right around the corner. Adam could almost hear their heartbeats and the slow and steady rhythm of each breath as they were lulled into a false sense of tranquility by a long and boring shift.

Adam peeked around his corner. There were two, standing at the end like statues, facing the center hallway where his target lay hidden. He closed his eyes again. Once he made this move, there would be no turning back. The building would be on alert.

He began a clock-like meter, counting in his head a metronome pulsing softly, reminding him of the passing seconds and controlling his thoughts with a mantra-like focus.

1…2…3…

Adam lunged out from behind the corner, sprinting down the corridor. With two quick shots, he took down the standing guards, but the three men in the center corridor would now be ready for him.

7…8…9…

He dove for the floor, sprawling his body lengthwise across it, sliding on his side past the center corridor as bullets soared above his head into the wall. He shot two more rounds, taking two of the men down, but the third, not a soldier, a man in a white lab coat, ducked into a side door, bolting it fast behind him.

13...14...15...

Adam jumped up and raced off towards the door and the flailing bodies of the two men whose blood now splattered across the white tiles and walls.

All these soldiers on this one spot. A black plated plaque beside the door read in Cyrillic letters, "Dr. Volkov: Examination Room." Adam retrieved a small explosive device and quickly affixed it to the door, just above the bolt. He lay down on the floor, and when the bolt detonated, he kicked the door in, remaining on the floor as a tranquilizer dart flew above and stuck itself into the wall behind him.

20...21...22...

The adjacent door opened, and an agent stepped out, raising a weapon. Adam sent multiple rounds through the door before the man could get off a shot. He continued firing at the old decaying wood of the door, making splintered black holes, until two more bodies fell slumped on each other, leaving the door propped open.

26...27...28...

Turning back to the examination room, he fired three shots, aiming low, beneath the procedural table, upon which his target lay, moaning. His bullets sank into the man in the lab coat, propelling his squatting body against the opposite wall with a thud.

Adam rose and pulled off his black mask. He stood over his target while the KGB doctor of torture gushed blood across the floor. The doctor looked up at him with his final breaths and as death settled in, a final, horrified recognition forever imbedded on his features.

32...33...34...

"Mr. McLarey, I'm here to take you home." Adam released the

restraints on McLarey as the diplomat groaned back to consciousness.

Four days earlier, Thomas McLarey, of the US State Department, had landed in Moscow on a diplomatic envoy carrying representatives from a variety of nations and creeds. At about the same time in the intelligence community, a vital transfer of time-sensitive intel from a Russian operative had been thwarted due to a handler's sudden disappearance. Time was crucial, and the operative, panicking, had seized an opportunity at a social gathering to relate his information to a totally innocent and unsuspecting McLarey instead. Adam had no idea what this information was, but when the operative suddenly vanished and McLarey told his fellow diplomats of the bizarre exchange between himself and a cocktail server, hours later, McLarey also disappeared.

This was a delicate situation. Soviet intelligence fiercely hunted whatever McLarey knew, and once they got it out of him, he would no doubt turn up in a traffic intersection with tire marks on his nice suit and smelling of Russian mafia vodka.

But these things happened on occasion, and such occurrences required a very particular kind of operation, one with intimate knowledge of the Moscow setting and a network of contacts to pinpoint a precise location on the man before his rendezvous with Moscow traffic. In the US, a call had been placed to a deeply clandestine and private organization known only as the Institute. Within three hours of McLarey's disappearance, Adam Walker had been dispatched to get him out, "preferably alive," his superior, Zeus had told him, "as the information he holds is very valuable."

*Well, that was the rub, wasn't it?* Adam thought, as he removed the restraints on McLarey's wrists. It all would have been so much easier to drop in and shoot the guy. But, with the valuable intel somewhere in his traumatized brain, the only way to get the intel from McLarey was to get McLarey home. And since he wasn't dead yet, chances were, he hadn't opened up. Now Adam would have to abduct his target safely from a Soviet hot house and orchestrate an escape for them both from the city.

"You must walk, right now," Adam ordered. McLarey leaned on him, and they limped down a hallway and around a corner. "Up one flight and you're all clear. Put this on."

Adam withdrew two miniature masks from a vest pocket and wrapped a strap around McLarey's head. He set the cup snugly over his face.

"Breathe only through your nose."

He pulled an identical mask over his own face and led McLarey into the stairwell. Four men lay unconscious on the descending staircase, weapons trailing from their paralyzed hands. Adam leaned over the railing. Dozens of similar unconscious arms and legs hung out from the steps below, gassed by the device he had earlier dropped to the bottom.

They climbed one flight. On the quiet seventh floor, Adam sat his charge down and whispered stern instructions. "I'm going to leave you. You must lie still in this sheet, probably for many hours. If you hear people, hold your breath. You survived many hours on that table in there. That tells me you've got a strong backbone. Now all you have to do is lay very still. Can you do that?"

"Just get me out of this place," McLarey said.

Adam covered McLarey up in a white sheet, carefully wrapping him for burial, and left him alone on the floor, disguised as one of the scattered corpses. He then lifted the heavy corpse whose burial sheet they had stolen and maneuvered back through the halls of white doors to the elevator. He dropped his load and pried the elevator door open. The elevator car purred as it climbed steadily to the sixth floor below, filled with Soviet reinforcements. Adam hauled the corpse he had stolen back onto his shoulders, climbed into the shaft, and eased onto the top of the car as the soldiers inside went charging out. He lay the corpse down on top of the car and turned to the dead man. This one was probably early forties, his final expression of agony well-preserved on his blue, lifeless lips, his last will and testament bequeathing his white fabric coffin to an American diplomat.

———

"Mr. Chaput." Robert Durand stood and extended his hand. "Thank you for coming. Please, have a seat. Can I get you something to drink?"

Henri Chaput shook his head as he lowered himself onto the chair in the lawyer's office. "No, thank you. I'm fine."

Durand struggled to find any similarity in the man's features to his five-year-old client, Kelli Bertrand. Henri Chaput was a young man, well dressed and handsomely shaven. His clothes were pristine, and he smelled of a woody cologne. The dark hair and eyes were certainly there, but Kelli's still infantile features were difficult to compare with the clean-shaven jaw and straight, thin nose that sat before him.

"I have to admit, I was very surprised to get your call," Durand began. "We had just about given up hope of finding any family. I'd already begun the paperwork to place the girl in an institution."

"The girl." Chaput seemed to jerk slightly. "She has a name, doesn't she?"

"Of course, of course. But I had assumed that—"

Chaput raised a hand. "Mr. Durand, I know my call must have come as a shock, but please try to understand. The news of Rachel's death came as a greater shock to me, and then to learn that she had a child, a daughter, just about six years old…it's too incredible. I had no idea until I saw your post in *Le Monde*. No idea at all."

The lawyer leaned back in his chair and studied the young, well-dressed man who sat so easily before him. His posture and movements were slow and subtle, calm and unalarming. He barely made eye contact as he watched his own fingers slide back and forth across the silver rim of the fedora hat on his lap.

"So, you knew Kelli's mother then. You were...intimately connected?"

"Kelli," Chaput repeated. His eyes rose, wandering across blank spaces on the office walls. "Her name is Kelli then?"

"Does that name have any meaning to you?" Durand asked.

Chaput shook his head, and a grin slipped up the corners of his lips as he returned to stroking his hat. "No. It wouldn't. Rachel and I, we parted badly. The dumb things you say when you're angry."

"If you don't mind my asking, how long did you know Rachel Bertrand?"

"We were together for two years."

"You're certain there weren't any other..."

"No," Chaput said. "If I'm being honest, I can't assure you of that. But it doesn't matter. She's Rachel's daughter; that's enough."

"Do you know of any family, extended family?"

Chaput shook his head. "Rachel was an only child, born in West Africa. Her parents were some kind of scientists, or teachers. I can't remember. But they died when she was sixteen or seventeen in a fire. Rachel chose to return to France and live with an uncle, I think her mother's brother, who himself died a while later."

"You don't happen to know his name?" Durand asked.

"I'm afraid I don't. She didn't talk about her family much. But this, to be a mother herself, this would have made her very happy."

"Of course. Now, I assume you'll be willing to submit to some tests, check out your story, background, that kind of thing?"

"Whatever it takes," Chaput said, smiling. "If you don't mind my asking, how did she die? Was she ill?"

"An accident. Stepped off a curb in Glasgow at the wrong time. Very quick."

"That's terrible. And Kelli? What is she like?"

"Well, she's a little girl, like most little girls," said Durand. "Mind you, I'm not the expert, since I've only met her after the accident. But those who know her say she was very normal, liked to dance ballet and play like any other child."

"Before the accident?"

"Naturally, she's been traumatized by her mother's death. That's only to be expected in one so young and with no family to support her. She's been demonstrating some strange behaviors. Just odd things here and there."

"Is she in any danger?"

"Oh no, nothing serious. Just little things, refusing to speak, eating very little, hiding. But I'm sure all that will pass with some security and time, don't you think?"

"Yes of course. But is she, I mean, is she..."

"I'm not sure what you want to know, Mr. Chaput."

"She's my little girl," Chaput said. "I want to know everything."

———

The morning after Adam's attack on the Soviet compound in Moscow, an unmarked cargo truck pulled up outside the compound gate, its warm exhaust hitting the Moscow air with dissipating white puffs. A guard approached the driver side window, checked some papers, then the vehicle proceeded around the building, where another soldier opened a gate and the truck came to a stop by a small side door. Two men emerged from the compound and unlatched the back. The driver remained in his seat, unwilling to leave his warm cocoon while the heavy, white-sheeted bundles were tossed one by one into the back. Five were loaded before they pulled the door back down, resealing the truck. At first, the driver backed out the way he had come, but this instigated a series of Russian shouts and flailing arms. With a wave and a shrug, he pulled around the back of the building to a rear exit and departed.

Adam drove the truck casually through the Moscow streets. He knew them intimately, paths he used to cross en route to a favorite *zakusochnaya*, where a friendly assemblage waited with a bowl of *schi* and some pirozhki in a dimly lit back room. He might have noticed some ongoing changes to the landscape he once called home: boarded-up doors and windows, vacant lots, disintegrating sidewalks. Hundreds of building-sized posters of Leonid Brezhnev, the newly elected President of the Supreme Soviet, swayed lightly in the brittle winter air. Beneath their unending stare, Adam drove past three extended lines of people waiting for groceries, their empty food pails dangling in their frostbitten hands.

He might have noticed these things. But only the Fokus mattered.

Eventually, he pulled off at an isolated spot and got out. Crossing around to the back of the truck, he unlatched the door and pulled it up. Six white-sheet bundles lay cold and motionless on the truck floor.

"Mr. McLarey? Are you here?"

# TWO

ABOUT THE SAME TIME AS ADAM'S JAUNT THROUGH A SOVIET compound, US Air Force general Douglas Savio stepped into the dark lobby of the San Francisco Opera House. Beyond the neat red rows of empty seats, chattering musicians unpacked and tuned their instruments on the bright stage, preparing for a rehearsal.

A hush swept through the space as a lanky teenage boy, hands in his pockets and shoulders slouched, shuffled past the violins and plunked himself down at the long, glistening piano. The conductor nodded. The boy wiped his nose and began waffling around on the keys while wind instruments played limpid melodies behind him.

To Savio, observing the rehearsal from the shadows, the boy was obviously out of his element. It seemed strange to hear the piano resound like bells through the massive hall at the touch of such adolescent and uninterested fingertips.

"Me too, kid," he said out loud.

"General?" A man with an earpiece seemed to materialize from the lobby shadows. "If you'll follow me, please, sir?"

They passed through the lobby and up two flights of stairs,

while the music from the stage echoed softly through the walls. At the back of the balcony, the man with the earpiece gestured to a private box, and Savio stepped through. A small man sat in the box watching the rehearsal. Dressed entirely in white, he almost glowed in the darkened theater. Glasses that reflected the lights from the stage below hid a black patch over one eye.

"Zeus?" Savio asked.

The man in white lifted his good eye and gestured to an empty seat.

Savio sat halfway off the chair. "Did you lose that eye in combat?"

Zeus grinned but returned his attention to the rehearsal, his hands folded contemplatively over his lips as if in prayer.

Savio scanned the cavernous space with all its darkened crevices. The musicians wound their melodies in an endless cycle of repetition. The pianist ran his fingers across the keys with an adolescent distain. Savio should have insisted on the office meeting. These things never work out with dignity. "I didn't come all this way to listen to some kid play Beethoven," he said.

Several heads on the stage tilted up from their instruments, peering curiously towards the darkened balcony.

"That kid is much more than he seems, General," Zeus replied in hushed tones. "And you won't find anyone else who can help you with this delicate situation in Paris."

Savio relaxed back into his seat. "Riley, the bigmouth."

Zeus smiled. "Don't blame the Senator too quickly. I know all about your little problem in France, and that questionable aerodynamics engineer. Senator Riley was right to send you to me."

"Well, I don't negotiate with code names in concert halls. As I already told him, I need to see your people if this is going to go through."

"Naturally. But as Senator Riley explained, the nature of our organization is deeply confidential. So, we are at an impasse."

The music on the stage below wafted between them like an

awkward separating mist. The pianist traipsed up and down across the keys in a senseless winding patter while the bows of the violins rose and fell like waves.

Zeus spoke again. "General, how badly do you need to know about that aircraft's capabilities?"

Savio said nothing.

"Then," Zeus continued, "our only recourse is to do something rather unconventional. I am willing to bring you to our facilities and introduce you to our organization, but only under my terms."

"And what terms are those?"

"Have you let your people know you will be incognito for the afternoon?"

"As was agreed."

"Then, let's just say that I have made other arrangements."

Something rustled in the shadows behind Savio, then something pricked his neck. Before he could swat it away, the music from the stage curdled and the bright lights began to stretch and swirl. He wanted to move, but he couldn't find his arms.

Through closing shadows, Zeus spoke. "Get him on the plane. I have to stay and speak to the parents."

Strong arms hoisted Savio up, his feet dangling somewhere below. Before he slipped completely into darkness, the little man in white looked up and whispered in a respectful echo, "And General, for goodness' sake, it's not Beethoven, it's Saint-Saëns."

---

General Savio raised a hand to his throbbing head as his mind crawled back to consciousness.

"He's coming to now," said a distant and unfamiliar voice. "He'll be fine in a few minutes."

"Thank you, Riggs. You can go." That voice was familiar to Savio, though clouded in his memory by waves of piano music.

"General. Welcome back. You'll want to sit up slowly, as the effects of the sedative can take a while to subside."

"What the hell?" Savio stifled an urge to throw up. He held his screaming head while trying to stand. "You drugged me."

"Yes, yes, sincerest apologies, but let's try to remain civil about it." Two shadowy figures guided Savio back to the sofa. "You'll need a minute to get your bearings. Have some tea. They say the caffeine helps."

"Tea?"

"Do you prefer coffee? I am a tea man myself."

Zeus, still dressed all in white, sat cross-legged in a navy blue wing back chair, tenderly nursing a cup on his lap. Two guards loomed behind him.

"I'll see you do time for this," Savio snapped.

"I doubt that. You will have to find me first. But, in all honesty, General, you were rather insistent with Senator Riley to get a full introduction to our organization. I have merely provided the means for your request. As the Senator tried to explain to you, we prefer to remain discreet."

"I get it. But I'm not in the habit of hiring incognito organizations. I'm sure you understand." Savio wondered if the two guards were there to keep him from jumping up and strangling his tea-sipping abductor. "How'd you lose that eye?"

Zeus gestured to a cup on the table between them. The knee-high, round table was inlaid with a bright mosaic of a self-absorbed bird. "Try the tea, really. It's quite calming."

"Is it drugged?"

His host laughed and almost spilled some tea on his nice, white pants. "No."

Savio sat on a burgundy sofa, Persian carpets of red, navy, and ivory swirls beneath his feet. On the walls around him, stone sculptures mingled between shelves of jewel-toned books and a handful of vibrant paintings.

A long, curved wall of floor-to-ceiling windows faced two

heavy redwood doors on the opposite wall, the side walls extending inward in diagonal lines, creating a triangular office space. Beyond the open doors, a handful of secretarial staff poked away at white typewriters and answered white phones. Not a stitch of color among them.

Savio slowly lifted himself off the sofa. Zeus waved off the guards. "Gentlemen, I think the General is coming around. Why don't you wait outside?"

Tall windows spanned the entire length of the widest wall, overlooking endless brown hillsides, and a dry midday sky. It could be California, or New Mexico, or Colorado. They could be anywhere.

"Why am I here?"

"That aircraft in Paris." His host and abductor always seemed to be grinning, like a child nobody should trust. "You were wise not to hire Enoki. I can tell you why. You won't find anyone else who can get you answers on him. Or that machine." Zeus leaned forward to set his cup on one of the bird's green and golden wings. "General. Allow me to welcome you to the Institute. It's time you learned about one of your country's most valuable resources." He rose and gestured for the door with a short white arm. "Shall we?"

A minute later, they stood before an observation window. Miguel Garcia, the fourteen-year-old pianist from the Opera House, sat on the other side, doodling on some papers. A Hispanic couple huddled in a corner behind him, the man dozing, the woman's head wrapped in a scarf, her fingers clutching a handbag. Above the trio, a large painting of yellow and orange geometric patterns hung mounted in a gilded frame.

"Miguel Garcia was raised in the slums outside of Guadalajara," said Zeus. "At five years old, he walked by a piano bar and listened for hours. Went back every day, getting closer and closer to the pianist, until one day, he climbed up onto the bench and started playing. Like most of these prodigy stories, the rest is the same. Eventually a teacher found him, and he became a local celebrity, bringing in money for his family. But as you might have seen today at the symphony, he's bored. He plays to support his family, but soon his passion for piano will fade, and he'll be back at the pub, or worse."

"He's a prodigy."

"Yes. Prodigies," Zeus continued, "they're always some kind of accident, aren't they? Miguel happened to be standing outside the piano bar. For all we know, there could be multitudes of undiscovered prodigies walking around us every day."

"Are you saying you can predict them?" asked Savio.

"No. But what if it's not so much that young Miguel is musical, as he's a prodigy? What if he has an unequaled ability to learn and master something, something else?"

"You mean, he's not really interested in music."

"That's fairly obvious. But, more than that, he might be a KAT."

"A cat?"

"With a K," said Zeus. "It's an acronym from the German: *Kind, Agent, Tod*. Child, agent, death, the intended life's plan of the original KAT. The Nazis really began identifying the prodigal patterns. Hunting them down. Cataloguing them. Of course, they couldn't risk talent like that falling into enemy hands, so they named them after their life-plan: train as children, live as state agents, and die. A sort of monastic servant of the Reich."

Zeus continued, "Our Institute is founded on the premise that everyone, every child, is born with a spark. We call that their forté." Zeus pushed a button on a wall panel and spoke into a microphone. "Diane, try giving him the exams orally and make sure he doesn't need a translator. Also, take the parents down for some lunch. They might be distracting him."

A young woman in a white suit entered the exam room and sat opposite Miguel. Zeus said, "We're testing Miguel today to see if he has the prodigy spark, or if he is simply a pianist."

"How will you do that?" Savio asked.

"It's a hunting expedition. We have to find his interest. Passion. Curiosity. Unquenchable curiosity, almost like a child or an addict."

"For?"

"Oh, it could be anything: chemistry, higher mathematics, engineering, medicine, botany. We have KATs in every field imaginable. He might be a simple Level II, master of one skill, or a Level III, master of all fields related to their forté, which is what you need for this Paris project. Or, he could be a Level IV, able to combine multiple fields intellectually for higher calculations and problem solving. Where he ends up really doesn't matter."

"But you'll know he's more than a musician," Savio said.

"Is there such a thing?" Zeus replied, smiling. He opened the door to the observation room, and they moved into a long white corridor with bright windows on one side and doors on the other. Between each pair of doors, a painting hung in a gilded frame, illuminated by its own personal spotlight. Each one so different in style, but so carefully displayed that Savio had to wonder if he was touring an art school.

As though reading his thoughts, Zeus continued. "The arts are a way the KAT nature manifests in youth. That's often how we find them. If Miguel has a great potential for something else, then we can certainly help him."

"Or he can help you."

They stepped onto an elevator and descended several stories into the earth. The door opened on a dimly lit corridor with a dome-shaped ceiling. Zeus climbed into a small, motorized cart, and Savio joined him. They drove past doors, with similar carts parked outside, marked as *Chem Lab 1, Hormone Testing, Biotics, Chem Lab 2, Engineering, Robotics.* In between the doors hung more framed artwork, each in its own gilded frame. Down dozens of offshoot corridors, Savio saw a seemingly endless labyrinth of more doors, carts, paintings, and people.

———

A few hours later, General Savio followed his host into a long room with a sloped bank and reinforced metal deflectors. A line of tables holding weapons waited for them.

"I understand you're a good shot, General," Zeus said. "Care for a little contest?"

"With that eye and those glasses?"

"It's only fair to let you know I don't need the glasses. I wear them to cover the patch. Seems to make people more comfortable. Try these." Zeus passed him a pair of earplugs. "New design from our people. Protect the ears but don't hinder conversation."

"What are the stakes?" Savio asked, taking the plugs.

"You have seen our facilities now as you requested. You know what our Institute provides. But our services are not contracted lightly. If you win, I will disclose the location of our facility, give you a car to drive yourself home, and turn myself in."

"You're feeling confident."

"If I win, you give me a contact." Zeus pulled a small, folded piece of paper from his jacket pocket and slid it across the table.

Savio lifted the paper and read the figure. "This place is all very impressive," he said, "But Paris isn't some art show."

"That little aircraft that now sits purring in a Paris hangar was built by a Japanese engineer named Kazuhiro Enoki," Zeus said. "A KAT. And you need to know what exactly he has been commissioned to build for our Soviet friends. Let me guess, you already sent in one team, but they had no clue what the thing does. Well, that's not surprising. Enoki is brilliant, make no mistake of that. But he is also unstable. We had to turn him away, and our Japanese siblings dismissed him as well."

"Unstable?"

"Unfortunately, with great genius often comes some minor inconveniences of nature. Certain weaknesses. Personality issues we don't mind, but Enoki tested extreme paranoid and borderline delusional. No matter how much potential he had, we had to turn him away."

"Well, now he's made a deal with the devil, and we're left with our trousers down. What the hell did he build? Is it globally catastrophic? Before it disappears in Ivan's back pocket, we'd like to at least know."

"Then you have a choice, General. You already sent your people in. The clock is ticking, I'm sure you know. Now, if I win, that's our price tag. An aeronautics KAT will be able to tell you what that aircraft can do. I guarantee it." Zeus lifted an M16 off the first table and passed it to Savio. "Feel free to take a practice shot with this one."

Savio took the rifle. He opened the breech, checked the magazine, and pushed the bolt forward. When he took aim and shot, a bright projection appeared on a wall above them with a magnified image of the target, his bullet well-placed in the third ring.

"All right," he said. "A little Kentucky windage." Savio lifted the weapon a second time. Center ring, on the line. He passed the gun to his opponent.

Zeus took the weapon, chambered a round, aimed and shot, the shot so centered it took Savio a moment to find it. Without even checking where his shot had landed, Zeus gestured to a table of shotguns.

"I suppose I get to choose?" Savio asked.

"You are the guest."

Savio lifted the Remington 870, inspected the shells, then fired, and the scattering of pellets gathered slightly left of center.

"You know, this all sounds like comic book material," Savio said, handing the Remington to Zeus.

"Doesn't all genius when we hear about it?" Zeus fired the Remington, and the projection showed a happy conglomeration of nine black pellet holes distributed around the center, with two stragglers meandering up to the right by about four inches. He clucked his tongue in disapproval.

"How about three taps with these?" Zeus said, stepping up to an assortment of handguns.

Savio lifted a Colt 1911 and took the three hits, pausing between each to realign his sights. He then watched his short, white-frosted host take the weapon with minimal concern and aim, his grin melting away for an instant, his face like a blank gray clay, his one eye squinting in a concentrated stillness. The three shots passed in rapid succession. Dead on. Again. Three shots, and only one hole in the target. An egotistical eyebrow raised, Zeus's grin returned, and he put the Colt down before quietly moving to the revolver table.

Savio lifted a Colt Python. "Double or single?"

"You decide."

Savio bristled at Zeus's nonchalant tone, as though it didn't matter which he chose. He chose double. His first shot landed close to perfect, but his second and third strayed to the right. He passed the weapon to Zeus and watched him fire again.

"I want to see that target," Savio said.

"Be my guest."

Savio strode down the range and inspected the targets, each so uncannily centered. He again studied his host, a miniscule man, looking like a cartoon with the patch and all that white. "You're one of them, aren't you?"

"A humble Level II," Zeus replied. "Master of a simple skill."

"You're remarkable," said Savio, and the man in the fancy white suit bowed his head slightly. "But I have concerns with some of your core philosophies. This kind of talent should be working for me."

"Can you train them?"

"Yes, I believe so."

"Can you guarantee that no one will ever misuse them? Try to breed them? Bribe them, or coerce them into acting against their reason or their will?"

"I can't guarantee it, but can you? Don't the ideals of this country—?"

"Ideals." Zeus held up an interrupting hand. "I was apprehended by the Nazis, you know. They laid a trap for me. I was honored, in a way. Very clever. Put me right into their prodigy program. Called it research."

"That's where you learned about the KATs."

"That's where I lost the eye."

"What do you mean?"

"They took it out. To study it."

———

Back in the triangular office, Zeus lifted a folder from his desk and passed it to General Savio. "His name, as you can imagine, is confidential. Codename is Eagle. He's a Level III aerodynamics KAT. One of your boys actually, very decorated. Graduated from a POW camp in Vietnam before we found him. He's mastered nine different fields in his forté: aeronautical science, aerodynamics, aeronautical engineering, aviation, rocketry, design processing, defense systems, etc. Plus, a slew of related fields: anemology, meteorology, atmospheric chemistry and physics, global climatology, and so forth. He's the best pilot we've ever had. Even built our testing lab for us."

"Can we send him in?"

"If anyone can tell you what Enoki has built, he can. But Eagle doesn't get sent anywhere. He never quite recovered from Vietnam. Lost any sense of patriotism; left the Air Force, even as a decorated pilot with a bright future. He stayed on with us for a while. Our resources fueled his passion, but we differed in philosophy. The truth is he's gotten…hippie. You know, peace, flowers, the government is evil and all that."

"Can he be bought?"

"Possibly," said Zeus. "He isn't exactly in the black these days.

But it's more than that. If anything went wrong, I mean, if there were any, entanglements..."

"What then?"

"Send another man with him," Zeus said.

"I suppose you have someone in mind?"

"Indeed. He's a defector, and our only Level VI operative."

"How many of these levels do you have?" Savio asked.

"Only five. Adam's talents were so unique, we created the VI designation just for him."

"A superboy? What made him jump ship?"

"Don't know exactly. He was young when he came to us, and disturbed. I brought him home. He was actually born on American soil."

"Damn defectors, you never know if they're playing both hands. Can I meet him?"

"I'm afraid that won't be included in your tour today. I believe he's delivering a diplomat to the airport."

# THREE

NATHANIAL HEMMEL LAY PROSTRATE ON THE LONG, SLEEK WING OF a small airplane, enjoying the simple beauties buried within the bowels of a turboprop engine. It was a beautiful day in San Diego, despite the corrupt government, the rising inflation, and the crumbling state of his small airfield. Any day one could spend in a turboprop engine was a beautiful day.

"Hey, chief! Somebody here to see you." His office boy, Jeremy Planket, called him from the delights of aeronautic daydreams back to the world of mortgages and other unpaid bills. Jeremy had shuffled into the hangar in his overworn bell-bottom jeans and now stood beneath Nathanial's wing.

"Who is it?" Nathanial asked without rising from the engine.

"Some tall, slick fella. Says he's an old friend or something."

"I don't have any friends."

"That's what I told him, but he won't go away. Says he don't have any friends either."

Nathanial blamed himself. Fourteen times a week, he thought that the gum-chewing twenty-year-old should probably be fired, but he never had the heart to actually do it. And besides that,

Nathanial hated talking to people on the phone. Or at all. And of course, he couldn't afford a real secretary.

"Well, tell him to go away. Probably wants to sell me something."

"What if he wants to hire us for something?"

At last, Nathanial peeked over the rim, his hand, holding a wrench, drooped atop the engine compartment. "You didn't ask what he wanted?"

Most women would call Nathanial Hemmel an attractive guy. Dark caramel bangs habitually concealed his warm brown eyes, and beneath the grease and perpetual five o'clock shadow, his clear skin bore a single mole on his left cheek. He had a hypnotic smile that could disarm an angry stallion if given a chance, but his habitual wardrobe of combat pants and a T-shirt should probably have been thrown in the laundry long before he began considering it.

Nathanial spent most of his hours in the bowels of planes and helicopters. When he did fly taxi service with his small stock of aircraft, he would put on his headphones and say very little to anyone. He passed his off-work hours in a log cabin, which he'd built on a small unviolated lake at the end of a jagged dirt road. He had an undemanding dog and a spiritual relationship with an eagle that nested near the cabin every year. He fished and worked on planes, and to anyone's knowledge, hadn't spoken to a girl outside of business in his lifetime.

In fact, the limit of Nathanial Hemmel's civilized contact had so whittled down over the years that the chubby, stock-shouldered, quirk of an office boy was gradually becoming his only remaining link to humanity. So, he kept him on.

A tall, slender silhouette of a man stepped through the hangar bay doors. He leaned against the doorframe behind Jeremy. "Hello, Nathanial." The voice swept up to Nathanial's wing like a menacing wind. He sat up.

"Adam."

Adam Walker stepped forward, his straw-colored hair, hazel eyes and narrow, set jaw momentarily glowing in the California sunlight.

"Uh, you still want me to tell him to go away?" Jeremy asked.

"No thanks, Jeremy. You can go." Jeremy obediently shuffled back toward the office.

"Wow. The great Adam Walker. It's been what, two years?"

"Three, actually."

"Well, how are you? Wait." Nathanial's lips tightened. "No," he said, wagging the wrench like an accusatory finger. "Whatever it is, no. And you can tell whitey-pants Peter I didn't say hello."

"That's very quick of you. Can you really afford to say that?" Adam scanned Nathanial's rusting and cluttered hangar with disapproving eyes.

Nathanial sunk back into the turboprop engine. "I'd rather die of debt. Speaking of fatalities," he continued, "how many body bags have you called for this week? Ten? Twenty? Seriously, how many Russian mothers got phone calls, all in the great name of freedom and talent?"

"In the spirit of freedom, can't you try to keep an open mind?" Adam asked.

"If you're too open-minded, your brains will fall out, or in your case, your conscience."

"There's a war going on out there, in the world," Adam said.

"Yeah, there's always a war going on." Nathanial fiddled with the engine again. "It never stops. Only now, all the soldiers are field operatives and secret police, and all the victims just doing their job when *pop-pop, sorry 'bout that, I've got a focus to keep.*"

"We still have enemies."

"Yeah, whose enemy are you?" Nathanial worked while a half minute of silence smoldered between them. Perhaps Adam had left. Probably not. The man could slither.

"Do you know what *Holodomor* means, Nathanial?"

*Crap.* Nathanial remained buried in the plane. "Let's see. *Holodomor.* No, never heard of it."

"That's not by accident. It means death by hunger. It's Ukrainian for 'starve to death.' Most people haven't heard of it because Stalin worked so competently to keep it hidden. It's been illegal to even say the word 'holod' in the Soviet Union. Illegal to say the word. The press called it the 'famine,' as though it was some natural disaster, a normal evolutionary purge."

"I've got a lot of work here."

"It was the largest scale genocide in recorded history. Right under our noses. If you can call it recorded. Stalin wanted their land. He sent soldiers to take all the grain and livestock, farming tools, everything they needed. It was so simple, so effortless, and so perfectly effective. Ten million Ukrainians, starving, forced into cannibalism. The streets lined with emaciated corpses." Adam walked around behind the plane. "I know who our enemies are."

Against the back wall of Nathanial's hangar stood a work-bench cluttered with a menagerie of filth: crumpled papers, soda cans, and an old greasy T-shirt in a lump. On a small AM/FM radio, rigged with a coat hanger for an antenna, a spider had taken up a substantial, unchecked residence. Above the table hung a framed picture of teenage Nathanial holding a trophy and wearing too much pilot apparel. He stood beside a biplane, his father's arm around his shoulder. Adam reached out and straightened the picture. His fingertips strayed delicately to another, smaller photograph, in a silver frame, standing apart on the work-bench, partially covered by wayward paperwork. Adam moved the scraps aside. The face of a young Vietnamese woman glowed with a naïve happiness, despite the shabby hovel behind her.

Nathanial stepped up behind him.

"Mai," Adam said, lifting the picture. "She was so very beautiful."

"Put it down, Adam."

"Sometimes I wonder if we ever really left that jungle alive,"

Adam said. "And everything since then has been some convoluted dream."

"In your case, a nightmare. No. I don't know what the hell happened to you. But I'm home."

"Are you? Have you really moved on?"

"I've got this place. And my cabin. I keep busy."

"Yes. So do I. Keep busy. But I sometimes wonder, what would things be like, you and I, if that day, I had been—"

"Don't finish that sentence. You and your damn focus." Nathanial stepped forward and snatched the picture from him. "Not everything in life is a matter of you blocking distractions out of your tiny skull." He set the frame back on its dusty throne and wiped his hands with an ineffective rag.

"Peter will pay you enough to catch up on your mortgage payments," Adam said.

"Well, isn't he a piece of work? I should kick you out just for snooping into my affairs."

"You should take the gig."

"That's quite a bit of dough. The mighty Zeus must be trying to impress someone."

"We need you to look at a plane."

"Look at a plane?"

"Tell us what makes it so valuable to its funders."

"I suppose its funders would be the proverbial enemies in this scenario." Nathanial glanced around his hangar. Dirty, unorganized, covered with junk. So many lost projects he wanted to get to some weekend. But at least was *his* mess. At least until the bank came to claim it all. "How long will I get with it?"

"One hour, in and out."

"That. I hate that. That's always just a party in a hat, isn't it? One hour, in and out. That means somebody's watching. I'm guessing that means I can't take it up?"

"Probably not."

"Probably not. Where is it?"

"France."

"France? Crimey. Can't you bring it here? Damn. I guess I'm supposed to be happy it's not in Leningrad."

"We only want you to take a look. No one else in sight. No entanglements. Very simple." "It's never simple. I hate this stuff."

# FOUR

KELLI WAITED IN A LARGE LOBBY CHAIR WHILE HER FATHER WENT TO the front desk to check out. Soon they would go together, but she didn't know where. Not to the little house in Allonville. She didn't want to go so far from the little house. What if they were all wrong? What if everyone had it wrong, and Maman came back looking for her? Kelli wanted to go back to the little house and sit on the step and wait for her. All day and night, she could sit there. It would be so quiet and nice. Maman would come back eventually.

Here, waiting for her father, the fancy Paris hotel tapestries, chandeliers, and mirrors overloaded Kelli with colors and lights. She wanted to shut her eyes, but something nudged her, as if from the side, reached out and poked at her, calling for her attention. Her mind dreamily slipped forward, out from the haze to a painting, five times her size, on the far wall. She rose and stepped softly towards it. Inside the painted world, misty ballerinas held flowing poses in a sunlit studio where wild garden vines tumbled through the tall windows. The foggy brush strokes trapped the dancers in a wonderful fading memory, like something else... *What was that thing I was supposed to do?*

The ladies in their long white tutus returned her gaze, the first eye contact she had made in weeks, and her insides surged unexpectedly awake. She wanted to move, to run? A voice sang out in a nearby room. She could see only strangers. But now someone called to her, this time a ringing piano accompanying the class. Oh, it was so beautiful.

# FIVE

NATHANIAL LEANED AGAINST THE BACK WALL OF A PARIS FBO hangar, with only his sunglasses and leather jacket to hide him. A familiar chill ran continually up and down the back of his neck, less from the February cold than from the understanding that at any moment, his image could be drawing into focus on some sniper's rifle.

At last, the hangar door opened, then Adam signaled the all-clear. When Nathanial picked up his knapsack and gratefully slipped through, an unexpected blast of late afternoon sunlight from the open bay doors at the front surprised him.

"There was no one here?"

"No one knows about this location," Adam said. "Why bother placing a guard and draw attention to it?"

"Well, *we* know."

"Uncle Sam has been tracking him. But he doesn't know that."

"I thought you said the place was shut up tight."

"It has been," Adam said. "He must have opened the bay doors before he left, which is not good for us."

"What do you mean, not good for us?"

"He might be prepping for a test drive."

"I'd forgotten how you never say what you really mean. You mean, his funders might already be here and pop back in at any second with a shitload of Soviet gun power."

"You'd better get to work."

The aircraft stood alone in the nearly empty hangar. A trio of large crates sat by the bay door with tufts of packaging dangling from their lids, and a dilapidated motorcycle leaned against the north wall. A half dozen tools lay scattered on a single worktable with some pencils, books, and empty chemical bottles. Near a foldaway cot, Enoki's luggage spilled onto the floor alongside a half-dozen empty wine bottles.

"In and out in one hour," Nathanial muttered. "Real simple. How long do you think I have?"

"I'll let you know," Adam said, checking his Ruger 22.

At last, Nathanial glanced at the object of his mission. "It's a helicopter."

Adam assumed a watch position at the bay doors, scoping the tarmac. "Have you ever seen one that shape? Will it lift?"

"Yeah. Sure. If that rotor works. Weird looking thing. What's that disk for?"

"That's why you're here. And what are those?" Adam pointed at the shiny, smooth nubs protruding from each side of the main fuselage.

"Could be for weapons." Nathanial fell into his inspection. He swept studiously around her curves, the contours of the silver outer shell and glossy black bottom standing elegantly on an uncustomary three wheels. A helicopter that could taxi. Well, that's not so extraordinary. No, there was more to her than that. She was large for a single rotor chopper, and even stranger, the inner third of each blade disappeared into a central disk.

His fingertips moved down the fuselage until he lay prostrate beneath it. "This is very strange," he said.

"What's that?"

"Well, you probably know that for any aircraft to go fast, you want the outer surface as smooth as possible. But instead of one streamlined piece of metal, this outer shell, or at least the entire bottom, is actually constructed of hundreds of small cells. In themselves, they're smooth, dimpled mildly, and I don't know how they are held together. There are no outer rivets, but they are secure. To get that surface, each one would have to be constructed to very exact calculations. But why? That's got to affect airflow. So, this thing is not a speed machine. It does something, but it's not speed."

Nathanial pulled on the cockpit door and found the vessel unprotected.

The cabin was only large enough for a full back seat and some minor cargo. Where was all the space? Even more curious, he found no obvious weaponry, no guns, no missile launchers, just a handful of empty, retractable compartments. So, what had all the space? Engines? He warily opened a few panels and found electronics, mazes of wires, all carefully strung together, conveying a multitude of systems whose functions he couldn't begin to guess. He sat in the bowels of a monster.

———

Adam kept watch and the hour flew by uninterrupted, with Nathanial crawling under, in, and around his assignment, softy murmuring to himself. Eventually, Nathanial fired up the engine.

"How did you do that?" Adam called out.

A dim click, and Nathanial's voice rang through the hangar. "I'm good with planes." Adam gestured to turn it down.

A smooth motor started humming, and the tiny nubs that protruded from the sides of the helicopter stretched out into full wings, with smaller nubs pointing upwards at the tips. Nathanial came out.

"So, it *is* a plane," Adam said.

"Nope. Only one set of controls in there. That's pretty standard. And these," Nathanial gently patted one of the wings, "these aren't going to get you off the ground. Maybe in a pinch they could help you glide down, but I think there's another purpose for them. The truth is, I'm gonna need a couple weeks with this thing. Get deeper inside the electronics. There are so many systems going through its veins, I can't decipher what half of them do."

"Can't you guess?"

"Look, this thing is either a pile of highly advanced brilliance, or it's just, like, looney." Despite the concern in his voice, Nathanial beamed. "And even if I can theorize, how can we be sure that it works without taking it up? I need more time."

Adam returned to the hangar door. The FBO tarmac, off a branch of the main airport, was designed for private jets of the rich and famous. A handful of hangars like this one lined the avenue, some rented, others owned by corporations. Occasionally, a mechanic and flight staff appeared near another hangar, but generally the area stayed quiet and unpopulated. An airport baggage tractor approached with a cart in tow. It stopped near their hangar, and Adam nodded to a portly young man who deposited some barrels by the outside wall.

"Hey!" called Nathanial. "Come here a second, will ya?" Adam moved inside where Nathanial had the pilot door propped open with his foot. "Okay, it comes to this. I can't tell you much unless I take the thing apart piece by piece, or fly it in an unhealthy manner."

"Unhealthy?"

"Take her up and start pushing buttons. This is beyond anything I've ever seen, and there's no precedent for it. What should we do? Can you contact Peter?"

Adam shook his head.

"Well, I can take some Polaroids," Nathanial said, "and come up with some theories, but there is no manual for this thing. It came out of someone's crazy psyche, and either you get your hands on him, or we get our hands on the controls and I start experimenting."

"Couldn't there be some heavy weaponry?"

"That's the thing. I can't find any weapons. There's empty compartments, and some pretty sophisticated targeting systems, but no guns, no missiles, nothing."

"Then what's the use of it?"

Nathanial wiped his brow. "You know, Adam, just because you can't shoot something doesn't mean it's useless."

Adam stiffened, one hand held aloft, his other swinging around to grasp his pistol.

"What?" Nathanial asked.

Adam crept around the front of the aircraft, towards the bay doors, listening. Perhaps the breeze had shifted something. Something like an empty plastic barrel lying on its side. The wind must have caught it and nudged it over. Adam lowered his gun and jarred the barrel with his foot. "It's okay," he said. But it wasn't. Something in the very air had shifted, and Adam could feel the new presence with every hair on the back of his neck.

----

Because of the psychological trauma generally caused by Extraordinary Sensory Awareness, most medical professionals label it a 'disorder.' Among the talented, however, ESA is the rarest of jewels. So rare that only a handful had ever been cataloged with both the ESA and the Level V ability to master it.

At first, Adam assumed other children could hear the things he could: someone breathing erratically across the classroom, the heartbeats of nearby students, the ticking of the teacher's watch at the front of the class. He assumed everyone felt the warmth of a person's body heat from a few feet away.

But as he grew, so did the stimulus. The cacophony of sounds germinating with his adolescent knowledge of self twisted like menacing vines, depositing horrific, endless echoes in the cavern of his mind. Flavors and smells became so potent, they brought pain, chronic headaches, insomnia, terror, and perpetual trembling on a battlefield of endless sensory input.

Into his young cell of solitude and horror had stepped a woman. No one special really. Just someone who saw the clarity, followed the wind passing through the reeds, and restored the calm. She taught young Adam slowly, in that informal maternal way, to sift through the hoards, and fasten himself to one stimulus at a time. To build a cocoon of thought where he alone could allow admittance.

The Level V mind, when properly trained and honed, could isolate the sensory input and centralize his concentration on one thing: his prime objective, his directive. In Russia, they had called it the Fokus. But simple truth be told, the great Level VI, Adam Walker, could only be all he was to freedom and democracy because he had a mother who loved him.

Though he rarely considered that.

As Adam stood in the hangar door at the Paris FBO, nothing brazenly pervaded his space, but rather nudged at him, something subtle. It hadn't been there before, but now it watched him, hiding. Off and on, he could hear it, gently but too fast, different from him, muffled and small. Perhaps some sound or scent had drifted on the breeze from the nearby hangars. That had happened before.

But the scent overwhelmed him now, the perceivable unique signature on every human being, try as they might to smoke, drink, or soap it out. It wafted around him, fluttering through the hangar in unthreatening waves, sweet and light, like powder or beach sand.

"Adam, what is going on?" Nathanial spotted him creeping around with both hands on his weapon.

"I don't know... Start it back up."

"What?"

"Looks like you're going to get to take her up."

"Hold on. I thought we were just—"

"We can't leave it behind without answers. Be ready."

Again, the intrusive presence had moved, but he couldn't see it, couldn't catch it. It was sneaky. Very good at hiding. He inspected every corner, pistol ready, while Nathanial prepped for takeoff.

The sounds of the aircraft quickly filled the hangar.

Adam approached the three crates near the open bay doors and lifted the first lid. Inside was empty, but the scent entirely overwhelmed him now. He was closer, very close, and whatever, whoever, he sensed had stopped moving. He stepped to the second crate, his pistol at his hip, but found inside only the smell of grease and woodchips.

One crate remained. He lifted the lid, ready to fire.

"*Ce n'était pas mon père*," she said.

*He wasn't my father.*

# 2ND MOVEMENT: FOCUS

*"Now Kelli, recite the verse for me again."*

*"I don't remember."*

*"Yes, you do. Do it with me again. In English. 'If I am gone and light is dim, look closely on the dagger's rim.' Now you try."*

# ONE

ADAM STOOD STIFFLY, HOLDING THE CRATE LID AND GAPING AT THE tiny child. She was five, maybe six years old. She had deep, brown curly hair, a black coat, white tights, and a red beret. She trembled, hugging her tiny knees, and her large brown eyes peered up at him like moistened pleading jewels.

*Ce n'était pas mon père.*

He dropped the lid and stored his pistol, still slightly unsure of what he had just seen. Steps approached him from behind. Grown steps. And then a man spoke to him in French. Calling out from behind. Asking about a missing child. He and airport security were searching for…

Of course, the natural thing to do was point to the crate and say, "She's in here." The man would take the girl, and all three would leave without asking any more questions. That's what he should do. That's what he should have done. But suddenly Adam Walker's perception of the hangar, the breeze, and the smells of the girl all melded together, like objects wedged into clay. He couldn't clarify which one he was talking to. Whose scent he was battling, and who was lying to him. The sounds of the rotor activating on the helicopter rapidly melded into his muddled thoughts, creating an unexpected chaos that awoke the very nerves beneath his skin, kicking them all into fiery action, and his fleeting clarity into turmoil.

"Seems a strange place to take a little kid," Adam said. "Why'd you bring her out here?"

"She wandered off."

"From the main terminal? That's an awfully long way for a kid to wander by herself."

"Someone said they saw her. Right around this hangar actually. Have you seen her?"

"How old did you say she is?"

"I didn't say. She's five and a half, and—"

"And you're her father?" Adam could sense the man's growing frustration, *but then a worried parent might do that*. Adam's nerves surged as he fought to trust a potent and foreign sensation that he couldn't define. He imagined the hangar spinning, very slowly, like the rotor, and the ensuing chaos in his head continued to compel him to do the wrong thing.

Adam called out to Nathanial in English. "Niko, you seen a little girl?"

Nathanial used the mic. "You mean a little kid?"

The security guard nudged the father's arm. "She's not here, sir. Let's move on."

But the man persisted. "Do you mind if we just look around? I won't feel right until I look around. She's just a little thing." His voice faded as he wandered deeper into the hangar.

The guard offered Adam an apologetic shrug and followed.

Adam lifted the crate cover again. "*Qui est-ce?*" he whispered to the girl.

"*Ce n'est pas mon père.*"

The man approached the crates, and Adam closed the lid. "These are private property."

"Please, if I could just have a look."

"I'm afraid not."

"Well then perhaps you won't mind if airport security looks in them."

The guard rolled his eyes, grumbled, and stepped forward. Without thinking, Adam swiftly pivoted on his right heel and knocked him to the floor.

It had happened so quickly, so instinctually, the effort had even caught him by surprise. *What was he doing?* He stood momentarily immobile, his hands still raised in defense, staring in shock at the unconscious man. "Your daughter isn't here," he heard himself say. "You should go, now."

"Why do I think you are lying?"

"One of us is."

The man's fist slapped into Adam's right arm. Drawing back, the man then launched a series of precision strikes at Adam's face and gut, but never made his mark. Frustration mounting, he spun and kicked, but Adam bent and hit his grounded leg. Two more guards rushed in through the bay doors, shouting orders and pulling out weapons. Adam waved Nathanial out of the hangar, and he gladly taxied towards the sunlight.

––––––

For a moment, inside her crate, Kelli lifted the lid and peeked over the edge. The helicopter blew wind around as it rolled out the door. The tall blond man glided through the air, his motions effortless and graceful. He fought all the men at once, sending each to the floor or limping away. When he jumped, the tails of his long coat flew behind him like angel wings. One guard pulled out a gun, but the tall blond man grabbed his fist and flung the man around, aiming the weapon at the floor. The loud crack of the pistol made her jump, and she let the lid drop again.

––––––

The man who said he was the girl's father lifted a pistol from a security guard and held it up. "Look," he said in English. "I don't know who you are, or what you are doing here, but I'm just here to get the girl."

Adam stepped back, his hands raised. He gestured toward the crate. The man inched closer and took one hand off the pistol to lift the lid. Adam knocked the weapon away, sending it spinning across the concrete. Swinging himself around, he lifted his right foot, trailing his entire body through the air. His heel impacted the man's left temple, and the man crumbled to the pavement.

Adam stood over him, bewildered. Why did he do this? He didn't know the girl or the man. For all he knew, he could have just executed her parent. This was not his directive, or even related to it. He had gotten involved in something he had nothing to do with. All of this was...*off Fokus.*

And now what? Nathanial and the chopper were gone. Security men writhed on the ground. Down the access road, a posse of vehicles sped his way, lights flashing. He crossed quickly to the motorcycle and rigged the ignition, pulled out the choke. It turned over. It would do the job.

*Ce n'était pas mon père.*

Adam revved the bike and the posse advanced, encroaching shouts of angry voices ringing out between siren blares. Still, he held the bike frozen, its front wheel peeking over the hangar threshold.

*Ce n'était pas mon père.*

This had nothing to do with them. Security would eventually find the girl and return her to where she belonged.

Her pleading eyes besieged him. The tremor in her voice.

*He wasn't my father.*

Adam spun in another circle and stopped beside her crate. He lifted the lid and extended his hand. "You can trust me," he said in French.

Trancelike, she took the hand, and he easily lifted her tiny body onto the seat in front of him. The bike jerked and he roared off, swerving to avoid vehicles, but the girl wrapped her legs around his torso. He sped around the back of the hangar and up the parallel street towards the terminal. Another slew of security vehicles appeared, pinning them between the two angry mobs. A pair of gunshots pealed out from the posse. Threats in French projected through a loudspeaker.

The posse turned and pursued him back towards the main runway. He veered in and out of maintenance vehicles. A sharp turn almost tilted the bike on its side, and the little girl dug her fingers into his ribs. As they raced down the active runway, a massive airliner passed over their heads, applying full power into a go around and aborting their landing. Adam pushed the bike on despite the wind and heat. Once the plane passed, he could see Enoki's chopper, hovering off to his right. A rope ladder dangled beneath, curling back as Nathanial tried to match their pace.

"Hold on tight now," Adam called back to the girl.

Nathanial kept the chopper moving forward, trying to keep ahead of the posse, but when Adam reached up a hand for the ladder, the girl slipped away. Falling back onto the bike, he lost balance and swerved to a stop. The mass of sirens encroached to within fifty yards.

How to get them both on the ladder? He would have to trust the girl. "You must hold on, no matter what," he said in French. He felt her nod against his chest, and he started off again.

The runway threshold ahead closed in on them with an airport boundary fence blocking a busy highway. Nathanial only yards away, Adam again entered the aggressive rotor wash and deafening pounding. He let go of the bike with both hands and grabbed the ladder. For a moment, the bike left the ground with them, and all three swung backward in the air as Adam curled himself up to capture his lower legs into the rungs.

The bike's handlebar caught on the ladder and lifted off with them, its weight wildly tilting the ladder. Adam kicked at it repeatedly before it sailed silently back down to the runway, crashing and igniting the fuel tank. As the explosion rose up, Adam watched the vehicles, weapons, and angry faces converge around the small inferno and glare up at him.

*Who is this kid?* Adam wondered for the first time, and why had he gone to so much trouble to kidnap her?

# TWO

As they headed over international waters, Adam repeated a nonsensical phrase on the chopper's radio, and a voice responded with a mess of code phrases and broken snippets of intel. When finished, he gave coordinates to Nathanial for a mid-Atlantic rendezvous.

"Better to stay low."

"I want to check the altitude ceiling on this thing. What can it hurt?"

"Nathanial, we just stole a multimillion-dollar piece of machinery, and we're flying over international waters. Our Soviet comrades aren't above blowing us out of the sky."

The girl remained obediently seated with her back to Nathanial, where Adam had parked her. So still and quiet, even Adam almost forgot about her. However, a few hours later, while Nathanial approached a rocking aircraft carrier in the middle of the Atlantic, the girl's head suddenly popped up between them, and the chopper veered dangerously towards the salty blackness.

"What the—?" The trio wobbled in ungraceful silence as Nathanial quickly straightened the cyclic or pitch control stick. "Who is that?"

"Oh," Adam said. "We have a passenger."

"What? You never said anything about picking up any kid!"

"Calm down and level off. I don't know anything about her. She was in trouble."

"So, you kidnapped her?"

"Rescued."

After setting down on the carrier's deck, Adam removed his headgear and jumped out to make contact with the crew. Nathanial stewed silently in the cabin, waiting for the rotors to spin down. He turned back toward their guest. Despite the pounding rotor noise, it felt awkwardly silent with the little girl stiffly sitting there, her head down and her hands squeezed together on her lap. When she looked up at him, her eyes popped with a renewed terror, and she quickly scrambled out, opening the door with a disturbing delicacy and softness.

She crept up to Adam while he spoke with an Aviation Boatswains Mate in a yellow shirt on the undulating deck. She reminded Nathanial of a China doll, so pretty and breakable, her eyes almost lifeless, pointed intently at the deck floor. She clasped a bit of the Adam's coat and rubbed it between her fingers.

The crew scrambled around her to guide Nathanial and the stolen aircraft onto the elevator, where it would descend into the bowels of the newly commissioned Nimitz-class carrier. Once he got the all-clear, Nathanial jumped out and stormed around to confront Adam. "Who is she then?"

"I told you, I don't know," Adam said while checking off items on a clipboard for a yellow shirt. "She was in trouble. That's all I know for sure."

"What kind of trouble was she in?"

"She kept saying he wasn't her father."

"Who wasn't her father? The guy you decked?"

More naval seamen in yellow shirts approached Adam with questions and orders. "I didn't have time to get details," Adam said. "Security was coming. So, I made a choice."

Nathanial stepped away and scratched all ten fingers along his scalp. Even unexpectedly stealing the aircraft was too clean and simple. It was always something *moral* with these people. This had to be planned. How would Adam Walker ever decide to kidnap a kid on the fly? No. They had deceived him again. The mighty Peter Zeus, that cursed Institute, all those damn KATs.

The girl tugged on Adam's coat, but he ignored her and continued giving instructions to crewmen. An officer approached, and Adam gestured for the girl to hold still, but she shook her head and squatted. If the plan had included this child, then Adam was certainly taking a cool approach to her. He barely seemed concerned with her at all.

*Unbelievable.* Nathanial thought and reached for her hand. "Come with me," he said, but she jumped and span back away from him, hiding behind Adam's leg. "Adam, for crying out loud. You need to take her to the bathroom."

The girl buried her face as though hiding in the flapping fabrics of Adam's coat, her long black curls stretching like tendrils around her face and ears in the misty sea gusts, her arms held taut with an unnatural terror. Nathanial thought if he tried to grab her arm, he might accidentally snap it.

Eventually, Adam grew frustrated with the child clinging to his leg. He squatted down and held her shoulders gently. She seemed to loosen when Adam's eyes were before her, even through the growing shadows, so much so that for a moment, Nathanial wondered if they had met before this day. Of course, that would explain why she jumped on a strange aircraft with him. Adam spoke tenderly in French, with an unfamiliar voice. Was it tenderness? Or was this all part of a planned kidnapping and Adam just on-focus again? Nathanial harnessed a rising fury, momentarily mesmerized by the tiny thing listening to Adam. She was so out of place on this mighty swaying vessel, in the middle of a wild sea and a darkening night where grown people who must seem to her a swirling of sinister shadows and terrifying nonsense.

She should be at home somewhere. Tucked neatly into some little bed with something stuffed and furry.

An urge overwhelmed Nathanial to get the girl inside. Away from the sounds of the sea, the chaos of this windy deck, where nothing so precious and innocent should be standing. He would find a quiet room to sit her down, find her something, a cup of sweet soda, like some Nehi Grape soda or a piece of chocolate, and a National Geographic with some pictures of calmer places.

Adam gestured toward him, and the little girl looked up at Nathanial for the first time, her frightened brown eyes measuring her trust against the pressure in her bladder. Adam placed her hand in Nathanial's, and before taking another breath, he returned to the yellow-shirted officer.

Her hand felt absurdly small and cool in Nathanial's palm, and he wondered if she could feel his hardened calluses. As they crossed the deck of the great swaying vessel in the splattered dusk, her eyes stubbornly fixed on the deck beneath her tiny feet, as though looking up and seeing and accepting the chaos around her might trick her out of whatever trance Adam had laid upon her and awaken her into the spinning reality from which she kept her thin little shoulders pathetically hunched.

"I don't speak French," he said, holding the door. "Sorry about all that, I mean that shouting with Adam. I mean the other guy. The guy who speaks French. He's Adam. I'm Nathanial. You probably thought he was a nice, strong sort of person you can trust. You probably don't understand any of this. Well, he's an idiot, but right now, so am I for trusting him."

———

Peter had arranged for them to stay on the carrier for four days, reducing fuel stops on their journey across the ocean, and General Savio had ordered a direct and speedy route. There had been some minor upset with the ship's captain about having a child on board, of course. He had been notified of only two passengers and one aircraft, but Adam talked his way around it, and she ended up with priority seating in the wardroom all four nights, even though she never spoke a word to anyone and rarely ate anything at all.

The girl nurtured an unhealthy fidelity to her abductor, always preferring to be at Adam's side, holding on to some seam of his clothing. At first, they would sit for hours on the observation deck, Adam absorbed in some book to update his computer VI brain, while she stared blankly at the sea. Whenever Nathanial or anyone else approached, she quickly shifted her gaze to a random spot and tightened her fingers around the fabric. For sleeping, someone tried to arrange a private space for her with a female escort, but she showed such a countenance of horror and a death grip when Adam tried to leave her, that they all three ended up sharing a berth, with her on the bottom rack. Even then, tired though she must have been, sleep only triumphed when Adam sat on the floor beside her. And of course, the light remained on all night.

Nathanial remained close to this strange duo, instinctively wary of any Institute childcare. He read stories to her from some Reader's Digests he found on board. She couldn't understand, so he figured it didn't matter what he read. He took her on tours of the ship when Adam gladly ordered her to go. He showed her maps, machinery, or nautical instruments, talking endlessly, every word lost in translation, all the time him wondering, who is this kid? And what was the Institute's interest in her?

A few times, when she was more responsive, they sat together in the stolen chopper. He described the controls in great detail, using words like torque and lift, explaining concepts far beyond the grasp of a little kid. He let her hold the cyclic or the collective while he made sound effects, pretending they were on a dangerous mission. Though she never spoke, she occasionally began to make eye contact and even looked around the ship curiously, like a kid should. Once, in the chopper, the smallest beginning of a smile began to emerge, but it stopped quickly when, as though remembering something, she stiffened with a white horror, then jumped out and ran off to find Adam.

———

After taking off in the aircraft from the ship, they made The Institute in two more days, taking breaks for meals and refueling. When he slept, Nathanial let Adam take the controls. Whether eating or breaking for pitstops, the girl made no complaints and maintained her perfect silence throughout the long days, staring blankly out the window hour after hour, or lying across the back seat in trancelike sleep. As long as she had Adam in her sight, she was placid as a ragdoll.

At last, The Institute hangar doors ground open for them on the California mountainside.

The mighty Zeus stood in the hangar, the white spectacle, his hands in his pockets and a customary grin plastered on his face. How would he take the news of Mount Olympus's first kidnapping? At least Nathanial hoped it was the first time. Or maybe he already knew.

"Welcome home," he called out. "So, this is the beast. What secrets does it tell us, Nathanial?"

"I don't know."

"Even after all this time? You still have no idea what it does?"

"No, Peter. I was more concerned with getting it here after we unexpectedly stole it. Besides, I'm not a fan of pushing mysterious buttons at random altitudes. Not to mention the extra package in the back seat."

The air in the hangar seemed to quickly cool.

"Extra package?" So, Peter really had no idea. Adam stepped

aside, and Peter peered through the chopper's back window. "Is that…a child?"

Someone on the other side of the hangar dropped a metal tool with a series of resounding clangs. Peter's cloak of charm melted into such a pallor that his face momentarily matched his suit. "Well, Adam. A stolen helicopter, an angry coworker, and a botched mission. Okay, you're entitled to a few, but a child? Interesting that you left that out in your messages."

"So, you're telling me, you really had no idea about this?" Nathanial said. "About her?"

"Good heavens, Nathanial. What do you think, we've completely fallen apart ethically without you?"

"I don't know, Peter. Your top agent just collected a random kid from a Paris airport."

"All right. All right," Peter said. "Let's get her to some comfortable quarters, then you both can debrief me in my office as soon as you clean up." Adam opened the door and carefully lifted the dozing child into his arms. "Nathanial," Peter continued, "I'll ask you to stay around until we get this all sorted out. My general is still expecting answers about this aircraft. You'll be compensated, of course."

"Oh, no. No. I have a business to run, remember?" Nathanial lowered his voice. "This was supposed to be a one-day gig. I have a life to get back to."

"You have a hangar and a dog," Adam said, also whispering.

"Look who's talking. Do you even have any plants? How about a cactus, Adam? You know, you don't even have to water those."

"How you two collaborated long enough to escape the jungle will forever be a source of entertainment to me," said Peter. "Nathanial, I have not neglected you. We've got two reliable people at your hangar running things in your absence. I'm sure you'll find everything better than you left it."

Nathanial opened his mouth to object when a sudden explosion of sound from the loudspeakers cut him off. The all-campus alarm system blared through every inch of the hangar and every hair on their heads while a pedantic voice droned, "Unrecognized signal. Intruder alert."

Peter sped off to a nearby phone hanging on the hangar wall.

"What's going on?" Nathanial asked Adam as the girl jerked awake and covered her ears.

"Someone is sending a signal from inside The Institute." Adam put the girl down on the ground, where she assumed her leg clinging position and started shaking her head.

Peter shouted orders into the phone, the curled cord swinging beneath him. "Well, have you located it? What? But I'm in the hangar now. Are you sure? Check again." Peter scanned the hangar and Adam reached back for his pistol. Nathanial wondered if Adam's hand did that without his conscious consent, or if he still had to think about it. "I'm telling you I'm here right now and there is no—" Peter squinted ominously at the girl clinging to Adam. "Get a team down here."

"Oh, come on Peter," Nathanial said, stepping forward. "Isn't it more likely that giant hunk of stolen Soviet metal over there is signaling its mother ship? She's just a kid."

The hangar doors burst open, and five techs in jumpsuits dispersed with electronic equipment. One man, focused on a small device in his hands, said, "It's close."

Nathanial watched in horror as the device led him to Adam. The men pulled the girl from Adam's leg and she screamed, her tiny face stretching with terror. Nathanial reached for her, but two more men pushed him back. The others held the girl in place on the floor, scanning her with their devices while she clawed for Adam, who, along with his employer, stood motionless.

"Is that really necessary?" Nathanial repeated. "She's just a kid, Peter!"

"It's here." A technician held up Kelli's tiny wrist, and a golden charm bracelet sparkled in the light. "The signal is coming from this." He ripped the bracelet off, dropped it in a special envelope, and the team ran from the room.

Nathanial reached down and held the girl as she screamed the first words he'd heard her say. *"Non! Rends le-moi! Maman! Maman!"*

# THREE

Nathanial stood in the Institute shower, staring at the tiles while hot water ran down his back. Man, he hated this place. There were times, amidst his bills and the low-grade working conditions, that he wondered if he'd made a mistake by leaving. He could have done great things here with The Institute's facilities and funding. But today his ears just rang incessantly with the sound of the little girl's screams, crying out for her mother while Adam and Peter stood nearby like statues.

After the shower, he slipped out into the hallway to find the girl's room. Peter, the mighty Zeus, insisted that "artists shouldn't have to break focus to take the train home." To this end, he had installed hospitality rooms at The Institute for any KATs plying their craft into the dark hours. Adam stayed so often he had his own room, though Nathanial was sure there was nothing in it but hygiene products and a change of clothing. Certainly nothing like a cactus.

Nathanial gently knocked on her door, and the little face peeked out.

"Hi," he said, squatting down. "I was going to take a nap, but I thought I'd make sure you were okay first. Do you need anything?" She still wore the same clothes from their long trip.

"I'll ask Peter to get you some new clothes. Maybe I can find you a shirt or something to sleep in tonight. You don't understand a thing I'm saying, do you? Uh, are you hungry?" *What had Adam asked her before they ate?* "*Fem?* Are you *fem?*" He pretended to spoon food into his mouth. "*Fem?*"

Her eyes bulged.

"Okay, Okay. I'll get you something to eat. Something to, uh, *monjay. Monjay?*"

She stifled a tiny cough.

He shut the door gently and left for the cafeteria. A few minutes later, he passed her some fruit, crackers, and peanut butter as well as a small men's shirt for her to sleep in. He gestured towards his room down the hall.

"I'm just down the hall if you need anything. Umm…" He got up and ran to his door, knocking on it. "Uh, *bonjure*, Nathanial. Hello?" He leaned his ear over as though listening.

She bit her lower lip and disappeared into her room. He wondered if little kids knew how to use a shower. He would make sure one of Peter's secretaries showed her how to use it.

———

Two hours later, Nathanial met in Peter's office with Adam. The girl sat in the mighty Zeus's chair, stoically fidgeting with the trinkets on his desk. Peter dropped a stack of newspapers on the coffee table.

"Every major media hub in France and surrounding countries. Nothing. Not a word of an abducted child. No frantic parents, no massive search, not so much as ad in the classifieds. Gentlemen, there are no missing children in France today."

"What about the police?"

"Believe me," Peter said, "it's strange enough to explain a call to the French police *asking* if any children have been abducted in the last week, but even so, we called thirty-seven. Also, the Ministry of the Interior, National Police, INTERPOL, even France's Foreign Intelligence Agency. Nothing. No one presently has an open case for a missing girl."

Nathanial rubbed the stubble on his chin, partly relieved that there was no mother somewhere going crazy and that Adam hadn't screwed up as badly as he thought. But then, this was so much more horrible. No one was looking for her.

"Here's another thing," Peter continued. "Adam thought he might have killed the father." Behind Peter, at his large desk, the girl's head stopped moving, held still in the air above his trinkets, a tiny computer silently processing information.

"But there are no records," Peter said, "of any hospitals or morgues taking in a man of that description in the last week."

Adam sat straight and still; a glass of water balanced delicately on his crossed knee, a picture of cleanliness and pedigree hiding a mercenary. "I told you there was something fishy about that guy. So, what do we do now?"

Peter dropped onto the edge of a chair. "Well, this is new territory for us. We probably should bring her to the French version of Social Services, but I'm thinking that she's already been through that with the whole *'Ce n'était pas mon père.'* And then we may never know why a five-year-old child wears a golden bracelet with a tracking mechanism on it. No, somehow, I'm inclined to think she's caught up in all this, don't you?"

"The stolen helicopter?" said Nathanial. "No way. Why would that guy be claiming to be her dad right outside the hangar if he knew what was inside?"

"We should pass her over to the FBI," Adam said.

"Yes," Peter said. "They would know what to do. But it's a very delicate position you've put us in, Adam. Not an easy thing to explain, abducting a child. And then there's that bracelet."

Nathanial watched Peter mull over the quandary his Level VI

had brought back with the helicopter. Going forward would be without pay, nothing to gain for The Institute, a purely humanitarian effort. Her mystery could lead to more expenses, possible injuries, losses. On the other hand, if they gave her away, just dropped her on the nearest FBI doorstep, they could wash their hands like Pontius Pilate and say they did their best, but they would never really know if they had.

Nathanial leaned over and snatched some nuts from a bowl on the mosaic table. "I don't trust the FBI, or any feds."

"Does that mean you finally trust us, Nathanial?" Peter asked.

"Whether or not I trust you, Peter, is irrelevant. But she does. She trusts Adam."

Nathanial imagined Adam as totally disconnected from the girl, and probably even more disconnected from any sense of personal morality. But Adam did pick her up, whereas Nathanial had to admit, he himself might have walked away.

Still, Peter held the checkbook, and all the legal ramifications would fall directly in his lap.

"*Bonjour,*" Peter addressed the girl with his most diplomatic smile. "*Je m'appelle Peter. Comment t'appelles tu? Je veux t'aider. Dis-moi ton nom?*"

She looked up from the trinkets she was arranging on his desk. She knew he spoke to her, but she said nothing, as though her mouth had somehow forgotten how to form words. Peter exhaled and rubbed his eye. Nathanial could almost see the gears moving in his head. The mighty Zeus didn't cross a T without considering the potential repercussions to The Institute of the gods.

"Frankly, I don't see how I can get us out of this smoothly," he said. "If I bring her to the FBI, we'll have to explain the abduction, and then there would be legalities, red tape... There's no way to put a good spin on this for my contacts either. No one wants to be on the side of the abductor. I'll get a psych in tomorrow and see if we can't get her talking. Or that bracelet might give some answers. Interesting little trinket. It sent out a digital burst transmission for a passing satellite. Hopefully our signal interference stopped any connection."

"Why didn't it send out a signal before?" Adam asked.

"It might have, but then whoever is after her might not have fancied chasing you down on a US aircraft carrier."

"What about the chopper?" Adam asked, indicating the completion of the "newly abducted child" subject.

"Ah," Peter said. "Since we now have the precious item in our custody, we should spend some more time dissecting it. I owe General Savio a discourse. Nathanial, I would offer you whatever financial—"

"Fine," he said. "Whatever. As long as she's here, I'll stay. Now, I'm going to eat." Nathanial began to leave, but stopped in the doorway. Neither Adam nor Peter could even perceive of a single element of the girl's needs beyond their own concerns.

"Adam, would you—"

"*Accompagne-le. C'est l'heure du diner,*" Adam said without looking up.

The girl obediently ran to Nathanial and took his hand. They left together for the cafeteria, and as they waited for the elevator, Nathanial made a conscious note of the word "deenay," muttering it repeatedly it to himself.

# FOUR

ADAM SPENT THE EVENING IN THE INSTITUTE'S TRAINING facilities. By the time he returned to his room, Nathanial and the girl were already asleep in their respective quarters. Approaching his quarters, he grimaced at a small pile of laundry tossed on the floor outside his door.

It undulated. Softly.

It wasn't a pile of laundry. It was the little girl, wrapped in a blanket, sleeping on the floor outside his room. He carried her back down the hall to her room and put her in bed. When he pulled the covers over her, she rolled onto her side and went back to sleep.

He switched on the light in his own quarters, a space he had been using for almost seven years. The only things marking it as his were Peter's orders and a small sign on the door that read *A. Walker*. A simple store of neutral colored clothing, a plain square alarm clock, a few toiletries in the bathroom, and a small, temporary assortment of technical training books. All could easily be cleaned out with a few minutes notice.

He took off his watch, set it on the bookshelf, and laid his Ruger on the shelf above his bed. Actually, his loft in the city reflected this room, only bigger. Neutral grays and blacks, straight lines. Sleek, clean, expensive. Anonymous. No photographs or artwork, no flagrant colors, no pillows on the sofa. He didn't have a cactus.

He stopped a moment before the small mirror, regarding his face as though even that was not his own. In a way, it wasn't. In fact, since leaving Russia, he generally avoided mirrors. Reflections only reminded him of things he had left behind. Things that had to be purged for him to have his freedom.

He undressed and took a shower while these thoughts continued to nag at him. When at last under the sheets, he banished any more concern about his sparse belongings and set his mind to task. He stared at the dark ceiling planning out the next day: working with the electronics department to take apart the bracelet, continuing research for a missing child somewhere in the world, a missing child somewhere in the world…

When his bedroom door creaked slowly open, Adam shot up and snatched the pistol. The tiny silhouette of the girl loomed in the warm light from the hallway. She crept in, dragging a blanket over her shoulder. Softly, silently, she descended in an absurd spinning manner to the cool tiled floor, where she curled into a ball under her blanket.

Almost a full minute passed before Adam realized he was still holding the gun.

———

Because Nathanial had long since taken off down the runway of repose, Adam had to knock four times, open the door, and call out twice, then finally shake the pilot from his peaceful flight.

"What the heck?"

"Come with me." Adam tossed him his pants.

"What's going on? Is something wrong?"

"Come." Adam led a staggering Nathanial down the hallway and gestured inside his door.

"What? Is that the girl? Oh man." Nathanial rubbed his eyes. "Just put her back in bed."

"I already tried that. She came back."

"Did you post a guard at her door? Look, can't you just let her sleep there?"

"No. I can't sleep. I need to sleep."

"Yeah, we all do. Adam, you picked her up, so now you have to deal with it."

"I didn't see this coming."

"You can predict the direction of bullets, but that focus of yours can't predict kids, can it? It's okay. Let her sleep there. She won't bite."

"Take her home."

"What?"

"Take her to the cabin," Adam said. "You can bring her back in the morning."

"Whoa. Slow down. I'm not taking her to the cabin."

"You're good with her. You can sleep."

"Now hold on. I don't mind hanging around here playing guardian while you and Peter decide to do the right thing, but I ain't no babysitter. This is your problem." Nathanial sauntered off down the hall.

"Nathan," Adam said, "I can't be what she needs."

———

Nathanial's cabin rested in deepest mountain solitude, in the company of bears, elk, mountain lions, and smaller neighbors. Not an easily accessible spot for campers, it was too remote for most to hike or hunt, let alone consider building. A few seasonal cabins nestled around the ten-mile lake, but none within easy walking distance. Although every once in a while he could see a light across the waters at night, only Nathanial lived on the lake year-round.

He had built the cabin himself when working at The Institute and earning money instead of losing it. Naturally, it included a large dock with a chopper landing pad on which The Institute chopper touched down easily.

"Wait here," Nathanial said to Adam before running up the rock-studded path into the darkness. Through the blackened trees, the porch light appeared. Adam lifted the sleeping girl out of the backseat. Before leaving The Institute, he had woken her gently, and when he tried to lift her dozing body, she reached her arms up and around his neck. She'd slept serenely on his lap the whole flight. Now he carried her through the woods, treading carefully on the uneven path.

Adam had never stepped foot in Nathanial's home before. Four large walls of polished logs kept the cold mountain air out, with plenty of windows for daytime sunlight. The first floor opened up to a raftered roof, with a loft at the back for two small bedrooms and a bathroom. Beneath the loft, a wooden breakfast bar enclosed a small kitchen and pantry. On one side of the living area, a sizable flagstone fireplace towered over deep recliners and a bear skin rug. Beside it, a sliding glass door led to the back side of the cabin. The polished pine mantel over the hearth held a handful of trophies and a small stuffed fox. Above it, a large, spiritless elk peered down through black glossy eyes. Under a black iron chandelier, a heavy oak dining table flaunted its flowing contours and knots.

Adam noted the working sconces on the walls with relief. He had been afraid to ask about running water and electricity.

The layout and style of the cabin would have charmed any visitor, if not for the habitual decay of its sole inhabitant. Dirty clothes, coats, and towels lay carelessly tossed across the sofa, railings, and floor. A cluster of fishing poles leaned against a rocking chair, where an open tackle box spilled over onto the seat. Dead insects, dust, and dog hair covered the taxidermy mounts, and every available surface hosted half-filled coffee-mugs and forgotten scraps of crumpled paper. The beautiful oak dining table was blanketed with clumps of rags, dirty dishes, miscellaneous tools, and paperwork, all frosted with their own personal layer of dust. In the kitchen, Adam assumed there were no dishes in the cupboards, because so many were piled in the sink and on the countertops, crusted with dried remnants of ancient meals.

Carrying the girl, Adam followed Nathanial up the staircase and along the railed balcony to the second bedroom, navigating past lumps of dirty clothing. Nathanial went ahead, picking up what he could, tossing old piles onto new piles and muttering periodic apologies.

He opened the door and flicked on a switch. The room would have been charming but for the dirt laying in unperturbed layers on the bureau and nightstand, and the invasive smell of mildew. The twin size bed served as storage for some binoculars, a rifle, some ammo, and a giant pair of fishing waders.

"Sorry," Nathanial said. "I'll just get this off here..."

Adam silently thanked himself for never having any hobbies. Nathanial retreated with his bachelor gear. Adam sat, resting the girl's head on his shoulder. When he pulled back the bedspread, a cloud of dust exploded into his face. Nathanial returned in time to see it dissipating under the lamplight.

"Oh man. I'm sorry about that."

"Take this." Adam passed the sleeping child to Nathanial. He folded the corners of the bedspread up and rolled the whole thing into a ball before setting it on the floor. He checked the sheets for dust, smells, or creatures, while Nathanial stood by, mortified, swaying the girl gently back and forth. Nathanial laid her down, then the two men stepped back, deeply hoping she would wait until morning to awaken.

Adam returned downstairs and sat at the bar. He pushed a pile of dirty dishes aside and pulled something out of his pocket.

When Nathanial approached, Adam slid a check across the counter. "Buy some food tomorrow, and some clothes."

"You're giving me money?"

"I've seen your checking account."

Nathanial trembled with anger. "You and Peter had no right to"—he scanned the check—"whoa. How much clothing do you think she'll need?"

"It's for anything she wants. More expenses will arise, and we have no idea how long she'll be here." Nathanial wanted to object. "I have money," Adam said. "Use it. I know you'll do what's needed. Besides, you were right. This is my problem. I made it. The least I can do is fund it." Adam swept the wreckage of Nathanial's quarters with disgusted glance. "Tomorrow I'll have a cleaning crew sent up here."

"I can clean it up."

"You will need to take care of her. Let's get the food."

They headed out the front door and back down to the dock. "How will you get out of here?" Adam asked. "Peter will want you back tomorrow."

"Oh, the Jeep is out back. And the float plane. You know, Adam, I feel a little weird about this, don't you? I mean, a bachelor taking a kid to his secluded cabin in the woods? Shouldn't we have one of Peter's girls take her in tomorrow?"

"I thought of that, but she's already comfortable with you. It's probably best to keep building on that. I can vouch for you."

"No, you can't."

They reached the chopper, and Adam passed out a sack of food they'd swiped from the cafeteria. "I assume the phone still works? And running water?"

"Yes. Yes. Everything works."

Nathanial stood on the dock, and watched the chopper lights disappear into the night sky. A chilly wind jostled his bangs. A storm was coming.

# FIVE

BOOM.

*Wake up!*
*We are green witches in the sky,*
*Stomping rooftops as we fly.*
*Looking for children — Crunchy to eat!*
*Squash them to pieces their elbows and feet...*

SO THE WHISPERS SAID.

Kelli's eyes opened to a darkness — then a light flashed. *Boom!* Horrible loud noises. *What is that smell? Where am I?*

She jumped out of bed and pressed her back against a wall. The whispers echoed distantly, like hisses and spits.

*Something is rumbling up above.*
*Do you hear them, my tender dove?*
*Pattering down of whimpers and wails,*
*a thousand-million fingernails...*

BOOM!

She covered her ears and screamed, but the sound dissolved into another blast. She couldn't take it apart! It was too many! Were they giant bugs? They were getting louder. Coming closer. She felt along the wall, for anything, any clue, anything familiar. Her foot caught on something and she fell down, slamming into a cool wooden floor.

*It's a snake! Hiss!*

She kicked at it madly, pulled herself up, and ran, slamming into another wall. The room flashed into view and disappeared again. *Is this where the dead people go?* She flailed about the darkened wall with trembling hands.

*Where is the switch? Where are the lights?*
*Come see me, sweet, crispy delight...*

She found something round and cool, a doorknob. Another terrible CRACK from above, like a whip people use on horses, only a hundred feet long and held by something wicked. *Maman, I want to come too!* She pulled herself through the doorway. FLASH. Another room, much bigger. Grasp onto something, a railing. Keep from falling over, plummeting down.

*Grope, we are behind you now.*
*Girls can't run, they don't know how.*

They were coming. The bad people, with their giants and witches. They were angry. She had tested them with the question about the poets, and they were coming. *Flash!* A staircase. More groping, clinging, short gasping breaths now. One, two, three, hold on—FLASH. No! Falling, hitting things hard, fist and arm, then her head, moving too fast to stop, nothing to grab onto, tumbling over. How far would she fall? Would she fall forever?

Down, down to a landing. The falling stopped with a searing on her back, shoulder, and leg.

Then another mighty flash and horror. Creatures! She saw them for just a moment. Wicked things hanging on the walls. Glowing eyes under twisted horns. Demons watching her, waiting for her, licking their lips, their black eyes glowing with sinister hunger.

Flash Crack BOOM!

She saw a door across the room. Beyond the black-eyed monsters on the walls. It was her only hope. Get out. She limped. *It's just a dream. It's not real. Maman and the little house are right outside.* She pressed her hands against the glass. Streams of tears rushed down. A latch, a knob, flailing in random, un-clever motions.

*Why won't it open? Why won't it open?*
*Whiney wiggle and whiney writhe.*

They were not whispers now. They were upon her, their wretched cackle. The rotten smell of their steamy breath, right behind her.

"Maman!"

The horned creatures above flashed into view for just a second and then hid again inside the darkness. She saw another door but tripped and fell again. Soundless screams. *Get up! Get up!* The door. A demon with glowing eyes above it, guarding. Run! *The knob, turn it, pull, pull.* At last, it opened. Wind and pellets hit her face, soaking and chilling. She has to go, find the little house and Maman. No time for shoes. Just run, run, run!

————

Nathanial stirred awake. *Now what? Thunder? Oh, damn. Please don't wake her. Wait, that wasn't thunder. Something fell. Was it inside?* Rain pounded on the roof in gushes of water bullets. *Anything could have fallen. Just go back to sleep.*

*It wasn't thunder.*

His weary body rose, with jolts cramping through his legs. He groaned and forced himself up. The storm raged fiercely around the little cabin, cold winds wailing through the night forest. But the air, cold, fresh, wet air, blasted unabated through his open front door.

---

She ran. It was the only thing to do. The sole message, the directive, the one focus. *Run.*

Wet prickly things whipped her face and bare legs. Sharpened rocks and aged roots stabbed her feet through the mud and needles. Coldness numbed her to the pain. She stumbled on something and fell into pinecones and thorns. Mud under her fingernails, trees with scratchy bark, dark things whipping her face, the taste of blood.

"Maman, where are you?"

*Get up. Run.*

The ground changed. Freezing water gushed past, biting her naked feet. She fell and scrambled, hands in the mud, frantic, holding onto the branches, or vines but moving slower now. Pulling herself up. So cold.

At the top, she sank to her knees, shivering, blinded by darkness and whipping water. Her breath would not come in. She started choking, coughing on the cold, and wind. Her jaw shook with violent rage. So cold here. The howling voices all around her. She was dying.

"Maman!" She tried to call out, but she could not hear her own voice anymore. It blew away with the wind, like all of her.

Something snatched her arm. *A witch!* She struck at it frantically. It was strong. She screamed louder and kicked her legs, pulled herself away. It was too strong. It had her. It held her. She wept and trembled and then another flash, a gentleness. It wrapped her, then they were rocking, rocking. A coat thrown over them both. Warmth amid the icy surge, sturdiness. Maman had come. She held her as she died.

*"You can trust him."*

"It's all right. I got you. I got you, kid." Back and forth. Her eyes stopped searching. Back and forth, shielded from the ice. She could trust him.

# SIX

NATHANIAL WRAPPED THE GIRL TIGHTLY IN A HUNTING JACKET AND carried her home through the storm. Bracing against the onslaught of freezing rain and the slippery ground, he followed the sporadic appearances of light from the cabin. Drenched, chilled, and panting heavily, he laid her on the sofa, removed the wet jacket, and rewrapped her shivering body in a wool blanket. He then set his stiff hands to work on a fire. Soon, its hopeful glow embraced them, and the wildness outside sounded further and further away. He looked back at her trembling body on the sofa. For the first time since they had met, her eyes were on him.

"It's probably not a good idea to leave you in those clothes. I'm gonna get some dry clothes. Don't go anywhere. I'll be right back."

He ran upstairs and rummaged around for a clean shirt and towel, swearing that he would do laundry weekly after this. Back in front of the fire, he sat her tiny shivering body upright and unwrapped the now wet blanket and soaked shirt. The logs in the fire popped and cracked as he dried her off and rubbed her hair with the towel. Blood oozed from scratches on her hands, arms, feet, and face.

"Oh, man, kid."

Upstairs again, he searched for first aid, fumbling through closets and drawers, cursing himself for never assigning anything to a proper place. This time, her big brown eyes followed him all the way down the staircase and across the room. He treated her wounds and carried her, now redressed in a dry shirt and wrapped in a new blanket like a burrito, back to the sofa. She objected to nothing, but only kept her eyes steadily on him.

He sat on the floor beside her. "We'll stay right here the rest of the night," he said. "I'll sleep here on the floor. You get scared, you shake me. I'll even leave the lights on, okay?"

She rested her head on the pillow, but her eyes stayed on him, unnaturally wide, keeping vigil. He watched the crackling fire, hoping he'd done everything right. The wounds, the hypothermia, he felt pretty good about all that. He wished he could speak French. Where were her parents? Why weren't they searching for her?

Adam, that coward. The Institute… He should have seen this coming. He should have been sleeping guard in the living room.

Behind him on the sofa, her big brown eyes had closed, and her breaths came now, soft and steady.

———

Kelli awoke to the smell of something meaty and the sound of sizzles. The light of morning flooded the same room that had been so dark the night before: the fireplace, the fur on the floor, the monster over the mantel. She lifted her head and followed the sizzles.

*You can trust him.*

The dirty room smelled like dog, but outside, some chimes rang, a cool breeze wafted through pines, and sporadic chirps and flutters passed an open window. She rose and tip-toed towards the bright sunshine. Outside, an endless lake reflected trees and clouds like a giant golden mirror.

"Good morning," he said. "Are you hungry? Um, *fam*? *Fam*?"

She shivered.

He laid out some plates on the bar. She climbed up onto a stool and scrutinized the food, picked up the fork, poked. He was watching her. He'd been so nice. She took an ever so tiny bite, put the fork down, and as if it had never been any other way, said, "This is terrible."

Nathanial choked. "Uh, yes," he said, coughing. "Yes, it is terrible. It is." He pushed the plate away from her. "I'm sorry, I'm not a cook. But you speak English."

"Well, your French is h-h-h-orrible." She scanned the cabin, shaking her head with disapproval. "And this house is a mess."

He clutched his arms across his chest. "Yes. Yes, it's a mess."

"Do you do anything right?"

"Uh, yes, I do something very well, actually." Settling down now, he rubbed at his cheeks, then got up and tossed her a jacket. "Put this on."

She followed him outside and down a rocky path lined with tall pines. The dock wobbled and creaked when they stepped on it. The waters barely noticed.

"Is it glass?" she asked.

"No, it's water. Pretty cold, but if you look down, you'll see the rocks on the bottom and maybe even some fish. We can bring some of the uh, breakfast to feed them later."

She searched for fish while Nathanial unleashed the dingy from the dock. When he stretched out his hand to her, she took it and stepped into the boat. He rowed them out to a small plane sleeping on the smooth waters. It made strange hollow sounds when they climbed aboard.

She waited in curious apprehension. The plane bobbed up and down, gurgling on the water. The lake was so perfect, so smooth, she couldn't believe the machine would leap from it. But the engine grew louder and louder until they began gliding along the surface like a bug, speeding faster and faster until swiftly, as if by magic, they rose up into the air.

Flying was not a new experience. She had escaped Paris on a swinging ladder and traveled halfway around the world in an endless helicopter ride. But all that had been a means to an end. A way to escape the bad people.

Nathanial swerved around slopes blanketed in green pines and dipped into rocky ravines, turning sideways to pass through and burst free. The rising sun spread pinkly across some lingering clouds, and Kelli felt lifted up high into them before plunging and rearing back at the very surface of the glassy lake. A herd of sheep with big, round horns crossed an angled slope. She came so close to falls of white gushing waters, she wanted to put her hand out the window and touch the sprinkles. This wasn't moving from one place to another. What Nathanial did with a plane wasn't so much flying as painting. No, it was like...

"You dance," she said.

"See," he said into the headset. "I told you I could do something right."

She smiled, and her cheeks felt stiff. But up here in Nathanial's sky, not to smile would be wrong somehow. Maman would have wanted her to. A soft mist of rain began to fall, and a rainbow appeared between the mountain peaks. Kelli gasped and pointed towards the brightest end. "Look! Can we fly through it?"

Nathanial gestured for her to take the controls. "You can try."

# 3RD MOVEMENT: DISTRACTION

*"There are things about me that I've never told you. But you have the right to know. Once upon a time, before you were born, I was different. I had gifts, and I was very focused."*

# ONE

FOURTEEN-YEAR-OLD PIANO PRODIGY MIGUEL GARCIA SAT hunched over a microscope in The Institute's electronics lab. He peered through the eyepiece at a bundle of wiring on the stage. A piece so tiny it was worthy of respect. He respected it into the wee hours of the night. He wouldn't sleep until he understood it, no matter how many people came to get him—unless it was the lady with the shiny hair, around whom he seemed to lose the ability to combine subjects and verbs in any language.

Miguel had found his forté.

The testing process had almost destroyed him. He had begged his parents to take him with them when they left for Mexico, but a handsome check from the man with the eyepatch had convinced them to allow Miguel to stay for a few more days of testing. At the time, Miguel was plain tired. Tired of stupid questions he didn't care about, and tired of feeling like a dummy. When he started whining, they had offered to "try something else." So, no more tests. Then it was the tours. One boring room after another, forced to sit by each "specialist" and listen to incessant talk about things that sounded like Chinese, even with a translator. Three days sapped the remainder of teenage patience. But then the man with the eye patch said someone "noticed a pattern." *A pattern?* Miguel had thought. *Like boredom?*

"Try one last thing," Zeus had said and promised that afterward, Miguel could go home with their blessing, and another fat check.

Now, a week later, Miguel didn't want to go anywhere. He didn't care if he never saw Mexico again. He wasn't even terribly partial to seeing daylight again. At age fourteen, the former piano prodigy knew utter contentment, three floors underground, staring endlessly through a microscope at the second most beautiful thing he'd ever seen.

What had they done? These clever people, they had left him here in the electronics lab.

"Just explore," the white-suited man had said. "Have fun. This is Dr. Evelyn Bambartini. She will get you whatever you want."

Dr. Bambartini was a tall woman in her early thirties with deep black eyes and shiny raven hair. She moved like seawater through a midnight canal. Her curves made the male cockroaches in the facility tremble, and her smile was more potent than a nervous shotgun.

"Deal," Miguel said.

Tonight, Dr. Bambartini would return to kick him out and force him to do stupid things like sleep and eat, mercilessly locking the laboratory door until morning. The woman seemed to derive comic entertainment from Miguel's metamorphosis, always smiling and laughing around him.

"I know you," she'd say in a symphonic Italian accent. "You think they talk only to you. The wires. The beautiful wires."

Dr. Bambartini understood him. Or maybe she was in love with him.

The funniest part was that one small week ago, Miguel Garcia didn't know the first thing about electronics. Like most people, he had lived his entire life flicking light switches on and off, sadly ignorant to the wonders behind every wall socket. The movement of it, the force, the simplicity, drew him in fiercely, and like a new addict on a dangerously potent narcotic, Miguel couldn't stop from learning more and more. Everything he could absorb, in as little time as the days allowed, he did. The beautiful Dr. B had given him books to read. They even found some in Spanish, and every morning she arrived with more. He got to sit in daily on lectures and classes in a suddenly simplified English, and other Institute technicians and masters arrived regularly in the electronics lab to sit with him, feverishly going through textbooks and manuals, like they were all suddenly one big family and everyone derived personal delight in Miguel's guidance and instruction. It felt like riding a thrilling wave that began every morning and charged on through the unnoticed passing hours of each day. Concepts he never knew existed: circuits, vacuum tubes, transistors, diodes, charges, generators, relays, transformers. It was melodical, like a wonderful song that gets stuck in your head over and over, only you never want it to stop. The more he learned, the more he wanted to know.

Miguel had lost his slouch. Fellow institute employees got nods, smiles, and hellos as he bounced down the halls. In the cafeteria, he sat with KATs from all departments, full of questions, listening with an insatiable hunger to conversations in a language he was suddenly picking up much faster.

Tonight, the object of Miguel's obsession was a tiny heap of wiring encased in a bit of jewelry, of all things. Someone, some incredible mind, had woven an intricate network of processors into the chain links of a tiny golden bracelet. These processors could send out a signal all the way to space. Miguel likened the little metal network to the finesse of a Renoir, and the fire of a van Gogh (the man-in-white was making him take an art class).

As he studied its magnificence, something strange passed beneath his lens. He sat up and enhanced the magnification. Using a pair of tweezers, he moved a tiny golden charm back into his line of sight.

"Time for bed, kiddo." Bambartini startled him, which was not surprising in itself, but he didn't dare look away. He pulled the tiny shining dagger off the microscope stage and examined it with his own eyes. Nothing but a thin line of edging along the grind.

"Wait, Doc. I found something *extraño*. I think you should see."

———

Nathanial's ski plane rolled into The Institute hangar around two in the afternoon the next day. After the fun flying, he and Kelli had landed at his airfield, where he noted with mild bitterness that things were probably going better without him. They hopped in the company Jeep and went out for a real breakfast, where Nathanial got Kelli's story, along with a delightful tale about three banana fairies and a giant toad.

Next was shopping. Where to go for a kid? The mall, right? Everything is at the mall. So off to the Fashion Valley, and Nathanial told the five-year-old she could buy whatever she wanted. She picked a felt hat covered in pink sequin butterflies, and a gargantuan bell-shaped, purple-tulle tutu that fell to her ankles and projected five inches off her waist in full circumference. It was so thick that Nathanial thought she could do the tarantella, and he'd never know she had moved her feet.

"Uh, don't you need like, regular stuff?"

"That's what this is!"

"I mean like, socks, pajamas, that sort of thing?"

She admired the purple tulle bursting from her waist in all directions. Underneath it, she still wore a man's shirt with a belt wrapped around her waist. "We could get that too."

Together, they marched into the children's section of a JC Penney and got a cart. Kelli tossed in thirty-six pairs of underwear, twenty-eight pairs of socks in a variety of exciting colors, and four pairs of sleek sunglasses. They moved on to day clothes, all of which she had to model for Nathanial, who laughed and shouted, "Sure. Get it!" to everything.

A stylish young clerk with a sweet California twang approached the parade. "Do you need any help?"

Kelli yelled from behind a curtain. "Non! *Nous sommes* fine! We're fine. *Merci!*"

"Actually, help would be great." Nathanial stumbled through a story about his niece and her jet-setting parents. The clerk responded with professional enthusiasm. An hour later, they left with four pairs of new shoes, tights, dresses, pants, shorts, shirts, a cardigan sweater, a pullover sweatshirt, a hefty windbreaker, a swimsuit, and three pairs of pajamas.

Before they checked out, the clerk asked if he had considered stopping at the drugstore. She wrote up a list of everything, from children's shampoo to Tylenol, a toothbrush, and a thermometer. He felt like a super dad, or maybe a super-guy-taking-care-of-kidnapped-girl. He didn't know what he felt like, but it sure felt fun spending Adam's stinking money.

After the mall, all the bags were packed into the back of the Jeep, along with the cartload of toys they had picked up on the way out. The bags rustled as Nathanial whizzed around San Diego suburbia, the little princess finally wearing some decent clothing and a sharp new set of shades.

After a quick stop back at Hemmel Air to pick up his dog and transfer all the bags to the float plane, they headed out to The Institute. Kelli was scheduled for a psych evaluation, and Nathanial had to come up with some answers on the mystery chopper or he'd start getting cool glowers from Peter's remaining eye.

Adam and Peter found them in the hangar at about three in the afternoon. Nathanial lay buried in the bowels of the chopper, with open manuals, files, books, and a myriad of Polaroids of the inside mechanics of the craft scattered across the floor around him, while country music blared from a nearby radio. A massive mound of shopping bags carpeted another plot of the hangar floor with pink, yellow, and purple spilling out chaotically between stuffed animals. With two pairs of sparkly sunglasses perched in her hair, the girl sat amidst the bags, redressing three Barbie dolls, while Props, Nathanial's mutt, jumped around, yapping up a storm while leashed to the landing gear of the multimillion-dollar Soviet helicopter.

Peter smiled at the girl. "*Bonjour.*"

"*Bonjour.*" She did not look up from her Barbie.

Peter and Adam stopped. Peter asked, "*Comment vas-tu aujourd'hui?*"

"*D'accord. Votre français est beaucoup meilleur.*" Okay. Your French is much better.

"*Merci,*" responded Zeus, the Level II leader of The Institute.

"Hey, Kelli!" Nathanial's voice disrupted their enchanting discovery. "Can you pass me that wrench you were playing with a minute ago? The silver one, with the turny thing on it?"

Kelli rose, stumbling on her tutu. She sashayed to a wrench on the floor, picked it up, did a pirouette, then dropped it into Nathanial's waiting hand. Peter and Adam watched spellbound as she sashayed back to her place and contentedly plopped down amidst her pink and purple chaos.

"You speak English," Adam said.

"I had to. His French is h-h-horrible." She rolled her big brown eyes in disgust.

Peter snorted a chuckle and knocked on the windshield of the chopper. Nathanial's head popped up. "Oh, right. Hold on, I'll be right there." Nathanial swaggered around the front, the Polaroid camera in his hands. "Okay, her name is Kelli, and she lived alone with her mom in a place called Allonville, France. Went to school. Took ballet, all the normal stuff, pretty ordinary little kid life. Her mother's name was Rachel Bertrand, and she worked somehow in banking. Tall building with mirrored glass windows. She might remember the name of the bank if you ask her, but it was in

Amiens. Anyway, about three months ago—" He stepped away and lowered his voice. "About three months ago, her mom died."

"How?" Peter asked.

"Hit by a taxi in Glasgow while on a business trip. Kelli never met her father; says he was lost in the war, though I'm not sure which one. She has no other relatives that she knows of and has spent the last three months in the care of an elderly babysitter, while a lawyer named Durand searched for some family."

"What was she doing at the airport?" Adam asked.

"That's where it gets interesting. So, she's about to be planted in an orphanage, when about three weeks ago, out of nowhere, a man shows up claiming to be her long-lost daddy. The lawyer does all the tests, runs everything through, and finally packs her off with him. Hey Kelli, what was the name of your fake daddy again?"

"*Monsieur Chaput*. Henri Chaput."

"Chaput. Right. A couple of days later, Chaput puts her in a car and they head for the airport. Kelli has no idea where they were going, and she never finds out. See, on the way she remembers something her mom taught her, a little trick question to ask if anybody ever claimed to be daddy. Guess what? Missyure Chaput didn't know the answer. So, Kelli bolted when they got to the airport, and you know the rest."

"So, Chaput. That was the man I met in the hangar?" Adam asked.

"And probably killed? Yes."

Adam caught his breath in his throat. He'd been holding on to the vanishing hope that he hadn't done the wrong thing, that somehow his instincts had been right about the girl's situation. Now he wasn't sure. What if the lawyer was right? He had probably done blood tests. What if this guy Chaput really was her father? Had Adam killed her only surviving parent? Had he done that?

*"Ce n'était pas mon père!"* Kelli shouted from her spot on the floor.

The men regarded her with unified surprise. "Yes," Adam said. "Why did he call his daughter 'the girl' and fight like he'd had combat training? Why was there nothing reported to the police or the newspapers? Where did Chaput's body disappear to?"

"And most importantly," Peter added, "why does a five-year-old wear a bracelet that's signaling a satellite?"

"That's another thing," said Nathanial. "Kelli had never seen that bracelet until a week before fake daddy showed up. It was willed to her by her mother. She certainly didn't know about the signal."

"All right, Nathanial, well done. I'm impressed. We'll get to work right away on finding that lawyer." Peter stepped toward the chopper. "Now, how about this mystery?"

"That is going to be the harder one to solve. What I can tell you is that there are multiple avionics programs that I have only begun to uncover."

"Avionics programs."

"For example, when Kelli and Adam grabbed onto that ladder in France, I should have had to readjust to accommodate the weight, only I never got the chance. It took me a while to find it in all the other wiring going through this thing, but there's an automatic system that tracks weight and adjusts the flight controls. And, despite its size and unusual shape, this thing flies beautifully. The fly-by-wire system responds to the slightest touch. However, even that's not the real mystery here. This is." Nathanial sat in the cockpit, propping the door open with his foot. "Whenever I flick the switch to extend the wings, this program starts up automatically."

He indicated one of the three screens on the control panel. "It's a navigation system, and it's waiting for me to tell it where I am. Watch." Nathanial typed in The Institute's latitude and longitude coordinates. Immediately the screen lit up with a list of geographic characteristics. "You see that? It's like he's programmed all that information in. Now with radar and a half-wit pilot, I can't see why you'd need any of that."

"And you think there are more of these mystery programs on board?"

"Oh, I know there are. And most haven't been invented yet."

"Well, that's not surprising, given who built it," Peter said. "Can you tell what each program does?"

"Eventually, but that's not the larger picture here. They aren't in themselves anything useful. I mean, certainly not worth all this trouble."

"So, what's the point, in other words."

"The point, I think, is that they all tie together somehow into something bigger, some larger system, but I can't figure that out until you tell me what this is." Nathanial pulled a small, black cube out of his pocket and handed it to Peter. "This is one of the cells making up the fuselage and hooked intricately into the various avionics on board. If your guys in engineering or elec-tronics can tell me what this does, then I might be able to tell you what the chopper does that makes it so valuable to your Russian friends."

"What is it?" Peter asked.

"That's what I don't know, Peter. Getting one off was a real mess. See if some Level IV engineer can figure it out, or send it up to your brainiacs on the fifth floor."

Peter took the cube. "Well, that might be enough to stave off my General for now. I am certain he's aiming warheads in our direction as we speak."

"You told him our location? Wow, I didn't even know where this place was for the first six months I worked here."

"I said 'in our direction.' He was here partly at night, so I assume he could read the stars." Peter drew his attention back to Kelli, playing on the floor amidst her treasures. "Well, Nathanial, I guess we owe you a big thank you. How did you get her to talk?"

"Not sure, really. Fed her some bad food, chased her through an ice storm in the woods? Or maybe it was just my French."

"It was the French," she called out. "Terrible. Yuck."

"Well, thank God for bad French. I'll find out what I can from this Durand lawyer. Adam, would you take our little guest to her consult with Dr. Loring?"

Adam. Nathanial had forgotten him. It was creepy how the guy could be so silent and quiet, he could disappear in plain sight, like you just imagined him. But he was still there, leaning on the chopper, watching Kelli play. He squatted down amidst the chaos and said something to her softly. Without hesitating, she took Adam's hand and they left together. On the way out of the hangar, she stooped to grab an enormous brown bear in her other arm.

# TWO

"THERE'S NOTHING WRONG WITH THE GIRL, EXCEPT PERHAPS SHE hasn't mourned the loss of her mother yet." Dr. Shirley Loring, the Institute's Level III psychiatric specialist, spoke in placid tones as she and Peter walked through a third-floor basement corridor. Behind them, Nathanial was distracted by her lab coat blending in with Peter's whites. "So, you should be watching for that," she said, "and when it comes, you should encourage it. Don't try to cheer her out of it. It'll be very healthy for her to cry."

"Why do you think she stopped talking?" Peter asked.

"Many children stop communicating when something traumatic happens. It usually passes, with the help of loved ones. Captain Hemmel is to be commended for helping her."

"Bad French," said Nathanial.

"You're too humble, Captain," Loring said. "That would not have been enough. She must trust you."

"Well, I know it wasn't my clean house or my cooking."

"So I've heard," said Peter, holding the door to the electronics lab for them.

Inside the lab, the lights dimmed, and an image appeared projected on the back wall. Dr. Bambartini, a few electronics

KATs, and two of Peter's white-clad assistants waited. Adam sat behind everyone, while Kelli played on the floor with a young Mexican boy wearing a lab coat that was too big for him. Kelli spied Nathanial, jumped up, tripped on her tutu, and bounced between the chairs to take his hand and lead him to a seat.

"All right, everyone is here," Peter said. "Let's see what we've got."

Dr. Bambartini stepped to the front. "The six lines of characters you see here on the wall were microscopically engraved in the various charms on Miss Kelli's bracelet. We would never have found them if not for the astute attention of our newest KAT, Miguel." She nodded towards the boy on the floor. "We compiled them and sent them to PS for analysis."

Nathanial had forgotten all the nicknames in this place. One almost needed a directory of acronyms to participate in a cafeteria conversation. PS was "Problem Solving," Peter's think tank on the fifth floor. A handful of snobbish intellectuals who didn't have a useful skill to boast of but were reputedly gifted at unravelling everybody else's snags. The fifth floor always horrified Nathanial: no grease, no dirty hands, no jumpsuits, no smell of fuel. Just luxury sofas, chalkboards, coffee machines, and middle-aged men in sports jackets lounging around trying to appear esoteric. Half of them smoked cigars as though they were a sixth finger. The others swirled something stronger in those fancy mugs, though Peter swore it was prohibited (a rule Nathanial was sure got overlooked if Peter thought it would hasten a solution for a client). Besides, if they were so good at problem solving, why didn't they conjure up an end to world hunger while they were up there? Stinking Level IVs.

Bambartini's voice called him back to the lab. "This is what they sent down a few minutes ago." She gestured to the image on the wall behind her. "As you can see, first are some precise coordinates for latitude and longitude." The image shifted to an aerial shot of South Manhattan. "Directing us here, a building between

Nassau and Broadway in the financial district of New York City. The next line traces a numerical pattern one would take if pursuing a specific address in the building on foot: zip code, street number, floor number, and suite number." The image shifted to a company logo.

"Miles and Jeters Security," Bambartini read. "A storage facility in the top five floors of the building. One of the oldest in New York. They hold everything from safe deposit boxes to items of extreme interest. They have regular clients from all the major galleries in New York, jewelers, hospitals. Even the CDC is on their roster. They are considered an impenetrable fortress, and in the seventy-three years since they opened their doors, have never had a successful break-in."

"Sounds like a challenge," Adam said from the shadows.

"Well, we may not need to break in," Bambartini continued. "The next row of numbers is a complex account numbering system. We've already called Miles and Jeters, but this is a highly secured account. They wouldn't give us any information over the phone. This afternoon, Peter commissioned an operative out to New York, but all we know now is that it can only be accessed in person, and most likely by the right person."

"What's the next line?" Peter asked.

"We don't know. We can guess it's an entry code to access Kelli's vault, but it's possible that it has nothing to do with the account and might even be code for what's inside it."

"When you say account," Nathanial said, "you don't mean money, right? We're not talking about a bank."

"That's right. It's possible there could be money stored there, cash or bonds, et cetera, but we're talking about a storage facility, Miles and Jeters will take only physical properties."

"How do we know what's in the vault is for the girl?" Adam asked.

"I suppose we don't," Bambartini admitted. "Dr. Loring, do you have any new insight?"

Phyllis Loring sat in a back row next to Peter, holding a clipboard with her notes. "Well, you can probably ask Kelli herself. But as she's otherwise engaged at the moment" —Kelli and Miguel had descended into a scenario of distracting noises with the bear —"I don't mind. The bracelet was a gift to Kelli from her mother, postmortem. She never saw it before about a month ago. The lawyer in charge of her mother's estate gave it to her."

"I spoke with Durand at length this morning," said Peter. "He confirmed the instructions in her mother's will to open a security box at the Banque De France in Paris. The bracelet was the only thing stored in the box."

"Wait, the bracelet was stored in a security box? Why didn't it send out signals before?" Nathanial asked.

"No outside power source," Bambartini answered. "It has a self-contained regeneration system based on solar light and physical energy. That is, it recharges itself whenever it's in motion and daylight. So, immobile in a dark box, it would have no power to send out a signal."

"So, it has to be worn to have power?" Nathanial asked.

"Yes, but it probably goes without saying that this little piece of jewelry is far beyond current societal abilities," said Bambartini. "Everything about it exceeds all standards of commercial and military norms. Also, we have satellites actively in use, but not many other organizations do at this point. I'm guessing our friends at the Apex made this little system."

"The Russians?" Peter said. "Surely not. I can't imagine Drozdov successfully keeping satellite technology from his superiors."

"Peter, this little bracelet is too good," said Bambartini. "It took us several hours to unravel all the pieces. It's the kind of thing we would come up with and keep in-house and only use ourselves. It's KAT technology."

"Technology," said Peter, sighing. "We used to know a KAT by their abilities. More and more, we know them by their devices."

"KAT technology?" said Adam. "Enoki is a KAT. Peter, two KAT ops at the same airport at the same time?"

"Well, that doesn't mean it's Drozdov," said Peter. "He's not the only other big fish in the pond these days."

"Whoever they were," Adam continued, "they were on fire to get the girl. Plus, all this parade of making it look legal. Ask the lawyer if we can't get a look at those blood tests. I'll bet it's all a smokescreen to get into that vault."

"But the mother set all this up," said Peter. "The bracelet came from her. So, can we assume these codes were from her as well? Perhaps it was the mother's connection to whoever was chasing her at the airport that we need to investigate. What was the mother's name again?"

One of Peter's assistants checked her notes. "Rachel Bertrand, sir."

"Rachel Bertrand. Let's get a writeup on her. Find me a picture, and the obituary. Get someone in Amiens to look her up. Who was Rachel? Where was she born?"

"It's not that complicated, Peter," Adam interrupted. "Whatever they want, it's big, and it's in that vault. Get what's in that vault, and the girl can go back."

"Kelli," Nathanial said.

"What?"

"We know her name now, so I think we can stop calling her 'the girl.' Right? But wait a minute. If this Chaput guy isn't her father, then who is?"

"He probably died at war like her mother told her," Adam said, "and what she left in that vault is causing her daughter's troubles."

"But why would her mother do that?"

"That's irrelevant," said Adam.

"What? It's part of the whole equation," said Nathanial. "It only makes sense to ask why a mother would leave a Last Will and Testament spiraling her child into danger."

"Whatever her mother was thinking is not our business."

"Excuse me? Adam, you made it our business when you abducted her from that airport."

"Nathanial, be careful. The girl is going back."

"Kelli."

"She's going back."

"What the hell is the matter with you? I mean, you *did* have a mother, didn't you?"

Someone in the room let out a snicker, then straightaway pretended it was a cough.

"Gentlemen." Peter occasionally could access an incredibly intimidating operatic voice. Before Kelli's arrival, The Institute rumor-record listed its last appearance at more than eight months ago, when breaking up an argument in the chemistry lab about missing sodium chloride containers.

"*Ce n'était pas mon père,*" Kelli whispered so softly that the words left an echoing silence in their wake for several motionless moments in the electronics lab. No one had noticed that the antics with Miguel and the bear had ceased minutes ago. Now the silence shamed them all.

"Perhaps it was the bracelet," Miguel said. "I mean, maybe the mom didn't know about the signal, like someone used it to find her and she didn't know. And maybe she never thought she'd die so suddenly like that, or that Kelli would stop talking like she did. She made all these plans, hoping Kelli would be bigger, stronger. She couldn't plan on Kelli just being a kid. She didn't think of that, you know?"

"Miguel, thank you," Peter said. "So, we can assume since the mother went to so much trouble to get the bracelet to Kelly, that its value is not the charms themselves, but the message they contain. The engravings are probably from mom, but the signal was from, well, whoever was at the airport."

"Which would make sense," Bambartini said, "because the signal is very complex. It would only be activated when in direct light, and even then, a very specific satellite would have to be in the right place to pick it up. I'm guessing they would only get a signal every few hours. If the people at the airport had used the bracelet's signal to find her, they were very lucky in their timing. She would also need to be relatively stationary for their satellite to catch the signal."

"And not locked away in a dark security box for years," added one of Peter's secretaries. "Or speeding across the Atlantic on a carrier."

"Evelyn," Adam asked, "do you have the bracelet reassembled? Can I see it?"

"Yes. I disconnected the tracking signal, though I left the mechanism. We'll certainly be using that recharging system ourselves." She leaned over a nearby table, picked up the bracelet, and passed it to Adam.

"Maman," Kelli said, seeing the exchange.

"Okay," Nathanial said, wishing he could solve everything by flying it out into the sky. "Evelyn, what is that last bit up there? After all the numbers."

The remaining line of figures projected on the wall was the strangest. *Le Troisième—l'index.*

"The third one. Index finger," Peter translated. "What could that mean?"

"I know," Kelli said, still covered in shadows.

"Well, what does it mean?" Adam asked.

She rose from the floor and crossed to him with delicate steps. "Are you my papa?" she asked.

"No," he answered.

"Then I cannot tell you." Kelli returned to the floor near Miguel and the big bear.

"Kelli, we can't help you unless you tell us what it means," Adam said.

"Maman made me promise many times. I can only tell it to my papa."

"But your papa is dead," Adam said.

"Adam!" Nathanial started.

But Adam continued. "Surely your Maman would want someone to help you."

Kelli held the stuffed bear closely. She rocked slightly back and forth, squeezing it, and glanced up at Adam, her big brown eyes catching the light of the projector. "I promised her," she said. "I cannot tell."

"Adam, let me see that bracelet one more time," Peter said.

Adam fidgeted and turned in his seat. Confusion on his features. "I, don't seem to—"

"I am very sneaky," came the soft, voice of the girl with the hypnotizing eyes. "Much sneakier than you." She waved her hand in the air, the bracelet dangling from her tiny wrist like a golden trophy. She collapsed over her knees, giggling.

Nathanial really liked this kid.

"Well, I think we've covered what we can," Peter said, rising. "We'll meet up again when we hear from New York. Miguel, take Kelli back to the hangar, will you? Wait with her until Captain Hemmel gets there."

The meeting broke up, and the lights came on.

"Are you all right having Kelli in your home?" Peter asked, approaching Nathanial. "She seems to have bonded with you."

"It's fine. I'd like to take the chopper with me. Now that I've had a look inside, maybe some quality flying time will help me understand it better."

"That's fine but…" Peter paused, glancing towards the door as people left. "Careful where you tread. You were more out of line with Adam than you know."

"Too hard on the one-man SWAT team? You'd burn a small village to keep your pet on focus."

"That's not true, Nathanial. You do it to me, too. Why?"

"Please don't play psych, Peter. I'm just here until we get Kelli home." Nathanial moved to leave the room, but Peter blocked him.

"A ten-year-old Adam Walker held his mother in his arms when she was shot three times in their home. The only reason he lived was because his mother gave her life to save him."

Nathanial's neck stiffened. He didn't want to hear this. He'd never heard anything about Adam's past except that he was a defector, and until now, that was all he cared to know. "How do you know that?"

"I was part executor of the estate. I still had to let him make the choice himself. He did not choose me, so I let him go. I've never once asked. What state was he in when he found you in that cage? Nice healthy Russian boy out for a walk in the jungle? Yes. That's what I thought. When he betrayed and fled Russia, I'm guessing it was for a very good reason."

# THREE

It happened around six o'clock in the evening. Nathanial had returned to the hangar to ensure that he could, in fact, fly the stolen chopper home with one block removed from its underside. He was prostrate on the ground beneath the fuselage when he heard it. A guttural sort of growl. So foreign, so inhuman, at first, he thought he might have imagined it. His mutt, Props, slept contentedly on the concrete a few feet away. Perhaps it was some piece of machinery grinding to an unenthusiastic halt for the night. He shrugged it off and went back to the blocks.

The second time was longer, followed by two shallow puffs. *Kelli.*

Nathanial rolled out and knelt. She stood alone in the center of her new treasures, the massive tutu protruding from her tiny waist, a Barbie doll dangling carelessly from a hand. She regarded her piles with a furrowed brow and dropped her head backwards, releasing a terrible sound. It poured from her like an angry spirit and cast itself through every corner of the hangar.

She flung the doll across the hangar floor and began ripping at her tutu, pulling at it furiously from every side, yanking and tearing with tiny useless fingertips until she sank to her knees with an inhuman moan.

Nathanial noiselessly laid whatever tool he was holding on the floor. He crept through the toys. *Don't try to stop her. Let her cry.*

This wasn't crying. This was aching. Wishing her own death. Reaching out, he pulled her to him, pressed her against his greasy coveralls, and began rocking.

Something bothered him. He had felt the same nagging when he grabbed her on the stormy mountain but had been too frantic to pay attention. It was a familiarity. A song on the radio out of the blue, transporting one backwards through time and space, to another person, another life, a memory of the way things were supposed to be.

It had been long, so long, since he had held anyone in his arms. So long since he had even reached out and touched another human being on purpose. It had been years. How had years passed? *Years?*

The distantly familiar feeling of human tenderness came back like a series of waves, buffeting back and forth, holding him down until he prayed for air, then releasing him long enough to wish it back. It overwhelmed him, the forgotten sweetness shunned by the memory of violence and death.

But this, this should not have been left behind, should it? Had he meant to leave it *all* behind? How wonderful it was to reach out and willfully love. How could he forget this? Why did he push it away? *Who had he become?*

They rocked together, careless of the clock, until her trembling subsided and her tears and sobs abated.

She mumbled something, but he didn't catch it. "What'd you say?" he asked.

"Barbie."

"Oh yeah, I'll get her. I'm sure she's okay." Nathanial rose and hunted among the chaos for the victim of Kelli's rage. "Yeah, there she is. Hey, Barbie, you okay?" He held the doll to his ear as though listening. "Oh, I'm glad to hear that. That's good. No. She's real sorry. She's having a rough time, you know. Maybe you can help her out a little." He handed the doll to Kelli. "Here you go." Kelli held the doll tightly, whispering tearful apologies in its tiny plastic ear.

―――

Just a few weeks before Kelli and Nathanial shared their words with the Barbie doll, far beneath the streets of Communist Moscow, a tiny alarm softly chirped to life. Nothing obtrusive, just a sweet-sounding beep or a ding. Perhaps even a warm, inviting buzz, softly reiterating itself every thirty seconds beneath a tiny flashing light until someone had the decency to notice it. At first, Oleg, the Apex chief of satellite communications, assumed it was some malfunction, something being misread into the newly upgraded system. But it was a fiendishly persistent little alarm, rather like a fly that one can only shoo away for so long before picking up a swatter to address the problem.

An hour later, when Oleg peeked around the Apex conference room doorframe at his superior, he tried to subtly flash his eyes in a beckoning manner behind their guest, a visiting KGB Intelligence Officer. Drozdov tried to ignore him. Oleg then began waving like a moron in the doorway, hoping this was as important as he thought it was.

"Excuse me, gentlemen. I will return in a moment." Konstantin Andreevich Drozdov exhaled hotly, then strode through the door, leaving his moderately important guests.

On the books, Drozdov's official label in the echelons of Moscow's bureaucracy was research. *Researcher.* It had been true once. Drozdov, a young man just out of school, had indeed found himself decomposing in a musty basement assigned to the analysis and archival requirements of heaps of appropriated Nazi paperwork. But deep in those hours of solitary confinement, he had not panicked, as so many others had. He had not despaired of his lot and begun the obedient march of routine. Instead, he had found something, a virtual treasure trove, which in the haste of post-war healing, had been forgotten, overlooked, dismissed. *Talent,* he had said to his superiors, *would be the future of Russia.*

Today, the Apex facilities, buried far beneath the streets of Moscow, bustled on through the midnight hours, providing the most advanced and progressive services, technologies, and break-throughs to his people, his country, and their mutual ideals. Every Soviet operation had at some point commissioned his people. Well-stacked in favors and decorated in honors, with no political aspirations and no military obligations, Konstantin Andreevich Drozdov was the freest man in 1977 Russia. He was a living Soviet icon. *Researcher.*

Towering over his satellite technician, Drozdov could never discern whether Oleg was really that short, or merely the victim of some lingering inferiority complex. He stifled the familiar urge to grab the man's shoulders and force him straight, if only for the satisfaction of reminding him not to interrupted important visitors.

"This morning," Oleg said before Drozdov got a word out, "while updating the interface with our new signals, I came across an older pattern that predated our last system. I couldn't find it in any of the logs, so I checked the backlogs. Nothing like it. Nothing, dating back three years. But then, I remembered the signal booster you gave me when we were using the E-layer ionospheric refrac—"

Drozdov subtly readjusted his glower. "Oleg, my guests wait."

"Remember when I started here, you told me to watch for a specific spectrum signal?"

Drozdov searched his memory. Yes, he had given Oleg a spec-trum to look out for. *What was that about?* His gaze drifted through the technician, sorting through memory, years of daily duties, years of service to land on a face, a face that pained him to remember ... *Kira.*

"Where is she?" Drozdov asked, leaving the IO officer guests to be dealt with by some-or-other secretary.

# FOUR

## New York City, 1972

RACHEL PEERED THROUGH HER BINOCULARS. "REALLY? TWO THUGS in a Pontiac GTO?" She held her position out of sight around a corner. A river of rush hour traffic flowed down Broadway between her and the goons. "What do they do, sit there all day, waiting for somebody to show up?"

That meant a lot. They weren't top operatives, not for such a remedial duty. She could assume they were just local thugs with pistols and knuckles.

"Give me a break."

But there they sat, conveniently parked ten feet from a phone booth. All day. Everyday. Waiting for—who? Had they actually put the pieces together? Probably not. Because this, two heads in a Pontiac, this was just an insult really. No, there had to be more to it. There had to be someone inside. Someone watching the account who would call the thugs with a description of who to tackle at the exit.

She should have guessed the LOCK had a tracking device. Drozdov probably put a tracer on his toothbrush.

Rachel suffered a terrible wash of doubt. Her beautiful daughter, in her twenties—or thirties, that would be better—in her thirties, would finally return to open the safe and…be attacked unexpectedly at the exit.

Rachel shook the vision off. This was all just insurance. By then, she and Kelli would have had all the necessary conversations together, mother and daughter, and this whole plan could be dismantled and thrown in a dumpster.

But what if something *did* happen before then? Rachel was far too clever to assume the best in any situation. She knew better. Should she relocate the vault? Surely any tracking mechanism on the LOCK, the device which lay sleeping in her vault on the 38th floor, was dead by this time. If she moved it, Drozdov could no longer trace it. But could she move it? Could she get this set up again?

No, the goons in the Pontiac were surely not working alone. There had to be someone on the inside, someone in the Miles and Jeter's offices, watching Rachel's vault and calling the two goons on that conveniently located payphone the moment anyone accessed her account. No. Moving was impossible. The vault would have to stay put, and Rachel would have to concoct an alternate plan to protect her daughter.

*Dammit.* She shouldn't have included the LOCK in the vault in the first place. Should have gone with her instincts and just left Kelli a message. But she had to have it, didn't she? Had to have the LOCK because…because they were still inside her. Despite all the training, conditioning, and manipulation. Despite every mantra spat at her mind and soul. Despite every unquestioning act of obedience to her Soviet comrades, despite all she had endured and all she had done. There was still something inside her, in the very cellular make up of her organs, something that couldn't be squelched by any earthly power. Something she couldn't outgrow, reason away, or mature past. There was still something inside her of those damn nuns.

Rachel Bertrand, aka Kira Konstantinovna Voronina, remembered very little of her early childhood, her real childhood, before Konstantin Andreevich Drozdov and the great Soviet states. She remembered women with blue habits, living in a small brownstone surrounded by deep green. Green under gray. There was a narrow, walled lane with a tall stone spire and a magical mossy wood.

She had forgotten all the rest, save the uncanny precision of ritual that carves a memory no earthly force can will away.

Most of the nuns' holy indoctrination, Rachel had triumphantly stamped out. She grimaced to think of the childhood hours spent on Catechisms and useless Latin recitations, the translations of which they never bothered to teach her. However, if she tried right now, on this city sidewalk, with the car horns blaring a few short feet away, she might still be able to—*passus sub Pontio Pilato, crucifixus, mortuus, et sepultus, descendit ad infernos...*

Ritual had imposed an impression that no eraser could remove. Take, for instance, the hostess gift. The Sisters muttered "Never go anywhere empty-handed" almost as frequently as Matins. Always bring something: a cake, some flowers, a Bible, honey from their hives. That was why she had to leave the LOCK.

A lifetime later, Rachel, or Kira, mother and retired Soviet special ops agent, stood baffled on a city sidewalk, because she couldn't ask the Americans to take her daughter without a gift. As if Kelli weren't enough. But there it was, undissolved by decades of Soviet entrenchment, along with a ritualistic ability to chant some Latin verses, and *you never go anywhere empty-handed*. So, on the off chance that Kelli might ever find herself without a home, Rachel was sending her with a gift. A huge gift. The LOCK that she had stolen from Drozdov when she left Moscow forever.

A gift that now came with two goons sitting in a GTO.

She stowed the binoculars, put on her big Audrey Hepburn sunglasses, and pushed her cumbrous stroller away from the corner. She crossed at the sidewalk and pushed past the phone booth and the GTO. She had changed the color of her hair, in case they had a picture and a genie. Good grief, what a waste. Those two heads were stiff with boredom.

From inside the building, she peeked out. Not even a glance from the Pontiac. When the elevator doors slid open, courteous businessmen moved aside to make room for the young mother. She smiled her best Jackie O. "Thirty-three, please."

The receptionist desk at Miles and Jeter was flanked by two armed guards. She asked to open her vault and presented her numbers. The woman lifted a phone, and Kelli began whining in her stroller. She would be hungry soon. Babies could be terribly unaccommodating during fieldwork.

A short man in a double-breasted suit entered the lobby and warmly greeted her. "Madame, would you like to access your vault?"

"Actually, could we meet privately first?"

They passed through a set of etched-glass doors into a secretarial hub. A row of desks faced a line of management offices. Staff glanced up from typewriters and greeted the stroller with customary smiles and coos. Rachel wondered which one would be phoning the goons in the Pontiac.

"Please have a seat."

Rachel lifted Kelli to her shoulder and sat before the large carved mahogany desk. "I have a few new stipulations I would like added to my vault."

"Well, that's something. We've already allowed you to install your own safe. What else are you thinking?"

It was highly unlikely that this man was the plant, but… "May I request another person, also from management, be present?"

The manager lifted his phone, and a moment later another suit entered, taller, with a thick brown beard and wire-rimmed glasses. "This is Mr. Downing. Can he act as a witness?"

"Yes, thank you," Rachel said, offering Mr. Downing her free hand. "Gentlemen, after today, I will no longer be able to access my vault. I will turn the administrative powers over to my daughter. Mind you, I am hoping she will never need to access it, but if she does, she will need certain arrangements. First, there must be a film projector and a screen in the room."

"A projector and a screen?"

"Yes. I have already ordered both items to be delivered here next week."

Downing raised a curios eyebrow, but men seldom argue with a woman carrying a sleeping baby.

"She will also need a telephone with a private line."

"I guess that's not unreasonable, given how much you pay us to maintain your account. A few extra stipulations are not out of the question. We'll have someone type it up and—"

"I've already done that." Rachel pulled an envelope from the stroller. "If you would both sign here, and then I will need a few minutes alone with my safe."

The manager took her to a private elevator, flanked by guards. While they waited, Rachel removed a long strand of fabric from the stroller and fastened Kelli to her. She pulled out a purse and left the stroller at the elevator entrance.

They emerged on the 38th floor into a blank hallway with reinforced metal doors and guards at each end. At vault 18, the manager typed in a security code and used three different keys to open the heavy door.

The vault reached almost forty feet high. Safes were bolted to three of the walls with electric alarm systems running between them. Even the floor was state of the art technology, monitoring any significant changes in weight. Not dependent on any city power, the facility had its own generator in a separate suite and a backup generator at a location known only to three people.

When the manager left, Rachel climbed the rolling staircase up the north wall. Naturally, Kelli began complaining.

"Yes, I know. You're hungry, and this is no fun, is it?" She gave a pinkie to the chubby fingers and felt their warmth blindly clasp her.

The uniformly black safes all bore simple combination locks except for one. Safe number 36294 stood out; its face a puzzle of mechanisms that Rachel had designed herself. The safe innards clinked with approval when she entered her codes on the keyboard. She rested her index finger on a tiny plate of glass, and a thin line of light moved slowly beneath. The door popped open. She deposited the reel of film, and an index card.

"Okay, sweetie. This won't hurt a bit." She held Kelli's finger on the glass while the thin light passed below. When the safe was closed for good, Rachel sat on the stairs to nurse. "Well, that's really as good as a momma can do, I think. Don't you?"

Kelli fell asleep at the breast. Rachel wrapped her up and headed back to the main elevators. She got out on the 22nd floor and pushed the stroller into an accounting firm. A receptionist asked if she needed help.

"No, thank you." She approached a man in the waiting area. He was in his early twenties, with newly clipped hair, a smooth shave, and wearing a nice pair of tan bell-bottoms. "Jonathon Corduan?"

He rose and extended a hand. "You must be Ms. Bertrand. It's nice to meet you."

"How are you with babies?" She unwrapped Kelli from her cocoon.

"Uh, babies?"

"It's very simple. All you have to do is carry her out of the building and three blocks south to Beaver." She passed him Kelli. "Beaver and Broadway. Got it? If anyone asks, you're daddy out for a stroll. Make something up. Smile, be proud, show off your beautiful daughter. Preen. You can play happy daddy, right?"

Jonathon stiffened. "I'm not doing anything illegal, right?"

"No, but I'm glad you asked. Shows I can trust you." Rachel pulled more papers from the stroller. "Here's her birth certificate with my name on it, and here's my passport with my picture. See, I'm her momma."

"I don't know about this."

"Good heavens, I asked for an actor. Can't you pretend you know what you're doing for three blocks and an elevator ride? Happy daddy, right? Happy daddy?"

"Well, sure, I can do daddy." His posture improved; he bounced and started cooing to Kelli while they waited for the elevator. "What if she cries?"

"It's three blocks. It won't kill you."

"Right. Okay. Can I ask what this is all about?"

"If you must know, there are two men who will be looking for a woman with a baby to grab, torture, and murder. Your job is to get my girl out safely. Of course, if you don't show up, I will hunt you down and slit your throat."

"Are you serious?" The doors slid open.

"See you in ten minutes." Rachel swallowed hard as the young man got on the elevator with Kelli. It was a small separation for a greater purpose.

In a different elevator, Rachel retrieved a blonde wig and a black jacket from the stroller. She pulled off her red skirt and straightened the capris underneath. Checking her pistol one more time, she almost wished the goons would give it a try. When the doors opened, Miss Blonde strode out, purse swinging.

"Miss, you forgot something!" a suit called, pointing to the stroller.

"It was there when I got on!" she called back, and left Miles and Jeters Security forever.

# FIVE

**New York City, 1977**

COREENA DOUGLAS, NEWLY INVESTED LEVEL V INSTITUTE AGENT, felt her heart flutter as her yellow cab pushed its way through the rainy New York streets. The grip of rush hour traffic was beginning to relax. She didn't want to show up too early. Play it easy. Showing up right when they opened their doors would appear too eager.

Today was a big day. Her first field operation. Peter had offered it to her as a simple, low-risk opportunity to get her feet wet. She could play at undercover and do some investigating without the black hole of enemy territory. She knew this was kid's work, but she didn't care. She was finally playing the game. It *was* simple. Get in, give the numbers, see the vault, and retrieve the contents. Simple. But it would be fun.

The cab parked in a black puddle outside the building. Coreena paid her fare and darted across the splattered sidewalks, wishing she had thought to wear a raincoat. But being a little wet might be a cool part of her cover. She took great delight in using the word "cover" about something other than drapery.

In the elevator, she mentally rehearsed her nonchalant tone and dignified posture. Maybe dignified was too formal. Maybe just smile sweetly and complain about the weather.

The doors slid open on the thirty-third floor to a small lobby with a few armchairs and a receptionist desk. A large copper sign hung on the wall.

MILES AND JETERS SECURITY, EST. 1905.

Two armed guards flanked the receptionist. Coreena pretended not to notice the M1911 pistols on their hips or the Colt CAR-15 Commando assault carbine submachines hanging from their shoulders. Better not to look at them at all, or maybe that wasn't right. Maybe act intimidated, but only a little. A hint of grateful nervousness.

"I'd like to access a vault," she said to the receptionist.

"For an existing account?"

"Yes."

"Numbers and identification?"

Coreena retrieved the folded paper from her handbag and passed it across the counter, along with a driver's license identifying her as Kelli Bertrand.

"Security code?"

There it was. The next fifteen digits on the bracelet. Coreena had memorized them.

"Seven, nine, three..." She glared suspiciously at the guard on the left. "Do you mind if I write it down?"

The receptionist slid a piece of paper across the counter. "Wait here, please," she said after Coreena had written down the code. She disappeared through a set of glass doors and returned with a man in a double-breasted suit.

"Ms. Bertrand?" the man asked. "Not likely, I think."

"Not exactly," Coreena said. "Can we talk somewhere in private?"

He held the glass door open, and Coreena followed him through an office space lined with desks on the right and management offices on the left. Staff glanced up from typewriters as she passed. At the far corner, he led her inside a private office.

"What can I do for you today?"

"I'd like to access my vault."

"Of course. I have no reason to deny you access, Ms. Bertrand. Legally, you have all the right numbers. By contract, that's enough. But I have to admit to some reluctance."

Coreena feigned a little shock, but not too much. "Why?"

"Well, the woman who set up the account told us that her daughter might come back one day to open it, but..."

"Yes?"

"Well, you were just a baby the last time I saw you in this office. That was," he referenced his notes, "only five years ago."

"Oh." Coreena let out a big throaty laugh. "You must mean my baby sister."

"Your sister?"

"Yes. She's about six years old, but lives in France with Maman. Really, I hardly see her, now that I'm here studying. Maman's first husband, my father, died, you know."

"I know nothing about your mother beyond her account, and to be honest, it never occurred to me that there was another daughter. I assumed she meant the daughter that was here. The baby. Now, what was her name?"

"Adele," Coreena said. "My sister's name is Adele."

"Well, I guess I should show you to the vault then." He stood up.

*Victory!* She squelched any display of pride as they rode the elevator together to the vault.

Coreena watched, perplexed, while staff wheeled in a cart containing the projector and telephone. "Your mother asked us for a screen, but I think you'll find this wall serves adequately."

"I'm sure that will be fine."

The vault door shut behind her hosts with a leaden thump. She scanned the three walls of safes. 36290, 26292, *a-ha!* Too high. Atop the wheeled ladder, she melted with disappointment. This safe was different from the others, completely different. Worse, it was entirely foreign to her, a Level V KAT capable of penetrating any locking system thus known to man. She didn't even dare touch it for fear of setting off some defense mechanism. Someone had gone to a mass of trouble.

She heaved a furious sigh. Even with all the right numbers, she couldn't get in. The best she could do was get the layout of the place and report back to Zeus. She pulled a small photographic device from her purse, took pictures, and left the room, disheartened. Perhaps a better agent would have penetrated it.

She briefly stopped at the manager's office. "I understand that all of the securities on the account were set up by my mother. But since I am now the legal custodian, perhaps you could review them with me?"

Back out on the wet city streets, the rain had doubled. People dashed around, umbrellas or briefcases held aloft in a vain attempt to thwart the drops. Coreena didn't care if she got wet. *Doesn't it always rain on the flops?* She dreaded the phone call back to Zeus. Her first assignment, and she was outsmarted by a safe. *A safe.* Visualizing jibes in the Institute corridors, she passed between the New Yorkers, carelessly rushing about, fighting over cabs.

Funny thing rain. Without an umbrella, even a trained Level V can be off guard. Looking down, watching the puddles, avoiding water in one's eyes, just moving along quickly to the next dry spot and pouting.

Someone ran into her, knocked her off balance, sending her tripping into an alleyway. *Wait, was that an accident?* Four large hands dug into her shoulder blades and neck, yanking her backwards. Time to react. *I should react.* Something hit her head, and the dark shadow of a large man loomed over her in the mist.

"We been waitin' for you a long time, little missy," a voice said. "A long, long time."

Rain. Such a simple thing.

# SIX

NATHANIAL MADE UP HIS MIND TO SPEND THE NEXT DAY AT THE cabin. He and Kelli would exchange sterile hallways, machines, and adult conversations for pine-blanketed vistas, crystal waters, and the melodic buzz of bees. They would go fishing, hike up the mountain, watch squirrels, chop wood, feed ducks, and collect pinecones.

Kelli's meltdown had ended with a deep, hungover sleep. He had carefully laid her in the chopper and took off for home. *Home.* What a nice word that was. How infrequently he used it. With the sleeping child in his arms, he arrived at his front door to the startling sight of a clean house. The iron chandeliers had been dusted, the carpets beaten, the wood floors polished. All the miscellaneous scattered articles had disappeared, and the carved oak table stood proudly empty but for a crystal bowl sparkling in the light. He'd forgotten he bought that.

Adam must have shipped an entire crew in to overhaul the place. In Kelli's room, the linens had all been removed from the bed, laundered, and reset. The drawers had been cleared out and lined with fresh paper. Nathanial brought in her bags and moved the teddy bear and some of the toys up to her room. He flicked the light on in the bathroom. It smelled like citrus. *Oh, man.*

Downstairs, the refrigerator had been cleaned and restocked. *Someone went grocery shopping? Did Adam tell them to do that? Did Adam think of that?*

Nathanial couldn't imagine how much Adam had paid to make this happen. He wanted to be furious, outraged, but he couldn't find any honesty in it. His own pride seemed to dissipate in the night breeze. That little child, so alone and helpless, sleeping up there in his loft…Adam's thoroughness, and his own humility, were the least they could give her.

With that, Nathanial locked up his cabin, switched on the nightlight he had placed in the hallway, and let Props out. As he dozed off, he noted that the cool, crisp linens on his bed smelled like lavender.

Morning came for Kelli first. It must have. Who else would be cooking bacon? The five-year-old is using the gas stove.

Nathanial levitated out of the bed, grabbed a bathrobe conveniently hanging on the back of his door, and flew down the stairs. He found her standing on a chair, humming a sweet tune while fiddling with a spatula over a sputtering blue flame, a towel tied around her waist for an apron.

"*Bonjour,*" she sang.

"Uh, *bonjure.*" He didn't know whether to jump in and take over or pull up a chair. He pulled up a chair.

"Ugh," she said. "Just say good morning."

"You started it." Nathanial rubbed his eyes. "Right. Good morning. You're cooking."

"I have to," she said. "Your food is as bad as your French."

"But you're—five."

"Almost six."

"Oh, well, if you're almost six." He resigned himself to the ridiculous and sat back. "How'd you learn to do that?"

"*Quoi,* cook? Maman taught me. She taught me many things. I can sew, knit, swim, dance, sing, make bread, type, write my letters and numbers, and count to four hundred. Would you like to hear?"

"Hear what?"

"Hear me count to four hundred."

"Maybe later. What are you making?"

She got down, climbed on another chair, and opened a cabinet full of glasses.

Nathanial jumped up. "Here, let me help." He set the breakables on the bar. "Do you need anything else?"

"The dog," she said.

"Sorry?"

"I don't know where his food is. I let him out, but he's been crying ever since I started the meat."

"Oh right, sure. Hey, be careful with that bacon grease, it can really burn." He slid the back door open, and Props bounded in with a flurry of scampering.

After breakfast, they did the dishes together.

"You see, you clean right after and you won't be so messy again," she said, drying off a frying pan. "You have a very nice house. Now it's not so messy."

"Thank you."

"Would you like a riddle?"

"Sure," he said, his hands immersed in the soapy water.

"What is a worm that is cut in half?"

"Uh...I don't know."

"Two worms!" she blurted out. "You see? They are both worms. You can't say that for a fish or elephant."

"No, that's true. Or a monkey."

A half hour later, they drifted silently together in a rowboat. With their fishing poles hanging off the sides, and the mountains reflecting on the smooth lake, their quiet was disrupted only by an occasional dragonfly skittering across the water. Nothing was biting, but since Kelli had suffered a mild trauma watching Nathanial impale the worm on her hook, that was okay.

"Would you like another?"

"Another what?"

"Another riddle."

"Sure."

"What happens when you smoosh an octopus?"

"I don't know. What happens when you smoosh an octopus?"

"Nothing! They don't have bones. They are smooshy already."

"That's true."

"See. I tell funny riddles. Maman laughed at them."

A couple of hours later, they sat together atop a boulder watching an eagle search for prey above a hillside blanketed with firs. The warm sunshine drew pine aromas from the needled forest floor.

"Do you want another one?"

He didn't flinch. "Absolutely."

"Okay, what happens when you throw a stick at a dog that's really a statue, but it's not a statue at night because like magic it comes alive in the moon?"

Nathanial fell backward onto the boulder. "I don't know. What do you call a dog that's—"

"No! What happens when you throw—"

"Okay, what happens when you throw a dog—"

"No! You don't throw a dog!"

"So, you throw the stick at the moon, and—"

"You're impossible."

Two more hours passed, a wonderful waste of time. He chopped wood while she set up little forest houses for her Barbie dolls. He was about to suggest going in for lunch when Kelli's head popped up.

"What's that?" she asked.

"What's what?"

A moment later, he heard it. A plane. A small plane. Of course. Peter.

———

Something was dripping, echoing on hollow metal.

Coreena's senses awoke with a throb, a steady pulsing ache on the side of her head. The air was cold and damp, and her hands hurt. She tried to release them, wiggle them free, but tight, coarse fibers cut into her wrists. *What was going on?* She tried to stand but slipped on dampness, landing hard on her hip. More pain. Her feet were also bound. She was half-hanging, her arms above her head, the rest of her laying across a cold concrete floor.

Steam was hissing, a motor puttering. Something in her mouth tasted like grease. *What is this? Get it out!* Memory surged. *I was hit.*

A bolt turned and a door whined open. Voices, male with thick New York accents. "Gotta say, thought it was never gonna happen."

"Boss is getting paid. Something had to happen 'ventually."

"The sleeper watch."

"Boss is always right, Pippo. Remember that. Just do what you're told."

"We been waiting what, five years for that stinking phone to ring? Lorry read like a thousand comics in that parking spot."

"But ain't the boss gonna be so pleased with us."

"You sure we got the right one?"

"Hey, what do ya think, I'm stupid? Green sweater, black purse."

"And what about this?"

"Yeah. Nice piece."

"How many New York ladies you know carry one o' them? That ain't no dainty lady piece. This girl here, she's somebody."

"Yeah. I just never thought she was gonna be so stinkin' cute."

Male fingers on her chin, then warm wet breath near her ear smelling of garlic and beer. The man pulled off the blindfold.

A bare light bulb, a corded string clinking. She was in a basement with no windows, large rusty pipes, a water heater in a dark corner, a breaker box, broken crates.

A stumpy man leaned on the stair railing, rolling a twisted scrap of foil between his fingers. Stripes of black hair lay combed over his pale scalp, and a well-settled scar dug into his upper lip. Pippo was thinner, with dark red hair and a clipped beard that he rubbed pensively, as though studying meat in a butcher's case.

"Hey. How's yah head?" the stumpy one asked. "Huh? You took quite a nasty fall there, sweetheart."

"All right, little lady," said Pippo. "I'll take this off, but only if you promise not to scream. You don't want Uncle Baldo to give you another knock on the head, do you? No screaming."

He removed the gag. Coreena inhaled and stretched out her jaw. So, Pippo and Baldo. *Great. This is great.* It hadn't even occurred to her that the place could be staked out. *For crying out loud, this isn't East Berlin. Can't a girl take some things for granted? This is why Peter says it's never simple. That vault is extremely valuable to someone. But who? The New York mafia? No, these guys were just hired thugs. Watchdogs.*

Pippo's hand stroked her cheek, and she flinched away.

"Hey. We got us a lady on our hands. What's your name, pretty lady? I'm Pippo, and this is Baldo. Say hello, Baldo."

"Hello."

"And you know what? You're just the cutest thing I seen all day." Pippo's fingers wandered lower, down her neck and across her breast. She jerked away.

"Stop that! Don't touch me, you pig!" She bit at the air fiercely.

"Uh-oh, I think we got a fiery lady, Baldo. Did you just try to bite me?"

"What am I doing here? What is this place?"

Pippo's hand came down without warning, and the searing

pain spread through her jaw and into her throat. For a few electric seconds, she couldn't breathe. She tasted blood. He held her face in his right hand, his thumb and middle finger digging deep into her cheeks.

"You are our guest, little lady. So, we expect you to behave, y'understand? No biting. Bad doggie."

"Pippo!" a new voice called from atop the steps. "What the hell are you doing?" The older man stepped through the door, tall and built, with dark eyes and deep frown lines that ran all the way to his jaw. A tuft of gray hair peeked out from under his black fedora, and his long, black coat was buttoned to the top. He descended the steps and stood over Coreena.

"Can someone please tell me what's going on?" she said.

"Sure," he said. "You accessed an account today at Miles and Jeter, and we know somebody who's been looking to get into that vault for a long time. He's very eager to meet you. That's what's going on."

"Wait, an account? I didn't access any account. You've got the wrong person."

"Yeah," he said and sighed. "I'm glad it's over already. He won't be long, tomorrow at the latest. Listen you two idiots. She's not to be harmed, understand?"

"What if she acts up?" Baldo asked.

"Just don't make a bloody mess. After all this, we don't want to blow it in delivery."

The man climbed back up the stairs, Baldo and Pippo dragging behind. Mercifully, they left the gag off, but they did remember to turn out the light.

————

Kelli traipsed back and forth to Nathanial's kitchen, gathering utensils, napkins, plates, and drinks, as though she were a hostess at a fine tea party. Peter's guests had barely fit into Nathanial's plane: himself, Adam, Bambartini, and a representative from the PS Department, who carried the large sack of grinders Peter had brought for lunch.

Dr. Geoffrey Fines, Level IV PS, was a forty-something with thinning gray hair, scant eyebrows, colorless lips, and angular nose. He nibbled on the edges of his sandwich and sipped his Tab and had an annoying habit of apologizing at the end of every sentence, making it difficult to remember he was a genius of great mental strength.

"Would anyone like a riddle?" Kelli asked, once the food was served. She sat at the table, only visible from the shoulders up.

Nathanial smiled at his sandwich. *Here we go.*

"Oh, that would be very nice," Peter said, "I love riddles." Peter had his good points.

"What happens when you sit on a cloud?" Kelli bit her lips together.

"That doesn't make sense," Adam said. "You can't sit on a cloud."

"Adam! Have another pickle." Nathanial tossed a pickle spear at Adam's plate. "Go ahead, Kelli. What happens when you sit on a cloud?"

Her bulging eyes moved slyly back and forth, holding the stage like a drum roll. "You go swimming! Because it's water!"

Only Adam didn't laugh. "It doesn't make sense."

"Adam," said Peter, "I believe that's the point. Thank you, Kelli, and for serving us all so cordially."

"*Ce n'était rien,*" she cooed.

"All right, let's get down to it," Peter said when lunch was finished. "Geoff, tell Captain Hemmel what your people came up with."

"We've been studying that little cube you removed from the aircraft," Dr. Fines began. "Electronics took it apart. Physics department had a go at it, and then it got sent to us, but we've only got a handful of theories. Sorry."

"It's a very complex little unit," said Bambartini. "Difficult to imagine hundreds of them, all pieced together on the fuselage. It must have taken painfully precise calculations and experimentation to bring it all together."

Kelli retreated to the kitchen to refill water glasses.

Fines continued. "The cube has two apparent functions. First, a large intake portal at the center draws in air from the atmosphere. Then another mechanism separates the moisture from that air, expelling the dried air particles through a dispensary valve at the back."

"Moisture?" Nathanial asked. "You mean like water?"

"Yes. Sorry, a sort of miniature dehumidification system."

"That seems strange," Peter said. "What's the point of taking the water in from the air?"

Nathanial put down his sandwich. "What happens to the water?"

"Through an intricate network within the cube, the water molecules are isolated and submitted to a series of magnetic charges that radically alter their ionization."

"Ionization?" Peter asked.

"Yes. The atomic charges of their electrons."

"Hold on, Geoff," Peter said. "Are you saying this thing is nuclear?"

"No. Not at all, sorry. It's definitely manipulating the electro-molecular makeup of the molecules, but it's not splitting any atoms, so to speak."

"What happens to the re-ionized molecules?" Nathanial asked.

"They're shot back into the atmosphere through six tiny portals. We believe this process creates some kind of charge outside of the fuselage. Sorry, an energy pulse, of sorts. And since the cubes are so small, each one would produce a pulse that overlaps the others. We can't be certain without testing it, but we think it might be a type of—"

"Refraction charge," Nathanial cut in.

Kelli returned to the newly silenced table with some water glasses. Nathanial stood up, took three steps toward the door, stopped, turned, then stopped again and turned in a sort of hesitant robotic dance. "I think I know what it does," he said at last.

Peter perked up.

"I mean, I think I know what it's supposed to do. What he was trying to do. But…"

"But what?"

"Well, how much of a lunatic was this guy? Because the only way to be sure, is to take the darn thing up and push the button. It may be the single greatest achievement in aviation history, or it could burn up and disintegrate the pilot to smoldering bits."

"Have you seen this technology before, Nathanial?"

Nathanial gazed out the front window at the chopper resting peacefully on his dock. "At some point, you get tired of pushing air around," he said. "Propulsion, jets, airflow, friction. You're always just battling the atmosphere, like it was an enemy. What if you could stop pushing through the atmosphere and become part of it?"

"What do you mean?" Peter asked.

"What if, instead of pushing a vessel, you could use the charges already naturally present in the atmosphere, just the molecules in the air itself, to create a sort of capsule that a craft could ride, like a car on a roller coaster, only all encompassing. I was researching electrorefraction when I left The Institute, but it was a fool's errand. There were so many irreconcilable factors, I couldn't get it past the preliminary drawings."

"Why not?"

"Well, first of all, to encapsulate an aircraft with the energy needed to propel it along an electro-refractive wave, you'd need a mechanism three times the size of the ship itself. It never occurred to me to reduce the pulse inductors to smaller fragments surrounding the fuselage. It's brilliant."

"Please catch us up with your brilliance," Peter said.

"Theoretically, air molecules already have electronic charges. If you could isolate and encapsulate a vessel within those charges, you would no longer be pushing against the air, you would be one with it, riding it, like a bolt of lightning almost."

"Nathanial," Peter asked, "are we talking about light speed?"

"Not quite. But fast. Real fast. And there are tons of irreconcilables, like changing terrain and weather and friction. How do you protect the aircraft? That's why I wonder about the water."

Even Kelli, who had returned to her seat, seemed engaged in the conversation she couldn't possibly understand. All eyes fixated on Nathanial, as though watching a suspense film or waiting for lottery numbers.

"The only thing I can think," said Nathanial, "is that by re-charging the water molecules and shooting them out into the atmosphere, it creates a buffer to protect the aircraft from the friction caused by the pulse. Like, he's making a barrier or shield. Some kind of hydro-refraction shield. The problem is, I'm not willing to risk my life to find out whether it works or if this Enoki guy was just a nut."

The room sighed. Peter fell back into his seat. "Then that's the best we're going to get until we find a suicidal pilot. Nathanial, let's say it did work, that it was a viable new propulsion system. What do you think it would do?"

"It would change the world. Anyone who had this would hold an unmatchable military power. There would be no way to stop them. But if it went global, it would impact life as we know it. Travel, business, the whole world. It would transform everything we know. So, to be honest, I'm hoping that machine out there is just some crazy guy's fantasy and nothing more."

"Well, he must have made quite a case to the Russians to get them to invest in it."

"It's a prototype, right?"

"As far as we know."

"Then it should be destroyed before a real nut job gets their hands on it."

A grave silence swept through the cabin while everyone contemplated the Armageddon sitting on Nathanial's dock.

"What will you name it?" Kelli asked.

"Name what?" Nathanial said.

"This very fast helicopter that Monsieur Adam stole from the Russians."

"Uh, well, we don't know if it's very fast yet. It might just be very dangerous."

Kelli bounced in her seat. "You should call it *Le Pèlerin*."

"Luh peler and?"

"*Le Pèlerin* is the fastest bird."

"If she means the peregrine, she's right," Dr. Fines said. "The peregrine falcon is the fastest bird in the world. She's very smart. Sorry."

"And how do you know so much about birds, Kelli?" Peter asked.

"Madame Girard had a book. The albatross is the biggest. *La stern arctique* flies most far, *le corneille* is most smart, *la grue* can fly up the most—"

"Put it back," Adam interrupted.

Kelli stopped her bird list.

"I'm sorry, Adam, what?" Peter asked.

"I wasn't talking to you," Adam said. "Put it back."

In the seat beside him, Kelli released a sinister smile and hunched her shoulders up to her ears. "I am very sneaky."

"I knew you had it."

"You didn't see me take it. I am too sneaky for you."

"Put it back or go for a swim," Adam said.

Slowly, grinning all the way, Kelli lifted her right hand above the edge of the table.

Everyone had a cookie. Kelli had distributed them, one to each plate. Adam's cookie was missing. Ever so deliberately, she reached across the table, continuing a staring contest with him all the way. "Just remember who is too sneaky for you." The hostage was safely returned to Adam's plate.

"I knew she had it," he said.

Nathanial asked, "Do we know anything about that vault?"

Peter's smile melted. "Yes. Well, I am concerned. I should have heard from Coreena by now. She was due to go in at 8:00 a.m., New York time. That was almost seven hours ago."

"You think something went wrong?"

Peter only fiddled with his glass, swirling the melting ice cubes. "Miles and Jeter confirmed that Coreena came early to access the vault and left less than an hour later. Yes, I think something has gone wrong."

Nathanial wished he hadn't said that in front of Kelli.

# SEVEN

Coreena had several hours in the darkness to consider her fate. Whoever was coming for her would have many questions she shouldn't or couldn't answer. They would likely be more professional than Tweedles Pippo and Baldy. If she had any hope of surviving this, she had to get out before the contact arrived.

She scanned the basement for anything that could unbind her. Upstairs, a sports event played on a television, punctuated by cheers and groans from the men.

What if she couldn't get out of this? She felt panic start its merciless program: heart rate jumping, chills spreading down her limbs.

*Think, Coreena. This is what you trained for. You're a Level V with the equivalent of fourteen degrees in your head. You can think your way out of a stupid basement.*

She tugged on the pipes, checking for instability. She kicked at some, but the noise might jar the bozo boys. But maybe that wouldn't be such a bad thing. She kicked harder, making a raucous din until chairs scraped against the floor above, followed by swearing and footsteps.

Light assaulted her eyes, but she had to adjust quickly. She would only have one shot at this. She readjusted her position to provide ample enticement. Had to make him think it was his idea.

Pippo leaned on the doorframe, a beer bottle dangling from one hand. "Little lady. What are you doin'? We can't hear the game up here with you bangin' like that. Am I gonna have to come down and teach you a lesson?"

"Let me out of here. You have the wrong girl."

The light poured across Coreena's bound and semi-prostrate body, accentuating her curves. Pippo might have thought about it for a second, although, maybe, a dim voice in the back of his intoxicated brain was reminding him to heed the boss's warning. But how hard could it be to keep her "unharmed?"

"Hey Baldo, gimme some space, will ya?"

"What are you doing?" Baldo shouted from the room above.

"Just give me a minute. I need to teach the lady a lesson."

"Don't hurt her, moron."

"Oh, I'm not gonna hurt her." He reached for something in his back pocket. "But she might make a little noise."

"Ah, go ahead."

*Go ahead. What men of honor. Go ahead, Pippo, come on down and teach me a lesson.*

Pippo pulled a dagger from a worn, leather sheath. He shut the door, stumbled down the steps, and pulled the cord on the light bulb. She winced and felt herself tremble. He bent down to set his bottle on the floor, then knelt and held up the blade.

"It takes a real man to attack a woman who's tied up," Coreena said. "Do you really need that?"

Pippo was far too advanced in his delusion to be offended. "Oh, this ain't for you," he replied, slithering down to her level, his hot breath stinking of booze and cigarettes. "I'm gonna have to unbind your feet now, ain't I?" She allowed a look of disgust to cross her face, which wasn't difficult. He dragged the tip of his blade across the tops of her breasts. She wanted to spit on him, but she couldn't let him get angry and hit her again before she was able to defend herself.

"Please...please don't do this."

"I love it when you ladies beg."

He dropped the dagger on the floor and put his hands on her breasts. He pulled her shirt out of her pants and scraped his greasy fingers against her smooth, naked skin. She shut her eyes and tried to control her breathing. Nothing Peter had taught her prepared her for this.

He reached for the dagger. Coreena writhed, objecting and whimpering. He held her legs with one knee and cut through the ropes binding her feet. She squirmed but did not give him reason to hold her feet down as he knelt between them and reached for his zipper. He never got it down.

Coreena's right leg hit him on the left side of his head, knocking him against a pipe and stunning him enough to throw off his balance. He straightened and she took her second hit, pivoting her right leg underneath her while holding on to the pipe behind her head. Contorting her torso into a violent twist, she swung her left leg straight up, undercutting him right at the bottom of his jaw. With the sound of a faint crack, Pippo's head flipped upwards and froze in midair for two eternal seconds before his body slumped onto her, his face landing near her crotch.

Precisely at that moment, Sir Baldo peeked around the corner of the door.

"Stop it! Stop it!" Coreena whimpered to the corpse between her legs.

Baldo didn't even flinch. "Eh, good for you pal. Blomberg just struck out." He turned back and shut the door behind him.

Coreena exhaled. There wouldn't be a lot of time. Pippo's reputation with the ladies was surely not one of extended promises. Mustering her strength, she flipped his body off her and reached for the dagger with her feet. So this was why Peter had insisted on all those acrobatics lessons.

A moment later, she stood over the body of her would-be rapist, rubbing her wrists. "Thank you, Pippo." She grabbed a fistful of his slick hair and lifted his dense head. "I'll always be grateful you were such a pig." She dropped him onto the concrete and picked up her purse and the dagger, before heading up the steps. If her calculations were right, it was about time for the seventh-inning stretch.

———

After the sun dipped below the mountain crest, Nathanial started the fire. The guests had left in Enoki's chopper hours ago, and Kelli had enjoyed the rest of their quiet day, generally behaving in a healthy, childlike manner until collapsing in her bed for a nap. The warmth of the fire felt nice on his skin, and the crackles reminded him how wonderfully quiet his cabin could be.

A soft gurgle came from her room. He peered at the balcony, wondering if he should go up there or leave her alone. He would want to be left alone, but he wasn't a kid, and he chose this alone crap.

He climbed the steps and nudged her door ajar. "Hey kid. You okay?"

Her tiny figure lay outlined in a fetal position under the covers. He sat beside her and waited. The various toys and stuffed animals had now been carefully placed about the room, so easily transforming his lifeless space into a little girl's habitat.

"*Elle me manque,*" she whispered, "*tant.* When will it stop, the hurting?" Tiny tears rolled down her reddened cheeks, her eyes pleading and hopeless.

He didn't need to speak French to understand what she'd said. "Well, I don't know that it ever really stops, Kell. You just kind of get used to it, I think."

Her eyes widened. "Do you know someone there too?"

Nathanial wondered what Kelli's idea of "there" was. "Yeah. I know some people there too."

"Are they in the pictures on the wall? On the staircase?"

Nathanial winced. Why on earth did he hang up those pictures? They served no earthly purpose aside from a sick personal torture. Surely it would have been saner to burn all the pictures, but somehow the cabin hadn't felt complete until they were up there on the wall, a daily screaming testimony.

"Show me?" Kelli flipped off her covers.

A minute later, Nathanial stood on his staircase, carrying her piggyback. They studied the frames while the fire crackled behind them. She peered over his shoulder and pointed to one.

"That's my dad and me, and my two brothers, Michael and Joshua."

"They are gone?"

"Josh died in Vietnam. His chopper was shot down. And Michael, he died in a prison camp not far from me, actually."

"My papa died in a war, too. We never had a picture of him. Maman never had any pictures on the walls. Where is he now?"

"My dad? He had a heart attack not too long after I got back from Nam."

Kelli leaned sideways to look at his face. "How old are you?"

"Me? I'm twenty-eight, no, twenty-nine now. Yeah, twenty-nine."

"Oh, you're old."

"Thanks."

She studied the wall again. "Don't you have a Maman?"

"Yeah, of course. Everyone has a mom. Let's see." He stepped down and stopped before a wedding picture. "Here she is. That's my mom."

"Is she gone too?"

"Not exactly. She's sick. I mean, she doesn't remember me. I can visit her, but she thinks I'm trying to kill her. It's better if I stay away."

"Your Maman does not remember you? That's the most terrible thing I ever heard."

"It's not her fault. She's just real sick. That's all."

"When we get there," asked Kelli, "will she remember you?"

It took him a second to understand where "there" was. "Oh yeah. She'll be fine there. We all will."

Kelli studied the wall and asked questions: weddings, grandchildren, young Nathanial. "Who is that?" she asked, pointing at a last, small picture.

"That…" Nathanial hesitated. He never talked about this stuff. He didn't remember choosing to talk about these things with her. *How had they gotten this far? Why the heck did he keep these stupid pictures up for anyone to see them? Why was this girl in his house?* Her arms were growing heavy around his neck. He wanted to put her down. "That was my wife."

"You had a wife? You were married?"

"Hey, it's not that surprising. Don't get all bent out of shape. Yes, I was married. Very briefly, but yes."

"Were you so messy?"

"I guess I deserve that. No. I wasn't so messy."

"Did you like it?"

"Did I like what?"

"Married. Did you like it?"

"Yeah, I liked it. What's not to like? I liked it a lot. You can't tell in the picture, but she was pregnant there."

"You mean she had a baby in her belly? What was her name?"

"Well, the baby was never, I mean I never got the chance to—"

"I mean your wife. What was her name?"

"Oh. Mai. Her name was Mai."

"Like the month?"

"I believe it was a type of flower. Mai."

"She was very beautiful. You know a lot of people there."

That was truth. There had been so many burials, so much black. For a while, he felt like a regular at the local funeral parlor. The staff there called him by his first name and would ask "How ya' been?" What a dumb question. But the funeral farce showed up every time: people with food and flowers, handshakes and embraces, and firm, uncomfortable pats on the back. Everything was so sorry, so sincere and so meaningless. When the last guest left, there was a terrible awesome quiet. So, keep busy. Start a business. Build a cabin. Hammers and nails, saws and screws, plans without goals. So many ways to keep busy.

"Nathanial?"

"Yes?"

"Do you think, if we find a picture of Maman, that I can hang it up here on your wall?"

Nathanial stepped down and squatted, releasing her legs. She slid off his back onto the landing.

"We should probably get some dinner going." Something was making a sound other than the fireplace, a gentle tapping on the roof and windows. "I think it's starting to rain. I'd better go out and check the dock. Make sure we didn't leave anything out there."

"Okay."

———

Kelli watched through the window as Nathanial's silhouette stumbled down the darkening path, his hands in his jean pockets and his shoulders bent. He disappeared into the darkness as the droplets began tapping on the windowpane and the sky erupted into a distant rumble.

She waited a couple minutes, but he did not return. Without thinking, she snatched a gray woolen blanket, ran out the front door and down the jagged forest path. She found him at the dock, sitting on the edge with his feet hanging off and his eyes lost.

Crickets filled the woods with their twitters. She sat and wrapped the blanket over both their shoulders, sealing them together in its warm cocoon. She wrapped her arm through his, and they watched the drops make circles on the darkened water.

When the rain picked up and the breeze shifted, Nathanial stood and bundled the blanket over his arm.

"Come on kid," he said. "It's raining on us."

# EIGHT

Two weeks earlier, Konstantin Andreevich Drozdov also had a contemplative and quiet moment with Kelli, one she hadn't even known he was there, sitting outside a small café in Amiens, France.

"There was absolutely no sign of the mother?" he asked his assistant sitting with him, his words materializing as puffs of white vapor in the chilly morning air.

"We dug up the grave. It was definitely Kira, and she's dead."

Some lingering traffic and a few well-bundled pedestrians clutching briefcases studded the morning street. The fresh taste of daybreak mingled with gas fumes and coffee grounds. From his seat, Drozdov could easily witness the scene across the street through the lawyer's conveniently large front window.

The tiny child named Kelli sat stiffly on a sofa with her hands folded in her lap. Underneath her red hat and black coat, she wore white tights and shiny black shoes. She clutched a worn ragdoll with scant brown hair. Her legs did not swing off the edge like a little girl's should. Nor did her eyes wander about curiously full of imagination. Instead, she remained coldly fixated on a vacant spot of the floor near her small valise. Next to her, an elderly woman nervously blotted her nose with a handkerchief.

"How old is she again?" Drozdov asked.

"Five years and nine months, give or take a day."

"Incredible." He sipped his coffee and mentally wrangled with the whole scenario. Kira, his Kira, killed by a taxi? *How was that possible?* "What name was she going under?"

"Rachel Bertrand. An investment manager at a local bank."

Drozdov repeated the name aloud. *Rachel Bertrand.* It was familiar somehow, but he couldn't place it. "They are buying the story?"

"We had enough paperwork to drown a small village, but we hardly needed it. The lawyer practically hugged Serebryakov and wept. He was about to place her in an orphanage."

"No orphanage."

"Yes sir. But let's hope Serebryakov can do his job."

Yuri Venediktovich Serebryakov was not one of Konstantin Andreevich's own people. He was not a KAT. But all Drozdov's best undercover operatives were engaged elsewhere, and it wasn't a terribly demanding role for the KGB veteran to play. Stationed undercover in France for over ten years, Serebryakov had shipped back to Moscow a few months ago for a transfer to analysis. So, he was experienced, and excellent with the French. And anyway, this wasn't high espionage. It was a child. Surely anyone with half a brain could pull this off. Even KGB.

"What about the blood tests?"

"Also taken care of."

"Science. No one argues with it."

Across the street, behind the window, the lawyer bounced out of the conference room holding a file folder. A young man in a nice suit followed him. *Serebryakov.*

"What name did we give him?"

"Chaput. Henri Chaput."

The lawyer squatted before Kelli and introduced Serebryakov

to the girl. Drozdov watched her head tilt away from the agent as her shoulders stiffly rose towards her ears. Serebryakov gestured to her doll, reeking of smiles and charm. He gently touched her hand, but she only stiffened further.

*Don't push her, you idiot.*

The lawyer covered a few final formalities and after a minute, the girl stood, her wide, unblinking eyes continuously fixed to the floor. When Serebryakov led her to the door, she followed unquestioning, almost trancelike.

When she stepped outside, Drozdov finally got a good look at her in the crisp morning air. She was lovely, simply darling, like a porcelain doll all dressed up and brought to life. She had Kira's eyes, and brown curls that bounced above her shoulders under her little red hat. But her face had been stripped of its childhood cheerfulness. *Poor thing.* He would take her home to her family. She would have a home, a country, a purpose, and all that he could give her. She would be the future of the Soviet State.

# NINE

ADAM NEEDED HIS FOCUS. HE ALWAYS NEEDED HIS FOCUS, BUT HE would not be alone on this mission. He would be accompanied by the omega of distraction, the sorceress of tangents, the queen of disruption: the almost six-year-old he himself had brought bustling into their ordered world in a moment of delusional distraction.

"Do you feel safe?" he asked. They hung, strapped together in the Institute training facility, by means of an intricate harness made especially for them.

"*Oui*," she said. "Can we swing?"

"No." *Can we swing?* What was this? A trip to the park?

"It would be fun."

"No swinging. You have to be serious. No talking at all."

She pressed her lips together tightly and nodded, but her sneaky little eyes glistened.

This whole situation was absurd. Bringing a child on a dangerous assignment, breaking into a highly secured vault. The farce of it had triggered Adam's first-time balk at Peter's orders. He had to be joking. She could get hurt, lost, they could both get caught, end up in jail, his identity revealed, the perils to The Institute, the mission obliterated. These and other logical, sensible, compelling, and intelligent arguments were thrown at Peter across his fancy desk, with a mildly panicked demeanor and a candid vocabulary that couldn't have failed to incite the necessary sense of horror.

"Adam, what else can we do?" Peter had said. "The girl won't budge. Besides, you heard Coreena. There's a scanner on the thing the perfect size for a finger. Only one person can open that safe, and it's her."

"Surely we can get a photograph of her fingerprint and scan that?"

"There's no guarantee it would work, and failure might trigger an alarm. You know all this."

"Well wouldn't that be better than bringing her along?"

"Not necessarily. We've probably only got one shot at this. If you trigger any alarms, they'll find the vulnerability in the ventilation system and patch it immediately. Besides, we still wouldn't know what *Le Troisième* means."

"Well, push her some more."

"I'm open to suggestions."

"Have you threatened her?"

"I take it back," said Peter. "For goodness' sake."

"We could drug her."

"Adam, what's gotten into you? I'm not drugging a child. Even I respect her for standing her ground. Every friend she has in the world is pressuring her to tell us that code, and she won't do it. She's got grit."

It was true. So easily led this way and that, never any arguments, never any complaints, eager to please, happy to serve, Kelli and her "I cannot tell you" had made an alarmingly definitive declaration regarding the clue labeled *Le Troisième.*

Each of her new associates had tried in vain to persuade her. Nathanial had pleaded.

"Please stop asking me," she said. "Maman made me promise a thousand times. How can I tell you?" Her tears had stopped him.

Peter, Adam, Dr. Bambartini, Dr. Loring, they had all tried.

Miguel had refused. "If she doesn't want to tell us, we shouldn't make her."

So here they were, Adam and Kelli, practicing for the ridiculous heist. First, they had crawled through the mockup of the ventilation system, using crates made to size by Peter's people. Adam had insisted on total darkness to simulate the reality, hoping it would scare her into talking. She trudged through without a complaint. Now they hung together from the ceiling of the gym, and she thought it was all very fun.

Adam pulled a cord, slowly lowering them down about twenty feet. She started humming, and he glowered so fiercely that she caught her lower lip between her teeth. He stowed his flashlight in a vest pocket and pulled a firing device from a holder between his shoulder blades.

"Once we're at the right height, I will fire this at the safe." He ran some loose cable through a circular attachment near the muzzle.

"*Qu'est-ce que c'est?*" *What is that?*

"It's a magnet. It will latch onto the safe right above yours, so I can pull us over using a system of interlocking cables."

"What if the magnet is not so attracted to the safe?"

Adam employed his firmest voice, the scariest he could be without a gun. "I'm only talking now to tell you what will happen. When we're in the vault, you mustn't talk at all. Once we're there, I will lower us, then you will type the password."

The magnet latched easily to the corresponding metal that had been mounted, for their purposes, on the wall. Adam opened a crank on the device and began winding, gradually pulling them closer with a soft ticking sound. He unhooked and stowed the device back in the holster before lowering them down to the safe. He reached for the flashlight, but it wasn't there.

He felt around for it. He searched the ground below, in their straps...

"Kelli, you have to be serious."

"Yes," she said, "it is *very* serious how sneaky I am, and you don't even see me. Ve-ry snea-ky." She held up the flashlight.

He snatched it out of her hands and resumed his *focus on the damn safe*. He flicked on the light—whoops. *Wait.* Fumbled and lost his grip. The flashlight tumbled down in slow motion, rotating silently through time and space in a graceful descent to the padded floor.

An electric chirp and a voice over an intercom. "Did you just drop something?"

This was not going to work. They were both going to die.

Kelli kicked her legs off the wall and started spinning them around in circles. "This is so much fun!"

Adam used his own legs to prevent any broken bones when crashing into the wall.

———

An hour later, Adam returned the naughty imp to the air hangar. Even the walk through the facilities had been debilitating. Kelli either insisted on holding his hand, looking off in a million directions at once, or racing ahead, pretending to be an airplane or a butterfly. He was trying to figure out which when she complained it was impossible to flutter with human arms.

Inside the hangar, they found Nathanial embedded in the *Peregrine*, more books and Polaroids scattered across the floor. Bambartini and the new boy stood outside asking questions. Kelli took off and disappeared behind a hanging tarp.

When the pilot emerged, the universe slipped further into disorder.

"What?" Nathanial said.

"You cut your hair." Adam realized he hadn't actually seen the guy's eyes since he'd left the Air Force.

"Oh, right." Nathanial ran his hand across his atypically professional head. "Yeah, Kelli did it, actually. Then we cleaned up the mess—*right afterwards*," he added as though repeating a sermon.

"And you're wearing clothes."

"What are you talking about?"

But Adam was right. Nathanial was wearing grown-up clothes. Not the standard cargo pants and a dirty T-shirt. A nice pair of khakis and a plaid short sleeved shirt. Had he *ironed it?*

"Kelli wanted to go to church."

"You went to church?" Adam asked.

"Well, I think she wanted to go, 'cause of her mom, you know."

Adam felt an urge to pull out his own hair, get rid of hair altogether, lose all memory of hair. Go bald. "Nathanial, I think you're having a midlife crisis."

"It's not a midlife crisis, it's just a life. Oh, and that reminds me." Nathanial ducked back into the *Peregrine* and returned, cuddling a small pot in his hands. "It's a gift, from Kelli and me."

"It's a cactus."

"Baby steps, man. You don't even need to—"

"What are you doing?" Adam asked.

"What do you mean?"

"She doesn't belong here."

"Neither do I," said Nathanial. "We should make a great team."

"How many things can you be in denial about at one time?"

"That's rich, from you."

"Nathan, you can barely hold your own life together."

Nathanial lowered his voice. "Look, I know this seems crazy. I know that. I don't expect you to. I don't expect *anyone* to understand."

Music interrupted him. Someone had turned on a recording. *What now?* It was a piano concerto, delicately tinkling from behind the tarp where Kelli had disappeared.

"Oh—Oh—" Nathanial brightened and patted Adam on the shoulder. "Here it goes. This is great. You've got to see this. Come, come see this. This is great."

Several Institute employees, including young Miguel and Dr. Bambartini, moved into place next to Enoki's chopper. They stood or sat in a makeshift audience formation, exchanging glistening glances, rubbing their hands together, or folding arms across chests as though holding in some outward eruption.

"I need to get back," Adam said.

"Yeah yeah, in a minute." Nathanial pulled on Adam's arm, nudging him stiffly into place on the edge of the spectators. Nathanial took the cactus and placed it on the floor, gesturing. "Sit. Sit." Adam did not sit.

Nathanial plopped himself down on the floor dead center, hugging his knees and nonsensically watching the tarp with everyone else. *What were they waiting for?*

The piano and orchestra invaded the workspace like a brush stroking an empty canvas, a diverse swab of colors with no order to them but their mutual inappropriateness.

Adam remembered something he had forgotten, though he didn't know what. It was something important, but it had no face. Only a strange unintelligible sentiment that reminded him of being on the harness with Kelli, or watching her flutter through the halls, or her expectant eyes gazing up at him as she tugged on his pants, or told a riddle that made no sense. The room of his waiting coworkers offered no answers.

She appeared slowly, moving at first in teeny, tiny steps high up on her toes, her little feet close together under the big, fat tutu that bobbed around her legs. Her arms curved above her tilted head, her hands hanging at her wrists like leaves on a summer branch. Her gaze fell down over her still infantile nose, and she glided in a smooth line across the concrete hangar floor. Her path curved around and back toward the center, where she stopped and took a statuesque pose, her eyes vague as she waited for the music to release her. He had never seen her so serious, or perhaps she was always serious.

When her cue came, she moved. A tiny blob of pink and purple tulle. Her eyes lost in visions outside of this world, her arms swimming as if in water, and her feet in weightless space. Balancing gently in one position and another, she became a consummate flowing vision.

There was no moment when Adam stopped to judge her, compare her to other dancers, analyze her moves and her style, or criticize. There was an honesty about her dance that vanquished all waste. She was the most beautiful thing he had ever seen.

Things began slipping. Like loose snow layered atop a mountain crest, slipping off: sunlight, daffodils, stars and planets, everything purposefully ignored, every wonderful distraction, birth and death and mothers' kisses, orange blossoms and fathers' hugs, time wasted, idle laughter, debtless favors. Such a powerless and vulnerable tiny whiteness, filtering straight through and conquering. The mighty, reliable Level VI. How easily seduced in that quiet, shining glimpse of clarity. Years and years, lifetimes, choices and identities crumbling, falling and dissipating like dandelion fluffs on a breeze, wafting away in a twinkling, leaving only a fading trail of distant forgetful echoes. In his dreaming, she tiptoed to him directly, sensing his surrender, and he too was dancing. He always had been, as if it all mattered very much. Entranced, he lifted her and held her spinning above him in the air where she belonged, where she had always been.

"Hello," she whispered.

Adam put her down.

"You are a good dancer," she said as they moved together in a circle. "Do you believe in beauty?" she asked when he returned her curtsey with a bow.

"Yes."

"Have you been in love?"

"Yes."

"Was she pretty?"

"She looked like you."

"Adam Walker was in love?"

Adam lifted his eyes toward the invasive voice where the stranger with the haircut sat staring. Kelli continued her dance, unmarred by the interruption from the audience. The music also continued, though the room felt densely silent despite the full orchestra. Blood rushed through Adam's face.

"We leave at five a.m.," he said. "We'll stop over twice and run the op the next night. She should bring black clothing." Adam escaped, knowing the eyes that followed him to the door quickly turned away, forgetting him as soon as he was gone. He wouldn't forget. He couldn't. Didn't anyone understand this would be dangerous? They weren't ready. How could they be? There were remaining details to plan, and potential obstacles to consider. What if something went wrong?

Two hours later Adam stood, almost sick, staring at calculations, timetables and graphs, blueprints and schematics, his eyes glazing over for the hundredth time in as many minutes. The crawl through the ventilation system. Nothing indicated there was any security on it, but he would have to be ready to back out quickly. The blueprints meandered off in chaotic directions, white lines cutting through blackness. *Was there another exit route if something went wrong? Where would a butterfly go in all this chaos?* It wouldn't, he thought. A butterfly would die in such a dark, enclosed space. It would get lost and shrivel up in some dusty corner.

He traced his finger through the mess of white rectangles, passing through each floor, calculating potential routes. Above a series of electrical rooms like stacks of cocoons, he discovered a separate line out. Two floors above, leading to an electrical room or some storage, and butterflies do flutter…

They really don't fly like other insects. They sort of bobble up and down as they go, fluttering. To flutter. What else is that verb used for, besides butterflies? Do flags flutter? That's not really an accurate use of the word. One could say that flags flap. But butterflies flutter. That's what they do. What they are meant to do. They are the thing in the universe that flutters. An entire verb created, conjugated and preserved merely for the flight pattern of something so insignificant.

———

That night, Kelli sat near the fire, contentedly entertaining Props while Nathanial fiddled with a transistor radio.

"Darnit," he said.

"What's the matter?"

"Oh nothing, just the batteries are dead."

She got up and came to him, softly touching his rough knuckles. "Don't worry. You'll see them again in Heaven."

He swallowed. "Yes. Yes, we will."

She went back to Props. "Nathanial."

"What's up?"

"I don't want to go in the vault. I will get lost. The bad people will get me."

"The bad people? You've said that before. Where did you hear that?"

"Maman."

"Ah. Well, you don't need to be scared. Nothing to it. I'm flying you in and out, and you're not going anywhere without Adam. He's the best. And there aren't going to be any bad people."

"In the *Peregrine*?" she said.

"The what?"

"You know, the very fast helicopter that the crazy Japanese man built and Monsieur Adam stole from the Russians."

"Wow. Uh, the *Peregrine*? Is that what we're calling it? Yes. We're taking the *Peregrine*. Why?"

"It will bring us home faster." She stroked Props. "Why does Monsieur Adam speak French and you do not?"

"Ah. Well, that's a little complicated. He's very special, or annoying. He can learn lots of stuff very easily. He speaks a lot of languages. I only speak two."

"Two?"

"English and Airplan-ese."

"That's not a language."

"Oh yeah? Someday I'll speak it and see if you understand me."

"He wants me to tell him the secret."

"Well, yeah. That's Adam. But he won't let anything happen to you."

"I will be scared."

"We're all scared sometimes."

"He's not scared of anything," she said.

"I'd say he's pretty scared of you."

"That's silly."

"Listen, before you know it, it'll all be over, and you can come back here. I mean if you want to." He rested the radio on the side table, and they watched the fire together while the crackling embers slowed.

"Nathanial?"

"Mmm?"

"Do you know who the three poets are?"

"The three poets? Is that the secret question for your dad? I'm sorry Kell, I don't know the answer."

# TEN

ABOUT A WEEK EARLIER, WHILE ADAM AND NATHANIAL WERE having their first introductory encounter with the *Peregrine*, in the private hangar in Paris, Kazuhiro Enoki, the *Peregrine* designer and chief engineer, sipped nervously from a glass of soda in the airport café, his eyes darting back and forth through the terminal. A large man in his early sixties strode up, dropped his hat on the table, and sank into the opposite chair. He had a square shape, bulky shoulders, and a solid jaw with the beginning of a double chin and an unapologetic cleft. Below his graying brows, his eyes set firmly, as though perpetually disappointed.

"*Déesse en volant?*" Drozdov said. "Really, Kazuhiro? Is all this necessary?"

"Shh! What's the matter with you?" Enoki eyed a nearby janitor, mopping outside the men's room.

Konstantin Andreevich Drozdov glanced over at Erik and his two other agents leaning on the opposite wall, folded newspapers under their arms. "So, where is my machine?" he asked.

"Machine? No. She is a goddess."

"Where's my thirty-million-dollar *goddess*, Kazuhiro? When do I see her divinity at work?"

"Today. She is ready. Like a bride, she is ready for you."

"Today? That wasn't the arrangement."

"Arrangement has changed. Today."

Konstantin Andreevich Drozdov understood when he contracted Kazuhiro Enoki that he was working with instability. But instability was something the Americans were not willing to employ, so he had gambled on a contract that could easily prove suicidal. However, if it worked, it would be the greatest accomplishment of his career. More than once during the last months, he had considered whether Hitler had been foolish to murder all the crazies. Perhaps the brilliance in lunacy could be harnessed with the right money and patience.

"She is here," Enoki said.

"What? Here?" This time Drozdov did look around. "At the airport? Where?"

"First, final payment."

"You really have no idea how these things are done."

"I know how these things are done, Comrade Drozdov. I bring you to her, then my brains spill all over hangar floor. Then you fly into Russian sunset. I know how these things are done."

Drozdov swallowed the urge to reach over and snap the man's little Japanese neck. Now the public meeting spot made sense. He was far less likely to take a bullet in the middle of international tourist central of the Paris airport.

Drozdov weighed his options. He could probably disperse his men and find the damn Goddess himself, but for the public airport. Enoki probably had it stashed in some remote private hangar. Even with his diplomatic pass, Drozdov wouldn't have access, and his men would be restricted, questioned at every point, and possibly captured. In Enoki's defense, this was a brilliant tactical move.

"You don't know what you're asking, Kazuhiro. Money like that takes time to assemble. And you're not my only appointment today."

"Perhaps you would prefer if I call my American friends again?"

"That's a dangerous business, tossing threats around. I've invested more than money in this little Goddess of yours."

"She is yours," Enoki said. "Today or not at all."

The guy was calculating. He knew that international airports were not easy landscapes for Soviet ambassadors. By the time Drozdov did find his way to the aircraft, Enoki would be long gone with it.

Drozdov sighed and fell back in his seat. This scene should not have surprised him: a last thread of lunacy in the long, agonizing quilt of dealing with Enoki's brilliance. Inwardly, he hoped he could get it all over with today. Then the sun might actually set on Enoki's brains all over a hangar floor.

The money wasn't a terrible problem. He could call the Paris safe house to get it transferred. He even had Erik here to pilot the thing and deal with Enoki.

Enoki's demands weren't really the problem. The problem was Kira's girl. The tiny fragile thing who he had stashed in a luxury hotel with Serebryakov until he could make the paperwork plausible. She was scheduled to depart on his private plane in three days, when the necessary documents and IDs would at last be assembled to get her past the customs at the FBO. It all had to be so sparkling pristine. The girl was traumatized, didn't speak a word of Russian, and worst of all, Soviet diplomat Konstantin Drozdov hadn't arrived in Paris with a five-year-old. The briefest inspection of her and her newly found father could prove catastrophic.

But then Drozdov hadn't arrived with Enoki's aircraft either. Enoki's anxieties might have just opened a window. Perhaps he could get the girl off today in Enoki's Goddess. She wouldn't be getting on a Soviet diplomatic plane. She would just be going for a harmless helicopter ride with her new father in a private aircraft. A harmless helicopter ride that would never return to French soil.

Enoki wasn't some Soviet bureaucrat. He was just an engineer who had rented a hangar.

"I'll need some time," Drozdov said. "I have to make some calls. Transfer the money, and I've got a couple passengers."

"She will keep any passengers, Comrade Drozdov. They will be quite safe with her flying over iron borders."

Never kill off the crazies before they deliver.

# ELEVEN

Serebryakov had found Kelli behind one of the long drapes in the sitting room of their suite. Curled up into her customary knee-hugging position, she didn't even look up at him when he delicately pulled the curtain back. By this time, he knew better than to move to quickly or disturb her. Heck, she could sit there staring at a slowly moving spot on the Persian carpet until they left. It seemed a shame to waste all this expensive décor on someone who didn't even notice, but Drozdov had insisted.

"Just get her safely home, then my people can take care of her."

Serebryakov didn't say so to his superior, but he felt a little uncomfortable with this whole scenario. The girl must be important somehow. She must know someone or have something. Still, despite his unwavering fidelity to his country, and his undercover experience, he just didn't like this. Misleading a kid into believing her dead father, Henri Chaput, magically appeared to save the day. It didn't feel right. Even to a *podlets* like him.

"What kind of music do you like, Kelli?"

No answer. Never any answer. Serebryakov had not spent any time with children, but it didn't take a psych to know there was something wrong here. There weren't any scenes, wild tantrums, or breakdowns. One might expect all that, even welcome it, but this kid never spoke a word, never even made eye contact. She stared. She stared out windows, at walls, at the floor. When he tried to talk to her, the stare shifted down and to the side. *Away.* Whenever he left her alone, even for a minute, he would return to find her huddled tightly into a ball in some new corner or tight crevice: under a bed, inside the bathroom counter, between the desk and the wall.

It was like she was constantly trying to make herself smaller and disappear.

That first night in the hotel, he nearly had a heart attack when he found her bed empty. Frantic, he called the hotel staff to engage in a search. They found her, asleep inside her own closet tightly woven into a fetal position on the floor.

On their second night, he didn't call the staff, and later found her curled under the kitchenette table, a puddle of yellow urine slowly streaking across the tiles.

Serebryakov attempted a variety of tactics to draw her out. He spoke to her in his most charming voice, telling her stories about her mother. He took her to eat pastries. She stared blankly at the mound of crème and chocolate on her plate until Serebryakov told her to eat it. He took her to visit a park, and they took long silent walks together. He would point out the ducks, but she would only look when he told her to. So, he started telling her to.

On their fourth day in Paris together, he took her to the Louvre. She followed him from room to room like a spirit, but this time, she looked up instead of down, her quiet mind somehow captured by the artwork. He patted himself on the back in the Impressionist room, when she stopped immobile before a blurry painting of two boats floating away from one another on an evening bay. It didn't seem extraordinary to Serebryakov; a few careless strokes of a rectangular brush had swiped the boats into existence. Still, she fixated on it for almost an hour, her eyes focused for the first time as though they were searching for something between all the slabs of blue and gray. He tried talking to her about the picture, about Impressionists, about the colors, the boats. Eventually, she glossed over again and wandered out of the room.

Soon after, they found the modern art, Serebryakov's favorite. Kandinsky's abstracts, Dali's absurdities, melting figures in stark frontiers, Rothko's drowning in colors and Fontana's sculptures of inharmonious drippings, holding just a remnant of something human.

When he turned to point something out to Kelli, she was gone.

He rushed back out, retracing his steps, dodging spectators until he found her huddled beneath a drinking fountain, shivering. This time, it took fifteen minutes to coerce her out with promises they would not go back into that room. *Damn trying to help this kid.* They would remain alone together in the hotel until Drozdov's plane was ready at the end of the week.

So, it was isolation with a steady dose of uncomfortable instability. To make matters worse, Drozdov had ordered no cigarettes. Had even gotten him a whole new set of clothes so he wouldn't "smell" bad. Serebryakov hadn't had a fix in five days, six hours, and twenty-seven minutes when he got the call. His nerves seared with relief when he heard the voice on the line report that their rendezvous and departure had been moved up. This silence charade would be over today.

———

Serebryakov left the hotel checkout desk, sat Kelli in the lobby, and ducked into the men's room. A young man dressed in jeans and a pullover stepped out of a stall and secured the bathroom door. "Your orders have changed."

"We're checking out now. Are we still going to Orly?"

"Yes, but not to Drozdov's plane. Bring the girl to the main terminal. When you get there, leave your luggage in the car and transfer to a private limo that will be waiting. The paperwork for entrance to the FBO and precise hangar will be in the backseat."

"Can't you just give it to me now?"

"Still waiting on the exact location. By the time you arrive at the terminal, it should be there."

"We'll never get her through customs, even at the FBO."

"You don't need to go through customs. You're not leaving the country."

———

Serebryakov returned to Kelli still sitting alone in the lobby, then took her valise and led her outside to a waiting car. When he joined her in the backseat, all at once, as though it had never been any other way, Kelli's eyes met him in a clear glare. Serebryakov almost forgot to speak French. "Kelli? Are you okay?"

"Yes."

He smiled, his first sincere act of their acquaintance. "Well, that's great! It's so nice to hear your voice. Do you want to ask me anything?"

"Yes."

"All right. Anything. Ask me anything."

Her posture evolved, straightening and growing into a sort of hover from so far beneath him on the large open seat. "Can you tell me please," she spoke very slowly, and clearly, as though ensuring there would be no misunderstanding, then, like a mighty tower bell, "Who are the three poets?"

"The three…"

He had been ready. They had given him backstory, and he'd been silently practicing all week. He had stories about Rachel, with family and lineage and hometowns, where he studied, and what he did for a living, anecdotes and pictures and family jokes, well-rehearsed and piled full of lies.

"Come again? The three poets? I know a lot of poets. Do you

like poetry? French poetry? Do you write poetry?" He rambled on, filling the baffling silence with his wit.

Kelli's eyes widened momentarily and then narrowed, retreating back to their sightless stare out the car window. Slowly, her legs ascended onto the seat where she held them tightly, as though squeezing the very life from them, and she began to tremble from the extreme effort of it.

The driver lowered the partition and asked where to. Serebryakov slumped back onto his seat. "Orly International Airport," said the man claiming to be her father.

# TWELVE

As soon as the car pulled up to the airport curb, Serebryakov hopped out. A man in a trench coat, who appeared out of nowhere, touched his shoulder. "Your car is already here, sir. Follow me. Don't worry about your bags."

"Thank you. Okay, honey," Serebryakov said, reaching for Kelli. "Let's go now."

Serebryakov grabbed her ragdoll in one hand and took Kelli's hand in the other. Her hand went limp at his touch.

The sidewalks and drop-off area bustled with people coming and going. Kelli's tiny vulnerable hand in his revived a cringe at this whole deception. He hastened between the travelers, following the contact. The private car was parked near the end of a sidewalk. The trench coat opened the back door, and Serebryakov helped her inside.

"Kelli, just climb in," he said. "Everything's fine. We're just going to take another quick ride to a very special plane. It will be fun. I'll be right back." He placed the doll on top of the paperwork on the seat beside her and shut the door, then grabbed the trench coat's sleeve and pleadingly whispered something in his ear.

The contact smiled, then Serebryakov stepped behind a pillar to light up. The outside air and smells of the airport would surely ward off any residual smokey scent from his clothes. His fellow agent stood by the limo door watching him with a sardonic grin. "That bad?"

"You have no idea."

Oh man, it felt good. Just what he needed to calm his nerves and finish this damn job. It was bliss. A few precious moments to self-maintain that ended too soon with the butted remains pressed under his heel. Calmer and back in control, he returned, nodded off the trench coat, and opened the car door. "Okay, Kelli. It's time to—"

The girl was gone.

———

Kelli clutched Petit Pearl close in a tight fist and fixed her eyes on Maman's skirt, the red one with the tiny white flowers that she wore sometimes on Sundays. Kelli had to work hard to stay with her, following the red swirling fabric back across the streets, through the moving cars and into the terminal. She almost lost her, between all the other legs and luggage, and then it was up, up, up the long flight of stairs.

*No, that wasn't right. This skirt didn't have any little white flowers.*

Maman passed again, now wearing her black pants and her sleek black heels. Kelli navigated the forest of legs, clutching Petit Pearl to her pounding chest. The multitude of noises muddled together, swirling into chaos inside her head. She wanted to cover her ears and block it all out, but she couldn't let go of Petit Pearl, and Maman was moving so fast through the whirlwind of colors and mesh of sounds.

*Maman, attends!*

———

"You lost her?" Drozdov seethed in the bustling airport, reddening lines darkening his face. "Do you have any idea how important this was? *Mat tvoyu.* She's a child. A child. Did you scare her?" "She was always scared, sir. I'm not sure she's completely stable."

Drozdov cursed himself for not using a KAT. A KAT never would have messed this up. Hell, a kindergarten teacher never would have messed this up. "Never mind. We have to find her. *You* have to find her, or you'll be pulling a rickshaw in a Siberian outpost for the next thirty years."

"Yes sir," Serebryakov said. "Under the circumstances, perhaps we should engage the airport security. They might be able to start an alert."

Drozdov knew that getting security involved would give them clearance and access to an entire network of eyes and cameras. However, it would also trigger a series of interrogations that only Serebryakov would be able to partake in, and right now Serebryakov was his leading moron. Without help, Drozdov's people would undoubtedly come up empty-handed, and possibly arouse suspicion. He could feel the precious seconds ticking by, his thoughts straying to a vision of little Kelli alone on a bus, headed back towards central Paris. Serebryakov's cover was still perfect. He was her legal father in France. The authorities couldn't question that.

"Do it," he said, but then suddenly Drozdov clutched Serebryakov's arm. "No, wait. We're forgetting. I'm forgetting." Drozdov leaned over to one of his agents. "Get back on the pay phone and call the Paris safe house again. Tell them to get Oleg on the line. I need to talk to Oleg immediately. Then we contact security."

––––––

*Follow Mama. Follow Maman.*

Kelli stopped outside a restroom. How strange that someone had parked a tiny, open car right here in the hallway with all that luggage packed on the back. Kelli thought it might be nice to cuddle up between those big bags. To hide, to disappear. But no, she and Petit Pearl must stay right here and wait for Maman... *But Maman would not be back. Maman was never coming back.*

———

"Sir, we have Oleg on the line for you."

Drozdov rose from the airport café table, grateful to put some distance between himself and the Japanese nutcase. With a nod of his head, he sent Erik to take his seat and make sure Enoki stayed put. He crossed the airport corridor to the pay phone, and one of his men passed him the receiver.

"Oleg. Remember the signal you found? I need you to find it again. Right now. Drop whatever you're doing and do a search. How close can you get?"

"Your timing is good. Our satellite is coming into range. If the transmitter is not moving, I should be able to give you coordinates within a few meters," Oleg said over the miles of lines from beneath the streets of Moscow. "But it will take me a few minutes to locate a map of the airport."

———

Luggage wobbled around Kelli as the cart wound its way through the terminal. It burst through another set of doors and she clutched Pearl tighter. She should have stayed and waited for Maman outside the restroom. Where was she going?

The chaotic sounds gradually faded, and the cart came to a stop. The driver got out and walked away. Kelli pushed a bag off, slid to the ground, and ran behind another cart, and then another. They were everywhere, a forest of little open cars for her and

Petit Pearl to hide in. One reminded her of a small tractor, pulling a cart full of big barrels.

*Come on, Pearl, that's where we can hide.*

Pearl crinkled strangely in her clutch. From between her chest and Pearl, a cold, crumpled piece of paper dropped onto the driver's seat. She must have picked the paper up accidentally when she reached for Pearl in the car.

Someone was coming. She ducked between the barrels.

*Pearl, we can hide. It's dark here...*

———

"Louis, what the hell man?" said a passing airport employee. "Gus sees you loitering around, you're in for it."

"Well, what am I supposed to be doing?"

"You're a ramp rat, idiot. Just pick a cart. That one's been sitting here for like three days. Get rid of that shit. And check the boards for any pickups while you're out there."

"Well, where does this stuff go?"

"Seriously? Use the directory like the rest of us?"

Louis lifted a crumpled paper off the seat and flattened it. "Enoki. *Déesse en Volant.* What is that?" He carried the paperwork to the maintenance and delivery boards and ran his finger down the long column of private hangars currently being used. "There you are, Goddess."

———

Drozdov tried to remain calm as his diplomatic limousine drove at an infuriatingly diplomatic speed away from the main terminal of Orly International Airport. The long, sleek car crawled through the maddening traffic and down the highway to the private road of the FBO.

Oleg's signal had traced the girl's bracelet, and Serebryakov was presently engaged convincing the airport security that he'd heard someone say a little girl was wandering around the FBO. It was uncanny how Kira's girl had somehow wandered right onto the very lane of hangars where Enoki had stored his Goddess, as though Kira herself had reached from beyond the grave, forgiving him, helping him to find her to bring her home.

None of this was going to be quick and easy: the traffic, the paperwork at the gate, Enoki explaining why they were visiting the hangar. Russian passports weren't granted friendly access to tarmacs they weren't supposed to be on, and Drozdov's private jet stood useless on the other end of the airport. They would need to gain access as Enoki's guests.

The Japanese engineer sat next to him in the limousine, muttering some mantra over and over under his breath. Erik sat opposite, his legs crossed in that easy manner that only a Level VI can carry off. Erik had no tolerance for instability and eyed Enoki narrowly, as if waiting for the slightest signal from his superior. Drozdov had to be very careful. If he nodded his head the wrong way, the Japanese genius would be dead before they reached the gate.

———

The wind jostled Serebryakov's hair as the airport security vehicle moved along the tarmac. He had explained to the French police that his newly found child was mildly unstable and required more supervision than he realized. He also claimed a maintenance man mentioned a little girl wandering around the west side private hangars, and they had gladly bought the story. If the girl showed any resistance, he would claim mental instability, and no one would argue. No one wants to deal with a mental case.

The security vehicle pulled up in a lane between private hangars, and the party of four split up to search. One guard accompanied Serebryakov. Oleg had given Drozdov coordinates of the girl's location, pinpointing this avenue of private hangars off the main airport. At least he hadn't lost her completely. At least she was still at the airport. But how she had gotten this far from the main terminal was baffling. Serebryakov recalled the endless hours in their hotel room while she sat disinterestedly, staring out windows at the Paris skyline. Eventually, he would have to tell Drozdov about the little interview regarding poets in the taxi. But for now, he just had to find her.

Approaching the hangar, Serebryakov first noticed the odd and unique aircraft firing up for an imminent departure. A man stood near the entrance. Tall and slender, with straw-colored hair and angular facial features, he stood motionless, peering into a wooden crate.

"*Tiens! Bonjour?*" Serebryakov called.

The man didn't turn around. Serebryakov didn't want to overreact in front of the security guard, but he thought he might have seen the man stow a weapon.

"I am sorry to disturb you. We are looking for a missing child," he continued in French. "We have reason to believe she was last seen in this area. Have you seen her?"

The man didn't answer. Perhaps he didn't speak French.

# 4TH MOVEMENT: CHOICES

"In the safe, you'll find a phone number. It's very important that you call that number, right now, before you leave. I've never met him. I don't even know his real name, but I understand now that, well... I was about to say 'he's a good guy,' but I don't know if there really is such a thing anymore. Good guys, bad guys. At some point, I've been both. So, what does that make me? Maybe, in the end, there are no good or bad guys. Maybe instead, we're all just trying to get back to ourselves somehow, like in living, we all got lost along the way."

# ONE

SEREBRYAKOV WAS NOT DEAD. ADAM'S FINAL LUNGE AT THE MAN IN the Paris air hangar had caused a concussion and two teardrop fractures in his neck, but he was not dead. Days later, the man Kelli had known as Henri Chaput lay unconscious at a private medical facility. Nearby, sitting in constant surveillance, Drozdov ran the gingham skirt of Petite Pearl over and over contemplatively between his fingers, as though touching it would bring him some answers, some contact with the girl, with truth.

While Kelli was dreaming of witches in Nathanial's cabin, Drozdov had ordered that the unconscious KGB agent, Serebryakov, was never to be left alone. If he should wake, even for a minute, there might be something, anything he could report. Most hours, Drozdov sat in a shadowed corner of the sterile room, perpetually vigilant for any sign of awakening. Like the incessant drone of Serebryakov's monitor, Drozdov mentally relived the scene at the airport. The girl, the chopper, Enoki, the strange figure on the motorcycle, and Kira.

Wounds long since healed now burned afresh. Kira. So faithful, so constant, so ideal. Then one day, gone. Recruited to France? No. The idiot French government never even knew she had crossed their borders. Working in a bank? Kira? What had happened here?

*Serebryakov, wake up dammit. Wake up, you fool, and tell me something.*

Why had the little girl run away? Was she frightened by something Chaput had said?

Despite his present desperation, Drozdov caught himself smiling at the girl's little doll, which she had somehow dropped into an empty storage crate in the Paris hangar. Hadn't Kira been only a little older when he'd rescued her in Dublin? Oh, that tiny precious little ballerina. He hadn't even been there to find her. In Ireland to research that terrible violist. *Poterya vremeni.* What was his name? But in those days, he never wasted a trip. Fueled by an endless store of youthful energy, he would visit the local watering holes, spark gossip in the hotel lobbies, and pretend to be a potential donor at the art schools.

Kira, imprisoned on such a hopeless path, the little ward of some sisters of something or other who were delighted when Drozdov took an interest. He was younger then and could pull off an adoption himself, no need for any half-wit KGB.

Serebryakov did not move for five days. Move him too hard, move him at all even, and it could kill him. First, he began to moan sporadically. A nurse came in and offered a painkiller, but Drozdov refused. More hours of solitude, the repeating playback of memories, the darkness and the soft beep of the monitor, until finally his eyelids lifted.

"Comrade," Drozdov spoke in his gentlest Russian. "Can you hear me? You are safe." A groan, eyeballs moving around the room. Recognition.

"Do not try to move. You are badly injured. Your neck was broken. But you are lucky; the spinal cord was not damaged. You will walk again soon, my friend."

The patient's eyes closed. One hand lifted to his neck, feeling the brace.

"*Tovarishch*, comrade, can you tell me your name?"

"Yuri... Venedik-tovich... Sere-brya—" He tried to stifle some coughs.

Drozdov exhaled with relief. "And who am I?"

"Konstantin Andreevich Drozdov, special research advisor to the Politburo. You want to know about the girl."

An aging nurse opened the door and gasped. "*Il s'est réveillé*!!" The door closed, and her steps faded off down the corridor.

Drozdov seized the isolation. "Yes, comrade. Anything at all that you can tell me."

"I will tell you what I remember, but I don't know that it will help."

The doctor arrived too quickly, and meticulously examined and questioned his patient for ten minutes. He ordered Serebryakov's head be elevated and that he be hydrated, but to Drozdov's relief, he also encouraged conversation.

When they were at last alone, Serebryakov described the scene in the Paris hangar as he remembered it, especially the tall, fair-haired man who had so expertly beaten him. When he finished, Drozdov sat back, disappointed. Serebryakov's story ended with a death toll. No answers, no clues, except that the thieves were, by Serebryakov's estimation, American. No leads, no direction to go but home, empty handed.

It was time to address the ramifications of losing Enoki's chopper. Commissioning it at all had been a huge financial gamble. Apex funding didn't run so deep. There had been markers called in, IOUs filled, and now it was stolen. Like a hungry old bear, dread crept stealthily out of the dark places. Humiliation from faces he had long held in his debt. Removal from his post, or prison, or worse.

The door softly opened, and the unnatural hallway light poured in around the shadow of a tall and slender man. Erik had come to relieve Drozdov.

A deep, drowning gasp came from the body of Yuri Venediktovich Serebryakov. His breathing and heart rate escalated, and monitors blared out warnings. Erik and Drozdov stepped forward as the doctor burst through the door shouting orders. He gave the patient a mild sedative, but Serebryakov struggled to resist it, frantic. He would not be calmed. He drew in his strength and lifted his right hand in an unquestionable line towards Erik. "The man from the hangar!"

Drozdov pushed the doctor aside despite shouts of disapproval, leaning over the patient's flinching body. Serebryakov grabbed his arm, gulping in air with a frantic fury.

"The man from the hangar!" he said again, his arm still pointing at Erik. "That's him!"

# TWO

For five nights, a small black helicopter waited atop a Manhattan high rise, its occupants vigilant.

"That's them," Drozdov said at last, pointing to the screen. "It has to be."

In the cool darkness outside their sedate chopper, a tiny floating light appeared on the horizon above the skyscrapers. It gradually grew larger until the unmistakable chopping of a rotor passed directly overhead.

In the back seat of the helicopter, Kazuhiro Enoki muttered something prayerful in Japanese.

"I've only seen it in the daylight," Drozdov said, "but I believe that's your beauty, or your goddess, or whatever you call it."

"Yes." From Enoki's fingertips, a new sound flowed onto a computer keyboard. *Tip tap tip-tip tap.* "You did it. You found her." Enoki retreated into the depths of his focus. The computer screen, sturdily affixed to the backseat of their small cabin, responded without bias, its yellow glow pouring across his eyes.

A part of Drozdov was disappointed to see Enoki's Goddess. Though he had hoped the chopper would make an appearance at the heist, Adam and the girl would have been enough. If Adam was working for the Americans, that meant that Zeus had the craft. Infuriating. Drozdov had the balls to pay for it, and Zeus had stolen it. But if he had Kelli or Adam, the right amount of pressure meant one of them would talk.

Tonight, chopper or not, a lifelong rivalry with a faceless enemy would finally end. The LOCK, Kira, Adam, and the girl. One of them would lead Drozdov to the only thing he wanted more than Enoki's chopper: the illusory Zeus and the American Institute of KATs.

Erik sat up as the chopper passed over them. "Look at that. You were right."

Of course Drozdov was right. Four years ago, he had bribed, coerced, and blackmailed his own agent into that vault. Stacks of safes and one specially made with a locking scanner just the size for a finger. That damn safe. Within its impenetrable mechanisms lay something so precious, so valuable, that his career, his reputation, and his life had hung in a perpetual limbo for the day that some faceless person would access that cursed account.

He posted Mafia thugs out front to wait for the owner's return. He had a plant in the offices, feeding him the paperwork and watching the vault. Once a woman had come, but she had slipped past his network. Since then, over five years had passed, and no living soul had even once approached it. Drozdov could only ever guess who had built it and tucked it so securely in the impenetrable fortress of that high-rise.

Until last week. When he got the call from his New York thugs. All at once, Drozdov remembered where he had heard the name Bertrand. Kelli Bertrand. That was the name on the paperwork of the vault. Kelli Bertrand. Now, with the revelation that Adam was the stranger at the Paris airport, and the woman who attempted to access it, Drozdov knew with absolute certainty that there would soon be a move on the vault. All he had to do was wait.

*Who are the three poets?*

Serebryakov's story ate at Drozdov in every quiet moment, sitting atop this high rise, waiting for the inevitable to appear in the New York sky.

*Who are the three poets?*

What did it mean? Only minutes later, the girl had fled in the Paris airport. It was this question, Drozdov had no doubt, this odd and inconsequential chain of words that held the answer to everything. Somehow it was all connected. Kira, the girl, the LOCK, and now Adam.

Had Drozdov not been there in the Paris hospital room when Serebryakov woke up pointing at Erik, his Level VI surely would have strangled him.

"I was with you and that Japanese lunatic the whole time," Erik had said.

"Erik. It wasn't you."

"Then what the hell was he talking about?"

"It wasn't you," Drozdov had repeated, like a patient mantra, hoping Erik would figure it out for himself. "We never found a body," he said at length.

"What?"

"Your brother tricked us. He defected."

Drozdov knew this was the first Erik had considered anything but the foil. After all, it had played out so perfectly. There had been a funeral, commendations, and condolences. There was a grave, an empty grave, but such is often the case in their work. That wasn't enough to stop Erik from weekly visits, or was it monthly now? Had it been that long? Yes, now that he thought of it, years had passed without notice, by streams of work-filled days.

Internally, Drozdov had always suspected it, always kept the possibility open in his mind. Nothing was impossible with people; faithfulness was such a rare quality, even rarer than the ESA that made the brothers and Kira so unique. Fidelity, gratitude, honesty.

Were these even realities, or simply convenient lies we told ourselves?

"No," Erik had said, so quietly Drozdov almost didn't hear him over the hum of Serebryakov's monitors. "There is some other explanation."

Drozdov had watched with sympathy as Erik struggled to digest such a simple and evident truth. It was alarming sometimes, how innocent they could be. What little innocence that had somehow remained with Erik melted away right then in Serebryakov's hospital room, as if he was mourning the loss of his brother a second time, only now aflame with betrayal.

"We both saw that ship explode," Erik said.

"Be assured of it. He is alive, and working for the Americans." He could not help Erik. Betrayal is a private pill that must digest slowly.

*Who are the three poets?* Was it some sort of code?

Betrayal. It was Kira. Of course. Drozdov shamed himself for not thinking of it before. His pride had kept him blind to the truth. Kira had done all of this. Even the missing LOCK. He could see that now. She had manipulated every detail so perfectly, even from the grave. This whole scenario was her very ghost coming back to taunt him. Kira had taught the girl something, some secret code to keep her from him.

*Tip tap tip tip tap.* "I need to be closer," Enoki said at length.

"Not yet," said Drozdov from the front seat of the chopper. "First let them complete their mission."

When the *Peregrine* landed atop a nearby building, Erik jumped out and ran to the nearest ledge. He peered through binoculars to watch two figures emerge. "It's him," he said as Drozdov approached. "It's Adam, and they brought the girl."

"Of course. They can't get in without her." The two black shadows, one tall and one miniscule, dashed across the roof and disappeared into a ventilation duct. "Now, we wait again," said Drozdov, returning to the chopper.

"I still don't understand why we can't just blast at them while they are vulnerable," said Enoki from the backseat, momentarily coming out of his stupor.

"As interesting a prospect as that might be," said Drozdov, "one cannot just start blasting at helicopters on New York City rooftops without raising alarms. Besides, I've waited a long time to get in that vault. Tonight, Adam will get in there for me."

"It's ridiculous. Whatever is in there can't be worth such risk."

"I have absolute confidence in your ability to reign in my aircraft," said Drozdov.

"She isn't designed to be caught."

"You know, Enoki, if you were so desperate not to lose her, you might have fitted her with some tracking mechanism to begin with. As the sole funder of this venture, it would have been okay with me."

*Tip tap tip tip tap.*

# THREE

THE DARKNESS INSIDE THE VAULT WAS ABSOLUTE. WHENEVER KELLI opened her eyes, she had to blink again to be sure she'd opened them. They hung as comfortably as possible from the ceiling of vault 18, while Adam worked on the magnet device by memory. The quiet, the darkness, and the solemn nature of her companion lay siege on Kelli's imagination, converting her confidence into frozen terror, and her lips into saintly silence.

She tried to imagine herself back in the cabin. The smell of burning embers, crickets outside, and Nathanial reading her a story—the one about the green eggs. She liked that Sam character. He was very sneaky. Still, the reality of her location made it harder and harder not to cry. Her companion would not like it if she cried. Instead, she clung to his torso, listening to the gentle thump-thump of his heartbeat and the slow and controlled swoosh of his breathing.

"Thwop!" The device fired its magnet. The gentle clicking sound of the little crank pulled them along the new cable, closer to the safe. She clung tighter to him, having made the mistake of briefly opening her eyes into the hopeless cold of pitch black.

This place was terrible.

———

On the roof, Nathanial waited in the cockpit. So far, everything had gone according to plan. With a few phone calls, Peter had subverted any potentially curious air traffic controllers so he could land the *Peregrine* on the Manhattan high rise without interference.

The unlikely duo of a Level VI and an almost-six had disappeared about twenty minutes ago into a ventilation unit. They were already probably finished worming their way through the intricate labyrinth of cold metal vents, and right now were most likely in the vault. Soon, this whole nightmare would be over.

Adam had reprimanded Kelli sternly three times in the *Peregrine* and once on the roof to not speak anymore. He really was a blockhead. Anyone could see she was terrified. He should have been thanking her for requesting a pitstop before they got to the vault.

Nathanial checked his watch. Just a few more minutes, and this whole mess would be over. Man, he hated this stuff.

———

"All right, it's time. Give me your right hand." Adam switched on a small flashlight and carefully set the girl's index finger over the glass scanner. He pushed the button, and a tiny light flashed, followed by a soft humming. Another button launched a series of soft whirrs and a clink. "You have to sit up for this."

She reached for the keyboard with a trembling hand, but first shot Adam an accusatory glance. He rolled his eyes and looked away.

At last, the safe door popped open. Adam removed two small

boxlike items and left the door open on purpose. There would be no doubt that the contents were gone.

He switched off the flashlight, returning them to the darkness.

"Are we done?" she whispered.

"Yes."

"Can we go now?"

"Yes. Wait, no. I have to tell you something."

He reached in a back pocket and winced away from a sudden bright flash. She had found the flashlight.

"What's that?" she asked, glaring at the small white handkerchief in his hand.

"Kelli, you're not coming with me." He snatched the flashlight, leaving it on, and returned it to his vest.

"What do you mean?"

"It's time for you to go back where you belong. It's time to go home."

"You mean to the cabin?"

"No, back home to France."

Her eyes widened to a horror-filled stretch. He felt her body tense up on the harness.

"It's going to be all right. You'll see."

She shook her head. "You're going to leave me? But I don't like it here. The bad people!"

"No. No one is going to hurt you. You're safe now."

He held the handkerchief over her nose and mouth, securing his hand on the back of her head. She squirmed violently, a flood of terror in her eyes pleading with him, but it was like fighting a kitten. Easy.

"Just relax, it's going to be okay. Relax."

Her body fell limp. She had trusted him, and he had lied to her. It was simple. Hanging there, alone in the darkness with her tiny frame slumped on his, a distant piano sang a melancholy melody, and she twirled for him in her massive purple tutu. She didn't belong in their world. Anyone could see that. This was the cleanest way of returning her to hers.

Carefully, he slid her limp weight off his knees and onto the cold vault floor, then pulled on a cable and ascended into the darkness above.

# FOUR

When Adam returned to the rooftop, Nathanial was already in the cockpit and the *Peregrine* rotor was throwing its wind. Adam opened the back door to stow his equipment and give the illusion of buckling in a child. Nathanial was so eager to get going, he didn't even turn around. Adam shut the door and ran around the front. Headsets on, the pilot received an explicit "Go," and the *Peregrine* rose off the roof, soaring above the New York skyline.

"Everything go okay?"

"Yes. Fine."

"What was in the safe?"

"Don't know. Two small items. We'll get into that later."

"Of course. Kelli okay?"

Adam feigned looking backward. "Asleep." It wasn't a lie.

Nathanial chuckled. "Figures."

A warning alarm sounded.

"What's that?" Adam asked.

"Looks like another chopper by the speed, but it sure is gaining on us."

"Authorities?"

"Unlikely."

Adam monitored the screen, watching the encroacher shorten the gap between them. "They certainly are cutting it close."

"What the hell?" Nathanial tightened on the cyclic as the foolhardy chopper swept past within a few dangerous feet. "That was no accident."

The attacker quickly turned for a head-on collision.

"Nathan!"

"I got it! I got it!" Nathanial dodged veering right and accelerated rapidly. "What is going on, Adam? Who is this?"

"I assume it's whoever abducted Coreena. They want what I stole."

"Yeah, and maybe their stinking helicopter along with it. When am I gonna learn? It's never simple."

———

"Now just to clarify, why can't you force them to land?" Erik asked.

"She is not easily forced. Not so vulnerable."

"Then what the hell are we doing here?"

"I know signals," said Enoki. "They can interfere. We must force them higher. You keep her over land. When the fuel is gone, they will land. She can do it, over *land*." Enoki spoke but did not look up from his screen.

*Tip-tap, tippity tap.*

As they rocked from side to side, Drozdov considered whether the thieves might not know what they stole. Could that whole scene at the Paris airport possibly have been a blind heist? No, Adam's presence changed everything. Adam would be working for Zeus now, and that meant the slithering American KATs had their paws all over Enoki's aircraft. KATs were KATs, no matter where their allegiance.

"We'll draw too much attention up here," Erik said. "Staying lower would keep us in the dark."

"Too much air. Thinner is better. Higher is better," Enoki muttered.

"Seems a lot of risk, when I'm perfectly happy to blow them out of the sky."

Drozdov had allowed Erik to bring a weapon at his insistence, and he had to admit, Erik was right. This whole affair could be dealt with in an instant if he just nodded his head and took the controls.

"You can rebuild that thing surely," Erik continued. "One swift trigger pull, and a lot of problems go up in the night."

Drozdov could claim the chopper was destroyed by malfunction and then pick up the pieces of his investment. The LOCK would gratefully be destroyed forever, and Erik would certainly enjoy watching Adam go up in flames, but...

"You must not let them engage the drive!" Enoki shouted.

"Drozdov, we don't even know if that drive works," Erik said.

*But Kira, your little girl...* "Get as close as you can, Erik."

———

Every time Nathanial had an encounter with Adam Walker, he inevitably found himself the target of someone else's weapon. But this time he wasn't vulnerable on the ground in a hangar. He pitched the chopper forward sharply and shot away from the attackers.

"Can't we go any faster?" Adam asked.

"I told you, this thing wasn't built for speed." The pursuer came at them from behind, dangerously close. Nathanial compensated, and the *Peregrine* wobbled precariously. "Who builds a helicopter for the Soviets without any weapons?"

"If I didn't know better, I'd say you want a gun," Adam said, holding onto his seat.

"Right now, a few guns would be great. Is she buckled in back there?"

"She's safe. Just keep your focus forward.'"

"Don't tell me what to do with my focus!" Nathanial pulled up and turned abruptly back towards the city.

"What are you doing?"

"If I can't shoot 'em and I can't outrun 'em, maybe I can outmaneuver 'em." The *Peregrine* pitched downward again as Nathanial accelerated back into downtown Manhattan. "Whoever's back there, they're good."

Adam's right hand instinctively crept up towards the cyclic controls on his side.

"Touch those controls and I break your arm," Nathanial said. Adam retracted his hand. "He's good, but I'll be damned if he is as good as me."

They sped back over the financial district. At Battery, Nathanial reduced their altitude, and they sunk between the buildings, coming within mere feet of the cars on Trinity place. He moved swiftly, avoiding streetlights and media signs without leaning too far and chopping into the abdomen of a high rise. When he got to Liberty Plaza Park, he made a surprise sharp right turn. The attacker passed, and Nathanial headed west down even tighter Cedar Street, hoping to confine his opponent.

It was late, so there wasn't a lot of traffic on the streets, but two helicopters madly playing chicken around sharp city corners would hardly go unnoticed. Taxi drivers peered up from steering wheels as the choppers sped past, blowing newspapers and stray napkins into white vortexes. Intoxicated club patrons lost their precarious balance and stumbled off sidewalk edges as a storm of wind and sound disarranged their already spinning heads.

This was not like flying in the mountains; one slightly inaccurate gesture of his hand and they would end up a smoking hole. As the seconds ticked away, Nathanial came to grips with the obvious reality that his pursuer was both a fanatical and worthy opponent. There was a good chance that he wouldn't be able to best him. Additionally, there was only so long they could keep this race up without the authorities coming out to play, and then it would get really messy. Somebody was bound to have a gun.

"We haven't got the fuel for this," he said into his headgear. "We're not out yet, but we certainly can't keep this up indefinitely."

For a few moments, he dodged his tail at Times Square by faking out a move up Seventh Avenue, but at the last second veered off over Broadway, turning them completely on their side and shattering some lightbulbs on a tall marquee flashing "Sugar Babies at Camp." He recovered the controls quickly but not without a warning glare from Adam.

Now he had to make the insane decision of when to break free from his current path as the two choppers careened furiously up Broadway and Seventh Avenues respectively.

Adam peered down each passing cross street to catch a glimpse of the enemy. "He's staying with us."

Nathanial pulled up short and turned west down 54th for a rapid swing left, putting them back in the direction they'd come on Eighth Avenue. Perhaps he could lose them long enough to make a landing back on the Battery docks and either evacuate the *Peregrine* with Kelli and the goods, or disappear off the assailant's radar completely.

They had only gone a few blocks towards safety when he had to pull up again, surprised by the assailant unexpectedly pitching around the corner of 47th, throwing the *Peregrine* violently off its equilibrium.

"Dammit!" Nathanial clutched for control. "Adam, I'm running out of ideas. I don't suppose we could call in the cavalry?"

"From our stolen Soviet aircraft? Too many questions."

"Well, maybe Peter can turn on the charm and make some of his magic phone calls. Surely that would be better than going up in smoke."

"They don't want to blow us up."

"Then what do they want?"

"They want what's in my satchel. They want you to land. Is there a chance of that?"

For a few seconds, the distasteful question hung alive in the air between them.

"Did you bring a gun?" asked Nathanial.

"I always bring a gun."

———

"Can't you fly any gentler? She's a finely tuned instrument of precision and balance. Not some American pickup truck."

"Easy does it, Erik. Precious cargo," Drozdov warned. "This isn't personal, remember."

"The hell it isn't."

"Listen to him! You push too hard. Stay close and burn their fuel," Enoki said, fighting to keep his arms on his keyboard. "Almost there." *Tip tip tap.*

The chopper rocked with the fury of the chase.

"All right, Enoki," Drozdov asked, "he's moving back out of the city. How is this going to work?"

"Just keep close. Very close."

Erik veered around another corner, and Enoki had to clutch his keyboard to keep it from falling.

"We don't know if they're running out of fuel," Erik said, "and we can't keep this up indefinitely."

*Tip tap tip tap tap.* "Not a lot of fuel storage, and ascent will cost them. Wait, I have her."

———

"Oh, this guy is really ticking me off. What's his game?" Nathanial had left the city streets to outrun his pursuers up the Hudson. He glared down at his instruments and pulled aggressively on the collective. "What the hell?" Two orange lights started flashing and an alarm sounded.

"What is it?"

"The collective. It's not responding."

"Has it done that before?" Adam reached down and tried the lever with no success.

"No."

"A malfunction? Are all the controls locked up?"

Nathanial veered left. "I've got steering and velocity, but—" Adam and Nathanial were sucked backward as the *Peregrine* pitched and rapidly began ascending. "Dammit! We're going up."

"How are you doing this without the collective?"

"I'm not pulling us up. Someone else is."

———

With great satisfaction, Drozdov watched Enoki's helicopter veer upwards in a rapid ascent out of the pilot's control.

"There they go," Erik said. "I'll have to get you to show me how to do that."

"Follow them, and stay close."

———

"I don't get it. Why push us up?"

"They know something we don't," Adam said. "Something about the drive."

"Who knows what that nut put in this thing?"

"We could try shutting down the engines to cut the power."

"That might release the collective," Nathanial said. "But then it will be about time for our fuel to run out." Seconds passed as they quickly ascended into the night sky. Nathanial frantically tried to regain control.

"We could engage the drive."

The *Peregrine* rocked slightly in defiance of its rapid steep ascent.

"You understand that we could just blow up into a fiery blaze," said Nathanial.

"Or it could do nothing?"

"Oh no, it's going to do something. But I can't predict what."

"They sure are fighting to get this thing back in one piece."

"This thing, plus whatever's in your satchel there, not to mention the sleepy girl in the back seat. Dammit, I don't see any other choice except to land and hand them everything they want."

"They'll kill us all."

"Well, in a few minutes we might be dead anyway."

"Can you do it?" Adam asked.

Nathanial took a moment to process out loud. "First, shut down the engines to kill the power. Hopefully the collective comes back online. We'll start dropping, but the drop will be good. We can use it. If the drive works as I think, there will have to be a minimum amount of forward speed for it to engage. I've already got the Institute coordinates programmed into the drive. While we're falling, we restart the engines, get the power back on—"

"Do we need the engines?"

"I don't know, Adam! I've never tried anything like this before. And this is not what you'd call optimal circumstances. If we're lucky we've got just enough fuel for that. Extend the wings, retract the blades, and pull up, then..." Once more, he considered the ramifications of landing, the potential battlefield of bullets with tiny Kelli in the middle. "Then we engage the drive."

———

The vault's floor was weight sensitive. Of course, Adam knew that when he left her there. The girl would not be alone for long. As soon as her tiny body hit the ground, a sensor gleefully leaped to duty. Behind the steel and concrete, the signal spanned across thirty yards of circuitry to a small and otherwise inactive computer monitor, where something starting flashing.

Sidney, a dozing security officer in his mid-fifties, jerked up, spilling a half-eaten bag of chips on his blue shirt and knocking an open paperback to the floor.

"You gotta be kidding me. Those stinking floors." He flicked on his walkie-talkie to reach another guard several floors up. "Murandi, you up there?"

"Yeah, Sidney. Where else would I be? Some of us can't be sleeping."

"We got a floor trigger," Sidney said over the walkie-talkie. "Vault 18. Probably another dumb rat. You hear anything?"

"Besides your whining voice, not a thing."

"Those floor sensors are way more hassle than they're worth."

"You gonna lift your lazy carcass and come up here anyway?" Murandi asked.

"Roger that. There'll be a signal to general and a phone call in the morning." Sidney got up, brushed any remaining crumbs off his trousers, and shuffled onto an elevator. Once upstairs, he grumbled as he entered a code and retrieved his keys in the dim hallway.

He met up with Murandi, who turned the handle on Vault 18, and the door ground open. Murandi's flashlight beam shone around the smooth, even floor in the cold darkness.

"Wait, go back," Sidney said, seeing something. "What was that?"

"What the hell?"

"That ain't no rat."

# FIVE

"WE'RE LEVELING OFF," NATHANIAL SAID. "TAKE THE CONTROLS AND buy me thirty seconds."

Adam grasped the cyclic while Nathanial began what he believed were the preparations to engage the Hydro-Refraction Drive, as he was calling it. If he was right, it wasn't terribly complicated. The onboard computer first had to have the latitude and longitude of their starting and intended locations. He suspected these coordinates were crucial, because when he engaged the drive, he would no longer be in control of the aircraft. The *Peregrine* would need to know where they were going and any ensuing change in terrain elevation.

"Okay, shutting down the power now."

A section at a time, the panel lights disappeared into darkness. The engines quieted as the rotor began descending in pitch. The cyclic went dead, and Adam released it. "Now comes the hard part," Nathanial continued. "Get ready to drop. But keep alert. We need to restart the engines as soon as we're moving and get those wings out."

"Get ready to drop?"

Nathanial took the controls back. "Drop, Adam. Like, hold the hell on."

———

"They're cutting the power," Enoki said. "Probably trying to get the collective back. Clever. But at this point, they must be out of fuel. They won't have enough speed to engage the drive. Now they will have to land."

Drozdov waited for the lights to switch back on inside Enoki's chopper, but instead it slowed significantly, pitched forward, and dropped out of view.

"They're committing suicide!" Erik shouted.

As the vessel plunged downward towards the earth, Erik pitched forward to pursue, but even his ESA eyes had trouble picking the *Peregrine* out in the black night sky. Drozdov and Enoki clutched their seats as the chopped descended at a danger-ously rapid rate. At last, the lights inside the *Peregrine* reappeared just in time to see the nub-wings extending from its sides like a stretching cat. Meanwhile, the massive rotor blades that had been steadily slowing slid away inside their disc cover.

"Oh no," whispered Enoki into his headset. "How very clever."

Drozdov whipped around. "What do you mean, oh no? What are they doing?"

"Stop them," Enoki said. "Shoot at them!"

———

Falling, electricity shivering though skin and skull…

Adam had jumped out of many planes, but for some reason, rapidly descending in a heavy vehicle over which he had no control was considerably more terrifying. His stomach whirled as Nathanial reached for a lever beneath his foot and snatched hold of the cyclic, pulling it towards him doggedly, fighting against wind and gravity, trying to get a lift with the slowly extending wings. Twenty or so thousand feet didn't seem so far to fall, as the scattered lights on the dark earth grew farther and farther apart beneath them.

"Come on. Come on, you stubborn Japanese monstrosity." Nathanial winced, pulling on the flight control. Adam felt the aircraft begin to submit ever so slightly. The drop decelerated as their nose edged up an inch at a time. Just as Adam thought he could see the trees beneath them, their angle shifted, and the black horizon grew steadily back into view.

The entire aircraft began humming. A strange conglomeration of bluish particles assembled in the air around them, glimmering as they multiplied across every window. Adam felt drawn into a daze. He wanted to reach out and touch each tiny spinning electric particle with his fingers.

Trembling, Nathanial checked his watch. "Well, I'd say it's been nice knowing you," he said. "But you've been a real pain in the ass."

———

"Stop them!" Enoki hollered. "Shoot them!"

"What can I do?" Erik said. "He plummeted out of the sky. Wait, he's pulling up finally."

"Don't let him pull up. Don't let him pull up!"

Erik checked for permission, but Drozdov's eyes remained steadfast on the bluish light slowly engulfing the *Peregrine*.

"No," said the Japanese genius whom The Institute had labeled as unstable. "You're too late."

———

Detective Riley Kirkpatrick's long desired promotion to Detective at age 52 had been a welcome honor and a gratifying change. He had earned the new position after twelve years on the streets of Midtown South, where the dregs of New York society convened in one foul spot to do their worst to themselves. Even this neighborhood was better. Lower Manhattan quieted down in the evenings, after all the big money bulls went home to their high rises and Long Island cottages. Compared to Times Square, South Side detective was a job to sit back and relax in. Of course, it had come with the third-shift price tag. Every officer had to do their time.

He stiffly eased his bottom into the squeaky wooden chair at his small aluminum desk. Tonight, half the staff was out with a stomach flu, so everyone had to cover extra duties for the officers in the latrine. So far this evening, Kirkpatrick had interviewed three prostitutes, two muggers, and a man who reeked of bourbon and kept calling out "Yes General!" with a shaky salute.

*Just like home*, he thought, as he sent the last mugger down to a holding cell and pulled out his open case files.

His phone rang. "Kirkpatrick."

"Hello, Detective. They transferred me from the dispatch. My name is Jason Stiles, and I am the Director of Security over at Miles and Jeter in the Equitable Building."

"What can I do for you, Mr. Siles?"

"Stiles. Well, it appears we've had our first break-in in seventy-five years this evening."

The detective perked up. "Has someone already been sent over?"

"Yes. Our security team has been through the place. We think we know how they got in. Incredible, really. Only one thing was stolen, that is, only one safe emptied. A personal safe. We can hold everything as we found it until you get here."

Riley considered the vacant office around him, eager to escape before any more oafs climbed the front steps for a slap on the wrist. "I'm on my way," he said, whipping his folder shut.

"Detective?"

Riley caught the receiver as it dangled over its cradle, its curled cord getting caught on his sleeve. "Yeah? What is it?"

"Well, it's just that, you should probably bring someone from Social Welfare."

"What are you talking about?"

"Or maybe The Department of Health? I'm not really sure. But you should bring someone with you."

"I thought you said you had a break-in on a high security vault."

"Yes, sir. But the perpetrator left something behind. He left something in the vault."

---

Three minutes. Though an insignificant fraction in the span of eternity, such few seconds transcend into an eternal wilderness of time when one is waiting to be reduced to a pile of molecules dancing about in the atmosphere.

Adam and Nathanial did not speak as the HR drive reached its full potential. Like seated statues, hearts pounding, their breathing forced into submission by the smallest remnant of intelligent will, each held something tightly in his hands: the flight controls and the sides of a seat.

A low pitch hum gradually ascended to an apex no whistle could produce, where it plateaued and remained, as though waiting for orders. The pressure on their backs released into weightlessness, dizziness, and disorientation. Where was up? Which way were they moving? What was happening?

Once, Nathanial tried to scan the instruments, but terror constrained him from letting go of his futile stranglehold on the controls. Whatever their fate, he could no more stop it happening than he could stop the drive.

Nathanial's haze melted in stages. He heard something beeping. Beeps, warning, signaling. Coming closer. Gravity returning, weight, pressure on his seat. His head dizzy. More signals, warn-ing. Breathe. A shove on his right shoulder.

"Hey. Snap out of it," Adam's voice said from outside the blur. "We're alive."

"What?"

"Wake up and fly."

Nathanial sat up as the last of the blue glow disintegrated into the dark sky. "At least we're still airborne. Where are we?"

"Checking that now. Some of the instruments seem to be dead. Is the engine...?"

"We're gliding, but we've got a bit of speed." He checked his watch. "Please tell me the radar is working."

"That's a negative."

"Great. Throbbing headache, dead stick, a new aircraft in the middle of the night with no certain indication of altitude. Where are we? Is there radio?"

"Dead."

Nathanial guided them downward, feeling a little hungover and knowing that he was actually spinning into dark nothingness and could hit ground anytime. "Well, what the hell is working?"

"There are some lights on, so it isn't a total power failure. Probably running on battery."

"Airspeed indicator is up, at least we can hope that's right. Altimeter?"

"Looks normal. Attitude indicator seems okay."

"Count our blessings."

Nathanial guessed they were probably low, and whatever the drive had done to the instruments, the radar altimeter wasn't reading much lower than when they left. Did the drive adjust for changes in altitude, or had it whipped all the instruments into an undependable frenzy? He searched for any sign of humanity beneath the dark, endless horizon. Thanks to a three-quarter moon and no clouds in the sky, he would at least see the ground as he came in. That is, once they got perilously close to it.

"I'm gonna need those Level VI eyes of yours. Who knows what that drive did to these instruments? Here's hoping we're not over a lake or something."

"Like an ocean?"

"Unlikely. We were heading west."

Adam was quiet for a few moments. "Okay," he said. "I see it, we're not too close. You're good for now. Uh-oh."

"Uh oh? What uh oh?"

"I see undulations," Adam said.

"You mean like waves?"

"No, wait. There's no reflection, it's ripples on the ground. Maybe rock formations? It's barren. Looks like a desert or prairie. There's a lot of empty space. It's not farmland. Something else. A large dark crevice, a river or a canyon maybe?" A few minutes passed in silence as they continued to glide downward. "There," Adam said. "Lights."

"I see it. Woo-ha! Good job, Adam! Love you Level VI guys."

"Maybe a mining community? I don't see any headlights or moving vehicles."

Nathanial continued to steer the gliding *Peregrine* towards the lights, grateful for any sign of order. "I'll just be happy if there's something paved. And of course, here's the magic question to end all questions." He reached down and pulled the emergency gear extension handle. Both men sighed at the sweet sound of the three wheels deploying underneath them. Enoki, whoever he was, had included a back-up power source for the landing gear. "Now use those magic eyes to find me a place to land."

"I can see a straight line of lights to the right of the town now. Probably a road. Keep towards the lights, and you'll see it too. Based on what I'm seeing, I think your altimeter is working."

"Let's hope no one's out for a late-night drive," said Nathanial. "We're not making any noise."

"How far do you think we went?"

"I have no idea. I'm not even sure we aren't in some makeshift Twilight Zone. She okay back there?"

"Fine. Still asleep."

"So, she missed the whole thing. Unbelievable, man's first jump into an electromagnetic pulse. She won't believe it." It was funny that Kelli had slept through that whole adventure. So consistent with her innocent nature, calmly dozing away, believing the worst part of her mission was over, while he and Adam evaded attackers and risked everything jumping into a scientific future. Nathanial wished he could go back in time and sleep through it all too. "On second thought," he said, "maybe we should skip the part about the bad guys."

He drew the road into his flight path, hoping the local authorities in the middle of nowhere were obsessed with highway maintenance. Adam called out occasional bits of information as the ground got closer, but Nathanial held the controls all the way down. When they made the final approach, touching the precious earth like a timid lover, Nathanial laughed with a triumphant howl. It had been a night of firsts all around, but it was finally over.

# SIX

DETECTIVE KIRKPATRICK STOOD SPELLBOUND IN THE DOORWAY OF Miles and Jeter's Vault 18, repeatedly interrogating the security personnel. "No one heard anything coming out of the vault?"

"No, sir. Quiet all night."

"And only one safe was touched."

"Just the one."

"And she was here when you came in. Just like that."

"We did make sure she's breathing. To be sure."

"When did the alarm go off exactly?" Kirkpatrick asked.

"1:42 a.m., sir."

"And you immediately went in the vault."

"No one person can access any vault. We had to wait for a man to come upstairs with entry codes."

The three men stood stiffly in the vault entrance, speaking in unnaturally muffled tones. Kirkpatrick had originally assumed the security men had made a mistake. Perhaps the kid was really a big doll of some kind, or a corpse. But even he could see her tiny torso undulating softly up and down with the delicate metered breaths of childhood sleep. "What was in the safe? Any clue?"

"No," the company manager said. "All safe contents are private. Measures have been taken to notify the owner, but..."

"But what?"

"Well, apparently the owner is deceased, and the safe was accessed by the heir recently. We haven't been able to reach her yet."

"Deceased. Great. Who was paying the rent?"

"The account is paid ten years in advance."

The detective asked himself why he found this scene so disturbing. This certainly wasn't the scum of Times Square. But there she lay, such a tiny little bundle, her dainty little snores whistling in and out of her baby-like nostrils. *What kind of nutcase brings a little kid like that on a job? And who do you call when you find a kid asleep in a high security vault?* He called a medic, naturally, but this required something more nurturing, more maternal.

Even though it was 2:00 a.m., Kirkpatrick had not been surprised when the receiver at the Holy Angels Orphanage in Brooklyn softly lifted, and a young novice promised to wake the Mother General. As he dispatched a unit out to Brooklyn to pick her up, he wondered what the average life span of a nun might be. Surely, it wasn't the same woman.

At 2:47 a.m., the elevator doors opened on the 38th floor of Miles and Jeter Security, and a painfully familiar gaze fell on him, the woman's aged eyes squinting narrow and her lips slightly pursed.

"I always knew that one day they'd try to send you back," she said.

In her late sixties, Sister Mary Immaculata's posture showed no signs of bending. Although the edge of her coif now hung several inches below his brow, her height somehow transcended constrictions of mere measure. She still seemed taller than him. He felt like an eleven-year-old boy caught painting a mustache on the Sacred Heart of Jesus. Not that anyone could ever prove that.

"Be not afraid, Riley," the Sister said. "Now, we are on the same team. Yes?"

"Yes ma'am."

She peeked through the vault door while a medic checked on the sleeping child.

The nurse rose and came out. "I think she's fine, Detective. Pulse, breathing, temp all consistent with a healthy sleeping child. Without waking her, I see no signs of trauma or struggle. She was possibly given some mild sedative. When I examined her, she rolled over and complained a bit."

"I guess it's time to wake her, then." Kirkpatrick and Sister Mary knelt down on the vault floor. "All right kiddo, come on," he said, lifting the child. "Time to wake up now. Sit up, there ya' go." Her head bobbed from side to side, and she groaned. "Hey, you thirsty? You want some soda?" He pulled a Coke bottle from his coat pocket. *Pop, clink, fizz.* When he lifted it to her lips, the sugary bubbles brought her to a groggy consciousness.

She opened her eyes, spit the soda on his face, and screamed.

———

To Adam's surprise, Nathanial did not immediately turn around to check on Kelli. When the *Peregrine* at last rolled to a stop, the pilot sat back, took a deep satisfying breath, and said, "We're alive." Then he removed his head set and jumped out onto the dark street.

Warm, motionless air filled a barren terrain of undeveloped rock scattered with black brush. Adam watched Nathanial bounce around like a little kid on Christmas morning, running towards two road signs perched atop thin poles. Their text glowed softly in the moonlight.

*Glen Canyon City, Utah. Colorado River Storage Project. Glen Canyon Unit.*

"Utah?" Adam said. "Is that real?"

"Adam, I timed our flight."

"How long was the drive engaged?"

"Just under two and a half minutes."

———

"*Ne me touchez pas!*" The girl pushed the detective away. "*Laissez-moi tranquille!*"

"Hey kid, it's okay. My name is Detective Kirkpatrick, and this is my friend Sister Mary. We found you sleeping here in this vault. Can you tell us how you got here? What's your name? Can you tell us your name?"

The girl only hugged her knees, pulling them up under her chin tightly. Her unblinking eyes moved from one unfamiliar face to another, her head jerking irregularly, like a mechanical gadget about to short-circuit, until she stopped moving completely and her big bewildered brown eyes glazed over at a spot on the floor.

"She speaks French," Sister Mary said.

"Oh. That's what that was. I don't suppose you do."

Sister Mary shook her head. "But Sister Elizabeth does. We can wake her once we're home. Though I think we've heard the last from this little one for a while. This child has been through something, Detective. We need to find out where she comes from, and quickly. Let's take her to the orphanage. In the morning, you should notify the papers."

The nun gently placed herself between the girl and her fixated spot on the wall. "I'm sure you must be very scared and confused. We are here to help you. We will do everything we can to get you back where you belong. I promise."

The girl flinched at the word "promise," but did not look away from the woman's neck.

"For now, we'd like to take you some place with a nice warm bed, a pillow, and some clean sheets. And there is a special basket filled with bears. You can pick one out. They will be very excited to see you. They love it when a new little girl arrives."

————

"Do you have any idea what we just did?" Nathanial asked.

"We flew from New York to somewhere in Utah."

"In less than three minutes."

"Are you sure?" Adam asked.

"What do you think, I forgot?"

"Well, things did get a little strange up there."

"No," Nathanial said, "not this. This is … this is incredible."

"So why did we stop?"

"Oh, I got that figured out already. We're in Utah, right? I'm betting southern Utah, probably passed over Moab and a whole lot of dry deserts. Low altitude flying, not a cloud in the sky. Okay, the drive runs using water in the air, right? Well, I'm guessing there wasn't enough to sustain it, so it must have had some kind of electric shock when the water ran out and that's what knocked out our instruments and the drive itself. We're also out of fuel, so I wonder if the drive needs fuel to engage as well."

"Okay, but if the water was so important, why not have a water storage compartment?"

"It does. I just didn't get it until now. I couldn't figure out why there were two fuel tanks, one big and one small. And where the smaller one fed into was a mystery."

"So normally, you would fly it on the water already in the air, but when the atmosphere gets too dry—"

"Exactly."

"Could you replicate this thing?" Adam asked.

Nathanial thought for a moment. "I could if I had enough time to study it. I might even be able to improve it. But I'm not sure that's what we should do."

"Why not?"

"Well, come on. This technology is decades beyond us. This is going to change the world. This will give anyone an incredible advantage over their enemies. Think about it. No radar's going to pick this up. You leave home, and five minutes later you're inside enemy borders. Then you drop your worst and take off without leaving so much as a fingerprint."

"Eventually someone will learn what this looks like on radar."

"Perhaps, but what are they going to do about it? Shoot it down? Tell you to knock it off? No, this is power, real power. Man, I know I call you a nutcase all the time, and when we stole this thing and kidnapped Kelli, I seriously thought you had slipped off the cliff, I really did. First her, and now this. Adam, can you imagine what would have happened if this got into the hands of the Soviets?"

"Hold on. If we're really in Utah, we went over the Rockies. That's over fourteen thousand feet above sea level. We should have crashed into a thousand bits."

"Enoki built an altitude adjustment program into the avionics. That's why I have to enter the starting and ending coordinates. I think he's got the program loaded with terrain elevation data for the entire planet, or most of it. I mean the guy is looney in a really brilliant way, you know?" Quickly changing gears, he turned. "Now let's wake her and go find a phone. Come on, slow boy!"

Adam watched Nathanial jog back to the chopper, really acting like a kid, running as if there was someone to get back to.

———

Before they left for Brooklyn, Detective Kirkpatrick took a decent Polaroid of the mystery girl. Mother General had ordered the picture be developed and released to the media without delay.

They drove back to Brooklyn in silence. Kirkpatrick pulled the cruiser up outside the Holy Angels Home, walked his charges to the door, and rang the bell for them. The girl didn't look around with curiosity or even fear, like a little kid should. Her eyes remained coldly fixed straight ahead and down, wide-eyed and empty.

Sister Mary's eyes, on the other hand, studied him coolly. "And Riley."

"Yes, ma'am."

"It's obvious you've become a very good sort of person. We are all children once." She hesitated before opening the gate. "Some of us, more than once."

"Thanks, Sister, and thanks for coming out." A novice appeared at the door. "I'll have something set up for the morning with the press."

The silent pair disappeared into the dim hallway beyond. As the door closed, he caught a brief scent of candles and something he'd forgotten about. He didn't know why, but whatever it was, he strangely thought it smelled like hope.

———

Adam followed Nathanial back to the *Peregrine* and watched him cup his hands to the rear window. He opened the back door, jumped away, and began scanning the rocky darkness. "She's not there. Did she get out when we did?" He started calling, "Kelli!"

"Nathanial."

"She did this once before. At the cabin. She woke up, didn't know where she was. I had to chase her out into the freezing rain. We both half-died of hypothermia. Kelli! Well, use those super ears of yours. You hear her anywhere? Kelli!"

"She's not here because I left her in the vault."

———

Though Nathanial had spoken English his whole life, Adam's words stood for a moment in the arid night air between them as a

filter between the simple phonetics from his lips and the compre-
hension of their meaning. Adam's voice was deliberate, his
composure controlled. The guy had never told a joke. Nathanial's
insides leaped up, swirling into panic and sickening horror. Adam
was telling the truth. The bastard had left that little kid alone in a
cold, dark vault.

"You have to know she couldn't stay here." Such gently patron-
izing tones. "She had to go home. We did well by her, freed her.
Now that the vault is empty, she will be safe. This is best for the
girl."

"Kelli," Nathanial said.

"What?"

Nathanial would not remember having the courage to make
his next move, his conscious mind never actually a part of it,
except for the ensuing pleasure it would give him for years to
come. He squeezed his right fist into a virtual hot iron and
propelled it with such speed, that even the precious ESA didn't
register its movement. Adam Walker spun around like a rag doll,
flopping to the dusty gravel in a gratifying position of humility
and shock. When he rose to all fours, he touched his cheek and
spit out a tooth, along with a mouthful of blood.

Careless of the stupidity of what he had done, Nathanial
kicked up a cloud of gravel at Adam's self-righteous face. "You
low-life-weasel-excuse-for... Don't you dare say that. You didn't
do this for her. You did this for you."

"What? How do you get that?" Adam wiped his hands and rose
to his feet.

"What the hell, Adam? You left her? You left that little kid
alone in that dark vault? What the hell is wrong with you?"

"There's nothing wrong with me."

"Oh yeah, now there's nothing wrong because you got rid of
the problem, didn't you? Hey, let me ask you something. How
come your super senses didn't see that blow coming? Feeling a

little off focus tonight? You may be able to see things the rest of us can't, but you are the blindest bat in the cave."

"This isn't about me."

"Oh, this is the book of you, Adam Walker, Level VI ESA. And I just keep letting myself get sucked back in." Nathanial dragged his fingernails through his neatly clipped hair.

"Oh, come on Nathanial. What did you think was going to happen?" Adam brushed himself off and spat out some more blood. "You were going to make her your consolation prize family? Did she deserve that? You can't even manage your own affairs."

Nathanial swung at him again, but his arm met Adam's midair. He pushed back and wagged an accusatory finger. "You're afraid."

"What?"

"She got to you. This fragile little, innocent kid came along and, and suddenly the ground starts to shake, and you're acting on instinct instead of orders. You're second-guessing things, stopping to smell the flowers, missing whole conversations."

"You're imagining things."

"Dancing with her in the hangar? Here's another question to mull around in that pea-sized super-boy brain of yours. That off-focus decision you made back in France? That one time you did something totally crazy. Not because it was part of the plan, not because it was a procedure, not because it was a necessary obstacle to your stinking directive? Didn't we just find out that might have saved the free world?"

"Coincidence."

"Oh no. Not you. Nothing random happens to you. You're so in control, you probably gave away that cactus. A five-year-old girl with big brown eyes completely unsettled your world, because, because she was beauty, and charm, and laughter. She was innocence and need and fear. She was everything that life is supposed to be, and you couldn't stand it. It made you feel things, think things, reminded you of stuff. Like your own mom. Been thinking about her lately?"

Nathanial took Adam's fist solidly in the gut. He bent over in shock, pushed him off, and struck out for his face again. Adam caught his wrist and twisted it around quickly, yanking his arm up behind his back.

"Nathanial, I know you're upset. But the truth is she should be in a real home."

"With a picket fence, two dogs, and a cat? Wow, you really don't get it." Adam released him, and he fell to the dirt. "She's not some algorithm. We were her story. You and I. And now we've abandoned her." Nathanial pulled himself up and started towards the lights.

"Where are you going?"

"I'm going to call Peter and get the hell out of here. There's got to be a phone somewhere."

"Everyone's asleep."

"Not for long."

# SEVEN

LIFE HAD NOT BLESSED PETER VAN DE SANT WITH ANY BIOLOGICAL children, but he nevertheless always felt as though he had somehow fathered a few hundred, all of them prodigies.

Like his nickname namesake of Mount Olympus, Peter — "Zeus" — nurtured a sort of paternal relationship with the KATs. He discovered them, guided them to their potential, and protected them, and when they threw the towel in his face, he never felt more like a parent. Over the years, he had cultivated multiple techniques to nurture their brilliance: the creative arts certainly, proper education, guidance, a culture of freedom, an unquestioning acceptance of their oddities, a system of mentorship and support. But there was also a strange, unspeakable need for something else. They needed him somehow. They needed him to be both strong and protective, as well as vulnerable. They needed to know they could hurt him.

The phone rang in Peter's bedroom. His wife, Jerilee, woke up first, assuming Peter would follow quickly, but his stubborn body lay beside her like a lump of breathing lead. She grumbled and swung an arm across his shoulder. "Peter, Peter."

"Right-right. Sorry, dear." He reached for the phone carefully, lest he push the wrong button and inadvertently connect to the CIA. "Yes. What is it?" He switched the lamp on.

"I have Captain Hemmel on the line, sir," came the soft voice of Rebecca, Peter's third-shift secretary. "May I put him through?"

"Of course." The line shifted over. "Nathanial? Everything go okay?"

At this moment, Peter was reminded of the bleaker side of parenthood and quietly strove to better awaken himself while Nathanial tossed out a wrathful chain of obscenities.

"Nathanial, calm down. I can't understand a word you're saying. Are you alright? Where are you? How did it go?" Peter checked his clock, the details of the mission foggily returning.

"No, we're not back. We're stranded in someplace called Glen Canyon City, Utah. We're running out of time. I need you to send a jet."

"Utah?"

"Look, it's a long story. I'll debrief you later."

"Give me the short version now."

"Someone was waiting for us at the vault. We were pursued, and I had to engage the HR Drive."

Peter straightened up in his bed. "You what?"

"We're fine, it's fine," Nathanial said. "It worked."

*It worked.* "Nathanial, what exactly do you mean?"

"I mean we just flew from New York to Utah in less than three minutes. That's what I mean. We're fine. Everything's fine except for wonder boy here. Listen, if you can get a jet out here with some supplies, I know I can fix her up in time."

"Fix her up?"

"Yes. Electronic failure, my fault. But I've figured it all out. I can do the repairs in less than an hour, then we can get back to New York before the sun rises. Superman here can go back in the vault and—"

"That won't work, Nathanial," Adam's characteristically sedate voice sounded softly in the background.

"It'll work fine, and you'll do it."

"I triggered an alarm," Adam said. "The floor was weight sensitive, remember?"

Only electric silence came through the line. "Nathanial?" Peter said. "Are you there?"

The phone reverberated with what sounded like the receiver being thrown across the room, followed by what Peter could only guess were large pieces of furniture crashing around, accompanied by a new parade of four-letter words.

"Nathanial? What's happening? Nathanial? Rebecca, pick up."

The bar brawl disappeared with a click, and the placid voice of Rebecca returned to the line. "Yes, sir. I'm here."

"Rebecca. Get Edgar to send a crew to Glen Canyon City, Utah right away. They'll need some supplies for the repairs."

"What if they don't have an airfield?"

"Get the standby crew in a cockpit right now. I don't care if they have to land in a canyon. Get someone out there before those two kill each other."

# EIGHT

KIRA HAD WON. FOR DROZDOV, THIS WAS THE END. THERE WERE NO more leads to follow. No more vaults to watch. No more satellite signals. With the last blue wisps of Enoki's drive dissipating into the night sky, Drozdov's hopes and plans had all, likewise, vanished.

Repeatedly, and in vain, Drozdov ran through the events of the previous. Where had it gone wrong? What else could he have done? Perhaps, perhaps, perhaps. Perhaps they should have over-taken the pilot on the roof, but he had no proof that Adam wasn't communicating from inside the vault. What if he attempted contact and they triggered an alarm intentionally? Perhaps he should have let Erik shoot at them. Destroy the drive, Adam, the LOCK, and the girl. No. He couldn't do that.

Adam. He had only caught a short glimpse of his former pupil, the traitor. Just the flash of a black shadow darting across a windy roof. The sight of his familiar elegance, like wind through swirling water, had triggered an unwelcome pleasure.

On the edge of his hotel bed, Drozdov sat with his shoulders slumped and his hands hanging limply between his knees, as though practicing invisible shackles. The television in front of him spouted off shallow American advertisements for soap and cereal.

Erik put a firm hand on his shoulder. "It's time to go."

The LOCK was gone. The signal had died off years ago while sitting in that stupid vault. All those years of surveillance, wasted. Now it was certainly in the hands of his enemies, of Zeus, and the Institute, wherever that place was. Drozdov's tenure in the echelons of Russian bureaucracy was coming to an abrupt and possibly violent end.

Drozdov reached for his coat. *Go where? Home?* This wasn't the old days with Stalin, right? Hadn't he risen to some position of security? Hadn't his programs at the Apex saved the day enough times over the years? So much so that he had even been allowed to construct the LOCK in the first place? Couldn't he expect to hope for some mercy from his comrades? Surely even the Politburo could overlook losing one small item.

As Erik reached for the television, a stream of words plunged into Drozdov's subconscious. "Stop!" he said, and Erik's hand froze above the knob.

*"In some stunning local news, last night the Miles and Jeter Security Storage facility in lower Manhattan saw its first successful robbery in over seventy-five years. The most startling characteristic, however, is not what the thieves stole, but rather what they left behind in the vault. An unidentified little girl about six years old was found sleeping inside the maximum-security vault. Authorities are currently looking for any information about this little girl or the thieves who left her."* A picture of a vacant-faced Kelli appeared on the screen. *"In other news, reports of a wild, late-night helicopter chase are coming in from all corners of the city..."*

Drozdov fell back onto the edge of the bed as the rest of the familiar story faded into background noise. *"On yeyo brosil"* he whispered. "Your brother."

"So, that's the girl?" Erik said.

Drozdov exploded with a fit of unbridled laughter. "He left her in the vault. Erik, he left her!"

"Why would he do that?"

"Because he is your brother, and he doesn't know."

"Should we send for Serebryakov?" Erik asked. "Have him show all the paperwork and start the whole thing again?"

"No." The laughter stopped. "We tried it above the wire. You go and get her tonight. Find out where they are keeping her, and bring her home."

Erik raised an eyebrow. "Casualties?"

"Whatever it takes."

————

By the time Nathanial eased the *Peregrine* into The Institute's hangar, he was on the verge of a nervous breakdown. Between worrying about Kelli, leaping into an electromagnetic pulse, and loathing his copilot, he needed a strong drink and to slug somebody again.

It had taken two hours for Peter's crew to find their way to Glen Canyon City. Two long, agonizing hours of sitting in silence, wanting to kill Adam. Then another hour to fix the electrical components on the *Peregrine* and load water into the second tank. Once airborne, he immediately engaged the HR Drive for an encore performance. About thirty seconds of bluish humming later, he could see The Institute hangar doors opening on the mountainside below, Zeus's white presence glowing in the morning light.

"Peter, did you approve this?" Nathanial stormed around the front of the chopper.

"I take it something went wrong."

"Peter, you had better not be playing me."

"Playing you?"

"Did you approve this?"

"Approve what?" Peter asked. "Did you get the contents of the safe?"

"Yes," Adam said, stepping from behind to pass Peter the satchel.

"Goodness. Adam, if I didn't know better, I'd say someone gave you a shiner."

"It was me," Nathanial crowed. "Peter, did you have anything to do with this?"

"Do with what? Where is Kelli? Asleep?"

"He didn't know," Adam said.

"Wow," said Nathanial. "You're a piece of work. You knew it was half-cocked, so you didn't even run it by your moral authority."

"Adam?" Peter said. "What could be worse than stealing a Soviet aircraft and abducting a child? You didn't set off any nuclear weapons in New York, I hope?"

"He left her."

"Left Kelli? Left her where? In the vault? Surely not." Peter fixed his eye on Adam without blinking, and his customary grin quickly descended to a stiffened horror.

"Come on, Peter, you know it was for the best."

The active working hangar around them spontaneously morphed into silence.

"Let me, one more time. Adam, you left that child inside the locked vault?"

"It triggered an alarm," said Adam. "Someone would have picked her up minutes after I left."

"What if it didn't?" Peter said.

"Why wouldn't it?"

"I don't know, maybe she wasn't heavy enough, maybe it wasn't working, maybe they turned it off? And even if it did trigger an alarm, who came to get her?"

"What does that matter?"

"It matters if it's some Marquis De Sade! Great Scott, man, no wonder Nathanial was so frantic on the phone."

"Everyone was so taken with her, even you. It was obvious that this was the easiest and most efficient way to return her."

"Obvious? What are you talking about?" Peter stopped himself, then removed his glasses and meticulously wiped them with a handkerchief. Nothing moved for endless seconds while technicians and aviators exchanged glances, eavesdropping from workbenches and inside engines, tools frozen in grease-covered hands. "You violated a directive protocol" Peter said at last. "You're suspended."

"You can't be serious," Adam said.

"Go home. I should have insisted on that before. For that reason, this is probably my fault."

"Come on, Peter. We both know I've done much worse."

"Much worse? What are you talking about? Why not quit your job and take up filing? We'll discuss this later. Go home."

For a moment, Nathanial wasn't sure whether Adam would obey Peter or kill him. But the Level VI was still very much a programmable commodity. Despite his breach of the previous evening, it was Adam's favorite pastime, his only pastime, to take orders. As his tall, imposing figure plodded angrily out of the hangar, Nathanial felt a little sorry for him. Even with Peter's condemnation, Adam couldn't see the real problem in his thinking.

Peter turned back to Nathanial. "Well, now what?"

"Let me go get her."

"Under what authority? She's probably in the hands of the police by now."

"Then let me at least go to her. Tell her, I don't know, something."

"We have to think this through, Nathanial." Peter started heading for the hangar door.

"You do."

"If I don't understand Adam right now, I have never understood why you mistrust me so. What did I ever do for you to lose faith in me, Nathanial?"

"Maybe not so much what you did, but what you failed to do."

"You mean rein Adam in? Really, that same old sermon?"

"Oh, hell no. You've reined him in so tight he can't even keep his head above water without permission."

"What do you think I just did?" Peter asked.

"I think I can't tell who got betrayed here," Nathanial said. "Kelli, or you."

"You have to understand that Adam's abilities require a certain espousal to a short leash. Without it, he could be very—"

"Dangerous? Yeah, I got it. Sometimes I wonder what's really different for him here."

"What does that mean?"

"Look, let me go get her, Peter. Show me that you understand why I have to go. I can take the *Peregrine* and be there in ten minutes. I can explain to the authorities."

"Explain what? That you're one of the two louses that left her in the vault? You're not thinking clearly. I know you grew attached to her; goodness knows we all did. She danced into this place and dropped sequins on everyone she met, myself included. But we have no rights to her. We're just the second people to abduct her."

Nathanial hadn't thought of that. Of course, Peter was right. He and Kelli had made a silent agreement, but the avenues of law and legalities were completely foreign to him, and on them, he had no license.

"They'll be launching a publicity campaign," said Peter. "If she talks to them, goodness knows what she'll tell them. But if not... I should call the lawyer."

"Lawyer?"

"Yes, Durand was his name, I think, in Amiens, in charge of her mother's estate. He's probably the only one who could get to her.

I'll have him flown in. He could be in New York by tonight or tomorrow at the latest. In fact, I should meet him there." Again, Peter headed for the hangar doors.

"What about the Chaput guy?"

Peter stopped. "Right. *'He wasn't my father.'* Well, I've already warned Durand, so he won't release her to them a second time, but..."

"But what?"

"Let's hope that Adam was right. We've got the contents of the vault, so whoever they were, they don't need her anymore."

"And if he's wrong?"

"Nathanial, what can I do?" Peter asked. "I'll call the lawyer. You'll see. It'll all work out somehow."

He spoke those words, but Nathanial understood his real meaning. Kelli was gone from their lives forever. Any case Peter might make for getting Kelli back was severely hindered by the fact that they had just dropped her in a locked vault.

As Peter headed out the hangar doors, young Miguel Garcia, the newly cataloged Level III electrical KAT, sauntered in, decked out in a white lab coat, which he probably wore in his sleep. "Where is little Kelli?" he said, looking around, then regarded Nathanial's expression. "The tall man. He did something, didn't he?"

Nathanial raised an eyebrow at the perceptive teenager.

"I didn't trust him," Miguel continued. "He's not right completely. You know? There's something wrong there."

Nathanial headed back for the *Peregrine*. He would need to refill both the fuel and the water tanks.

"Are you going to get her?" Miguel asked, following him.

"Not exactly."

"I'll come with you."

"No, you won't. You're fourteen."

"Almost fifteen."

"Oh well," said Nathanial, "if you're almost fifteen..."

# NINE

DETECTIVE KIRKPATRICK CALLED THE PRESS CONFERENCE FOR 1:00 p.m. at police headquarters, but by 12:30, the small, musty room was already stuffed with cameras and reporters eager to get the best angle on the abandoned little girl. At 12:45, Kirkpatrick moved the conference to the front steps of the building, and press members begrudgingly shuffled their equipment outside.

The girl had already arrived. He'd sent a courier to pick her up, along with Sister Mary, the French translator, and Sister Elizabeth. The little girl was very obedient, but utterly uncommunicative. She did not eat.

As the minutes closed in on the hour, a podium was brought to the top step. Riley reviewed his statement while the three ladies waited in somber silence, save the occasional clicking of Sister Mary's large wooden beads.

"Okay," he said finally, "if you Sisters wouldn't mind coming out, maybe hold her hand while I do the talking?"

———

The city air teemed with unfamiliar smells and disassociated sounds that Kelli couldn't unscramble. Hundreds of eyes beamed at her between camera flashes and clicks. The large policeman began talking, and then someone asked a question.

She wanted to look down, away from all the eyes, but something pestered her, chased her for her attention. Something was out of place between the legs and feet, catching her focus. A face, persistent and near the ground, a body squatting, darting from side to side in a clever unavoidable manner, constantly shifting to meet her gaze no matter how she turned away. It was looking at her, and it wanted her to look back.

Miguel. The boy from the hangar. How he got here, wherever here was, she couldn't guess. But there he was, crawling around between the legs of the reporters, waving and signaling to her. She paid careful attention to his gestures. It took him a few different attempts, but after a frustrating length, she shouted, "*Je dois faire pipi!*"

Someone gasped. The clicking stopped. The pictures stopped. Pens scribbling on handheld pads of paper stopped, and cameramen peeked out from behind their lenses. Kirkpatrick choked mid-sentence. Behind Kelli, Sister Elizabeth leaned over and whispered something in her superior's ear.

"Well," Sister Mary said, "we'd better get you to a girl's room then. Detective, if you would excuse us?"

Movement resumed. Reporters recommenced scratching on their pads. Cameramen got a shot of the little girl being escorted back into the station. Detective Kirkpatrick shrugged.

"So, she can apparently talk when necessity dictates."

Outside the restroom, Kelli gestured for Sister Mary to stay, and the nun took a seat. Kelli pushed open the swinging door and went inside alone. There were four stalls, all empty, except the last one. Nathanial stepped out, his eyes warm and full of apologies. Tears welled, her lips quivered, and she ran to him.

"Kelli, I am so sorry." He repeated it over and over as she clung to him, trembling. "I had no idea he was going to leave you." Reluctantly, he put her down and knelt, wiping the tears. "What he did was wrong, Kell. He should not have left you there. And if it makes you feel better, I hit him."

"You did?"

"Right here on the cheek. Left a big blue bruise and even knocked out a tooth."

"Why did he do that?"

"I don't know. He does things. But it was very wrong of him."

"Can we go back to the cabin now?"

"Kelli, I have no right to you. I mean, no one will give you to me. Do you remember Mr. Durand? He's coming here to get you."

She jumped back. "He will give me to the bad people!"

"No, listen. He didn't know they were bad people, Kell, and he can take care of you. He's the only person who can. He'll take you home, and then we'll try to work everything out."

"But you can't promise," she said.

"No, I can't promise. Here." He reached in his jacket pocket. "This belongs to you. Miguel reworked it, so never take it off. Even when you go to bed, leave it on. For me, okay?"

She regarded the bracelet silently, watching the tiny trinkets dangle from her upheld wrist. "When I am gone and light is dim," Kelli said, "look closely at the dagger's rim."

Nathanial felt himself falling apart.

"You have to go now, don't you?" she asked him. "It's going to be all right," she whispered, laying a small hand softly on his cheek. "Maman is here. She is here, you'll see."

"Yeah. Of course she is."

Kelli emerged from the restroom and took Sister Mary's hand. Together they returned to the orphanage, and no one noticed the glittering new addition dangling on her tiny wrist.

# TEN

**Moscow, 1971**

KIRA SAT ALONE, WAITING IN A COLD OFFICE. THE DARKNESS enveloped her so completely, she couldn't even see her own legs, or the gloved hands holding the Tokarev TT-33 on her lap like a purring kitten.

If it was just her, she could get out tonight; disappear in the wind, leave nothing but a misty legacy in Moscow's memory. Drozdov would never find her. She was better than him. But it wasn't just her. If anything should ever happen, if she should ever be taken out of the picture, he would find the child. He was a ravenous hunter, and he would keep looking. Without Kira, someone would adopt her and unwittingly put her in a dance class or give her some art lessons.

He'd find her.

Footsteps moved softly through the hallway just beyond the door, and keys shuttered in the lock. Slowly the office door opened and a silhouette of a man crept inside, crossing to the desk. Kira reached up and switched on the lamp.

Startled, the man looked up and stopped reaching for his

weapon. "Kira," he said, catching his breath. As the silent seconds ticked by, understanding descended upon him. "There is no Steamhouse Report, is there?"

"You're a double agent, Kuzmin," Kira said. She was going to miss these more tender moments of her job. Watching realization of doom slowly drown a target in terror. He remained frozen, waiting for the final moment to transpire, his posture hunched, his hands midair, cautious of the slightest flinch. She waved the gun towards a chair, and he stepped backwards, falling upon the seat with solemn acceptance.

"You're going to kill me?"

She laughed. "If I was going to kill you, I'd have done something much more... interesting." At the end of her crossed leg, she spun her ankle in three pleasurable circles. "No. Drozdov's going to do that. You're going to Paris on Friday," she said. "I was supposed to take that trip."

"I had nothing to do with that switch. You were needed in New York next week."

"Yes, New York is very unfortunate for both of us."

"Both of us? Kira, how can we work this out?"

"Oh, there's no working it out. You're soup. I've already sent the intel to Drozdov's intelligence chief. He'll get it at precisely 12:01 on Friday afternoon."

"That's four days from now. Why would—"

"He'll get it at 12:01, and at 12:03 you'll be dead. Unless of course, you get to Paris that morning and just conveniently disappear."

Kuzmin leaned back in his chair and folded his palms across his lap. "Something tells me, the intelligence officer could accidentally get that information before Friday."

"You're getting sloppy," said Kira. "If I suspected you, Drozdov does. You even cross the street towards the Embassy and you'll be splattered all over the sidewalk. I'm offering you an out."

"But he's sending me to Paris."

"It's a test. You'll be delivering something very useful. Your American comrades won't be able to resist."

"I see," said Kuzmin. "So, you want me to help you get out?"

Now she really laughed, a big loud rumble, and Kuzmin stiffened, glancing towards the door. "Oh relax," she said. "No one's in the building. What do you think of me? Thank you, but I can get myself out without any clumsy interference. No, I need something done before I leave." She waved the weapon towards a folder on the desk. "The file. Open it."

Kuzmin leaned over and slid the folder off the desk. "It's some kind of design plans. Is this for a weapon?"

"Not a weapon. A safe. I was going to take care of it myself, but now I'll have to change the location, which means I need you to get that item built for me and delivered to the address printed at the bottom."

"How am I supposed to do that?"

"Oh, I'm betting your friends who were so interested in the Steamhouse Report can get it done by Friday."

"By Friday? That's insane."

"And there's something else. I need to reach someone."

"In intelligence?"

Kira muttered a name, the sound of which felt like a sort of blasphemy, and though barely audible, it seemed to bounce in waving echoes off the spirits in the walls.

Now Kuzmin snickered and shook his head. "Who the hell do you think I work for? God? Nobody can reach him."

"I don't need to speak with him," said Kira, "just a secure way to reach him."

"What you're asking is not possible. The man's a legend, probably construed in Drozdov's crazy head. Give me something possible at least. You want someone in the CIA? You want your own handler? Someone at the embassy?"

"Zeus," she said. "By Friday."

# ELEVEN

**Brooklyn, 1977**

IF SOMEONE HAD SEEN IT, THEY MIGHT HAVE DESCRIBED IT AS A dance. Dressed all in black, Erik moved quietly down the dark Brooklyn sidewalk like a sleek panther. Perhaps he was part of a new street gang, or maybe off to start a third shift. Or perhaps he was just a shadowy figment of one's imagination and was never really there at all.

Approaching a high iron fence, he glanced around and searched the surrounding buildings for peering eyes, misplaced curtains, or strange lights. Satisfied, he climbed and landed soundlessly in the courtyard, disappearing into the darkness beneath a tree.

The risks were painfully small. Worst-case scenario, one or two security guards could be dealt with quietly. Everyone else, he estimated thirty or so children and about fifteen nuns, would not even be awakened. Perhaps one or two were keeping some all-night ritual, but he could surely find the girl and extract her without disturbing any meditative stupor.

At the rear service entrance, he retrieved a wiry tool from an inside pocket, and eight seconds later, he slipped through the door. The whole tiny, insignificant event was so quick, so silent, and so gracefully enacted, that if anyone seen it, they might have described it very much like a dance. *Brisé, brisé, chassé, assemblé, arabesque, round and round*, but not quite so.

———

Sister Mary knew this building like a spouse: the way it reacted to the rain and wind, what creaks sounded as it settled into itself each day, which trees in the courtyard dropped their foliage first, and what shade of red they would turn before they fell. The instant a siren cried out on the city streets, she knew where it was and whether it would pass close enough to wake any of the precious charges on the third floor. She knew it all so well, these sounds, those trees, these halls, these children.

Oh, the children. Always coming, growing, and then going away. Never staying, rarely looking back. Where did they all go? And the exhausting, insatiable need of them, the never-ending calls and the driving to the dirty, lightless places to retrieve them. Bring them home. Bring them, and then what? Pray, morning and evening. Cleaning, feeding, clothing, teaching. Constantly waging war against the powers of despair, fighting to sustain the glowing thread of hope that somehow, someway, some of them could one day heal.

*Oh, these walls.*

Sister Mary Immaculata stared up at the familiar nodules and crevices of her paneled ceiling. Something was worrying her, but she didn't know what. She had tried to brush it off, even said two Rosaries already. But it was persistently tapping at her thoughts, like a sneaky kitchen cat constantly flitting away. Something was not right.

She went over the checklist again: all the doors were locked, and all the children were in their beds—brushed, dressed, prayed, tucked. Nothing was skipped. Sister Agatha would be on the phone for the next four hours. Sister Veritas was on the children's floor. Mr. Simmons paraded the halls. Ovens were off. Heat turned down. Candles all checked. Lights put on outside. *Did the novices remember to put the leftovers in the walk-in? Did they remember to shut the walk-in?* She closed her eyes and pushed that irrational thought out of her head. There are four novices. Surely not all of them forgot to shut the walk-in.

She thought about the new girl who only spoke when necessity dictated. Detective Kirkpatrick had gotten a call from a man in California, and tomorrow another man was coming all the way from France to produce documents and lay claim to her. California, France, so much geographical intrigue for someone so tiny and fragile. She hoped Riley knew what he was doing.

But at least there was a happy end. The Detective, her reprobate of former days whose misadventures had landed in the book of big-fish stories shared with the novices every year. Riley Kirkpatrick was now a police detective, fighting crime, saving lost children. *Well then*, she thought as she straightened her bedsheets again.

"Oh, for goodness' sake," she finally muttered. "I surrender." She rose and put her feet on the cold linoleum floor, rolling her eyes at her absurdity. She wasn't sleeping, so she might as well check on the walk-in. And maybe a casual stroll through the bedrooms to take the count one last time. Then hopefully, sleep would be so gracious as to pity an aging lady.

———

The layout of the orphanage was traditional old school: four floors with stairwells at each end and another in the center. There was probably a basement, but Erik wouldn't need to go down there.

He used the west stairwell and found himself in a cafeteria. All the tables and chairs seemed so absurdly tiny. He had always been tall, even as a child. Surely, he never fit in one of those.

He peeked through a pair of swinging doors into the first-floor corridor. It was dark but for three small shrines, where empty kneelers stood silent before racks of flickering candles.

At the front entrance, the hallway opened up to a large lobby. A door on the far side cast a slanted rectangle of yellow light onto the tiled floor. Inside, a petite woman in a habit and veil sat hunched over what he assumed was a book. A glass lamp glowed softly near her head, and a telephone rested about six inches from her left elbow. On the wall above her, a crucifix. He could kill her very easily. He needn't. He wouldn't. But he could.

Back in the lobby, a tall statue of a woman regarded him with empty concrete eyes. Her hands were folded in prayer. A stone snake reached out beneath her shoeless toes, and a vase of flowers wilted at her feet. Erik had seen multitudes of such idols in different parts of the world, all so ornate, so tacky, and so wasteful. He turned away and darted up the central staircase soundlessly, like a cat.

———

Someone was walking around. By the footsteps, Kelli guessed it was the old security guard. She could hear something jingle too, his keys probably. That would have been enough, but the building had lots of creaks and scary knocks. The nun in the bed at the end of the line snored wholeheartedly, and a tree branch tapped the glass pane of a window three beds down. One boy had a mild cough, and another mumbled in his sleep. Maybe Chinese. All of the stimulation made it hard to sleep, and she was worried anyway. She imagined the warmth of the fire in Nathanial's cabin, glowing and popping softly. Oh, how she wanted to feel that warmth again. Just for a minute, so she could fall asleep.

———

On the second floor, Erik found only empty classrooms. At the west end though, a dim light seeped beneath a door. He pushed it ajar, and it released an unfortunate squeak. Inside was a small chapel with stained, wooden pews that could seat about fifty people, if most of them were children. Glass windows on the west wall, which probably added some color in the daylight, were now only smoky black outlines. Around the small altar, dimly lit by candles, more stone figures stood, holding random objects.

He was not alone. His Extraordinary Sensory Awareness could hear the steady breathing, and a human heart beating softly in the pew around the corner, asleep, or deep in some meditation. When he turned to leave, the door squeaked a second time.

"That you, Sister?"

The security guard, shuffling, moving now and approaching the corner. Erik slipped out into the dark hallway and pressed his back against the wall. The guard, stiff from sitting, hobbled carelessly to the door and opened it with a final deafening whine.

"Sister Mary?"

He was an older man, probably tired, and certainly not prepared for the stealth of Erik's arm slithering around his neck so quickly, he barely knew what was happening before his life was over.

*Everyone should hope to be so lucky in death.*

The body slid to the linoleum floor, and Erik dragged it back into the chapel. Not a sound was made. Not a soul awakened. Anything that could be stolen so unobtrusively surely wasn't a very valuable commodity.

———

Sister Mary used the west side stairs to access the cafeteria. She sighed when she peeked into the kitchen and saw the walk-in tightly shut and the counters empty.

*How foolish you are, Mary.*

She switched the light off and headed back up the stairs. Of course, she would stop at the chapel to pay her respects. It was rude to pass without at least saying hello.

―――――

In her bed on the third floor, Kelli heard something different now, an animal flitting smoothly, lightly. Did the nuns have a cat? No, it was heavier than a cat. Moved more air. She pulled herself up, listening. These sounds didn't belong. They were for her somehow.

―――――

On the third floor, Erik found a long room lined with small beds. He crept inside and stood to his full height, assuming all were asleep. If not, he would have to handle it creatively.

He could hear so many little heartbeats, faster than an adult's, but soft and rhythmic. Someone was snoring, a tree branch was scraping against a distant window, one child had a mild cough, and another was mumbling in Vietnamese.

Which bed? There was no way to know. He took out the handkerchief he had prepared and moved from one bed to another along the south wall. Some were situated with faces up. Some extended too long under the covers, and others were too small. The hair peeking out at the hem of the sheet gave others away. He narrowed it down to three possibilities, but one bed was empty. The sheets were rumpled, so someone had been in it. He touched it. Warm.

———

Sister Mary entered the chapel as she had a thousand times over the last forty years. So habitual, the steps and actions, that she barely noticed the door squeak or the smell of the candles anymore. She dipped her hand in the small bowl hanging on the archway and crossed herself absentmindedly before dropping down on one knee. Only when she was struggling to rise did she see the body.

———

Erik followed the scent of the bed. He couldn't be sure it was the right girl, but if it wasn't, he could come back. He swept out like a ghost and in the main hallway he found her, a tiny waif in a plain white nightgown, barefoot and motionless, like one of the statues. She stared as though waiting for him.

"Why are you here?" she asked him.

*Of course.* She recognized him. "I'm here to take you home, Kelli," he said, taking slow steps towards her.

"You left me."

"Yes. That was very foolish of me." Just a little closer.

"Why do you smell different?"

That made him pause. "I smell different?" He went down on one knee. Her body stiffened and her right hand came up slowly, her tiny, cool fingertips touching his cheek.

"You're not him," she said.

"No, I'm not."

A loud penetrating blare erupted through the entire building. A fire alarm. Someone had found the guard. The girl inhaled to scream, but he grabbed her and forced the drugged cloth over her face. She squirmed, but it was like fighting a kitten.

———

On the first floor, Sister Mary scampered into the phone room. "Sister Agatha, we have an intruder in the building. Call the police. Close this door and lock yourself inside and don't open it until the police come."

"But—"

"Do as I tell you, Sister."

Sister Mary didn't hear him coming. It was more of a feeling, a sense. She ran to the front door and placed herself in front of it. The tall, imposing shadow of a man descended the staircase into the light, a bulky load on his shoulder.

He stopped at the landing about fifteen feet from her, a figure of obscurity with the streetlight shafting through the large window behind him. The alarm blared painfully on, joined by the growing whines and groans of encroaching children.

"As God as my witness," Sister Mary said, "you will not take that child."

The shadow's free arm moved, and something pierced her throat with a fiery sting. A second bullet penetrated her chest like a hammer. She fell to the floor, shocked by the pain and struggling to breathe, her lifeblood gushing to waste on the stones.

He stepped over her, a tower of hovering darkness. "I don't believe in God."

# 5TH MOVEMENT: SACRIFICE

*"I don't know why I'm getting so emotional. You'll probably never even see this... You know, no one tells you when you become a parent how to do stuff. They just hand over the bundle and send you home. You do what you think is right... And you hope, somewhere, somehow, someone is watching."*

# ONE

NATHANIAL PULLED HIS JEEP UP IN FRONT OF HIS PRIVATE BUSINESS. He hadn't given the place more than a passing thought in two weeks. The simple trip to France for a one-hour gig had turned his whole life upside down, and in every way, he was exhausted.

"Well, did you see her?" Peter had asked after hanging up the phone in his office.

"Yes. I saw her. I'd say I'm sorry, but…"

"You wouldn't mean it. Well, do you think it helped?"

"Who knows?"

"Nathanial, I am sorry things didn't turn out the way we all might have liked, but I have to thank you. Children are not my specialty. Certainly not Adam's. I'm not sure what we would have done without you here." Peter grabbed an envelope and walked around his desk. "Your paycheck. You were with us far longer than expected. And it comes with an open invitation to rejoin the roster. That helicopter…"

"About that. What are your plans?"

"I haven't decided yet."

"What about the General, the guy who hired you? Don't you owe it to him?"

"I owe him a description," Peter replied a bit too quickly, and Nathanial got the distinct feeling he was being dismissive. "He certainly didn't pay us to steal it for him."

"But he helped you get it into the country."

"This wouldn't be the first time we've come up with something the world isn't ready for yet."

"Only you didn't come up with it."

"And neither did he." Peter returned to the seat behind his desk and began rifling through a file. "Nathanial, the man who built the *Peregrine* is out there somewhere and could build it again, or at least draw up the plans. We have to, at the very least, hold on to it. Just in case."

"Yeah. Just in case."

Early the next morning, Nathanial flew to the cabin. He stood in her bedroom doorway, staring at all her things, so colorful and out of place. Somehow the space was no longer his. He grabbed his keys and took the Jeep for a long gratifying ride to the airfield, looking forward to burying himself in an engine and some mindless manual labor.

Naturally, his office was in much better shape than he had left it. Someone had done the filing and vacuumed. Looking through the business of the last two weeks, he found nothing too substantial to worry about, just some repairs. Peter's people had taken care of those, along with a few rentals and charters. One thing caught his eye though, and he curiously leaned around the office doorframe and peeked into the hangar, where a white Learjet 35 sparkled back at him.

Nathanial had flown to New York in under three minutes before lunch. It was hard to get excited about a Learjet 35 after that. In fact, it was hard to get excited about anything.

A mechanic from The Institute had some classical music playing on a radio at the back of the hangar. "Captain Hemmel," he called out. "Zeus asked me to stay on until you arrived. Everything in order, sir?"

"Too much so. I won't be able to find anything."

"Ah, Mr. Hemmel, at last." A painfully familiar voice took Nathanial on a rapid rewind, past the events of the last weeks and all the way back to the reality of his daily grind. George Monroe, of The Golden State Credit Union, stood stiffly in almost the exact spot where Adam had appeared a week before. He held a briefcase in one hand and a suspicious looking envelope in the other. "Where have you been, Mr. Hemmel? I call your office and leave messages, but you don't return my calls. I visit your cabin..."

"My cabin?"

"Yes Mr. Hemmel, your cabin." Monroe strode forward like a fat fox approaching prey. By the time he got close, his glasses had inched down to the end of his nose, his bulbous eyes glistening hungrily above them. "Very lovely, actually, if one can get to the darn thing. Unable to reach you, I paid it a visit a few days ago to get a solid estimation of the value."

"The value?"

"Mr. Hemmel, you owe us a significant amount of money, and unless you can come forth with it by the end of April, we may have to consider—"

"Don't finish that sentence. I've got your money. I was away on business."

"What business?"

"I contracted out, and it paid well. I can sign the check over to you right now and get this all done with. It should catch me up on everything."

"Well, that is indeed some good news. I am glad to hear it. I don't know who we would sell that cabin to besides a mountain man of sorts."

Nathanial began the process of blocking him out while fishing in his pocket for Peter's envelope. When he opened it, he might have been alarmed by the number, but something else caught his attention. It was something being spoken, but not by the loan manager. Somewhere in the background, distantly broadcasting. It was coming from the radio.

*"Startling news from New York today of a horrific murder and kidnapping. A security guard and a nun were both killed last night at The Holy Angels Home, a refuge for orphans run by the Sisters of Charity in Brooklyn."*

Nathanial raised a hand to silence the loan manager's diatribe. "Quiet. I need to hear this."

*"Police are questioning witnesses today, but as yet have no suspects and no trace on the child, herself a mystery girl who appeared in a Manhattan security vault the night before. One of the victims, a Sister Mary Immaculata, found shot in the throat, was the Mother General of the convent connected to the..."*

Nathanial turned to stone. The room swirled. *The bad guys.*

"Mr. Hemmel, are you okay?"

The check in his hand felt cool and crisp. What could he do? Chase after her? Without Adam? He had just gotten out of this mess.

"You know," Nathanial started, clearing his throat as he folded the envelope and stuffed it back in his pocket, "I forgot that I didn't get the check yet. They'll be mailing it. I should have it in a couple days."

"Very well, Mr. Hemmel. I'll look for it in the next couple days," Monroe replied, suspicion dripping from his lips. "I'll see you then, in either case."

As soon as he was alone, Nathanial stumbled towards the office phone, stopping briefly at a trash bin to throw up.

---

"Tell me why I'm here again?"

"You are representing the people of Denmark in an international conference in Austin, Texas for children gifted in higher mathematics. Your name is Malthe Pederson, you are nine years old, and you are here on a special visa as a guest of the United States."

"Yeah, Dad. No kidding. I mean, what am I doing *here?*"

Konstantin Andreevich Drozdov raised an eyebrow at his son. The boy sat slumped on the park bench with his hands in his pockets and his bony knees swaying about aimlessly in front of him. His naturally resistant, adolescent eyes wandered disinterestedly over the dog walkers and joggers in the Houston park.

Drozdov knew better than to be goaded into another argument about insubordination. In the end, it would always be his own fault anyway. He had wanted a talented offspring, a KAT. And he got one. Fruit of his own loins. Son of Russia. Konstantinovich.

The rising Houston sun seared the city park, and Drozdov could feel perspiration gathering on his forehead and neck. Why would anyone ever choose to live in such a wretched climate?

"You remember that I learned Danish for this?" Iosif snarked. "And the colloquium is only two weeks long. Isn't pulling me out a bit of a waste after all that? Not to mention, dragging me halfway across the state to meet up with my oh-so-powerful Soviet daddy in broad daylight? What the heck? What was all that covert *dermo* for, anyway?"

"There will be other opportunities for math. Something more important has come up."

"Something more important?"

"I need your help with something very, delicate," said Drozdov. "It requires a child."

"A child?" Iosif gazed over the rims of his sunglasses. "And I'm the child in this scenario?"

"You're nine years old, Iosif. That makes you a child."

"I'm ten. Birthday last week? I knew Mom sent the box, but, oh never mind. So, let me get this straight. After everything we went through to get me here, you pulled me out because you need a dumb kid?"

Drozdov offered an apologetic shrug. "We are here in Houston for a few days. When we leave, you can return to the colloquium, if you want."

"We? Who is we?"

"Erik is with me."

"*Zamechatelno*. This just keeps getting better."

"And we have a girl with us. She's five years old, scared, traumatized. I can't get through to her."

"And you think I can? I'm good with numbers, not girls."

"You're good with problems, and I think perhaps with another child around, maybe she would be more comfortable. It's a technique I've used before."

"Wait, how many little kids — *Ya ne khochu znat*. What do you mean, start talking?"

Drozdov frowned, and Iosif's head fell backward. "Great. I go through all that work just to get saddled with a crazy mute kid. So, where is the little brat?"

———

A man's voice emerged from Kelli's comfortable darkness. It was not Nathanial. "Why is she crying?" it said.

There was pain, a throbbing made worse by the whimpering.

"The younger girls do that for some reason. Not so much the boys." That was a different voice, one she dimly recognized.

Someone groaned and whimpered. It was her. *Where am I?*

"You are safe and with friends." The first voice again, deep and soothing.

Her thoughts raced to catch up with reality. Maman... *Ce n'est pas mon père*. Swinging on the helicopter. Flying. The cabin, the man in the rain. *Don't leave me!* The nun. The little beds and statues. The tall man in the darkness. — *Who was that?*

Her tiny body sprang up as her ribs pulled outward, sucking in air, wheezing like she had been drowning. Her head pounded in angry revolt.

"*Pritormozi*, slow down there," the strong voice said. Someone had a hand on her back. Another hand was on her arm as she leaned over it, gagging. "You've been out for some time, so you shouldn't rush. Just go slowly. Everything is all right. Have a sip of this." He held a glass to her lips and she sipped from it. She was thirsty, so thirsty. She took the cup and drank, gulping. "That's it. Not too fast. Little sips now." She peeked over the rim.

There were three men. The one she recognized stood to her side, working with some needles on a dresser. He wrapped them carefully up in a small leather pouch.

The second man was just a boy really, older than her, tall and bony, with a thick nest of bronze curls on his head. He leaned on a doorframe with his arms folded and his face set in a disapproving sneer.

Then there was the third man, whose firm hands held her upwards, keeping her steady. Much older than the other two, he smelled smoky and had dark eyes that studied her. Atop his bulky, block-shaped shoulders, he had a head of thick, salt and pepper hair.

"Hello, Kelli," he said. "I know you must have many questions, but there will be lots of time for all of that. For now, you just need to know that you are safe and we are friends." He gestured to the tall man, who was now leaning on the dresser. "This is Erik. I believe you've already met his brother, Adam." He paused as though looking for a response. "And this is my son, Iosif. He is very eager to be your friend." The boy rolled his eyes and grimaced. "And I am Konstantin Andreevich, but if you like, I hope you will call me Uncle Kostya."

A shiver rushed from her scalp to her toenails. The tears stopped, and she felt the room slipping. Darkness enveloped her like the warm towel Maman wrapped her in after a bath. It was getting easier and easier to climb into. She could find it anywhere now, waiting in corners and under beds, or in vacant spots on a carpet. Darkness was the only constant in the world. It did not die. It did not lie. An echo told her not to go, some dissipating memory of a dock and a strong arm in the rain, but it wasn't enough to hold her from the powerful void. It was comforting, actually, how dark it could be in such a bright room.

# TWO

A *TIME* MAGAZINE HAD BEEN OPEN ON NATHANIAL'S LAP AT THE same page for two hours, his hands too busy fidgeting to turn away from an article that had something to do with hockey. Instead of reading, his skittering eyes continuously scanned the hotel lobby, wondering what a bad guy looked like.

Travelers with luggage and businessmen with briefcases walked past him. Exhausted parents checked in while children scattered chaotically about. Surely, they weren't the bad guys. Were they? How do you know a bad guy? He had seen bad guys before in Vietnam. But were those really bad guys? Was anybody bad, really?

He shook it off. This was no time for philosophical wanderings. Somebody was bad. Someone had killed a nun and kidnapped a little kid. Nathanial shuddered. The longer he sat, the less his chances of finding Kelli. He needed to find her. But how? More questions. More unknowns. Nothing but a useless catalog of hockey statistics.

Of course, despite his vigilant surveillance, there was probably a back exit somewhere where they could be coming and going easily. But no, she had not moved. Miguel would call the front desk if she moved. If she was wearing the bracelet, that is, and her captors hadn't tucked it in the luggage of some Houston traveler.

He couldn't call the authorities. He had no idea who these guys were. Hell, these guys could be the authorities. Any siege on the hotel would be insufficient if they were KATs. He'd lose her, and in a bloodbath, too. No. He had to be inconspicuous, covert. Man, he hated this stuff.

When he first learned of Kelli's abduction, Nathanial immediately called Peter, but an apologetic lady-in-white told him that "Zeus" was in New York. So, he called Miguel.

"It's not that simple, Mr. Hemmel. You have to be patient."

"You said we put a signal we could trace on the bracelet, so where is she?"

"The signal has to be relayed onto one of our satellites, and that only comes in every few hours," Miguel had said. "And she can't be moving. Once I've got a signal, I can probably hold onto it so long as she doesn't move too quickly."

"So, she's flying over the Iron Curtain as we speak? Is that it?"

"I promise I'll call you as soon as I get something."

Nathanial hung up the phone and cuddled the whole receiver in his arms. He lay down on the old brown leather sofa in the office and waited. It wasn't much later that evening when the ringer woke him. Miguel had a location.

Then there had been the sobering trip into his old KAT locker. He kept it hidden behind some crates at the back of his hangar. After three exasperating attempts at remembering the lock's combination, he knocked the damn thing off with a sledgehammer. He tossed aside old passports, research files, and old unfinished projects. Everything else, he stashed in a sack. There was no time for a plan. Just grab stuff you know how to use.

He remembered the lockbox. He had lifted the lid so slowly, as though something alive was inside, ready to jump out. His fingers closed around the dense metal grip, lifted it from its coffin, and stuffed it in the sack with some ammunition, hoping that it worked after so much idle time. Of course, it worked. The damn things always work.

After all that, stealing the Learjet wasn't really that big of a deal.

Nathanial rubbed his forehead. He'd been sitting in this lobby most of the night, fidgeting and generally feeling like a moron, but he didn't dare leave his post for a second. His thoughts ran unharnessed, like a subway car out of control, flitting past the same four stops: the need to sleep, an equally toxic pull to scamper childishly out of the building, the worry of what was going on in a room somewhere above him, and an overwhelming urge to pummel Adam Walker.

"Excuse me, sir. Are you a client here?" A bellhop leaned over him.

"Uh, sorry?"

"The manager has asked me to see if you need some help. You have been sitting in our lobby for some time, reading the same magazine. The lobby is for customers of the Grand Meridian, sir. If you do not have a room here, we will have to ask you to leave."

Man, he stunk at this stuff. His strongest asset in field work was that he would be so bad at it, no one would consider him a threat. "Only a client can stay?" he asked.

"Yes, sir."

"So, if I get a room for the night, then I can stay here and keep reading?"

"Yes, sir."

"Great, I'd like a room then." Nathanial got up for the first time in hours, stretched his legs, and headed for the front desk.

"Our maître-d'hotel will be happy to help you with that sir. If you have any bags, I can take care of them for you."

"Uh, yes. That's mine, there." Nathanial pointed to his duffel bag and pulled a random bill from his pocket.

The bellhop glanced at the cash and lit up. "And if there is anything else, I can help you with sir, anything at all, please don't hesitate to ask."

Nathanial generally didn't believe in miracles. In fact, one might say that if he believed in anything outside of aeronautics, it was the undependability of people. But if any kind of eternal power exists in the realm of men, and every dog has a moment when the infinite reaches down to touch the insignificant for one second, well, this was Nathanial Hemmel's second.

He had to check himself twice to be sure what he was seeing. Because this was a genuine, bona fide supernatural event, complete with conversion, redemption, and salvation blended in. He was so awestruck by the vision, he could barely take in a breath. A miracle incarnate was standing, in the flesh, right there in the check-in line. Adam Walker. Tall and blond, arrogant and graceful. Undeniable. Right in front of him, almost glowing.

Adam must have learned about Kelli's abduction and gotten her location from Miguel, then come to help retrieve her. He had come to undo the wrong he had started. Adam Walker had repented? Grown up?

Nathanial was so overcome that he might have started singing a Christmas carol right there. As he reached out his hand to grab Adam's shoulder, time seemed to slow down somehow, as though allowing him to appreciate this providential interference with sincerest gratitude. What should he say? *Maybe don't say anything. Just shake the guy's hand, darn it.* Actually, this probably merited some sort of manly hug moment, but Nathanial hadn't eaten since throwing up and couldn't stomach that idea. But who cared? Adam was here, and everything would be all right.

At precisely the instant his hand would have landed on Adam's back, a bellhop carelessly misguided a luggage cart, sending a load tumbling chaotically onto the lobby floor. Staff dispersed to tidy the unpleasant scene, and Adam's head naturally turned. For some reason that Nathanial couldn't fathom, his hand halted midair, his breath stopped, his mouth mute, locked up, paralyzed. *Why?*

Something was wrong, terribly wrong. He retracted his hand while a subconscious message called to him, something he should know, a picture in the recesses of his mind somewhere between fatigue and terror. He couldn't access it. He couldn't see it. *What was it that he needed to see?* He closed his eyes to extract the image from his subconscious and got a piercing light, a vision of pure, gifted insight, a frightening revelation sent by some unearthly maternal force to stop his hand, to save his life, to save Kelli.

*Where was the scar?*

Was he losing his mind? Inventing stories that didn't happen?

He made a fist. No, he was not losing his mind. He had hit Adam hard in the desert, a real heavy wallop. He was sure of that. It had given him the most satisfying two seconds of their relationship. And the blow had drawn blood, knocked out a tooth even. There should be a scar.

But the face before him showed no scar, no bandage, no scab, no swelling. Not even a mild discoloration. It was as if the strike had never happened at all. And suddenly he realized it was staring him down. As sure as the daylight in the air around them, Adam's face with his searing hazel eyes, regarded him without the slightest recognition.

"Can I help you?" the apparition spoke, using what was clearly Adam's voice.

Nathanial coughed and forced a smile. "Uh —no," he said, his eyes fixed unnaturally on the man. "No, sorry. I mean uh, I think you're up." Nathanial gestured to the clerk at the front desk. The man hesitated, considering Nathanial for a moment, but a dismissive look swept across his face, and he turned away.

Nathanial stifled the urge to hyperventilate, so grateful to be bad at covert ops. He inched closer to the man's back and listened to his conversation with the desk clerk.

"Are there any deliveries for room thirteen-twenty-seven?" Adam's voice asked.

"Let me check that for you, sir. Yes, there was a parcel dropped off this morning. I'll need to see some ID and you'll have to sign for it." The man pulled out his wallet and passed a card to the clerk.

"Okay, sign here sir," the clerk said before passing a small parcel over the counter. "Is there anything else we can do for you, sir?"

"That's fine. Thank you." The man swooped away with the elegance of a wild hawk.

"Can I help you, sir?"

Nathanial carelessly allowed himself to stare while the specter waited at the elevator.

"Sir? Can I help you ?"

When the stranger looked up, Nathanial clamped his mouth shut, smiled sheepishly, and waved like an idiot, then guiltily turned away. He was pretty certain he also blushed.

"Yes." Behind him, the elevator doors closed with a comforting swish. "Yes, I want a room. I've got a cousin already on your thirteenth floor. Any chance you can get me on the same floor?"

"That floor is entirely full, but I get you on the twelfth floor, only one flight down. Will that be acceptable? How will you be paying?"

"Cash."

———

For a pair of undercover Soviet officers in 1977, getting out of the United States undetected was a delicate business. Escaping with a recently abducted five-year-old was a task for a mastermind with connections.

As soon as he had seen the girl on the news, Drozdov had begun making calls. New York would be impossible, so he charted the plane to Texas directly after the abduction. The girl slept through the whole flight.

Houston would offer a more discreet point of departure by

sea. He then called a Mexican associate who provided a sprawling inboard cruiser and an invisible network of Coast Guard contacts who would look the other way. Drozdov and his party would slip quietly away during the night and rendezvous with naval comrades near Cuba.

But the boat was not available until Friday. They would have to wait out the four days in a hotel. Conveniently, Iosif was already in Texas, so one call to the math conference and another for a hired car ensured that Iosif would arrive in Houston before the girl even woke up.

Iosif's presence had definitely kept her calm and distracted, but she wouldn't talk. She *could* talk. She spoke at the press conference in New York, and she spoke to Erik in the convent.

"She recognized me," he had said, "and she wasn't happy to see me."

That did not surprise Drozdov. Adam's blunder had not only returned the girl to her family but detached her from any connection she might have made with him. All the pain and confusion since her mother's death had sent the poor child spiraling somewhere beyond reach.

On the living room floor, Iosif played enthusiastically with some marbles. He was a very clever boy, wordlessly playing the game in front of her. Sometimes her eyes would momentarily focus on the little glass balls rolling across the carpet, but barely reacting when they softly clicked together.

The doorknob turned, and Kelli stiffened when Erik entered. Drozdov never ceased being awed by the duplicity of the Level VI, so potently violent yet so graceful. The wisest decision he had ever made was to begin their training with dance. It put everything afterward into a framework of beauty. Everything became art, even death.

"Why does she look at me like that?" Erik whispered.

"Give her some credit. If people knew what you are capable of, everyone would look at you like that."

"Maybe. But why does *she* look at me like that?"

"It's frightening to see a double. Surely, you can understand that. And she's not completely in reality. Her mind is in a place of fear."

"Is all this worth it?"

"I'll get through eventually. Something will work, trigger a reaction. The truth is, I'm almost grateful she fears you so visibly."

"She won't try to run."

"Outward fear is a sign of humanity. She's in there somewhere. I just have to find a way to reach something other than the fear." Drozdov had tried to talk to her, make a connection, draw her out with play, jokes, or stories about her mother.

"You're a lot more patient than I am. I'd have chucked her in the looney bin by now."

"It's been two days, Erik. How ironic. You think you and your brother were a walk in the park?" Drozdov snickered. "No, there's a way in. We just have to be patient."

The only glimmer of her humanity had surfaced at the sight of some pictures of Kira he showed her. Her eyes had studied them longingly, but she didn't reach out and touch them as a child should.

"I probably don't even need to mention this," Erik said, "but there was a man in the lobby."

"Who?"

"I don't know, but," he lowered his voice again, "he seemed to recognize me."

Drozdov's face hardened. "Should we move?"

On the common room floor, Iosif's marbles connected, and he released a triumphant cheer. Kelli's inanimate eyes watched the gloating without response.

"How long before the boat?" Erik asked.

"Friday night."

"It was probably nothing. He certainly wasn't an operative."

"How do you know?"

"Hard to explain. But definitely not a threat."

————

The bellhop proved to be an easily manipulated asset. At the sight of a second fifty-dollar bill, he promised to call Nathanial with any information about room thirteen-twenty-seven. The first day, he called once. A small Asian man had gone into the room repeatedly, usually close to mealtimes. Another Ulysses produced the man's actual room number and valuable information from the hotel register. The whole party was set to check out on Friday evening, less than two days away. This gave Nathanial time to formulate a plan and run back to the Learjet for equipment, but he still had no idea how to get Kelli out of the suite.

At four o'clock in the afternoon, the bellhop called to say that suite thirteen-twenty-seven had requested all their meals from local restaurants for the next two days, to be delivered by hotel staff. Nathanial rushed downstairs to meet him in the service area.

The bellhop's name was Chad, and Nathanial guessed him to be in his late teens: old enough to know a good thing when it came along, but smart enough to know he should probably ask some questions before pocketing any more American presidents.

"So, what are we trying to do, exactly?" Chad asked.

"I need to get a message to someone. That's all, just a message."

"Which someone?"

"You've been in the room now. I know about the tall blond man, but who else is in there?"

"Maybe you should tell me that."

"I don't know. No — wait. Okay, the person I need to get a message to is a little girl about six years old and about so high." He held his hand in the air. "Brown curls, big brown eyes."

"The kid who doesn't talk?"

"Yes!" Nathanial tried not to hug the guy. "You've seen her. She's there then. Who else is there?"

"Uh, let's see, there's another man. Older, stocky with bushy eyebrows. Then there's another kid, a little older than her, a boy. I think that's it, unless someone's hiding in the bathroom. But man, the girl you're talking about, yeah, she's like disturbed or something. Doesn't even look at me, or anyone. Dude, I'm not sure you could get a message to her if you held a flashing sign in front of her nose."

Nathanial frowned. He hadn't thought of that. Of course, Kelli had retreated after Adam's abandonment and her abduction. "You'll have to do it," he said.

"Me? I don't know how to get the kid to look at me, let alone give her a message."

"That no one else knows about."

"What?"

"The message has to be covert. No one else in the room can know she's getting a message."

"Or what?"

Nathanial hesitated. He should tell the kid the truth. *There's a hit man in the room who will swiftly strangle you and dump your body in a sewage drain.*

"Hey, wait a second man," said Chad. "Should we be calling the police or something?"

"No," Nathanial came back too quickly. "They would only escape with her. Or worse. That man, the tall one. He's very clever."

"I don't know, man. This is getting a little freaky."

"Listen, all we need to do is get a message to the girl. Nothing else. Can you do that?" Nathanial was out of arguments. "I'll give you five hundred dollars if you can pull it off."

The boy's face lit up. "Five hundred bucks? How do I know you're for real? How do I know you're not gonna hurt the kid?"

"It's just a message."

"Well, what's the message?"

Nathanial hesitated. How to do this? How could he send a message so covert that 'super senses' wouldn't see it, but so plain that the five-year-old would? It had to be something very clever, something the Level VI in the room wouldn't get.

———

Drozdov didn't dare leave Kira's girl alone. He had himself only left the suite once, shortly after arriving, to purchase her some clothes. When he returned, his son met him at the door with a disturbed countenance.

"What's wrong?"

Iosif silently led him back into the children's room. The hotel lamp shed a dim glow on the girl's empty bed.

"Where is she?"

Iosif slid the closet door open. Her little body lay curled up tightly on the floor.

"Let her be." Drozdov sighed, blaming himself. He should have sent Erik after the clothes. From now on, only Erik would go out, and they would have their food delivered.

After that, Drozdov only gently prodded her. The pictures of her mother continued to draw some interest. When she thought he wasn't looking, she stole one from the table. He asked her about it, and the fear returned to her eyes. "My dear girl, you may have all the pictures if you want them."

He talked about Kira, telling stories and explaining his relationship to her, always using the name Rachel, of course. And Uncle for himself. Then he left her alone with Iosif.

It would happen. He would get through. He just had to wait, look for anything, any trigger, no matter how small or seemingly insignificant.

When room service knocked on the door, it was already 12:30. Iosif had retreated into the children's bedroom to watch TV. The girl had slipped in with him, where she would stare at blank points on the wall.

A bellhop rolled a cart in and laid plates of sandwiches and utensils upon the kitchenette table. Drozdov called everyone to come and eat together at the table. The regular meals would build small subconscious bonds, so long as he could keep Enoki from talking crazy and Erik from saying anything at all. Drozdov would engage everyone in polite chitchat to foster an atmosphere of comradery.

"Is there anything else I can get for you?" the bellhop asked once the table was set and all were seated.

"No, thank you," Drozdov replied without looking up. As he fished in his pocket for a tip, the boy gazed quizzically at Kelli.

"Is something wrong, little lady?" the bellhop asked Kelli.

To Drozdov's surprise, Kelli glared up at the bellhop. Her little brown eyebrows scrunched up with what could only be an accusatory signal.

"No, she is fine, thank you," Erik said, eager to remove the young man from the room, but Drozdov clenched a hand on Erik's wrist beneath the table. The girl glared at the bellhop. Oh, she was mad about something. Everyone could see that. And it was a beautiful thing. A thing that instantly silenced all movement around the table, electrifying the air as everyone watched, afraid to move, to uncast the beautiful spell.

"Hey," Iosif blurted out. "How come she didn't get a cookie?"

Drozdov again applauded the decision to drag Iosif into this scene. It takes a child to see the obvious. Every plate had a sandwich, a drink, silverware, a napkin, and a cookie. But Kelli's plate lacked the most important element of a five-year-old's meal.

It was incredible. To Drozdov, it was like watching a miracle in a silent motion picture. She was angry at the boy and letting him have it.

"Oh, that's all right, Kelli," Drozdov offered. "You may have mine." But as he reached to pass it, the bellhop interrupted.

"Oh, that's not necessary sir. I think I see one." He leaned in closer to Kelli, and Erik's hand slipped backwards, reaching for his pistol. Once again, Drozdov laid a hand on Erik's knee beneath the table.

The bellhop bent over, inches from her nose. His left hand flipped up beside her face and she cringed in disapproval. She watched in guarded curiosity as, with a quick flip of his hand and a cocky smirk, he pulled the missing cookie out from behind her ear.

Kelli's eyes sparkled, and the very far edges of her lips curled, ever so slightly. *Bingo!* Childhood delight. Innocence.

"You see," the bellhop said, resting the cookie next to her plate, "I am very sneaky."

# THREE

Ah, sweet anonymity. A precious invisible commodity, a warm cloak in the rain. These days of cold war, when ideals so easily became tyrants, anonymity allowed one to do one's job well, and yet to never exist at all. To save the world in the afternoon, then stop at the grocery store at night, pondering breakfast cereals.

Zeus preferred sweet anonymity.

It often made Peter Van De Sant wonder at how something so precious could originate by accident. He hadn't even thought of it himself. No, Peter's descent into the annals of the anonymous had actually begun as some long forgotten, offhand joke in a conference room. But, as though in line with destiny's plans, the nickname had ventured off with a flourish through each vent and wire of The Institute facilities, inspiring every janitor and secretary to call it out when passing in the halls. Until one day, Peter arrived at his office, quite surprised to discover it emblazoned on a small brass plaque: "Zeus." The king of the gods. Well, the plaque didn't say that second part, but naturally it was hard to avoid the reference.

Zeus hadn't ventured out of The Institute confines for much

more than a talent search in almost ten years. His sojourn to New York City had been humbling, to say the least. He left behind his conspicuous whites and used an assumed name, a false government identity, and a glass eye. He presented a well-constructed and plausible scenario to explain matters to an irate French lawyer and a baffled detective, without giving any information at all about Adam or the Institute, while pulling every diplomatic resource in his pocket to keep them from booking him.

He made no headway with the lawyer, Durand, who insisted that Kelli be found and promptly returned to "her people." He did manage to convince them both, however, that her abductors would be trying to escape the country, so they had coldly collaborated for hours to get Kelli's picture on every media outlet and border checkpoint. He had done that at least.

Nevertheless, the return flight to The Institute consisted of intermittent sleep, plagued by visions of horrible things happening to nuns and little girls in tutus. Throughout it all, his prodigy pilot's words echoed relentlessly, like a supertitle above the gory melodrama:

*Sometimes I wonder what's really different for him here.*

What did Nathanial mean by that? Adam would have been better off in Russia? Surely not. Still, what was he thinking, leaving her in that vault? Peter shivered. He had meant to do right by Adam after all, by all of them. Hadn't he? Had he willfully neglected something? Something that might have withdrawn the full potency of his Level VI asset? Peter couldn't see it. He had let Adam make his own choice after all, like Nathanial, like all of them. They had a choice. Wasn't that enough? Adam chose to do his job in full democratic freedom. He could quit any time, and Peter certainly wouldn't hold him back.

Yet, even as the California mountainside runway grew closer, Peter had a sickening feeling that he should have made Adam Walker get a cactus long ago.

His assistant Sondra met him at the hangar door with a

message from Bambartini. Immediately after re-donning his whites, Peter burst into the electronics lab. "Evelyn, what have you got? I need some good news."

"We've been coordinating with computer sciences ever since you dropped it off. It took some finagling, but I think we've finally accessed it."

"Accessed what?" Peter parked himself in a chair.

"The small black box that Mr. Walker retrieved from the vault. It's a very complex system of electronic information storage. It doesn't use any currently known digital linguistics. Basically, we could tell what should be done with it, but when we plugged it into our systems, it didn't even register. We were only able to get some nonsensical images until we encountered a few fragments of repeating digital algorithms—"

"Evelyn. You know I adore you."

"We built our own computer. A terrible bulky thing that wouldn't pass for KAT work by any standards, but it served to read the information on that particular device. We were able to access it, and we've been transcribing it for hours now. It's slow going because the mechanics are so crude. So far, we've only touched the surface of the images it holds."

"Images?"

"What would you like to know about our enemies?" she said. "It's full of blueprints. Every government facility in Moscow, Leningrad, and most of the Soviet states. Blueprints, technical data, production statistics and model numbers for planes, submarines, tanks, missiles, you name it. Technological centers, power plants, missile depots, satellites, computer systems, energy plants. It's a massive information storage unit. It's an incredible boon, like nothing we've ever encountered."

"The LOCK," Peter whispered. There had been rumors in the intelligence community for years. Peter had even been commissioned to find it three times, but no one could ever concretely prove that it existed. Drozdov had allegedly persuaded the Politburo to allow him to create it in order to streamline his work at the Apex with a single reference point, but Peter had always thought it was a myth. If it fell into the wrong hands, well, his hands, it would give The Institute a supreme advantage. "It's been sitting in that vault all this time? Didn't it have any tracking system on it?"

"Yes, sir. But the power source ran out, we estimate, about four years ago."

"Four years ago," Peter muttered. "Hence the need to monitor the vault. I wonder how old the information is now. Not that it matters. Sondra, call up Miles and Jeter and see if you can find out the last time that vault was accessed before Coreena. If they don't help you, try the detective." Peter rose and headed out, then turned suddenly. "How on earth did the LOCK get into Kelli's vault? Sondra, Adam also brought back some footage, didn't he?"

"It's waiting in your office, sir."

"Let's go take a look. Evelyn, make sure to copy that information as best you can."

"Unfortunately, that's not possible."

"Not possible?"

"Well, not yet. You have to understand, it's such a foreign method of technological communication. We would have to build another complete system to be able to duplicate it. We can do that, maybe in a month or so. Until then, we can only see the information on a screen. We've tried taking pictures of the screen, but they aren't very good."

"How is that possible?"

"It can't communicate with any kind of printer or media device. It doesn't recognize commands like copy and save. It took us two full days to get it to display to a screen, and then another 24 hours to decode and translate it. At this point, we can access it, but we can't duplicate it. That's the genius in its construction."

"And that's how Drozdov persuaded them to let him make it."

———

"Man, you really know this kid," said Chad.

"It worked?"

"Yeah, just like the last time. First, the whole cookie thing, which like, I thought you were crazy, man, but that really worked. I mean she was like, mad, and she looked right at me. I could tell she got all perky when I said 'sneaky.' Just like you said. It was wild, man."

"Okay, how about this time?" said Nathanial. "They didn't mind you coming back?"

"Mind? Heck, no dude. The old guy called the front desk and *requested* me. They like *want* me to bring all their meals from now on. Gave me a fat tip too."

*Don't let the tall blond guy know you're sending messages,* Nathanial thought. "Great. So, you brought them lunch. Tell me how that went."

"Just like before, I played it all cool, man. Super cool. Only this time, she was like looking at me the whole time. Like she was waiting for it, you know? I mean I got through to the kid. I really did."

"I got through."

"Yeah well, I did it just like you told me to."

"Tell me."

"Trust me, man. That older man, he really likes me. Practically hugged me when I got there, you know? All right, so after the food was all set out, I asked if I could get them anything else and then, right before I left, I said all cute and cuddly like, 'Would the little lady like to hear a riddle?' And her eyes lit up. It was crazy. She started bouncing in her seat like a little kid does, you know?"

"Okay, so you told her the riddle."

"Actually, I thought of some better ones on the way up. Like, how many spiders does it take to—"

"You told her the riddle I gave you, right?"

"Hey, relax, man. Yes, I told your dumb riddle."

"Tell me," said Nathanial. "Like you told them."

Chad let out a teenage sigh. "What part of the house has a floor but no ceiling? It's a really easy, dumb riddle, dude."

"What happened next?"

"Well, everybody waited. The girl was like half-smiling, you know? I could tell she got it, but the idiot kid blurted it first. The old man was mad. He gave him a real dirty look. But she got it."

"Great. I have another riddle for when you bring dinner tonight."

"Wait, I thought you wanted me to deliver a message."

Nathanial smiled. "You already did. You ready for the last one?"

———

"I want you to help me escape."

"So, you *do* talk."

"Of course I talk. Everyone talks."

"I knew it. Could tell from the look in your eyes."

"Help me escape."

"What? My dad would have my arms pulled off."

"You're his son."

"He says he's your uncle."

"I don't believe him."

"You probably shouldn't. But I'm still not helping you."

"I think you could."

"I could also march in the other room and tell them you're talking like a native of Leningrad. You'll love it in Russia, trust me. It's a blast. Now be quiet so I can watch TV."

"You're right. If I'm going to ask you to get into trouble with your dad, then I should have to give you something in return."

"You. What could you possibly give me?"

"I can promise to marry you."

"What?"

"Hush, they'll hear."

"Let me get this straight. If I help you escape, you will promise to marry me?"

"Yes."

"You're five years old."

"So?"

"Well, I'm ten. Girls are gross."

"You think so now. But when you're old, like the other boys, you'll want a wife."

"Can't imagine why. I'd never get to watch TV in peace."

"Don't you have a mom?"

That was a stupid argument. What did that have to do with anything? It was a universally known fact that moms were a kid's greatest impediment to watching TV. "Who says I would want to marry you?"

"Maybe you won't. But I can be your backup plan," said Kelli. "Just in case no one wants to marry you and you're old. I promise to come to Russia and—" Kelli clamped her mouth shut and stared at the floor as Erik's shadow appeared in the door frame.

"Thought I heard some talking in here."

"TV. People talk on TV," Iosif answered with one lanky leg draped over the arm of his chair.

Erik retreated, and Kelli reached over to turn up the volume.

"Think about it. No matter what, you are guaranteed a wife. No matter how old you get, or sick, or ugly, or—"

"Hey, you don't know what you're saying. I'm brilliant. They had me tested. And my father is one of the most powerful men in Russia. Who says I'd want to marry you?"

"I didn't say you would want to marry me, just that I would marry you if no one else would. But since you asked, I'm very smart too."

"So *you* say."

"I'm smart enough that we're still talking. I'm smart enough not to talk to your dad, no matter how many pictures of Maman he shows me. Have you seen the pictures of my Maman?"

Curiosity snuck into his eyes. She pulled the picture out of her sleeve and held it up.

"I don't know. I'd need a guarantee. Something to prove you're serious."

# FOUR

Iosif Konstantinovich Drozdov stared up at the paneled ceiling above his hotel bed, drumming his fingers atop his slowly undulating belly.

Thinking was his thing. Ten years old, and he'd already made it to three Chess World Championships. He couldn't win, of course, because his father wouldn't let him compete in the final rounds.

"Too high profile," he would say. "Anonymity is a gift, Iosif. If I could redo only one thing about my career, it would be to hide my identity from the world. It was vanity that allowed me to release it. Unlike Zeus."

Iosif had no idea who Zeus was other than a Greek god, but he guessed that was probably the point. He did know one thing for sure; the future of Iosif Drozdov's mind was completely and utterly in the hands of the great Konstantin Andreevich Drozdov, comrade of Russia, servant of the republic, decorated minister of defense and research, blah, blah, blah...

In the silence of the waning hours of the night, Iosif considered whether he would even be allowed to marry at all. Surely his father wanted progeny like everybody else. Even animals were allowed to have kids, right? Would the girl be able to find him when the time came, since his precious identity would be so safely guarded?

Iosif hated thinking about the future because he knew his, intimately. At age ten, he was the most pre-destined kid on the planet, his story a well-formed research paper. It wasn't a complex equation to solve, but a long-ago-published book with an indefinitely postponed, predetermined ending. His life and his future were, in essence, a bore.

At the foot of his bed, the five-year-old girl slept curled up on the closet floor. He hoped she had wonderful dreams, the brat. She had proposed, no pun intended, a remarkable equation. Not her marriage proposal, but a backup plan he had never considered.

He doubted she would keep her promise. Who kept promises? What was a promise anyway? Nothing mathematically trustworthy, that's for sure. Just a gamble, a bet on a human horse. He silently swore to himself that he would always keep his promises. He would never be a horse.

But as for the girl, her fidelity didn't matter. Her idea in its very proposition had already given birth to a concept, a theory of freedom. And this night, these very ensuing seconds while everyone else slept, Iosif would enact its historic origin. Engaging the first rebellious attack in a hot war of thought versus tyranny by solving her ridiculous quandary.

He would get the girl out of the suite without Erik knowing.

Erik. He was the problem, wasn't he? It all hinged on the watchdog. The stinking ESA would hear any click of the lock no matter how controlled, even from a deeply engaged REM sleep. Heck, his father had set him in the common area for exactly that reason. The man was a walking freak show, really. If Iosif hadn't seen otherwise, he would have bet anything the guy slept hanging upside down, with his eyes open and his ears turned out.

But perhaps, in these earliest hours of the morning, Iosif could trick the rodent into thinking it heard something when really it heard something else. He needed a sensory diversion.

Iosif had purposely left their bedroom door ajar when going to bed, so he didn't have to open it now. He had tested it after dinner to make sure there was no alarming squeak in the hinge. But the main door, the one to the hotel hallway, lay right in the middle of the living area, squarely between the two bedrooms and a mere fifteen feet from the dragon's sofa lair. At the risk of his own peril, he had already snuck out during the hours of silent darkness to lift the chain bolt and the other protective lock. Moving ever so painfully slow, gliding the parts through space without even their innards suspecting they had been moved. But the doorknob itself would certainly make a deafening click.

Iosif slipped his feet off the bed. He crept across the carpeted floor to the closet and gingerly slid the door open. How could something so tiny and fragile hold such a magnitude of annoying persistence? He touched her shoulder, and her eyes opened. She sat up groggily. He had already made her dress after his father checked on them.

Together, they crept into the living area and waited in the dark. They stared at the back of the sofa while the light of day gradually encroached, and Iosif listened for his diversion. Nothing, save a void of disappointing silence existed in the universe beyond the door. As the light increased, only seconds remained. When he heard it, Iosif would have to act without hesitation.

At last, a soft, distant elevator bell rang from the far end of the hallway. Two voices, Spanish. Hotel service workers, pushing a cart. Iosif jumped up, put his hand on the knob, and turned slowly, as far as he could without feeling the bolt engage. He held it there, frozen in his small hands. The voices came closer, and keys jingled. He turned the knob, and both children shot their eyes back at the sofa. No movement. Iosif delicately pulled the door to himself. It had a squeak, but earlier he had lathered the hinge with a pad of butter he'd saved from dinner. Cool hallway air invaded the sleeping quarters as they slipped out, and Iosif stuffed a sock over the latch bolt so it wouldn't click.

Between the air temperature, the maid's movements, and the sudden loss of heartbeats in the room, Erik's subconscious alarms would soon be going off. There wasn't enough time to get her to the elevator and wait for the car. A housemaid's cleaning cart with a deep laundry bin stood in front of them.

"Climb in," he whispered.

She obeyed without question, and he covered her with the sheets.

"Now don't get out until he runs past. When he comes, hold your breath. Wait until you're sure he's on the elevator and then go. And don't forget your promise."

———

Erik stirred. Iosif quickly removed the sock and allowed the door to shut as quietly as possible. Erik sat up and glared at the tense ten-year-old backed squarely against the door with an uncharacteristically rigid frame and hands guiltily behind him.

"What are you doing?"

"It's the girl," said Iosif. "I don't know where she is."

"What?" Erik leaped up and tucked in his shirt. "Konstantin Andreevich!" he called out and pounded on Drozdov's private door before disappearing into the children's room. "She's not in the closet?"

"No," Iosif said. "I thought I heard something. I woke up and thought I should check, but I don't know where she is."

Erik searched the bedroom and bathroom. He returned and pointed an accusatory finger at Iosif. "You little weasel. You better not have done anything."

Drozdov stumbled in. "What's going on?"

"I swear," pleaded Iosif, "I thought I heard something, so I got up."

"The girl's not here," Erik's said, throwing on a shirt. "She's gone. Can't have been gone long, if he's telling the truth." Erik put his shoes on and stashed his pistol. "I'll go down to the lobby. Someone was bound to spot her alone at this hour." He grabbed his jacket and flung the door open.

Drozdov passed him a small radio. "Erik, be gentle."

"I'll be gentle," he called over his shoulder as he took off down the hallway.

Iosif smiled inwardly when Erik took the bait and headed in the wrong direction.

"The bracelet," Drozdov said and dragged his son by the arm back into the children's room. "Help me find it."

"What bracelet?" Iosif protested, his arm burning as his father wrenched it. "Wouldn't she take it with her?"

"I certainly hope so. Help me look."

Strange that Iosif should fear his own father more than the hitman in the elevator. He could feel his hands trembling, so he put them in his pockets while his father studied his features, breath streaming in and out of his nostrils. Suddenly Drozdov turned and began rifling through Iosif's luggage on top of the dresser.

"Dad, what are you doing?"

Drozdov turned back to face him slowly, a golden charm bracelet dangling in his hand.

It wasn't a complex equation, but after so much previous experience, it remained an enduring mystery to Iosif why the force and density of his father's hand always caught him by surprise.

———

As soon as the elevator doors closed, Kelli flipped the sheets off and climbed out of the cart. She tumbled to the floor as a housemaid stepped from a nearby room. Kelli smiled, then jumped up and skipped down the hall. When the elevator came, she pushed the highest number on the panel and rode up to the top of the building.

The doors slid open onto an office space. No one sat at the large fancy desk and all the lights were off. On the far wall, an exit sign hung above a door. She pushed the bar, stepped into a dim stairway, and ran up three flights. The stairs ended at a heavy metal door held ajar by a rolled-up towel. Cool morning air and orange sunlight seeped through the crack. A final push and she stepped out onto the roof.

She found him sleeping in the northwest corner, his brown leather flight jacket draped over his torso.

"Those were terrible riddles," she said.

A smile stretched across Nathanial's lips. "You're here, aren't you?"

"You know he's waiting for us downstairs. We'll never get away."

One eye peeked open. "Hey, I'm good at one thing, remember?"

———

Erik burst out of the elevator on the ground floor and scanned the lobby. He started with the front desk, interrogating the clerk with a picture in his hand. He questioned the scattered early risers in the lobby. He ran out onto the street and scanned the sidewalks in both directions. She was five years old. How far could she have gotten? He asked the valet, a passing garbage man, and three people waiting for taxis. How could no one have noticed an unsupervised five-year-old out for a walk?

Unless she didn't leave the building.

———

"You know, Peter laughed at me when I built this thing," Nathanial said, standing over a strange network of wires and wrist-thick metal piping that lay sprawled across the southern corner of the hotel's roof. Nathanial bent down and started arranging the thin rods while he mimicked Peter's voice. "What's anybody ever going to use that for? Really, Nathanial. With your brilliance, I'd expect better."

"Will it take long?" she asked.

"I already put the frame together, but I couldn't risk it being seen from above or blowing away. So, we just have to spread it out and insert the battens. With the triangle and frame ready to go, it should take us about four minutes. Should I ask how you got out of the room? Just walked out, I suppose?"

"I promised a ten-year-old I would marry him."

"What?"

"I knew I couldn't do it without his help."

"Well, uh, who is this guy? Does he have a decent job?"

"He's ten."

"Well, is he from a good family?"

"Can I help with anything?"

"Sure. See this? Lift the biggest pole on each side and carry it as far as you can." She did as instructed, grateful to have something to do. The poles were heavy, but a subconscious clock continually ticking away the minutes gave her an unusual strength. Once stretched out across the roof, they resembled the wingspan of a giant green bat.

"Well, do you think he took you seriously?"

"Who?"

"The ten-year-old."

"Oh yes. He's very smart."

"Well, that's good to hear. And he helped you. That bodes well for him, but I don't know. I'll have to meet this guy."

"It won't matter. I keep my promises."

"Yeah, I bet you do."

"What is this thing?" Kelli asked.

"It's a titanium alloy and steel cable, fully collapsible Rogallo wing. See, I told you it was a language. It's a glider."

"Glider?"

"Sorry, I don't know the French word."

"You don't know any French words."

"That's not true. *Manjay*, I know *manjay*, remember?"

"You don't know any French words."

———

"I've lost her," Erik said into the radio. "It's impossible. No one has seen her."

"She's too smart for that. Try a different exit, a back exit."

Erik ran down the hallway adjacent to the elevators through a 'Personnel Only' door. Beyond it, he inspected every corner, pushing past maids and clerks through a laundry room, storage rooms and a kitchen to the far back of the building. He shoved a young man in a white kitchen coat against a wall and held Kelli's picture to his face. "Have you seen her?"

"Uh no, sir. Do you need help?"

Erik sped off. He reached the loading dock outside the service entrance and began questioning staff. He moved out to the street. Someone had to have seen her.

———

"So, we're going to jump off the roof on this?" Kelli asked.

Nathanial finished inserting all the battens into tiny pockets, firming up the sail. "That's the plan. You're not scared?"

Kelli shuffled towards the edge of the roof for the first time and peered over the ledge. "*Ça va.*" Dizziness washed over her at the sight of the tiny cars and people so far below, like pieces on a toy display. "Are witches real?" she asked, turning back.

"Witches? You mean like, green ladies on brooms? No, witches aren't real. Why do you ask?"

"*Peu importe.*"

"All right, English is gone. Come here," he said. "Lift your arms up for me." He weaved a series of straps around her legs and arms. "Now, I'm not gonna be able to take off with you in front of me, so you'll have to be on my back." He grabbed her shoulders and turned her around. "Don't worry. You can't fall, because you'll be in this harness. I'm gonna yank you around a little to get you into this thing."

"Will it work?"

"Of course it will work. Most gliders don't have these harnesses, but they will one day, I guarantee it. Another peaceful invention Peter will have missed out on because it didn't have a gun." He tightened the straps around her. "All right, that should do it."

Gently taking her hand, he led her under the wings and started affixing their harnesses to the frame. Kelli felt herself pulled off the gravel onto her toes. Her heart sped up.

"Now, can you grab onto my back?" he asked and lifted the triangular frame off the ground. She put her hands on his shoulders. "Oh come on, you can do better than that. Grab on hard now. It will help me launch if you're not flailing around like a sack of potatoes. Okay, okay, that's better, maybe a little less aggressive? No, no that's okay. I don't need to breathe. I'm good. Now your legs, until we take off, okay? Can you wrap your—" She dug her heels into his torso and buried her face in his neck. "Great, that'll do. As soon as we're in level flight, you can let go and just hang above me. Then you can hold onto the frame here if you want." He detached her trembling hands from his throat and placed them on the triangle, but when he let go, she immediately returned to the death grip.

"I guess we'd better do this before I black out. You ready?" He began rambling together meaningless strings of words. "No incline, but no upwind from the street…still air, probably a bit of a nosedive for the first few seconds…have her under control…one of the tallest buildings…other high-rises. I probably shouldn't have said that. I don't know why I'm telling you any of this. You don't speak airplane-ese now, do you?"

"*Maintenant?*"

"Kelli, it's going to be fine. Piece of cake."

He straightened the wings and stepped up onto the ledge, wobbling. She clamped her eyes shut, and he moved within a few short steps of the corner, the large wings wobbling back and forth above them. In the few breathless seconds before he stepped off, Kelli considered why she had ever left the safety of the room below.

# FIVE

"She isn't here either," Erik said into the radio. "I think she's still in the building."

"Iosif helped her. I will get him to tell me where she is." The radio went silent. Erik contemplated going back inside and sniffing every floor.

On the opposite side of the street, a woman cried out and pointed upwards. "Someone jumped!"

A murmur washed over the street as more hands pointed upward. A deliveryman jumped out of his truck, and service workers froze in place, loads of packaged food in their arms.

Erik didn't need a detailed diagram. His Level VI eyes could easily make out two figures, one larger and one smaller, soaring suspended together on a glider. Within seconds, they would waft out of his visual range.

A motorcycle approached, and Erik brazenly stepped into the street, his dangerous proximity causing it to swerve with a screech of the brakes. "Hey, watch out, man!" the rider cried out.

In one seamless move, Erik grabbed the man and flung helmet, head, and rider to the ground, sending the motorcycle spinning off on its side. The onlookers reacted with gasps, most frozen in terror, while some ducked behind parked cars or into empty doorways. The dismounted rider lay motionless on the cool morning pavement. Erik mounted the fallen bike and engaged the throttle. Above him, the glider silently slid between the buildings and rounded a corner, disappearing out of sight.

———

Kelli was getting used to strange sensations. At first, there had been the feeling of falling, seconds of belly butterflies, and an invasive whistling sound as air rushed past her ears. She might have screamed, but she couldn't remember. She clung to Nathanial. When they soon leveled off, and she could feel the weightlessness of flight, she allowed herself to let go and hold onto the beams as he had showed her.

They were flying again, soaring above the city streets and looking down on morning traffic alongside curious pigeons. Massive walls of glass and concrete swept past, some offering a shining reflection of herself and Nathanial, the pair of them, under their mighty green wing. How simple it all was, and how delightful. In and out they weaved between the buildings, tilting, forgetting where gravity was supposed to pull, curving easily around the corners of mighty fortresses. They flew on something that could not be seen by the tiny people, moving so slowly down below. Kelli dared not close her eyes for a second. She didn't want to miss anything else that was wonderful.

———

"You can't stay up there forever," Erik said from the waking streets. He jerked the bike around another corner, running his third red light and invading a sidewalk. As long as he could see the green wing, he could recover his directive. Nothing else mattered, not pedestrians, vendors, cars, or authorities. Only the Fokus mattered.

He came to a stop in the middle of an intersection. Where had they gone? A man holding a tiny dog on a leash pointed upwards down another street, and Erik spun off, leaving behind a barrage of angry drivers and a traffic cop hollering into his radio. Time was running out for both parties. Despite the lead of the glider, it was obvious that their altitude was steadily dropping.

———

Once clear of the larger buildings, Nathanial spotted something curious in a clear area of green. Massive colorful tarps lay flat on the ground, while others slowly expanded, tilting upright. Crowds of curious onlookers ambled nearby, taking pictures and shielding their eyes from the morning sunlight. Balloons, about a dozen of them, bright flames spitting into their reclining envelopes. Nathanial took them as a sign of safe harbor and headed for an empty patch of nearby grass.

As they approached the ground, Nathanial pushed the control bar out, tipping the glider nose up and stalling so he could land running, awkward though it was with Kelli dangling behind him. Once grounded, he hastily unlatched himself from the frame and began unfastening her harness, but he couldn't shake the stubborn lingering anxiety. Of course, they were safe now. He had done it. He could ditch the glider and take a cab back to the Learjet. They would be at the cabin in time for dinner.

As he unhooked the last of Kelli's straps, he lifted his eyes towards the streets they had just escaped. A tall blond man spun a motorcycle to a clumsy stop on the opposite edge of the grassy plot. He poised like a hunting dog, his eyes making painfully naked contact with Nathanial across the grassy expanse.

"What's the matter?" Kelli asked.

Adam Walker's figure began a steady march towards them.

"Come on!" Nathanial grabbed Kelli's little hand and sped through the park into the crowds. Across the street, a large delivery door to an industrial complex stood open. Lifting Kelli into his arms, he ran, paying little heed to traffic. He swept up the steps and plunged through the service door into the darkness beyond.

Machines. Blessedly loud, cranking machines melted and pounded metal articles on long cooling belts and climbing rollers. Pushing and pulling, clanking, snorting, steaming, and smelling of grease, cleansers, and molten alloy. The noise, the heat, and the smells would provide useful sensory distractions to hide them from the ESA. Nathanial ducked behind a massive grinding mechanism and dropped to the floor, holding Kelli close.

"Don't talk now," he whispered.

She huddled tightly to him, peering through towards the factory entrance. A tall shadow appeared, looming on the threshold in the morning light.

Nathanial felt Kelli inhale quickly. He lifted her and scurried deeper into the forest of machines, settling momentarily on the cool concrete behind a rattling network of metal cranks and steam. He peeked out the other side, towards the door. The silhouette was gone, but a new sound, a low steady grind, added itself to the cacophony of noise. Nathanial might not have noticed it, were it not for the accompanying loss of daylight as the entranceway door descended to the floor.

"Hey, what are you doing?" a male voice shouted.

Two quick cracks echoed under the high ceiling, despite the cacophony of mechanical sounds. Nathanial peeked back down the aisle. The tall figure was gone, but something on the floor, a dark puddle, flowed steadily forward beneath a motionless hand. Nathanial cuddled Kelli's head closer.

Something snapped loudly, and a machine began the gradual descent in pitch as it wound to a stop. Soon, a second part of their protective symphony began the same diminuendo. He was shutting off the machines one by one. Once the room was silent, every breath they took would lead him to them. There would be no hiding from his ears. They were trapped. They had to get out of the factory, and to do that, they had to separate.

"Kelli, I need you to crawl back to the door, then, very quietly, open it. There's probably a control switch on one side. Do you think you can do that?" A timid nod. "You mustn't push the button until you hear my signal. Not until I call out, like, like the eagle. Do you remember what it sounded like?" Kelli nodded again. "Once it starts to open, roll under and run fast. I'll be right behind you. Can you do that?"

With sedate obedience, she left his arms and began crawling back towards the door. A third machine fell victim to a power loss and began the descent into abysmal silence.

"Hey! Who the hell are you? Who—"

Two more muffled shots, and the protests stopped. Footsteps sounded, along with men's voices, as the remaining floor workers sped off, crouching, towards hidden doors, escaping the confines of the building. They would call for help, but it would arrive too late.

Nathanial ran, hunched over, towards the back wall. At the end of the aisle, bins of processed metal pilings sat on the receiving end of roller belts. He picked up two large pans and laid them on a moving belt, sending them towards a collision with a mechanism they would most definitely jam. When they hit their mark, the sounds would lead the phantom away from Kelli.

The back wall had no exits and little consolation besides a fire extinguisher and a pair of soda machines. An archway shined a rectangle of light across the factory floor. Beyond it, he found a storage room full of metal pilings, shelved ten and twenty feet high, with boxes and crates scattered in unorganized lanes.

Another machine petered to a mild hum in the factory behind him, and the encroaching silence grew deeper. Only seconds remained. He ran back to the bins and unraveled a large piece of sturdy rope knotted around its frame, pulling frantically at the fibers with his fingers.

*Clang — Yank — Clung — Clung!* The pans he had sent off met their mark. The stranger was coming.

Nathanial dislodged the stretch of rope and grabbed another pan before ducking back into the storage room. He squatted down among the racks. From behind a trio of the freestanding shelves, he peeked above a bin of metal scraps. The long slender legs of Adam's doppelgänger appeared in the doorway. As the shadow moved two steps away from the door, Nathanial shuddered, then hurled the pan to the far end of the room, where it landed with a clang.

The menace floated back toward the sounds. Nathanial crept back through the archway and strung the rope around a beam on the nearest rack. Standing back, he pulled on it gently, and it wobbled. Throw the thing off balance, and gravity would do the rest. He wrapped the rope around his back and gathered any remaining insanity he could muster.

———

At the front of the factory, Kelli had successfully reached the door and located a hanging switch. Three tiny pictures on it represented outlines of the door as open, closed, and midway. She stood trembling, the control ready in her tiny fingers. *Once it starts to open, roll under and run fast.* She could do that. He would be right behind her.

Then she heard it, a sudden high-pitched caw like an eagle. Her fingers turned the knob and the door began its grating ascent. She got down on all fours, but as she watched the rectangle of light grow on the concrete floor, something distracted her. *Something was not right.*

At the far side of the door, a darkness moved gently, spreading itself like a living blanket across the concrete. A terrible crash erupted from the back of the factory, followed by Erik shouting. She should pay attention to those sounds. There was something she was supposed to do, but the liquid on the floor had entranced her and was holding her hostage, her eyes unwillingly fixated on its gradual spread. *What is that river of darkness?*

Footsteps getting louder. A voice calling through the fog. "Run, Kelli!"

Her breath abruptly whipped out of her as a hard arm landed on her ribs. Nathanial swept her up and through the door into the fullness of the daylight. She was flying again, not like before, in the air, but rushing, frantic, and panting heavily, as they scurried between the cars.

———

Nathanial plunged into the crowd, glancing occasionally behind to catch sight of any lurking shadows. Vendors in makeshift booths sold mementos and sizzling delicacies, while someone made announcements on a distorted sound system. Colorfully dressed hippies reclined on blankets, smelling of incense and weed. A pair of clowns juggled batons and made balloon animals for impatient toddlers.

Nathanial approached a pair of teenagers leaning on a tree and puffing cigarettes. "Hey," Nathanial said. "Would you be willing to sell me your jacket?"

"Whoa. Dude, what?" The teenager laughed as smoke billowed from his nostrils.

"Your jacket! Look, I'll give you fifty bucks for it, and I'll give you mine. It's leather, see?" He took off his pilot jacket and tossed it to them, then pulled a wad of cash from his pants pocket with trembling hands.

"Whoa, man. Okay. Okay. I dig it. You can have my jacket. I'll take your money. That's a nice ride. I like it." The young man took

Nathanial's jacket and the money. "You know mine ain't worth that much."

"It is to me." Nathanial took the denim jacket with a large black dragon on the back and threw it on. "Thanks."

"Hey man, you okay? You need some help or something?"

"Peace!" Nathanial grabbed Kelli's hand and pulled her away.

————

Erik grabbed the factory wall and pulled himself up from the scattered remnants that had fallen around him. The tall shelf had tilted as he neared the door, throwing off boxes of metal scraps to the concrete floor and bringing down a second shelving unit as well. Before the worst of it fell, Erik ducked into an open space on the bottom shelf of another unit, wrapped his trench coat around himself, and covered his head as tiny bits of metal crashed around him like shrapnel. When the last of the debris hit the concrete floor, Erik carefully dug himself out from the shelf where he had curled up. His arms and legs stung with fresh cuts and bruises where metal fragments had cut though his clothing. He was dizzy, his ears rang madly, and he repeatedly spit out the taste a metal, the dust of which seemed to fill the air like a fog. His limbs whined as he climbed the debris, stumbling towards his directive.

At the entrance of the factory floor, his eyes adjusted slowly to the bright sunlight. His directive would be hiding in the crowds at the park. The people would be inconvenient but manageable. He strode, limping, between cars and pedestrians, his focus fueled by fury. Whoever this guy was, Erik was going to kill him.

————

Nathanial approached a vendor booth draped with colorful hats, scarves, and dangling earrings. He grabbed a pink, tie-dyed scarf and fished out some cash. While he wrapped Kelli's shoulders in it, she fixated on a blue and red velour top hat, picking it off the table and placing it on her head. Nathanial thoughtlessly threw down another twenty.

"That's too much," the man called out.

They headed into the thick of the crowds, closer to the awakening balloons, where inflation fans sent fiery blasts into the envelopes. Coming clear of a group of pointing spectators, he stopped short and tightened his grip on Kelli's hand. Their pursuer's green eyes beamed across the crowded grassy landing. Nathanial tugged Kelli into a flock of people and around the side of a semi-inflated balloon, where three men struggled to hold the crown line steady. He huddled with her behind a blue pickup and peeked around the back. The man scanned the crowd a few short yards away. Nathanial nudged Kelli to crawl with him along the underside of the truck as the man walked around the back bumper.

*What would he do when he found them?* Probably hold them at gunpoint and force them from the safety of the crowd. Nathanial was not what she needed right now. Adam was what she needed. Adam could face this guy. Hell, Adam *was* this guy.

The man's feet slowly moved away, and Nathanial pulled Kelli into his arms. He headed towards the closest standing balloon, red and blue with white sashes. It towered up into the air above them, booming with the hot puff off the burner.

"Hey!" he called out, running past the crew. "How much to take someone up for a ride?"

"Get out of here, mister. You're in the way. You're gonna get hurt!"

He put Kelli down and grabbed hold of the wicker gondola. "How much to take a passenger with you?"

"Sorry pal, we're about to lift off now. If you'll just get out of the way."

Nathanial stood his ground, clamping his fists stubbornly onto the basket. "How much?"

———

Erik lifted his radio to his lips. "I haven't got her, but I know where they are."

"Well, don't lose her."

"I won't. But there have been some complications. I'll need a pickup. I'll let you know." He returned the radio to his pocket. The police were already tailing him, first from the motorcycle chaos on the morning streets, and now the inconvenient mess on the factory floor. His hand reached up and touched his forehead, stinging from the bits of metal that had fallen on him. He remembered the man now. It was the blubbering idiot from the hotel lobby, who had so clearly recognized him two days before. He should have killed him then. Now he would have to do it with the girl watching.

———

"How much to take passengers for a ride in the balloon?" Nathanial asked the fifty-something man inside the gondola who was preoccupied getting ready to launch. The radiant heat pressed at them when the occasional bursts of flames spewed up into the envelope.

"Nothing, I'm taking a crew member with me. Promised. Come see us after we land, and I'll take your number. We can make an appointment for a ride."

"No, it has to be now," Nathanial said. "Right now. How much?"

"Sorry sir, not today. Please step out of the way."

For the second time that day, a crew member put his hands on Nathanial's shoulders and pulled him away, but he jerked back and grabbed the gondola. He reached in his pocket and pulled out the last of his cash. "Two thousand dollars?" He waved the wad of bills in the air, and everyone froze except the balloon, now fighting against the ropes.

"Two thou—are you crazy? Just wait 'til—"

"Two thousand dollars, cash. Right now."

It only took a moment of silence, and an understanding glance between pilot and crew, before the last of Peter's paycheck was spent in a gamble for Kelli's safety. Seconds later, all firmly ensconced in the basket, they were ready to release the gentle giant into the sky. Nathanial reached behind him and pulled out the damned handgun.

"I'm really sorry for this," he said to his host, "but you have to get out. I'll do my best not to damage it, and you keep the cash no matter what, but you have to go."

"Whoa. What the—? You're nuts!" The aeronaut lifted his hands to his shoulders. Crew members gasped, fighting with panic to hold the gondola to the earth. "Look, mister, there's propane in here."

"I'm going to count to five," Nathanial said, disbelieving his own, oddly steady hands.

"You don't know how to fly this thing."

"One." Nathanial released one hand from the weapon, reached up, and opened the blast valve on the propane burner. A surge of hot flames rushed into the envelope. "Two."

Deciding he really didn't want to be isolated in the skies with an armed nutcase, the pilot hurled himself over the side of the gondola and rolled to safety on the ground. He turned enraged eyes on Nathanial as the massive green balloon rose into the open air. As soon as it passed above their heads, the crew began running about, shouting for police.

Nathanial stowed the weapon, deeply grateful that the pilot had not called his bluff. He peered over the edge of the gondola in time to see Adam's figure rush beneath him, furiously jumping for the ropes. As the nefarious image got gratifyingly smaller, a sick feeling swelled in Nathanial's stomach. For the first time in all this mess, he had a moment to consider that familiar face. A face somehow both his friend and his enemy. He felt sick knowing that he still couldn't trust either.

―――――

The balloon rose quickly with silent elegance, gliding west on invisible wind. Amidst the panicked crowd, Erik pulled out his pistol and aimed. The man ducked into the basket. Erik squeezed the trigger, but he remembered himself and lowered the weapon before firing. The girl. He could only see the top of her stupid blue and red hat. Any shot at the man was a shot at her. Even hitting the fuel was not an option.

They were getting away. He was losing his target to a ridiculous balloon that could take them only where the wind blew. He could steal a vehicle and follow them on the ground, but back at the factory entrance, three police cruisers pulled up, lights flashing. Authorities would be waiting wherever the balloon landed, ready to arrest and protect them. He couldn't let them land. He had to catch them in the air. He had to go after them.

# SIX

ERIK SCANNED THE REMAINING BALLOONS. ONE PERCOLATED MORE eagerly than the others, impatient of its man-held harness. He pushed aside panicked spectators, moving so quickly that no crew members had a chance to object.

In the gondola, two men busily prepared for liftoff. Like a hawk, Erik swept in, his pistol low at his side. His free arm encircled the neck of the younger man, a teenager in a baseball cap, and wrenched him backwards out of the gondola.

From the weight drop, the balloon heaved itself upwards, forcing the crew to put their full strength into the ropes. Erik jumped into the gondola and grabbed the pilot, a portly man in his mid-fifties with a trimmed gray beard. Erik jabbed the weapon into his throat.

"Tell them to let go."

The man struggled under the pressure of the muzzle. His hands wildly gestured for his crew to obey.

A female voice cried out, "He has a gun!" and a new epic of chaos sparked through the park as the red and gold striped balloon began its graceful ascent. Once above the crowd, Erik plunged the man's weight forward over the wicker railing. His desperate attempts to claw at the wicker and leather did not prevent him from spiraling helplessly towards the earth, where his body landed on the grass with a horrific thump.

Without the weight of the pilot, the balloon leaped upwards at a dangerous rate. Erik grabbed hold of the maneuvering vent to compensate. He scoured the horizon for his target in the green balloon. It was already drifting apart from the others.

———

Peter Van De Sant came to work unusually early that morning. He had three agents out on operations, two important contracts to sign, and honestly, he couldn't sleep. He enjoyed strolling through the dimly lit corridors, sauntering into his empty office on the sixth floor, drinking his customary tea, and watching the sunrise over the mountainside.

"Is it true?" a ghostlike voice said from a dark corner.

Peter gasped. "Adam, you scared the daylights out of me."

"You left a message to come this morning."

"Well yes, this morning, but I didn't think you'd be here at 6:00 a.m." He bent over his wingback chair. "You know I'm not the young man I used to be. I could have had a heart attack."

"I forget sometimes. What other people can't hear."

"No, we don't hear heartbeats." Peter caught his breath as he took off his coat. "What did you say? Is what true?"

"What Nathanial said."

Peter had hoped to get his tea and be slightly more awake before having this conversation. He released his first paternal sigh of the day and lowered himself into the chair. "To which of the many colorful epithets Nathanial threw in your direction over the last two weeks would you be referring?"

"Are you my moral compass?"

Peter grinned. Of all the outrages that Nathanial had

dispensed, justly or unjustly, this was the one that left a mark on Adam's ego.

"It's partly my fault," Peter said. "You and I both know it's better for you to not struggle with ethics when you are pursuing an objective." He finally took his hat off and rested it atop his knee. "Adam, you are the good guy. Remember that."

"So, you tell me. Nathanial isn't so sure. Everyone can't be righteous. Even Drozdov thought he was somehow doing the right thing when he had my parents killed, or anything else he's done."

"We all have weaknesses, Adam. Every KAT has some flaw, personality quirk—"

"And this is mine? So, what happens when you do have a heart attack?"

"You'll find another compass." As soon as Peter said it, he regretted it. "No, that's not it. You'll be your own. Look, Nathanial didn't just get to you. I've spent my life supposedly protecting you all, so no one could take anybody's eyes out. Now suddenly I'm terrified that maybe..."

"Maybe what?"

"That maybe I took yours. Listen, why'd you leave Russia? I've never pushed you on it, but it's time to tell me."

Adam was silent for so long that Peter thought he might not respond. He waited, allowing the awkwardness between them to become obtuse while Adam's tall shadow slowly clarified in the hazy morning light.

"They asked too much," he said at last. "Something happened. With me, but I don't know what. They used drugs that made me forget. Drozdov told me a story, I was in an accident, that sort of thing. But I knew it was a lie."

"How did you know it was a lie?"

"They couldn't erase it completely. I had flashes, still do, that don't make sense. Memory fragments that weren't there before. And then a few weeks later, one of my colleagues just disappeared. She was part of it all somehow, she knew something I didn't and tried to tell me. She was acting strange, too. Acted differently around me. When she disappeared, I knew I had to get out. What could I have done that was so bad, they needed to make me forget it?"

Adam leaned against Peter's corner bookcase, his head bent at the neck, his hands in his coat pockets, reminding Peter of a caricature from a Norman Rockwell.

"I thought I was doing the right thing," Adam went on. "Leaving Kelli in that vault. What else were we going to do? Bring her to the authorities and explain? That would have meant questions about the Institute and explaining my actions and what we were doing at that airport in the first place. I figured we could leave her there and she'd just be found by security. I thought I was protecting you, and this place, and everything in it."

"And yourself."

"Now you sound like Nathan. Nobody is making any sense."

For a moment, in that dim morning light, his posture bent, Adam looked almost pathetic. Peter felt pathetic and submerged another urge to reprimand Adam for listening to Nathanial or thinking for himself. As the sun rose, it brought them both into a rose-colored light that demanded a certain honesty, like Kelli playing at his desk or running through the electronics lab or feeding them all lunch.

"There are things," Peter said, "that are more important than this place and what we do."

"We prevent wars, Peter. Nuclear wars."

"Yes, yes. I know. But what are we preventing the wars for? Just to save lives? Keep people alive? What about all the better things? The lesser things we don't even notice half the time."

"Like what?"

"Well, like, all the paintings on the walls in this place. You walk past them every day. Things like that sunrise out there, and all the stuff the hippies are ranting about. Flowers, peace."

"Weed?"

"Adam, can't you think of anything meaningless, useless, but priceless? Something more important than any talent or directive. Something precious."

"So, I am the bad guy."

"Bad guys, good guys. Listen to us. We're talking like five-year-olds. That girl left her mark. But you do have to believe in something beyond just your mission. You used to play cello, years ago."

"Another lifetime."

"It wasn't that long. But it could be anything. What about faith? Do you believe in God?"

"Should I?"

Peter laughed, but then shuddered. "Probably not," he said. There was only so far this conversation should go. He couldn't have his Level VI taking retreats to mountaintop monasteries. Adam needed perspective, not a conscience.

Peter lifted himself from the wingback and crossed behind his desk. The sun had risen, and the first of his secretaries now puttered around in the offices just outside his door. "I need you to find Nathanial."

"Is he missing?"

"Maybe he's just not answering his calls. He's probably furious with the lot of us, or humanity in general again. But I can't stop this sickening feeling that he's gotten himself into trouble. Go to the hangar, the cabin, anywhere he might be. He has a mother in a home somewhere; find her. Count all his planes, boats, cars. Who has the dog? Someone must know where he is."

"And when I find him?"

"Well, that would be enough for me. But something tells me, you won't."

———

Nathanial found the experience of being chased to his death in a hot air balloon alarmingly peaceful. Isolated in a basket, he floated, only minimally in control, blown towards the very will of nature, with no engines, just an unobtrusive flight burner, and the wind his master, pilot, throttle, and rudder.

Behind him, the small flock of balloons hung as if suspended on invisible wires. He felt mild concern at the sight of the red and gold offshoot, ascending into the same western bound current as his own, easing closer on a slow and steady path. He imagined the mighty Level VI in the tiny gondola, helplessly frustrated with the slow pace of the chase.

Then there was Kelli. The innocent little one, caught in the middle of all this adult mayhem. How her little limbs had trembled as he settled her onto the floor of the gondola, where she curled up straightaway in a corner and tucked her head between her knees. There had been no time for reassurances, just an immediate transferal of goods before he had to move on to more pressing matters, like commandeering a balloon at gunpoint.

The gold and red predator followed him past the city limits, past suburbia and over undeveloped terrain, before his pursuer made a judgment error by pulling too aggressively on his blast valve. His balloon rose dramatically out of the wind, following Nathanial into a higher current but in the opposite direction. A few minutes of wind and silence later, the Level VI's balloon rose into a third tier of the atmosphere, securing itself in the new, even higher path of wind. A tiny dot shrinking into the sky.

With the pursuing balloon safely at a distance, it was time for Nathanial to land. With the wind in control, he had to navigate carefully to avoid structures or electrical entanglements. The cords for the maneuvering vents and deflation valve gripped in his hands, he studied the countryside in the direction of the lowest wind current and began his descent.

Minutes later, the unexpected sound of a burner igniting made him jump. He searched the skies. A second time, the fiery blast closed in on him from an invisible adversary. He craned over the railing in time to see the last of the red and gold stripes slip above his green envelope *from the opposite side.* The Level VI had lifted up to the higher, faster current and passed far overhead, only to descend and return in the eastbound wind.

Nathanial pulled on the maneuvering vent rope, accelerating his descent. If he pulled any harder, the balloon would collapse into a dead drop. He was not nearly close enough for a jump.

Something jerked the balloon and the gondola wobbled clumsily beneath his feet as he felt the descent quicken. Up inside the envelope, the dark imprint of a man's body rested on the balloon's cusp. Outstretched hands clung to the edge of the deflation port. The Level VI had jumped from his balloon.

"Man, you guys are nuts."

Nathanial had to engage the burner to prevent the sudden weight from sending them careening into gravity. The man inched around the load tape, his arms and legs strewn wildly, kicking in the wind. Surely, he wasn't stupid enough to climb inside the envelope: the heat, the drop, and the disastrous effect of over opening the valve could be suicidal.

*What is he reaching for?* Nathanial felt another pull on the gondola beneath him.

Of course. The crown line, the rope attached to the very apex of the envelope, swung violently back and forth as the man began to climb down it. It was tied into an impossible knot on the burner frame. Nathanial reached into a flight bag, searching for a knife as the gondola rocked wildly. Finding a blade, he cut at the taught fibers frantically, no longer concerned with where the balloon would come down, only how soon.

---

When Erik finally got the crown line in his hands, he realized he would not be able to slide down into the gondola. The coarse rope would certainly burn up his palms. It would have to be a slow, controlled descent, moving in the same direction as the balloon itself. If the balloon got to the ground before he got to the gondola, the hostages could run. If authorities were waiting, he would lose them.

Gradually working down the crown line took incredible upper body endurance. Halfway to his objective, Erik curled his foot around the rope in an attempt to stabilize himself.

The line abruptly went limp in his hands, and instead of cleaving to the side of the balloon, Erik found himself dangling tenuously off the cusp, suspended upside down over the undeveloped Texas countryside. When he swung outwards, he could see some of the gondola, the briefest glimpse of the man's face, and the top of the girl's stupid hat.

Anything loose on his being slid out of place and tumbled to the earth below. Like his gun. Erik grabbed the dagger on his belt and on the next swing, he stabbed it into the nylon, creating an anchor. The burner ignited, and heat poured from within the balloon. He cut a rip in the nylon and maneuvered himself through, into the envelope, less than twenty feet from the skirt seam.

Erik now held the gash, hanging down the inside of the envelope. When he let go, he slid to the skirt, where he would have dropped to his death between the steel cables, had he not spread himself evenly across them. He inched his way down over the propane burner. It had not engaged since he entered the envelope. He felt the consequent descent of the balloon.

Where were they? The gondola was empty but wobbling furiously. Over the side, the man from the hotel lobby clambered down a rope. Erik wished he hadn't lost his gun.

*But where was the girl?*

She did not hang with the man, nor from any other rope. Erik spun around again. With a flaring rage and an unfamiliar modicum of respect, he put his hand on the red and blue hat, perched comfortably atop a propane tank. The girl had never been in the balloon at all. The man had left her at the park and drawn Erik into this ridiculous chase. This whole trip, the chase, the patience, the wind, the climb, had all been a fool's errand to take him farther from his target.

Erik glared over the gondola at his new objective. The ground glided past underneath, now only meters away. He reached for the blast valve. He would lift the balloon back up, making a jump to the ground impossible. But as his fingers closed around it, the balloon sailed right over the banks of a brown body of water. The man took a last look up at Erik before letting go of the rope and dropping into the questionable waters below. The balloon immediately leaped upwards at the loss of weight. Erik pulled hard on the deflation port line, ripping it almost halfway off, disrupting the ascent. Like an undaunted fox after its prey, he climbed onto the gondola side, assessed the water below, and jumped.

———

Many eyes cannot see clearly, though they see well enough: eyes that need glasses to go to the cinema, eyes that lose precision with age, or eyes that fade with disease or abuse.

However, these eyes, these tiny, five-year-old eyes, were well beyond what any optometrist would call 20/20. These eyes watched with intent, peering over the rim of another gondola high in the sky, squinting against the morning sunlight beneath the massive red, white, and blue balloon.

"When you land," Nathanial had said, "you must go to the police right away. Tell them to call the FBI and get Zeus. Don't ask for Peter, ask for Zeus, okay?" He had held her then, so firmly. Now she understood. She was to go to the police, as soon as her balloon landed.

The tiny scene of darkened shapes played out on the distant ground below her. The two figures of Nathanial and Erik emerged from a river that looked like a giant reflective brown serpent on the ground below. One man dragged the other into hiding while the big green balloon withered down far enough away to distract the flashing blue lights that were following it.

She was to go to the police as soon as she landed.

As soon as she landed.

———

The downwash from Adam's chopper made ripples in the lake as he landed at Nathanial's cabin. The pontoon plane bobbed easily, while a canoe and a dinged-up motorboat lay idle on a nearby shore. When the rotor slowed to a stop, everything felt as though it were sleeping, not even lifting a metaphorical eyelid at his arrival.

Adam had a vision of Nathanial hiding somewhere under a tree and "accidentally" misfiring a weapon in his direction. But that was just sarcasm. Nathanial would never willfully point a gun at another human being.

The visit to Hemmel Air had been fruitless. No sign of life, except the gum-chewing office boy sitting bewildered at a desk, unable to do anything but take messages and feed the dog. Adam rifled through the messages: two from Peter's secretaries, two from clients, and four from a loan manager named Monroe. At the back of the hangar, Adam found a ransacked storage closet, file folders thrown about in disarray on the concrete, and an ominously empty gun box. A cursory examination of the office paperwork told him that a client's plane was missing, a nice plane. Still, Adam held hope that Nathanial could just be out camping in some reclusive spot of wilderness. Without the dog.

The cabin was unlocked, but that could be normal. No dirty dishes lay piled in the sink, no trash in the bins, and only cold, settled ashes in the fireplace. He found empty luggage in a closet, and under the stairs, a sleeping bag and a tent.

A motor approached. Adam closed his eyes and listened. It certainly wasn't Nathanial's Jeep. It was something sleeker, something that had no business driving on the rough forest roads.

He withdrew his pistol, undid the latch on the side door, and slid it open. The vehicle pulled to a stop in the back, and a car door opened and shut. Heavy footsteps trod uncomfortably on the earthen ground, crunching stray leaves.

Adam lifted his weapon. "Stop right there."

A short, balding man released a high-pitched wail and tossed his briefcase into the pine needles. With one hand on his heart, he waved the other aloft as though it could block an unwelcome bullet. "Please, don't shoot."

"Who are you, and what are you doing here?"

"Who am I? Who are you flashing a gun at me? You put that cursed thing away."

Adam redirected his weapon into the woods and fired, sending birds into furious twitters.

"Wait! Wait." The man's eyes wandered constantly through the tops of the pines, as if eye contact would cause the weapon to spontaneously discharge. "Here, here!" He reached inside his coat pocket.

"Nope."

The man retracted his foolish hand. "I'm...I was just reaching for my card. I'm George Monroe. Golden State, Golden State Credit Union. I'm a loan manager, that's all. I swear that's all. Just my card."

"Keep your hands up and turn around."

Adam slipped his free hand inside the jacket and retrieved the card.

"See? See?" he said. "I'm just a loan manager. Just a Golden State—"

Adam lowered his weapon, and Monroe leaned on his knees with stubby wrists.

"I suppose he owes you money too?" Monroe raised an

objecting hand. "Please, whoever you're with, I don't want to know. Our creditors have a deed in lieu of foreclosure." A fat finger waved at the cabin and surrounding trees. "And it will be delivered at the end of next month." Standing fully erect, his head barely reached Adam's chin. He adjusted the glasses on the lower end of his nose.

"You're taking his cabin?" Adam said. "Didn't he cover the payments?"

"The fool. He said he had been paid by someone, but now he's disappeared, and so has the money. If we find him, it will probably be in a jail cell."

"I doubt that. When did you speak with him?"

"Excuse me, but considering you're on my client's property and you've just nearly killed me, I'll ask you to leave, please."

"How much does he owe?" Adam asked again.

———

It was unfortunate that Erik had to kill the guy, but he could see no way around it. If he let him live, he might be found. Then another police report, someone would spot the car on the road or at the rendezvous point, and on and on. So much hassle. Besides, after this morning's chase, Erik really wanted to kill someone.

The corpse he dragged across the gravel to its drainage ditch grave reeked of cigar and had more white facial hair than any civilized person should. The poor, unfortunate soul had pulled over to help a man in trouble. He spoke with such a deep drawl that Erik had to think carefully before responding.

"Uh, you need some help?" the man had said. "Is that fella okay?"

'That fella,' the unconscious body of Nathanial, lay strewn carefully across the side of the road where Erik was feigning CPR. He had managed to keep his captive subdued in the drainage pipe by slugging him every time he showed some sign of consciousness; enough pressure to knock him out, but never enough to inflict any permanent damage, really the only part of the morning he had enjoyed.

"Please," Erik said, his back to the man. "I saw him go down. Come do some compressions and give me a rest."

"Compressions?" The curious doomed character squatted low and stared. "Uh, I never heard of that. You sure you know what you're doing?"

"Yes, it's easy," Erik had said. "I'll show you."

Hesitant, but like any fifty-something Texan with an American flag T-shirt, he knelt down on his faded jeans for his own execution. Erik made it quick. That was the least he could do in exchange for the man's car.

Erik tore some strips off the man's shirt. He used them to bind Nathanial's hands and feet in such a way that struggling would only make them tighter. As much fun as repeatedly hammering the guy was, eventually he might hurt something, and he really wanted this guy alive when he got him alone. He used his last strips to blindfold and gag him before tossing him in the trunk, hoping that it got hot as hell in there.

---

"I lost her" was not what Drozdov wanted to hear when he finally picked up the hotel phone a few hours later. He leaned over to turn down the ongoing TV reports of mayhem in the Houston streets, describing everything from hang gliders to triple homicides.

"But I've got the man," Erik said. "He'll know where to find her."

*A consolation prize?* Would this ridiculous custody battle never end? "There are drawings of your face all over the television. Someone recognized you from the lobby. I've already had police here. Stay low."

Briefly, Drozdov contemplated leaving the hotel. But they were leaving that night anyway. Only a few more hours. The police had already come and gone.

Drozdov watched the chase play out on the television, flicking back and forth between channels. There was no mention of the girl being apprehended. Usually, children made great press, and this one was already famous.

An hour later in the hotel garage, Drozdov and Erik opened the trunk of the stolen sedan. The bound and blindfolded stranger within stirred at the sensation of cool air. Drozdov splattered a bottle of beer atop of him, while Erik unrolled a small brown leather pouch of syringes. The man's body flinched at the prick, but relaxed when the chemical took effect. They unbound him, took off the blindfold and gag, and carried him like a drunken idiot, his feet dragging between them.

The elevator doors slid open onto the long, dim hallway of the thirteenth floor. Naturally, Erik saw her first. Through the sunglasses he wore to hide his face, the vision so shocked him that he didn't dare say anything, lest the apparition spontaneously vanish. The battered man between them looked up and whispered, "No," and Drozdov saw her last.

Drozdov was not so surprised as delighted. He could see it all immediately. It had been quite simple really. Once the balloon had landed, Kelli had instructed the pilot to return her to the very hotel she had escaped. Of course, she knew the name; it was on every napkin and notepad in the suite. He could just imagine the balloon pilot's truck pulling up on the busy street outside and little Kelli jumping out before they could stop her, quickly running away, calling out a quick thank you and disappearing into the hotel lobby. An elevator ride later, she sat down on the floor outside the same door Iosif had snuck her through. She wouldn't want to knock. Iosif would naturally be angry with her. So, she sat and waited. Waited for them.

United in wonder, the trio of men froze in the hotel hallway as the tiny girl quietly rose from her seat on the floor and faced Drozdov, neither overwrought with emotion, nor lost in some dark blur. Kira's girl was everything he had planned and hoped for.

"*Ne ubivaite yevo,*" she said plainly. *Don't kill him.*

# 6TH MOVEMENT: REVELATION

*"Even now, after all these plans, I'm just left with hope. I hope I'm doing the right thing. I hope you find your way here safely. But mostly, I hope you find your story. I hope you find your dance. You were my dance, Kelli. You were my dance."*

# ONE

"Sir, Mr. Walker is here."

On the conference room wall, a screen flashed a repeating series of black and white patterns. Behind Peter, the projector clicked endlessly in circular oblivion while he turned a small index card over in his fingers. "Send him in."

When Adam entered, sleek and graceful, Peter slid the card across the table. "Recognize that?"

Adam picked up the card. "It's your safe number."

"The safe number," Peter said. "Is that what you all call it now? How ironic."

Years ago, decades now, in his paternal sensibility, Peter had set aside a phone number. With it, any KAT or anyone could reach him on a safe, untraceable line. All KATS had to memorize the number. Peter took great pains to protect it. Only a schizophrenic could unravel the chain of relays it went through to reach him, which ended, strangely enough, in the back room of a dry cleaner, six blocks from his house.

"That card came out of Kelli's vault," said Peter.

"Why was your safe number in her vault?"

"That's it, isn't it?"

Adam crossed to the endlessly clicking projector.

"Don't shut it off yet," Peter said. "You should watch it."

"What is it?" He switched it off anyway.

"Nothing really, just a bit of footage of Kelli's mother. She says goodbye and she's sorry, all the things a mother would say."

"You're not telling me something."

"Yes. Well, I'm afraid to tell you actually. You see, as it turns out, everything the mother did, all of it, the bracelet, the vault, the planning, the LOCK, everything, all of it—she was very smart."

"Peter."

"It was about me," Peter said. "Kelli's mother came up with this plan, in case anything ever happened to her. A plan to protect her daughter and tell her the truth about who her mother really was. 'Find Zeus, he'll take care of you,' she said. She didn't know that by using it, she would be sending her child into the hands of the very people she was hiding from. Miguel was right. She didn't know about the signal in the bracelet. And Kelli, I was supposed to protect her."

"It's not your fault."

"That's debatable. But speaking of protection, did you find Nathanial?"

"No. He's gone, and I believe he took a customer's jet. No one has heard from him in days. And there are some strange things too."

"Like?"

"Like he ransacked his KAT materials. I'm pretty sure he took a gun."

"A gun?"

"I spoke with a man who saw him hours before he disappeared, said he was upset about something he heard on the radio."

"So, he went after her. But how? Where could he go?"

Peter's secretary Sondra, in a flurry of white, hurried through the door. "Sir, someone just called down from communications. There's something you need to see." She ran to a large television screen at the far end of the room and turned on a live news report.

*"...a terrible stream of seemingly random and unprovoked homicides took place early this morning. Hours later, investigators are still piecing together the incredible nightmarish tale which allegedly began when someone jumped from a building with a hang glider. Though the suspects are still at large, the main perpetrator is described as dangerous and violent. Authorities have put together a composite sketch based on the numerous eyewitnesses. If you see this man, do not approach him, but immediately alert authorities..."*

Peter gasped. "What in the blazes of Hell?"

"Peter, I know where Nathanial is," said Adam, "and he's in trouble."

―――――

*Where am I?*

Consciousness returned with the unwelcome awareness of pain. Nathanial's gut lurched, sending forth a groan at the insatiable pounding, every beat of his heart a pressure bomb in his skull.

He felt terribly wrong. He was hanging. His arms pulled mercilessly at the sockets of his shoulders, his bound wrists taking his weight. The earth beneath him seemed to be getting farther and farther away, because his feet couldn't quite get a hold of it.

He lifted his head, trying to nestle it between his stretched arms. He felt warmth, off to one side, smelled something pleasant, like toast. He forced his swollen eyes to open past the throbbing, finalizing his return from the sweet land of darkness.

"Where am I?" he thought again, or perhaps he said it. Something blocked his left eye, pain, thickness. He tasted dried blood on his lip, and he saw only blurry blackness.

He allowed his body to swing a little from side to side, uselessly grabbing at the surface beneath his feet, failing to gain any real balance until he surrendered to the pressure on his wrists with a groan. The blackness was all-encompassing but spotty, as if through rough strands. His breath, as it accelerated into the first stage of panic, came back towards his face, hot and moist.

*Where am I?*

There were creaks and clacks, and something crashing far off. Footsteps. Something quickly pulled whatever was on his head. He squinted his swollen eyes against the onslaught of morning light. Had he missed a night? How long had he been out?

Once his eyes adjusted, he knew that where he was didn't matter. He was looking into the face of horror.

———

"Let me go to Houston."

"You're not thinking, Adam. Every hot-blooded Texan with a shotgun will be looking for you. It's completely insane. How could you have kept this from me all these years? A twin, working for Drozdov, no less. At least now I finally understand why you got in that limousine with him all those years ago."

"We're wasting time. If Erik has Nathanial, he'll kill him, or worse."

"Yes, I know. But you're not going. I'll send someone else. Maybe Coreena."

"He'll eat her alive."

"Then someone else. I have to think. Not that we even know where to send them. If your brother has half a brain, which we now know he does, he'll have left the country. If not, I may at least be able to slow them down. Now listen. Stay here. We'll sort this out. I'm going to make some calls and get your picture off the television and preferably burned, and then try to shut off travel out of Houston." Peter left, shouting out orders to his secretaries.

*Erik.*

It was a name Adam avoided. Another memory he couldn't

afford, another distraction. Only this memory he couldn't escape, because it was splayed hopelessly across every mirror. Erik, the only living family, the only human connection he had on this earth, could never even know he was alive. But now, if he does know the truth, he will certainly take out his anger on someone else.

He got up to turn the TV off. Stop the incessant glare of his brother's face. The empty film case lay open on the conference table, the mother's message.

He rewound the film and sat down. At first, there was nothing but an empty room, jiggling around as someone started the camera. Eventually she appeared, her back at first, dark curly hair like her daughter, walking towards a stool, and then turning herself onto it.

*"I guess I should start by saying, I'm sorry. I know if you're watching this, if you've found your way to this recording, well..."*

———

When Peter returned, he found the room eerily empty, the lone voice of a dead woman speaking softly through the projector. "Sondra, where did Walker go?"

"I don't know, sir. He just ran out."

"He didn't say anything?"

"No, sir."

Peter took two steps towards the message playing placidly on the screen. For a moment, he saw something humble and naked in the woman, something that would forgive him for failing her daughter, something uncannily familiar. "Sondra, shut down the building," Peter said. "Code orange."

"All the exits?"

"No one gets in or out. And the elevators, have them all shut down. Emergency power only. Send every available man to the hangar."

Peter scrambled back into his office as the lights faded and the alarm began bleating through every corridor of the complex. He opened the bottom drawer in his desk and threw some file folders to the side.

"All floors are on lockdown, sir. Is there an intruder we should put the alert out for?"

"Yes," Peter said, checking the magazine of his pistol. "Adam Walker."

———

"Where am I?" Nathanial persisted. It was an incomplete structure. Beyond rusted pillars and grates, he could make out deep moving blues. However, he couldn't feel himself moving, so he remained confused, a sensation his host would most likely use against him.

"Now that doesn't really matter, does it?" Erik said with a twisted smile.

Nathanial maneuvered his wobbling body to follow the man with his eyes. A small pile of wooden scraps smoldered neatly on the concrete floor. He stoked it tenderly with a long metal rod.

"You should know that I'm a particularly honest person," Adam's double said, not moving his gaze from the embers.

"Well, that's comforting." Nathanial winced.

Erik glanced up at him. "Has someone who looks like me been lying to you?"

Nathanial would have frozen with terror if he could have gotten a firm footing.

"I generally don't," the man continued. "Lie, that is. One of my few virtues. For example, I feel it only right that I should tell you how desperately I wanted to kill you yesterday after our little morning chase." He touched some scratches on his chin. "You were quite an annoying little bastard. And if it weren't for the girl, well, no use crying." He smiled at Nathanial. "I really would like to see an end to you."

"I'll take that as a compliment."

"That's how it was intended. I don't give them very often. Does my brother give compliments?"

Again, Nathanial felt a chilling tremble at the mention of Adam. Of course. Adam has a twin brother, and the son of a bitch never bothered to tell anybody. Nathanial cleared his burning, parched throat.

"Thirsty?" Erik asked. "Tell you what. We're going to play a little game here. I need you to give me some information, so I'll give you a nice drink of cool water for every answer you give me."

"Sounds like fun."

"Oh, it won't be. I'm impressed by yesterday, but deeply bitter. I imagine you are very thirsty though, so you might play along. Like I said, I'm honest to a fault. You tell me what I want to know, and we're done here, no matter how much I want to rip your little throat out and roast it on this stick. I'll even give you two indications of my sincerity before I ask you a single question."

"How nice of you."

"First, I'll answer your question. Where are we?" Adam's brother moved away from the fire and took a nonchalant seat on a squeaky metal chair. He sat with the same elegance that Adam did, crossing his legs delicately. The metal rod in his hands hung carelessly off to his side, its tip now glowing orange and yellow. "We are on an old, offshore drilling rig in the Gulf of Mexico."

Nathanial felt a fleeting relief at the fulfillment of the very human desire for understanding.

"See? I can be very accommodating."

"How comforting." The dryness in his throat was now screaming. "And the second thing?"

"Ah," Erik confessed. "Now that's where it gets fun. You see, most interrogators begin by asking the questions, give the victim the option of answering straight out and actually skipping all the bad stuff."

Erik lifted the glowing metal rod while he spoke, studying it a few inches from his face. "But most interrogators don't want to hurt their victims, and the person being interrogated usually knows that, and banks their silence on the misplaced hope that the interrogator will never act out the threats. Either because they haven't got the guts, or there's some kind of moral problem." Erik snickered. "So, it's a kind of psychological lie, you see? The victim is tortured for longer than necessary."

"I'm afraid I don't get your point." Nathanial found he was unable to remove his eyes from the fiery rod in Erik's hand, which had inexplicably taken on a character of its own, as though it was a third, silent participant in their conversation.

Erik rose and circled behind Nathanial so that if he lost a grip with reality for even a second, he would think it was Adam.

"It prolongs the cruelty. They think they'll escape without actually experiencing any pain, but the truth is, eventually the interrogator will use the pain against them. So, it's a sort of lie, a deception really."

"Your honesty is inspiring."

"It is, I know." Erik grabbed the back of his shirt, and Nathanial felt the fabric pull against his neck as Erik ripped it off him. The metal rod fell to the concrete floor with a resonant clang as Erik tore a piece of fabric and wound it into a cord.

"Sorry about this part. I generally prefer not to do it, but I do have very sensitive ears, so you'll have to forgive me." Erik forced the cord between Nathanial's teeth and pulled it tightly around his head, tying it into place. He continued calmly. "You see, if they would start with the pain, instead of the questioning, well then, the victim would have no doubt. They would know their interrogator did have the will do to it, and they wouldn't prolong the inevitable. Thus, shortening the whole process. It's very simple really."

Nathanial stopped breathing through the resounding screech of the metal rod dragging across the concrete.

"So," Erik said, "just in case you don't think I will do it..."

Nathanial screamed into the gag as the rod landed across the bare skin of his back with a wicked hiss, his entire body erupting into a screaming surge of pain. He flailed, twitching wildly in the ropes. His eyes welled with tears, and his nostrils filled with the gruesome odor of his own flesh roasting.

Erik walked slowly back around Nathanial's trembling body, listening with satisfaction to the sound of air sucking in and out of his nostrils. With one hand, he pulled the gag off, and immediately Nathanial gulped in a labored groan.

"You see? Now you know. So much better, don't you think? So, let's get to it shall we?" Erik's free hand reached up and held the ropes above Nathanial steady. "Now, when I ask you a question, you'll know exactly what's coming next: a nice drink of water, or my hot friend here. So, here's my first question. My only question, really."

Nathanial could not stop his body from shaking. The familiar hazel eyes of his old friend and new tormentor met him with a calm honesty.

"Where's Zeus?"

# TWO

"THIS IS ZEUS. DO YOU HAVE CONTROL OF THE ELEVATORS?"

"All deactivated, sir."

"Turn on surveillance and locate Walker."

"I had him, but he broke out of the elevator, and we don't have monitors in the shafts."

"Calculate any access points he could have used out of that shaft. He's headed for the hangar. Turn on car three, I need to get to the basement. One trip only, and monitor it closely."

"Will do, sir."

Peter sped through the serpentine hallways of The Institute, while red lights continued to flash. He dialed another channel on his radio.

"What the hell is it?" said a scruffy male voice through the static and blares.

"Riggs, this is Zeus."

"Zeus? *Zeus?* Really? What is going on? A nuclear detonation? Can't you turn this blasted alarm off? How am I supposed to get any work done?"

Peter was accustomed to ignoring his cantankerous chief of

medical staff, who anyone in the civilized world would have fired years ago, regardless of his diagnostic genius and surgical skills. But a Level III medical was a rare commodity, so Peter allowed the irksome personality to roll off his back since he was himself surgical enough to stave off any resultant employee riots.

"Riggs, I need you to do something, right now."

"Sure, why not? I'm just sitting here on my fat carcass eating cashews and reading magazines. Not like we're looking for a cure for cancer or anything important down here. Sure, what can I do for you, *sir?*"

"Do you have any tranquilizer darts on hand?" A silence ensued, during which Riggs probably rolled his eyes. "Good. Get one loaded, not too strong, and meet me in the North corridor outside the air hangar. You'll have to take the stairs and bring some security with you. And hurry." He ended the transmission, blocking any further objections.

The elevator doors shut, then a few sullen moments later slid open onto the same corridor that Peter had guided General Savio through a few weeks before. He jumped into a cart and drove down the winding subterranean tunnel, skidding past flashing lights and the unusually vacant halls. Peter sincerely hoped he was wrong about Adam's intentions, but after a sharp right turn, his hopes collapsed. Two security officers lay writhing, a panel missing from the ventilation system at the top of the curved ceiling. Farther down the same corridor, three more men helped each other up. Peter pulled the cart around a final turn and landed hard on the brakes.

The hallway was strewn with men, twisting and squirming. With outrage, Peter noted some minor appearances of blood. At the far end, past all the bodies, Adam was fighting off the last of six Institute security personnel. He jabbed his knee heavily into an abdomen, took the man's weapon, and aimed it at the door's electronic lock. With a quick pair of shots, the unit perished into a crisp buzz and a wisp of smoke. Adam reached for the handle.

Another gunshot reverberated through the cavernous hallways and Adam's hand froze, hovering above the latch, his fingertips centimeters from the bullet mark.

"That wasn't a miss," Peter said. "You know that." Peter took several careful steps, moving between wincing security personnel, his eye never wandering.

"Peter, let me go."

"You know I can't do that."

"You're going to shoot me?"

"Only if I have to."

"You don't understand. This whole thing. It's been a huge mistake. It wasn't the safe Drozdov was after."

"I'm not so ignorant. I can imagine. You recognized the mother, didn't you? Someone you knew? Well, what's done is done, and now, I cannot let you hand that technology over to our enemies."

"What's more important, Peter? You're my moral compass, you tell me." Heavy footsteps approached from the long corridor behind Peter.

"If I had any doubt about that, I wouldn't be here," Peter said.

Dr. Mordecai Riggs, a white coated, overweight fifty-some-thing, appeared, panting. Two security men accompanied him. Riggs leaned on the wall to catch his breath, digesting the scene splayed out before him. He held the tranquilizer in a trembling, stubby hand.

"Peter, don't do this," Adam said.

"I'm sorry, but you leave me no choice," Peter said. "Riggs, if you please."

The dart struck the Level VI's shoulder with a muffled pop. Adam never moved his eyes from Peter. His strong stance wavered visibly, and he tried to catch himself, leaning on the hangar door until his tall frame reluctantly slid down into the darkness.

Peter lowered his weapon, feeling like he had just shot some-one's eye out.

———

Adam came to consciousness quickly. The flat surface under him was cool, and he squinted at the bright lights in the familiar cell he had only ever seen from the outside. Three of the walls were white, but the fourth was a clear panel of synthetic plastic that The Institute had produced: bulletproof, fireproof, and with an added benefit of reflecting no ambient light. He sat up and winced at a headache. A tall glass of water sat on a small white stand next to him. Beyond it was Peter, so white he blended in with the walls.

"How long?" Adam asked.

"About forty minutes."

"Well, thanks for that, at least. Is that it then? We're just going to sit here and abandon them both?"

"I never said that. It's certainly not what I want. Surely you know that."

Adam slumped back against the wall.

"I think I know how to find them," Peter said. "I'm not sure yet. I'm waiting for someone to join us. You don't know this, but Nathanial returned to New York after I sent you home."

"You let him go?"

"Not exactly. But I understand he didn't go alone."

The door on Peter's side opened and a security guard showed fourteen-year-old Miguel Garcia in. The boy stood with hunched shoulders, his hands in his pockets, his eyes shifting around until they landed on Adam with obvious disdain.

"Miguel," Peter addressed the newest of his recruits, "I have something very important to ask you."

"Did I do something wrong?" Miguel asked.

"When Captain Hemmel returned to New York to see Kelli, I know that you went with him."

Miguel's eyes moved back towards Adam, who had now risen.

"Miguel," Peter said, "we have reason to believe that Kelli and Captain Hemmel are in a great deal of danger. We need to find them, to help them."

"To help them?" Miguel snapped. "She would not be in any trouble *si en primer lugar, no la hubieses dejado!*" He pointed an accusing finger at Adam.

"Yes, yes. Mr. Walker made a mistake. He knows that now."

"Now that he's in a cage."

"Miguel, we are losing valuable time. Kelli and Captain Hemmel are in trouble, and you and I are the only ones who can help them. Do you know where they are?"

Miguel's words spilled forth clumsily, descending in spurts towards his native tongue. "Mr. Peter *lo siento*. I should have told you, but the Captain, he told me not to say *nada a nadie*. I reworked the bracelet and brought it to her. You know, the bracelet from *su madre*. But now I worry, because he left *hace cuatro días* and I don't hear from him, *nada*. And today she is moved someplace strange, *no tiene sentido*, so I wonder, should I tell you, but I don't know what to do. *Por favor* Mr. Peter. I am so sorry *si hice algo malo!*" Miguel's confession ended with a collapse into a chair, hiding his face in his hands.

"It's all right, Miguel. Captain Hemmel shouldn't have put you in that position."

"What did you mean, it doesn't make any sense?" Adam said.

"I mean, she is in the ocean," said Miguel.

"Moving slowly, like on a boat?"

"No. That's what I mean. It's stopped still, in the middle of the ocean."

"Standing still?" Peter said. "What ocean? The Pacific?"

"No sir. *El Golfo.*"

"The Gulf. So that's how they're getting out. That explains Houston. All right. Miguel, here's what I want you to do. Go back and get me some exact coordinates on that bracelet, as precise as you can."

Miguel ran out, leaving Peter and Adam alone.

"Peter, let me go."

"The bracelet could be stowed on a buoy for all we know."

"It's not. It's Drozdov. He wants me to come to him. That's why he hasn't terminated the signal. It's me he wants."

"Yes, but that's not all he wants, and you know it. I'm going to let you go, Adam, but you can't take the *Peregrine*."

"He won't let me near her without it."

"Bring him this." Peter lifted the LOCK from the table next to him. "It's very valuable to Drozdov, and I doubt there is anything he wouldn't give to get it back. As much of a patriot as I am, I'm not even sure we should have it. You can take whatever you want, the fastest thing in our hangar, but you can't take the *Peregrine*."

"And land where? In the Gulf? I could be there in two minutes. I could have been there forty minutes ago."

"No. He's setting you up, don't you see? He's probably got them on some oil rig out there, and the only thing you can land with is a chopper. He knew that once you figured out who she was, you'd be in a big rush to get there."

"He still has Enoki. He could always rebuild it anyway."

"I doubt he'd get the funding."

"Is it only that you don't want Drozdov to get it? The *Peregrine*?"

"Of course, that's it. What else would it be?"

"I could destroy it. That's what Nathanial said we should have done in the first place."

"You can't guarantee that. You can't guarantee anything. You'll be battling your own brother, for crying out loud. Have you thought of that? Then he gets it all—Kelli, Nathanial, the chopper, and you. I'm some moral compass."

For a moment, Adam remembered standing in the hangar in

Paris, looking into the crate at the big brown eyes that had caused so much trouble. He reached out his hand to her. "Butterflies," he said to Peter.

"What?"

"Butterflies. They...flutter."

———

"It's actually a tricky thing, this technique. I have to be careful." Erik studied the glowing end of his instrument as though it were some refined piece of physics. "You see, if I hold it on your flesh for a little too long, or allow it to penetrate too deeply, well, believe it or not," he chuckled, "you probably wouldn't feel a thing. Of course, you'd be dead in a couple of weeks from infection. But right now anyway, you'd be quite comfortable." He shifted his gaze back to Nathanial's trembling and sweat-covered body.

Nathanial struggled to remember what normal felt like, a pleasure he had only enjoyed in ignorance. He wished he could look away from Erik's arrogant image, but as though he'd already succumbed to Erik's will, his eyes couldn't move from their fixation on his tormentor.

Thirst crippled his thoughts. Uncontrollable shaking possessed his limbs, and skin he had never seen and had hardly ever thought of screamed endlessly. His arms stretched at the shoulders beyond tolerance. The only remaining awareness in his hands was a mild tingling between the cutting fibers around his wrists. Breathing had become the real challenge to occupy all his gathered energy, reasserting his will to stretch his exhausted lungs in their continued pattern of in and out, prolonging the exhaustive process of being alive.

"Look," Erik said, "we're both tired. You're a mess. I bet you'd really appreciate a drink. I know the girl would be relieved to see you. She's probably worried. And let's face it, you have lots of open, healthy skin left for me to char. So, we could be here all day really. Is this necessary? Is he really worth it?"

Erik bent down and picked up a small colorless bottle filled with glistening, crystal liquid. Erik flipped open the bottle and tipped it to his lips, taking a careless drink. Precious drops scattered on his chin, and he wiped them away with his sleeve.

*Is he really worth it?*

What was Peter really? Just a man, with a job. A small insignificant man. Or was it The Institute they were after? Is that what they wanted? Destroy Peter and The Institute? *Why the hell not?* From his first moments back from war, Nathanial had been assaulted in every corner by the reality beyond all the noble lines about talent. That place was nothing more than a hive of puffed-up, self-absorbed, profit mongering egomaniacs. *He detested them.* Their non-flinching obedience to talent, hallways, and a small, half-blind man in white who decided what had value and what did not. Dropping a bomb in their general direction might be just the thing to satisfy a long-endured disgust. Surely everyone would get what was coming to them, including Peter. They had made their choices.

A vision of young Miguel Garcia, white lab coat and flirtatious smile, floated through his mind.

"Let's see," Erik pressed on, "how could I make this easier for you? I mean, I'd love something specific like latitude and longitude but, maybe that would be asking too much right now. So how about a name? You know, what people call him around the office. I am betting you know who Zeus is. If you didn't, you would have reacted differently when I first asked you. You really need to work on your facial expressions. In fact, you need to work on a lot of things. Or maybe you don't. Yes, I'm betting you generally don't do this sort of thing, do you? What are you, some kind of pilot? Ah. So, you're just here for the girl. Wow, isn't that noble. Or stupid. Have to think about that. So let me make this even

easier for you. Don't tell me where to find Zeus, or his real identity. Tell me where to find the one person I'm certain you know.
Where's *Adam?*" The name seethed past his lips, steaming. "You
know, looks like me, but not nearly as handsome. Half as good at
this sort of thing. Tell me where I can find the traitor. Where's my
charming liar of a brother?"

Nathanial gathered some remaining strength to find his
footing.

Erik rose, dragging his instrument along the concrete behind
him with a threatening ring that sounded like a never-ending
school bell. He removed the gag a last time, holding the rope
steady while his hazel eyes seared into Nathanial's soul.

"Where's Adam?"

Nathanial struggled to take another load of air into his
parched lungs. He understood with precise clarity what was
coming next, and his stomach lurched. As the nausea overtook
him, he slipped into a delusional warp. A moment of flashback,
unwilled and un-conjured, to a more serene place and time. There
was, for just a moment, a bright science lab, where he sat in an
endless biology class, listening to a droning lecture about Xs and
Ys. The hard stone table under his elbows drew him in magneti-
cally, while afternoon sunbeams poured down on his back from a
large window. The banal prof lectured on, as though Nathanial
were the only student in the class.

Having heard that it was possible to fall asleep with one's eyes
open, teenage Nathanial experimented with it desperately. But try
as he may, his eyelids only knew one path to repose. Oh, how he
tried it, longed to master it. How sleep had called him on, like a
lovely siren in a wonderful, pleasurable abyss.

But he could not will it. He could not will his body to do
something against its nature. He couldn't will it then, and he
could not will it now. Try though he might, wish for it as he did,
he could not stop his heart from beating its incessant argument

and leave him in peace. He was so close. So close to *there*. Surely it was right beyond a dim horizon now, and everyone else...

Sucked back over the decades into the misery of the present, Nathanial lifted his eyes to his tormentor and gave him the only answer he knew he could live with.

"Adam who?"

# THREE

ADAM DISENGAGED THE HR DRIVE LESS THAN A MINUTE AFTER typing in Miguel's coordinates and disappearing into a shimmering streak above The Institute. The bright blue wrapping of the drive slowly evaporated onto a natural brightness, silver sunlight reflecting off endless miles of undulating blue. As Nathanial had said, the *Peregrine* took about a minute to regain manual control. Likewise, when the engine didn't fail midflight, the wings retracted automatically, while the rotor blades extended back out, already spinning.

He had overshot Miguel's coordinates and had to double back, passing a massive luxury yacht bobbing on the waves. In the visible distance, a solitary, abandoned oil rig stood, rusted by an unending onslaught of surf and salty wind. Peter had been right.

He set the *Peregrine* down on the rig. While the sounds of the rotor faded, no one made any appearance, and he considered whether he should have landed on the yacht instead.

Near the stairs, an upright knife pinned a photograph to the landing pad surface. Adam freed the picture: three young faces smiled back at him, cocky, ignorant, and Russian, two almost identical, himself and his brother, and between them, a girl.

"Kira," he said to the wind and slid the picture in a back pocket. He climbed down the clanking metal stairs from the landing pad and caught a passing scent of something burning. Or maybe it was cigarette smoke.

Not much remained of the massive rig. All the heavy machinery had been removed years ago when the source of its black gold had dried up. It towered solitary, like a tiny ghost town, isolated amid the waves.

It was definitely cigarette smoke.

Approaching the main structure, he rounded a corner—

"*Privyet, bratishka.*"

Erik leaned against a doorframe, a water bottle in one hand, a cigarette in the other. "You never write. You never call. It would be easy to think a person was dead. And yet, here we are, together again." He noted the pistol in Adam's hand. "I think you can put that away." He took a drag off his cigarette. "You know you have a lovely grave. Buried with honors and all that. You should see it sometime, or maybe you already have. Been back visiting the old haunts without stopping in to say hello?"

"Erik, I'm..."

"Sorry? Oh, I bet you are, brother, on the other end of that pistol. I can just smell the remorse. Does truth ever come out of you?"

Adam lowered the gun. "Whatever Drozdov has told you, it's a lie."

"This from you." Erik pressed the smoking butt under his foot.

"Listen, Erik. Things happened, things you don't know."

"Really, Adam? Honesty? Sincerity? Aren't we a little old for that? You made your choices, and I've made mine. But for what it's worth, I appreciate your apology."

"I won't fight you."

"Oh, how noble. It's nice to know you draw the line somewhere. Are you going to shoot me instead? No, I know you better than that. If it makes you feel any better, I want to kill you so badly that I took out my frustration on your pilot friend down there." Erik tilted his head in the direction of the staircase behind him. "And it felt very good. But now you're here, as Drozdov said you would be. And now it's purely a matter of, how did he always put it? Redirected focus?"

"You have some scars on your face, Erik."

"So do you." Erik reached his free hand inside his jacket. Adam lifted his pistol again. "Oh please, don't insult me."

Erik pulled out a small silver remote and mockingly waved it in the air. Then, with apparent pleasure, turned the dial slightly, held it up for Adam, and with a cocky flip of his wrist, pushed a button.

"You have about twenty minutes. Drozdov's idea, but I love the symbolism, don't you? If you leave now, you can have the aircraft and your life. Go after your friend down there, and well..." He swung his arm back and hurled the detonator far out into the blue waves.

Erik regarded his brother a last time, as though waiting for something, a remark, a gesture, a decision, but instead, disappointed, he tossed Adam the water bottle and started past him towards the landing pad. "He's very thirsty."

Adam contemplated his hands: a pistol in one, the bottle in the other. Twenty minutes.

———

"You know they are lying to you," Iosif said to Kelli in her small room inside the yacht.

"Shhh."

"Shhh? What do you mean, shhh? You're on a one-way trip to Russia. You're going to be seeing a lot of me. You'd better get used to the sound of my voice."

"I know," she replied. Then she pulled herself off the bench and stepped closer. He leaned, hands in his pockets, against the door, his ten-year-old frame towering over her. The cabin felt bright with mid-day sunlight, and the enormous vessel rocked with mighty confidence. She came closer, such a little shrink, the crest of her head barely reaching his ribcage. He felt nervous. His pupils popped out and his head jerked back when she reached her tiny hand towards his temple, laying sweet, cool fingertips on the swollen bruise.

"No," she repeated. "Don't talk to me anymore."

"That's not your fault." He moved her hand away. "Anyway, I still have to uphold my side of the bargain, remember?"

"No, you don't."

"Will you marry me if I don't?"

"That was silly."

"You mean, you never meant it?"

"No, I meant it. But it was silly, that's all."

"I know how to get you off the boat."

"It doesn't matter. I promised."

"Wow. Didn't you hear me? They are lying to you."

She climbed back up onto the bench and stared out at the water. "Does everyone lie?"

"Don't be stupid." It hadn't occurred to him that the hard part would be convincing her to go along. This hadn't been in the calculations. She really was delightful. "Did your mom lie to you? How about your friend? Did he lie to you? I'm not lying. Do you think I'm lying? All right, I'll prove it to you. I'll prove to you that they are going to kill your friend no matter what they say. If I can prove it to you, will you do what I tell you?"

"Why are you doing this?"

"I don't know. Because it's obvious, I guess. You don't," he searched for the right words, "you don't belong with us. Now come."

He grabbed her hand and pulled her out into the narrow passageway and all the way up the stairs towards the stern. He stopped at the top, inside the door, and raised his finger to his lips. If she was who they said she was, she would have no problem discerning the voices. He nudged her into position close to the door, stood back, and waited.

———

Adam took off down the stairs of the oil rig to the lower level, leaving Erik alone. He found the circle of smoldering embers on the floor, some scraps of fabric, and the smell again, more precise. *Erik, what have you done?*

He heard a stretching sound from behind an open wall constructed of metal framework bars. A shadow dangled beyond them, as though held in a prison cell. The silhouette of a man suspended by his feet, swayed in the wind, his arms hanging limply. Beyond the bars, the platform edge dropped off to the sea below. Nathanial's body spun in slow motion, revealing the ravages striped across his back. Adam reached between the framework bars but couldn't grab a hold of him. "Nathan!"

He pulled at the bars and kicked them but found no weakness in the framework. Up above on the platform, Erik fired up the *Peregrine*'s engine for take-off.

Did Adam see Nathanial's torso expand, or had he only imagined it? Something clanked loudly above them, followed by a lengthy grating sound, and without warning, Nathanial's body plunged out of sight.

"Nathan!" Adam raced back up the stairs to the top level. Tearing off his jacket, he hurdled over two rusted structures and scaled an empty metal framework. At the edge closest to Nathanial's plunge, he pulled off his shoes, mounted the railing, and dove.

The cool water and surging waves were minor impediments compared to finding the target. Having plunged straight down with little resistance, only half conscious, dehydrated, charred, and tightly bound, Nathanial's head might have very well cracked on impact, or his spine shattered.

*Only the focus mattered.*

The salt water stung Adam's eyes as he pushed himself into increasingly cold depths. Long vines of slithering kelp waved off the legs of the rig like hungry serpents ready to consume them both in the murky waters. Adam soon felt his own lungs stretched against the unrelenting pressure.

Between foggy bundles of seaweed, Nathanial writhed like a fish on a hook. Adam swam, grabbed him from behind, and pulled. He summoned an unearthly will against the cold heavy water, the writhing cargo, the merciless current, and his own clenching ribs. He pulled, refusing to surrender, refusing to even contemplate anything but success. He pulled against the forces of nature and death, his free hand reaching towards the ever-distant mirror of brightness above.

———

"Why are you bothering with this charade?" Kelli heard Erik ask in the very consonantal Russian language. The sounds of the helicopter, recently landed on the far side of the yacht, were beginning to fade.

"Try to understand," Drozdov said. "Just to watch him move is its own reward. I am the hand that molded the clay."

"So you like to remind me."

"How much time until it detonates?" Drozdov said.

"A little over fifteen minutes, or nearly that."

"It's very important that the girl doesn't hear the explosion. I'll want her to see him before you put her down. Once it's done, we'll be home before the hour is up."

"Assuming the fuel and water tanks are full." That was another voice, wiry, nasal, and Japanese.

———

When they reached the surface, Adam held Nathanial from behind. He swam, barely staying afloat, choking on mouthfuls of salty water and persevering on mere will. He approached one of the legs and grasped a metal beam, catching his breath. About twenty yards away, the remains of an old grate landing bobbed in the waves, clanging against a concrete pillar. He dragged Nathanial across and up onto the wobbling metal structure, laying him on his side to choke up salt water. While he released the ropes around Nathanial's ankles, something gray and smooth glided past the wobbling grate.

He grabbed hold of a beam and swung himself upwards to sit atop it. He could feel the precious, fleeting seconds his brother had left him ticking away somewhere above. A network of beams intertwined above the dark blue, kelp-filled waters. From beam to beam he flew, around, above, and between in an elegant series of maneuvers so seamless that the astute pair of eyes studying him through far off lenses probably smiled with melancholy.

At the far end of the underbelly, he examined an old ladder, its base tapering off loosely into the waves, detached from its original catwalk but sturdy enough that it might hold Nathanial. How to get Nathanial to the ladder without going back into the water?

Silently, Adam wished for the simplicity of getting and American diplomat out of a Soviet compound in central Moscow.

———

"So, is it done then?" Kelli heard 'Uncle Kostya' ask in English. "Erik, you understand how to engage the drive?"

"Yes, yes. He will be fine. All you need to rebuild her is stored onboard. She is like a racehorse waiting for you." That was the Japanese man again.

"Yes, of course. She's perfect, just as you promised," Drozdov said. "And one of a kind. You don't have any other plans stored somewhere? No safety copies floating around? You might have saved some drawings? Some equations?"

"No, I told you. Everything is in your hands now. All plans and specifications recorded only inside her loveliness itself. She told me everything. Only to me. Anything else had to be destroyed."

"Erik, you're ready to pilot her home?"

"Yes, it's very simple."

"Perfection is simplicity," Enoki said, and it reminded Kelli of the things she'd read on the stones, in the field where they left Maman.

"Very well," said Drozdov.

There was a final bit of silence, almost awkwardness, but as Kelli bent to peek out, her body jumped at two loud cracks. She felt a chill as something heavy fell onto the wooden deck beyond the door, something big, like a sack of fish.

Shifting, and muffled grunts, then a windy moment followed by a distant splash off the port side. She wanted to peer around the corner to solve the mystery, but the ensuing silence stiffened her with terror. Iosif clutched her wrist, pulling her away from the sunlight and the strange series of sounds, back down the stairs into the shadows.

———

When Adam returned, Nathanial's breathing had evened out, and he recognized him. Adam pulled him upright, but he resisted, struggling to speak with drenched lungs and a parched throat.

"Nathan, get up." The bomb had to be found and deactivated. He needed to stay on target, keep moving, the seconds ticking. He needed to keep his...

"Adam," Nathanial said, his hands grabbing at him, as though drowning again, sucked down in the cold, dark currents of murky waters.

Adam let Nathanial grab a hold of him. "You're the good guy," Nathanial said, stopping to breath, as though at last locating himself in the air somehow. "Adam, you're the good guy."

# FOUR

**Moscow, 1971**

SOMETHING TERRIBLE HAD HAPPENED.

Kira held the paper in her trembling hand, numbly watching the tiny circle grow steadily darker for the third time. Though the lab was closed and silent, her mind spun like a busy street where strangers passed, shouting what she should do.

"Get rid of it," said the first voice.

*What an irrational thought. Wasn't this the point? Wasn't this what she had wanted? What they had wanted?* Still, it was the first thing she thought. *Get rid of it.* She knew enough contacts to make that happen pretty easily. Hell, she could probably make that happen herself.

"But I don't want to get rid of it," she heard herself say.

A second voice passed, reminding her that what she wanted was irrelevant. She should put on her coat and run straight to Drozdov. This was her job, her duty to her people. She had agreed to it without a second thought. Why was she suddenly hesitating?

"I'm not hesitating."

A third mocked her. *This is hardly worse than anything else you've done. We might even need you to do it again. Grow up.*

"I'm not hesitating."

Kira laid the paper down on the cold laboratory table and felt herself collapsing to her knees before it. She started laughing. She laughed so hard it turned to weeping, and she curled around onto the floor, hugging her knees. Kira Konstantinovich, who had once killed three men in one day with a trench spade, sat weeping on a laboratory floor. Terror seeped in on her like the ghost of an old, forgotten relative. Terror of a little brown circle on a piece of paper. Terror of Drozdov, her father, her everything. Terror at knowing that no matter which way she went now, things could never be the same after this. She could never be the same. Even after that last encounter, when she had left Adam alone, the doorknob still clutched tightly in her fist, she had looked at Drozdov with newly disturbed eyes.

"I'm not doing this anymore."

Something terrible had happened. And it wasn't this dark little circle telling her new life was growing inside her. It belonged to her. Not Drozdov, not the Apex, not even the great Soviet states. Brought to vivid life inside her, by some incredible chemistry experiment gone terribly wrong.

*Hide it.*

Terribly wrong, Kira pulled herself up. One by one, she burned all the test papers in a bin before washing the ashes down a drain. She cleaned the glass tubes from all three runs, wiping each meticulously before returning them to the stacks.

If she did this, she would be an outlaw in her own country. A traitor. The clock was already moving forward. How many weeks before she started showing? She would have to watch every angle. Hell, the man was probably going through her garbage. She could steal someone else's trash and fake a cycle. That would throw him off. But what else would he think of? She would have to be three steps ahead of him, long into the future, because Konstantin

Drozdov would always be watching, waiting for the slightest vulnerability.

She lifted her right arm. The golden charms on her bracelet suddenly glistened with a new disdain. Drozdov had trained her well. The bracelet, his graduation present, each trinket a memento of all she had mastered, suddenly came together to form a golden shackle. A shackle of things that had never really belonged to her. She removed it from her wrist and dropped it in a pocket.

She could do this, even if she only had a week.

# FIVE

IOSIF PULLED KELLI DOWN THE PASSAGEWAY, PAST THEIR CABIN. HE opened a different door, pushed her inside, and closed it behind them. It was a mirror opposite of her cabin. He lifted something off a dresser.

"This," he said, indicating a small object shaped like a rocket with a pointy end, "this is for you. See in there?" He held it up. "See that liquid? That's not much, that's how I know it's for you. You're little. One prick of this little needle here and you'll wake up tomorrow in the Kremlin."

"But how?"

He lifted the larger object and demonstrated. "You place the dart in, right here, like this, and then snap this shut, and then you hold it like this. You'll have to use both hands." He grabbed her hands and forced the weapon into them, sculpting her tiny cool fingers around the large grip. "Then you aim and pull right here— stop! Not now. Save it for him."

"For who?"

"Don't you get it? They're going to put you to sleep and blow up your friends. You won't hear the explosion. You haven't got much time. Now, this won't do for the deranged rhinoceros, so you'll need more for him."

He carefully rested the dart gun on the dresser and reached for a new syringe and a tiny glass bottle of a yellowish liquid. Kelli watched, fascinated, as he filled an empty dart with the liquid, this time halfway to the top. "This will do for him. After you shoot him, refill it with this and use that on my father."

"I don't understand. If those are the ones I have to use, why don't we put that in the gun?"

"Because first you have to shoot me."

"What?"

"It won't hurt me."

"I can't do that!"

"Look, we haven't got time to talk about this. Just aim and shoot. When he sees me on the floor, he'll think you did it and assume I had nothing to do with it. There's a dingy boat on the starboard side of the ship. I've already half disengaged it for you. Crawl under the tarp and hide inside, then when you're ready, crank down the last cable and hold on. It will drop you into the water. Hopefully, your friends will have either found the bomb or gotten off the rig. I'm sure they have help on the way, but you might have to pick them up in the water. Do you know how to turn on the motor?"

"I've seen it done. Nathanial had one. He let me steer."

"Good. By the time you get to them, help should be on the way."

"What about you?"

"I'll be fine."

She again reached for the bruise on his temple, wondering how many others had already faded away. "Come with me," she said.

Again, he moved her fingers aside, and a wry little smile stretched across his thin lips. "Thanks, but I have a mom."

"Oh," she said. *Of course.*

"Talk to me," Adam said. "It will make the climbing easier."

"Thirsty."

"There's water on the landing. I know it's safe because Erik drank some in front of me."

"Yeah, me too."

Nathanial's tormented arms resisted each move up the precariously hanging ladder. Adam didn't need a ladder, and like a monkey, he swung and jumped from beam to beam behind him. Getting to this point was a testament to Level VI brilliance. With the rope from Nathanial's feet, Adam had affixed a swing to a central beam. He used it to swing Nathanial over the open patch of water.

"Thanks, by the way, for letting us all know about your psychotic, evil twin. I don't suppose the magnanimous Zeus knew?"

"He was...annoyed."

"Poor Peter. He didn't want you to come, did he? Didn't want to risk his precious aircraft."

"We disagreed."

"Well, there. Snowballs can make it in hell."

"Climb, Nathanial. And Erik didn't use to be sick. I probably had something to do with that. So, I'm sorry about that too. For what it's worth."

"You're getting very good at apologizing."

"Just a few more."

"Apologies?"

"Steps."

Nathanial pulled himself up another rung, his arms throbbing and his shoulders like hot irons. "So, you know, don't you?" he said. "You know why they're after her."

"Yes."

"Well, talk. It makes climbing easier."

"He wants her."

"Drozdov? Why?"

"Her mother was a VI, like me."

Nathanial stopped to let his arms rest. He hung between the rungs of the metal framework while seconds of gestating silence slipped away. Finally, he asked the question that was already hanging in the breeze. "You knew her mother?"

"Her name wasn't Rachel, it was Kira. She was my brother's fiancée." The crashing waves filled any gaps in Nathan's imagination. "What you don't know, what Peter tries so desperately to keep secret, is that what I have, the ESA, it's passed down the family line. In fact, there's evidence that all the upper levels might be hereditary."

"So, is that maniac Kelli's father?"

"Erik is sterile."

Nathanial started feeling guilty prying into Adam's family business, sick, psychotic nutcases though they may be. But Adam continued on.

"Kira was with my brother when I left, but they weren't what you might call exclusive. You love to pick on the moral attributes of the Institute, but you are naïve, Nathanial. Drozdov ran a very different ship than Peter. Morality was the bad word. And when you grow up under Drozdov's supervision, like Kira and Erik did, the sky is the limit for what you're willing to do. Kelli's father could be any one of a number of KATs, or non-KATs for that matter. Hell, Kelli's father could be someone from an assignment. But the Kira on that film from the vault, she was a different woman than I knew in Moscow. Kira was unquestioning obedience. Drozdov's most trusted asset. The woman on that film, she was just—"

"Disturbed?"

"She was a mother trying to protect her child. Somewhere along the line, something in her must have snapped. She must have hidden her pregnancy from Drozdov and escaped to protect

Kelli from him. That's why she disappeared, right before I left. This whole thing, the vault, the bracelet, Kira set the whole thing up so Kelli would find Peter. His safe number was in the vault."

"So, Miguel was right. She had no idea about the tracer on the bracelet, and by using it, she was putting Kelli right into his hands. Did Drozdov kill her mother?"

"It's possible," said Adam. "It's more likely she just died in an accident and the bracelet was triggered by the lawyer. All right, stay there."

Having reached the platform, Nathanial clung to the farthest outer edge of the metal frame, trapped underneath the floor. When Adam reached down to pull him up, he screamed from the agony in his arms.

———

Kelli closed the cabin door, her tiny fingers trembling and her eyes welling with tears. A dark, low voice snuck up behind her, and her whole body jumped with the fright.

"Kelli. Oh, precious girl," Drozdov said. "I am so sorry. I didn't mean to frighten you. I shouldn't have come up behind you. Oh dear, now you are crying. I haven't been around a little girl in a long while. You know, you are very different from little boys."

He squatted down beside her and gently held her shoulders in his large warm palms. He wiped away a gathering tear in a genuine act of kindness, completely ignorant of the revelation lying an inch away, behind the door.

"Kelli, you asked me to promise that I would let your friend go in safety. I know that you care for him, and I would never hurt him, so come with me now. Would you like to see him?"

Her head popped up. He took her hand and led her back down the passageway and up the stairs where she and Iosif had stood only a few minutes before. When they came outside, her eyes adjusted slowly to the bright sunlight. Brownish-red splotches were smeared on the otherwise pristine wooden deck. He stepped over them as though they weren't there. At the port side railing, he held a large pair of binoculars to her eyes.

"Now you have to find the rig. Move along the horizon, where the water meets the sky. Once you find it, you'll see your friend there on top, and help soon on the way to pick them up."

"There are two big circles."

"Oh, of course." He laughed. "You have much smaller eyes than I do. Here, let me adjust it. That should look better. Do you see one circle now?"

"*Oui*, but they are heavy. Wait, I see it. I found it. It's there." She let go with one hand and reached in front of her aimlessly.

"All right, look on the very top platform. Do you see them?"

"The boat is moving. Can you stop it?"

"No, I'm sorry, I can't stop it. But if you keep trying, you'll find them."

Desperately she searched, frustrated to the core by the massive vessel rocking and the heavy glasses wobbling around. When she found the top of the rig, for a few precious seconds she held it in her view. The two tiny men moved in and out of focus like cartoon characters. Nathanial sat slouched over, no shirt on and one arm folded over his chest. Adam ran about the massive structure with long graceful strides. He was searching for something.

———

"What the hell are you doing?"

"I'm looking for a bomb."

"A what? No, he promised Kelli he wouldn't kill me."

"He lied. That's what he does. He weaves lies, in and around each other, until your whole life is a patchwork from his twisted imagination. And you believe him. She will believe him, because she's young, alone, and afraid. Everything he tells her is comforting and makes sense."

Nathanial sat in the cool shadow of a looming structure. "What do you keep looking for out there? Is Peter sending reinforcements?"

"Yes, but they'll be too late. There was a yacht. I passed it when I arrived. It's Drozdov. Just his style: big enough to land the *Peregrine*, and close enough so he can watch us."

"How much time do you think we've got?"

"Two, maybe three minutes. Nathan, I can't find it. We have to get off this thing."

"I just got up here!"

"I hoped I'd find it."

"But how? Don't say swim. Dammit, Adam. Nope. No, I'd rather blow up." Nathanial closed his eyes and dropped his head against the rusted metal structure behind him while Adam ran off in search of the bomb.

———

Being little has its disadvantages. People can deceive you, lie to you about any number of important things. And it can be very frustrating too. No one believes you half the time. You can't take care of yourself, and you don't get to decide where you go. Being little can be very difficult.

But little can also be an asset. Little can be cute, even disarming. She had seen it before, only subconsciously, but she was a very perceptive child and learned from everything she saw. She only had to see something once to know how it worked. Big people could be hypnotized by littleness, unexpected expressions, a glint in the eyes, a giggle, all maneuvered like the controls on a helicopter.

For example, after she lowered the binoculars, she smiled softly at the big snake and said, "Okay. Should I go back to my room now?"

He said yes, the slithering liar, so she toddled down the stairs and skipped down the hall. She could feel his cold reptilian eyes on her all the way to her room, where she turned back, smiled again, and shut him out.

She took her doll, Pearl, and the pictures of her mother. There was no time to find the bracelet, and she had given it to Iosif anyway. At the stern end of the passageway, she encountered a crewman who eyed her with suspicion. She hugged Pearl closely under her chin, twinkling at the lug over the doll's matted head.

Other workers were on the deck too. She opted for skipping her way to where she needed to be. No one stopped her. She placed herself out of view. Large triangular blocks sat wedged under the wheels, a final solution to a final problem. She reached underneath and pulled two of them away, then opened the door and tossed everything inside. As always with this thing, she had to skootch herself up.

There was never any doubt that she could do it. With a clear and structured plan, it was all very simple.

She just had to focus.

———

Something was wrong. Drozdov had been doing this long enough to sense when the stars weren't aligning in his favor, and Drozdov could feel it, like a spider whispering in his ear.

But it was absurd. Adam was on the rig; he could see him there. A few more minutes and he would be dead, for good this time. By now, Erik would have knocked the girl unconscious and loaded her and Iosif onto the helicopter. The LOCK was safely deposited at the bottom of the Gulf, along with the Japanese lunatic. Yes. He, Russia, had persisted and emerged triumphant on all counts. Despite the plans of a deceitful mother, an interfering traitor, and an ignorant American institution, he had won. But not quite so.

Perhaps it was the way she had unexpectedly smiled at him. It had pleased him, but it was out of character. She was clever. *Was she playing him? Surely not.* She was only five years old. He checked his watch. Erik should have come to get him by now. What was taking so long? On the opposite deck, the rotor blades now blasted at full speed. Drozdov climbed back down the narrow staircase to the cabins and knocked on Erik's door. When no one answered, he pushed it open, but something blocked it. He forced it ajar. Erik and Iosif both lay in a twisted heap, unconscious on the floor.

Drozdov gasped and fell backwards into the hallway. At the front of the ship, the chopper's rotor continued accelerating. In seconds, it would be ready for takeoff. He pulled himself forward, shouting orders in crazed Russian that the crewmen could not understand. He blasted through the narrow passageway, clutching at walls and stairs, his voice bellowing for someone, anyone, to understand him. To do something, to intervene, before Kelli Bertrand became the greatest colossal underestimation of his career.

———

"I'm not jumping in a giant wave pool of shark-infested water."

"Shh! Hear that?" Adam's eyes glossed over, his face twisting subtly into the oddly curved squint of his focus.

"No, super ears, I don't hear anything, except perhaps a timer ticking in your head."

Adam straightened; his eyes peeled towards the sea like a hunting dog. "It's her."

Then Nathanial heard it, softly at first, gradually growing. Such a familiar sound. "It's who?"

"It's Kelli. She's coming for us."

"What, in *that*? Now I know you've lost your balance. If anything, it's your lunatic brother coming to finish the job, or at least pop them all off to Mother Russia."

"It's her, Nathanial." Adam's face was aglow as Nathanial had never seen it, smiling widely, panting with giddiness, laughing. His sparkling hazel eyes did not waver from the slowly approaching aircraft. "She's coming to rescue us. To rescue you." Adam grabbed Nathanial's arm and pulled him.

"Adam, you need to get a grip. She's bright, I'll give you that, but a five-year-old cannot fly a helicopter."

"She's a six."

"Fine. A six-year-old cannot fly—"

"Not six years. She's *a* VI. Don't you get it? That's why Drozdov wants her so badly. She's me; she can do anything." Adam pulled him along, bounding around the rig, following the *Peregrine's* jagged flight path. "We have to get up to the landing pad."

"This is crazy. That's not Kelli in that thing. I don't care what level she is. She can't fly a helicopter."

"You only say that because you don't know. You can't know what it's like." Adam reached the landing pad and shoved Nathanial up the stairs. "To be able to do anything, to learn anything, to master anything, just from seeing it once, from feeling it or smelling it once. And the crazy part is, *you* taught her how to do it."

"I'm sorry to interfere with your delusions here, but you know that flying a helicopter is more than an intellectual experience. You can't learn it from watching, or being told how it's done."

"Did you let her hold the cyclic?"

Under ordinary circumstances, of course, Nathanial never would have let a child hold the cyclic, but they had spent so much time in the cockpit together...

"How about the collective? Didn't you spend hours with her on the carrier, talking what you thought was nonsense to a kid who didn't understand you? You didn't even know she spoke English."

"None of that means she can do it all at the same time."

"That's exactly what it means."

"It's not possible. For crying out loud, she can't even reach the pedals." But as they reached the landing at the top of the stairs, the *Peregrine* jerked off course twice and then ungracefully redirected itself.

"Look," Adam said, "she just figured out the steering."

The *Peregrine* continued towards them in a straight line now, a ladder flopping wildly underneath, just like at the Paris airport. Nathanial spoke so quietly, only the ESA could hear. "She can't hover."

"Did she watch you do it?"

"That's not the same. She's going to have to pass over us."

"Then we'll have to jump. But we'll throw off her balance."

"No, we won't." Nathanial couldn't believe his own words. Surely some spirit from this haunted rig had somehow possessed them both and was talking nonsense to the wind in the moments before Drozdov blew them to hell. "We won't throw of her balance," he said. "There's a program that automatically compensates."

Nathanial cringed at Adam's laugh, open and guttural, as though engaging muscles he hadn't used in years. The *Peregrine* veered slightly to the left and away from the platform.

"She's going to miss us."

"We're going to jump. Come on, Captain." Adam rested a hand on Nathanial's charred back, forcing him into a run.

"I won't make it!"

———

When the rig exploded, Nathanial's already tenuous grip on the flailing ladder failed. He slid right past Adam, who, hanging by his knees, caught him. Nathanial hollered in pain, his legs swinging madly above the sea. Eventually, he twisted around and hugged the ropes, his eyes clamped shut while the heat of the massive inferno reached out and singed his cheeks.

Adam climbed past him into the *Peregrine*, where he found the tiny pilot calmly perched on the edge of her seat, balancing two wheel-chocks under her toes. He did nothing to disturb her focus but set about pulling Nathanial to safety. "All right, Captain," Adam said when Nathanial was safely in the cabin, "get up and fly."

Nathanial climbed into the cockpit next to Kelli to take the cyclic in his hands. Kelli let go slowly, her gaze fixed rigidly on the only corner of the windshield she could see. She pushed herself back in her seat and folded her hands in her lap with an almost trancelike expression.

"You did good, kid," Nathanial shouted over the pounding rotor. "You did it. It's okay."

Behind them, Adam finished rolling up the ladder and closed the hatch.

She must have made her decision back on Drozdov's yacht. She must have brought it with her and hidden it between the collective and her seat. She must have picked it up while Nathanial was checking the controls. She aimed it squarely at her third target. Adam finally sat back and she marked him, void of expression from the other end of Erik's dart gun.

"Kelli, wait," Adam said, seeing her.

"I hate you," she said.

"I know."

Nathanial only noticed Kelli afterwards, the dart gun dangling in her hand, tears crawling down her cheeks as she began to cry, like little girls do.

# SIX

NATHANIAL WAS LYING ON HIS STOMACH IN A BRIGHT WHITE ROOM. The careful pinch of an IV irritated his right wrist, while various monitors beeped and whirred softly behind him. He didn't dare twist to look at them. Something was on his back, something that hurt like hell, blisters, now fully swollen and furious.

"Good morning, Captain," the familiar voice said. "Welcome back."

Nathanial's eyes slowly came into focus on Peter, almost invisible in a hospital chair, his hands folded atop his knee.

"Where's Kelli?"

Peter nodded towards a corner, where Kelli lay, draped across a stiff armchair, a light blue blanket wrapped around her. "She's fine. Been sleeping since I got here."

"When was that?"

"Oh, a couple hours ago. Took us a while to find you. Very thoughtful of you, dropping Adam in that graveyard, unconscious."

"It was an open space. I wasn't thinking my clearest."

"You were thinking pretty clearly about some things," said Peter. "Got yourself here, took a cab."

"You've been busy."

"Even thought to have the driver pick you up in the center of town. Can't for the life of me figure out how you hobbled there, bus maybe? And how did you pay for that cab? I know you didn't stop at home. Adam says you didn't even have a shirt on your back when he found you. It's quite a little mystery."

"You're impressed, I can tell."

"So where is it?" Peter asked.

"Ah. What was that, thirty seconds? Although you've really been asking since I woke up. I'm fine, by the way."

"Doctors say so." Peter shifted uncomfortably in his seat. "I don't suppose you'd let me transfer you to The Institute. This place is mildly primordial."

"Thanks, I'd rather live with the scars." Nathanial turned back towards Kelli. "I've seen enough of you people."

"Honestly, Nathanial. What are you going to do with that thing? Take it on vacations? You have no right to it."

For the first time in their acquaintance, Nathanial wondered why Peter always wore the whites. He looked like some kind of comic book character with that patch.

"Actually, I have a signed letter of agreement on my back. And honestly, Peter, what are you going to do with it? You have no right to it either. What took Adam so long to get to us, huh? Once you found out where I was, didn't you just pack him off in the *Peregrine* with some of your omnipotent orders? Adam, take the fastest thing we've got. Oh wait, I almost forgot, we have the *Peregrine*. Jump in that and go save Nathanial. Chop chop."

Kelli stirred in her sleep and rolled over as if the very nature of the conversation had wrestled her from her sugarplum fairies.

Nathanial lowered his voice. "Why don't you put those brainiacs on the fifth floor on it? I'm sure they'll come up with something."

Peter sighed and mournfully studied the floor beneath him, tracing the pattern of vinyl squares with the toe of his shiny white shoe. "Well, there's still the other problem. Kelli has to go back, of course."

"What?" Nathanial's head whipped up so fast he pulled something in his neck. "Didn't Adam tell you? She's a level VI."

"Yes, I know that."

"Well, don't you have to protect them? Protect the KATs? Isn't that your creed?"

"Protect the KATs in The Institute. Free will and choice are still requirements."

"Oh, don't start spouting that crap off to me. She's five years old."

"And a citizen of France."

"So? Pull some of your magic strings and make it happen."

"Nathanial, I am flattered that you think I have so much power in high places. Defense, security, intelligence perhaps. Matters of state, not so much. And you have to understand the lawyer who represented her mother's estate is not happy with us. In fact, he's very unhappy, what with all the abductions and abandonments and Adam's double running around Houston murdering people. He's gearing up for a fight. I would have to mount a legitimate legal battle of some kind. I'm not even sure how I would do that and maintain…"

"Your precious anonymity."

"Surely even you can understand that protects more than me?"

"What about Kelli? Won't that lunatic still be looking for her? If she goes back into the system, he could be waiting. He got his hands on her once. And what has she got to go back to anyway? Strangers?"

"You've only known her a few weeks yourself."

"At least I know her."

Peter rose and walked around the foot of Nathanial's bed, studying Kelli. "It's rather impressive, don't you think, how something so small and fragile came into our world and stirred us all up." Peter lifted Kelli's blanket up over her shoulders.

Nathanial's stomach turned. "Oh man. Why do I get the feeling your phone calls would be so much more effective if I handed over a certain aircraft?"

"You have this incredible way of making everything we do sound so wretched."

"You have no right to that thing, Peter, and you shouldn't have it. No one should. Honestly, I've got half a mind to destroy it. The world is too sick and messed up to be screwing with that kind of technology."

"Yes. After what you've been through, I can imagine. I'll leave you alone to think about it, and I will keep trying, I promise you that. For her sake." Peter began to leave, but he stopped in the doorway and turned back. "You know, for what it means to you, I do think you would have made a good father. You are still a young man, unlike some of us. You might give it a try someday, you know, the traditional way."

Peter left. Nathanial watched the sleeping child next to him. How long before they came to take her? A day or two? A week?

Later that afternoon, a nurse brought in a box of board games, clean clothes for Kelli, and a fold-up cot. When he asked where it all came from, she said a courier had delivered them, signed for by an A. Walker.

# POSTLUDE

# ONE

ADAM STOOD IN THE BRIGHT CALIFORNIA SUN, LEANING AGAINST HIS car, his eyes hidden behind thick black sunglasses. From his distantly comfortable spot, he could observe the lively little scene inside Nathanial's hangar.

Kelli skipped around, giggling wildly, with a wrench in her hand. She hid behind some landing gear and abominable Nathanial surprised her from behind (which, Adam thought, wasn't really possible). He lifted her, screaming, on his shoulder and spun her around until she called out something and he relented. Her wobbling, dizzy feet back on the ground, more giggling erupted when she smashed her nose on a helicopter door.

They were too concentrated on their unimportant task to notice the audience. But it couldn't last forever, and eventually, Nathanial emerged in his gray coveralls, trotting into the sunlight.

"Hey," he called out. "What are you doing out here? Why don't you come inside?"

Adam continued to watch. Kelli picked up a tiny bicycle and rode around the hangar in circular patterns, singing something French in a flute-like voice.

"She hates me."

"I know. She'll get over it. Thanks for the bike, by the way."

"How long did it take her to ride it?"

"She can fly a helicopter. How long do you think it took? Listen, I'm sorry about the whole graveyard thing."

"I understand why you did it. What I don't understand is why you stole the *Peregrine*, and what you hope to get out of it."

"I stole it? Hey, you started that, my friend."

"Peter could make good use of it, Nathanial."

"And good money."

Adam changed the subject. "When is she supposed to go back?"

"Two days."

"Does she know?"

"We've talked about it a little. Peter…"

"He's done everything he can," Adam said. "He has to protect The Institute's anonymity, but I don't think your actions have influenced him. He's mad. But he's not vindictive. Besides, he likes her."

"Right. Just like Drozdov."

They watched Kelli play contentedly until she felt the stares and stopped her ride. Her little face scowled at Adam, and she quickly disappeared into the shadows.

"Look, Adam, you've been very generous."

"Not really."

"My mortgage…"

"I had to fix my mistake."

"Yeah, that's what I keep telling myself." The warm California sun shone almost too brightly on them, and the distant sounds of cars passing on the nearby interstate only added to the natural movement of time, the steady pulse of normalcy returning. Somewhere inside the hangar, a phone rang, but Nathanial didn't move. "Adam, I've never asked you for anything. I mean, you don't owe me anything, of course. But all the contacts you've made, all the people you've worked with. I've got to believe you could pull a string somewhere. I know you don't think I can do this."

"I was wrong about that."

An explosive clanking erupted from inside the hangar, and Kelli hollered out a question.

"No!" Nathanial yelled back. "Put that down; I'll deal with it in a minute!"

"What about her real father?" Adam asked. "Has she said anything? Given you any clues?"

"You'd probably know that better than her. No, she just keeps asking me that stupid question over and over. I've told her I don't know the answer, but she keeps hoping, I guess."

"What do you mean? What question?"

"The question her mom taught her, that clued her in about Chaput? You know, the one about the three poets?" Another boom and Nathanial tore back into the hangar. "I don't care what level you are, you're not handling jet fuel!"

Adam remained abruptly stiffened at the car, his senses momentarily blocked by some internal computation. While his mind swept through ancient closets, his neutral, ever-controlled body slid down the car door to the pavement like a stiffened rag doll.

*The one about the three poets.*

For some unconscious reason, his hand reached inside his jacket pocket, and was searching nervously, as though he had lost it, and only had to find it again. The tiny pocket morphed in a cloud of panic, into a massive cavern of emptiness. Where was it? Whatever it was, he needed to find it quickly. It was the answer to everything. It would solve the past riddles and answer the long-dead betrayals. It could protect them. It could protect them from the future.

At last, his fingertips found their target and he pulled it out. It was a business card.

*Thomas McLarey, US State Department*

# TWO

A DELICATE CHILL IN THE EVENING AIR TICKLED THEIR EARS. SOON they wouldn't be able to hike without jackets. During the colder months, Kelli might get itchy in his small quiet lifestyle in the woods. It was beautiful, winter at the cabin; she would like that. But it was also isolated.

They wandered for a long time, crunching leaves under their feet and occasionally stopping by the lakeside to watch hawks glide over the amber waters.

"Kell, is something wrong?" Nathanial asked. "You haven't said anything since you got back. I mean, that's okay, but I guess I thought... Oh come on, you're killing me here."

"Nothing bad happened."

"Okay."

The breeze passed through the trees again like an ancient spirit eavesdropping on their conversation.

"We learned our colors and counted to twenty," she said finally.

"Oh, wow." He flopped down on a nearby stump. "I guess I hadn't thought of that. Yeah, that's first grade. Man. Kell, you have to go to school. You know that's part of the deal. I can't keep you if you don't go to regular school like the other kids."

She kicked at some pine needles and a frightened chipmunk scampered out from a leafy hiding place and rushed across a fallen trunk. "I liked the stories," she said.

"Well, there you go."

"The sixth graders dissected a frog."

"Yeah, I bet that sounded interesting. But you know we can't let you skip too many grades. You understand why we can't do that, don't you?"

"Yes, I know. The bad people." A woodpecker tapped vigorously on a nearby limb. "I made a friend."

"Well, that's great! You played together and had fun? There you go. That's something. Well, what's her name?"

"Charlie."

"Charlie. Uh, maybe we can get you some special time in the library or something too. You like to read, don't you? We'll figure something out, you'll see. Say, what did your mom do? I mean, didn't you go to school and learn your colors and shapes in France?"

She picked a crumbly stick off the forest floor and broke it into tiny pieces. "We can't go backward. Can we?"

"No, Kell. We can't." He extended his arms and lifted her onto his lap. "Hey," he said. "I've got a riddle for you."

"Oh no."

"No, it's a good one this time. Listen, what's blue and black and sometimes gray, no matter how fast you fly, you never get away? What? You hear something?" Soon, he heard it too, a chopper was approaching. They started toward home.

By the time they came through the clearing, the chopper was already lifting off the dock and swinging back out over the lake. Nathanial ran around front waving, but it flew off over the hilltops, the chop-chop gradually fading until the mountain forgot it had ever been there at all.

On the front stoop, they found a small package. Kelli opened it while Nathanial started dinner. *"C'est parfait."* It's perfect.

She beamed with pleasure at the framed photograph, instantly recognizable to them both. Nathanial leaning over the desk, signing the adoption papers, Kelli standing underneath him, reading. He had forgotten that someone had taken a picture. Rifling through the packaging, he found only a brief, hand scratched note.

*"Don't tell her it's from me. Congratulations. A."*

After dinner, and once the dishes were cleaned and put away, Nathanial hung the picture on the staircase, right beside the one of Kira.

"Nathanial," Kelli said with a familiar cocky ring. "I know the answer to your riddle."

# ACKNOWLEDGMENTS

To my husband, Gary, for continuing to put up with the crazy writing nonsense. *First, you're a musician, and now you want to be a what?* You are the love of my life.

To Terry Borton, for reading the first monstrous manuscript and not telling me I was an idiot. Lieutenant Colonel Mark Reidinger for believing in me every-single-time-we-talked-about-it and for fixing the New York escape problems. (Like six times) To Michael and Barbara Parsons for telling me I am a writer over and over and over and to Courtney Egbert for getting Kelli out of the hotel room.

To John and Laura Givens and Anna Maslennikova for all the Russian tips, especially for fixing the names and the political jargon. To Jackie Sand, my wonderful French teacher. To Gilma Fouts for the Spanish translations and suggestions.

To Sandy Reay, William Nuessle, Lynn Maloy, Heather Murphy, Kristin Masbaum and Craig Hoffman for Beta reading for me and for all your wonderful feedback and suggestions.

Thank you, Captain Tom Burke for answering flying questions and for directing me to JB. Thank you, Captain John Berkstresser, for your invaluable info on the inner workings of airports and FBOs. To Kevin Warren, helicopter pilot and instructor, for cleaning up the airport scene in Paris. To balloon pilots Robert and Carolyn Willbanks, Kevin Cloney, and Kevin Miko, and hang glider pilots Briggs Christie & Red from Hanggliding.org. To JS Morrison, author of *The Perfection of Fish* and expert on cold war, Russia and spies.

For help with all the firearm questions, thank you to Paul Paradise at Paradise Sales, The Firearms Trading Post, Colorado Springs, CO.

Special thanks to my first copy editor, Nikole Register at Register Edits, LLC / registerediting.com. Thank you, Annette Wood at annettewoodgraphics.com for the beautiful cover. And a hearty thanks to my final editor and formatter, a wonderful person to work with, Dave Pasquantonio.

To my *anonymous* Beta reader, for writing my first review, which I keep on my piano to this day. To each artist God sends a muse, but sometimes he sends a retired, New York, Jewish lawyer. Every writer should be so lucky to have a stranger place such faith in them and donate so much thought and time. I can honestly say this book is *so much better* because you stepped on the scene. Thank you for snapping me out of my darkest hours.

Finally, thank you to my beautiful daughter, for enduring endless conversations about helicopter plots and telling me such wonderful riddles. You are the greatest adventure of my life.

# ABOUT THE AUTHOR

**Valerie Niemerg** is a retired opera singer who performed leading roles with regional opera companies around the United States. Now a breast cancer survivor and a veteran foster mom, Niemerg divides her time between her two children, her music studio, and her writing. "Elly Uncomposed," her first novel, is available anywhere you can click.

# ALSO BY VALERIE NIEMERG

Elizabeth Kirtenpepper loves the opera. But she never wanted to be in one. Certainly not a real-life opera. So, when a strange magical twist of fate transports her into *The Marriage of Figaro*, Elizabeth finds herself swept out of the orchestra pit and into the scullery of the ruthless and domineering Count Almaviva.

Stuffed into a corset and forced to wear impractical shoes, Elizabeth meets Figaro, Susanna, and the whole cast of memorable characters, but no one is sticking to their story, and a strange, hooded villain is running through the estate, unraveling every bar line and fermata of Mozart's score! Elizabeth will soon have to summon her own inner diva to vanquish calamities from leprosy and sexual politics to revolutions in Spain. But the reticent little pianist from Kansas may just end up changing her own story as well, when she discovers that **everything she ever really needed to know...** she learned at the opera.